PLAYING WITH FIRE

Stephanie Harte

HEAD ZEUS

An Aries Book

First published in the UK in 2022 by Head of Zeus Ltd,
part of Bloomsbury Publishing Plc

9 7 5 3 1 2 4 6 8

A CIP catalogue record for this book is available
from the British Library.

ISBN (E): 9781800245808
ISBN (PB): 9781800245785

Cover design © Cherie Chapman

Typeset by Siliconchips Services Ltd UK

Printed and bound in Great Britain by
CPI Group (UK) Ltd, Croydon CR0 4YY

Head of Zeus
First Floor East
5–8 Hardwick Street
London EC1R 4RG

WWW.HEADOFZEUS.COM

To my brother and sister-in-law, Keith and Joan.
Thanks for all your support.
You two are simply the best!

I

Mia

December

One wrong decision was all it took to change the course of a person's life.

I clutched my new husband's arm; my fingers were digging into the fibres of his cashmere coat as he led me away from the limousine. The heels of my shoes sank into the surface of the sodden grass with every step I took.

As silent tears rolled down my cheeks, I tore my gaze away from the spray of red roses covering the top of the golden oak coffin and cast my eyes around the black-clothed congregation, wondering why the sun couldn't have shone even for a little while. Sunshine somehow made everything better; its warm rays had an uplifting quality and gave a person hope for the future. Life had to go on despite our heart-breaking loss. Death was inevitable. We couldn't hide from it. Right from the moment we were born, the clock started ticking.

Today was a sombre occasion, without the weather playing a hand in magnifying the sadness by matching the mood perfectly and making a blue day even gloomier. As if funerals weren't depressing enough, the rain pelted off the sea of black umbrellas that were a necessary part of the dress code. Mourners huddled together around the graveside while we watched the casket being slowly lowered into the ground. My tears started flowing freely; I couldn't get my head around the fact that I would never see my dad again. I felt my knees buckle as the realisation hit me. Jack wrapped his arm around my waist as he did his best to support me. I allowed myself to lean on him; this was by far the toughest thing I'd ever had to do.

As the congregation started to disperse and people walked back to their cars, I couldn't help noticing that the graveyard seemed eerily quiet. The silence felt loaded, ominous, as though it was foreshadowing something bad. That sent a shiver down my spine. I couldn't deny I was on high alert. The last time the family had gathered together in the same location, it had ended in tragedy. No wonder I was feeling edgy

2

Kelsey

One year earlier

'What are you doing?' Scarlett asked as she walked towards me.

I turned my head and looked over my shoulder at my younger sister. 'Shush! Keep your voice down, or you'll blow my cover. If you must know, I'm spying on Dad's newest recruit, and I don't mind telling you, I like what I see.'

'Let's have a look then,' Scarlett said as she sidled in beside me.

I had a bird's eye view from my vantage point on the landing of the parquet-floored hallway below. Dad was like the lord of the manor as he welcomed the bodyguard into our family home. Scarlett and I had to stifle a laugh when she peered over the bannister and began fanning herself with her hand.

'He's smoking hot,' Scarlett mouthed.

That was an understatement; this man was sex on legs, the embodiment of the phrase tall, dark and handsome. 'Hand's off, I saw him first.'

'This is my wife, Amanda,' Dad said when Mum came into view.

She glided across the herringbone flooring, looking effortlessly chic in a pair of grey, wide-legged trousers and a pastel pink, crew-neck jumper. Mum was a natural beauty and had an ageless appearance.

'I'm Todd Evans, pleased to meet you,' the bodyguard said, extending his hand towards the lady with pale blonde hair and glowing creamy complexion women half her age would envy.

'Pleased to meet you too, Todd,' Mum replied, her lavender-blue eyes shining.

'Why has the idea of giving him a hand job suddenly sprung into my mind? I wonder what he's like in bed,' I said, tilting my head to one side.

'Dad would kill you if he heard you talking like that. You're the spawn of the devil.' Scarlett giggled then linked her arm through mine.

'You better believe it.' I laughed.

The two of us stood grinning with our eyes fixed on Todd. We watched as he followed Dad down the flagstone path at the side of the striped lawn until he disappeared out of sight.

3

Davie

Ipaced along the pathway, rubbing my hands together as I led the way to my office space at the bottom of the garden.

'It would freeze the bollocks off you today,' I said over my shoulder.

When Amanda and I had bought the house, I'd originally planned to turn the workshop into a man cave, but due to its secluded location, the place was better suited to being my crime headquarters. It was ideal; much as I loved them all dearly, I'd be out of sight and out of mind of the women in my life.

'Take a seat,' I said, gesturing towards the black leather sofa at the far side of the office.

Todd wiped his feet on the mat before he closed the triple-glazed door behind him. As he parked his bum on the seat, I walked over to the sideboard, took out a cut-glass decanter and two tumblers, and poured us both a hefty measure of single malt.

I handed Todd a drink then held my tumbler towards his. 'Cheers, son, welcome to the firm,' I said before we clinked glasses.

'Thanks, Davie; I'm excited to be working with you.'

Todd's reply made me laugh out loud; he seemed genuinely shocked by my response. He might have been a former Royal Marine, a tough guy, but he was arrogant, a real cocky little shit. I wasn't sure if that was a good thing or a bad thing.

'Let's get one thing straight, shall we, son – you won't be working with me; you'll be working for me,' I corrected.

It gave me great satisfaction to slap the hired muscle firmly back into line, and I had to suppress the smile that wanted to take over my face. We weren't forming a partnership. Money equalled control, and I was the one paying his wages. I wanted to make sure he got that; I didn't like having to repeat myself.

'Understood?'

'Yes,' Todd replied, before placing his untouched whisky down on the glass coffee table, then held his hands up in front of him. 'Sorry, my mistake.'

It hadn't gone unnoticed that his apology lacked empathy. I knocked back my drink while I tried to gauge the measure of the man I'd hired to protect my daughters. First impressions count for a lot, and I wasn't at all sure I liked the person sitting opposite me. But then I reasoned, I wasn't adding him to my social circle; as long as he did his job, that was all that mattered.

'Like I said, your main duty will be to look after Kelsey. She works for a party planning company running events for influencers and reality TV stars. She's an attractive girl and has been the target of a lot of unwelcome attention thanks to her job, mingling with overzealous fans of the Z-list celebrity wannabes.'

Todd took out a notebook and pen and started scribbling in it. 'You don't mind if I make some notes, do you?' he asked when he saw me looking daggers at him.

'I'm not sure how I feel about you recording sensitive information regarding my girls. What if it fell into the wrong hands?'

I liked to keep things simple and never put anything in writing, so there was no evidence to find. The last thing I needed was somebody creating an unnecessary paper trail.

'Rest assured; I'm not doing this for a sinister reason.' Todd waved the small black book around. 'It's a strategy I use until I get to know the clients I'm looking after. I can't remember every tiny detail to start with, so this is invaluable until I learn the ropes. Having something in writing, which I can refer back to, helps me do a better job.'

'I get what you're saying, but that still doesn't answer my question. You make a lot of enemies in this game who would sell their granny in return for some dirt on me or my family.'

'What I've written down is confidential; I'd never share it with anyone,' Todd reassured.

I wasn't sure I believed that; everyone had a price. I regularly used the tactic myself. If I was having trouble trying to part one of my more reluctant customers from their cash and possessions, I would gather intelligence about their family members. Knowing all about their nearest and dearest was a great tool to have in my arsenal if I needed to heighten the stakes.

I eyed Todd suspiciously. He could just be displaying the traits of a highly organised individual with meticulous attention to detail, but I hadn't employed him for his pen-pushing ability. I wanted him for his background; he'd been trained to deal with threats and security challenges, all of which were relevant in his current role. Even though he'd explained his reasons, I still didn't like the idea of him documenting every word I said. In my business, putting something in writing made it official, and that had a habit of coming back to bite a person on the arse.

'When you're not tailing Kelsey, keep an eye out for the other two. Let them go about their daily business, but use your judgement and accompany them when the need arises. My eldest girl, Mia, won't give you any trouble; she's as good as gold. She works as a yoga instructor at the local gym. Unless she's teaching, she doesn't often venture out without her boyfriend.'

Todd nodded and began jotting in his book again. His pen tore across the page like he was an overeager journalist trying to document every detail of a scandalous scoop. Watching him made the palms of my hands start to sweat. I'd had enough of this bullshit.

'Do yourself a favour and put the book away before I'm forced to ram it where the sun doesn't shine.'

Todd's lips parted as though he was about to protest, but he must have thought better of it when he clocked the look on my face. If one of my employees ever questioned my orders, it would be more than their life was worth to do so. Whether it was intentional or not, he was pressing my buttons, and I could feel my temper coming up to boiling point at an alarming rate. I'd always been a fists-first type of person, and I was too long in the tooth to worry about anger management at this stage in my life.

I got up from my seat and walked over to the full-length windows to put some distance between the two of us so that I didn't end up terminating Todd's contract on his first day at work. I'd primarily employed him because of the constant threat to Kelsey but also to watch over the rest of my family. I'd almost recruited a different minder, but he was getting on a bit, so I'd opted for a younger model. On paper, Todd Evans was the badger's nadgers, but only time would tell if he was the real deal.

I turned away from the view of my manicured garden, collected my tumbler and went over to the sideboard. 'Do you want another drink?' I asked as I poured myself a large scotch.

'Not for me, thanks.'

Todd's answer had gone some way to redeem his actions. I didn't want to see him drinking while he was on duty, and he hadn't disappointed me. I'd noticed the single malt I'd given him earlier hadn't touched his lips.

'I'm meant to be filling you in on my girls, but for the life of me, I can't remember where I got to.' I rubbed my thumb and forefinger over my goatee, but my mind had gone blank.

'You were telling me about Mia,' Todd replied.

I nodded. 'Mia's her mother's daughter in both looks and personality. She's an absolute angel.'

I loved my girls equally, but there was no denying the other two would be more of a challenge, Kelsey in particular. It was my fault she'd turned out the way she had. When she was tiny, she used to raise hell; we should have stamped on it, but we never checked her because I saw so much of myself in her. And if I was totally honest, I liked her spirit; I didn't want to break it. She had a fire in her belly. Why would I want to put that out?

I took a sip of my drink while I considered my next words, but there was no point in pussyfooting around. Todd would soon find out, tact and diplomacy didn't enter into my vocabulary.

'My middle girl, Kelsey, has always had a wild streak. Ever since she was a nipper, she hasn't followed the rules. She's a rebel and has a nonconformist attitude. I can't imagine where she gets that from.' I laughed, knowing she was a chip off the old block.

Todd listened intently, but I could see his fingers twitching in his lap now that I'd put a stop to him minuting our meeting, and he didn't have a notebook and pen to hold on to.

'As for Scarlett, she's the baby of the family. She has red hair to match her name and is a drama student, so I'll let you form your own conclusions. Suffice to say, she can be overly dramatic, and she gets huffy when things don't go her way. She's like a hybrid of my other daughters. Generally speaking, she toes the line, but she has a mischievous side. Because she loves to please everybody, she has a tendency to be easily led, which Kelsey exploits at every opportunity.'

Todd was going to have his work cut out for him; he was getting well paid, but it wasn't going to be easy money.

'Thanks for the low-down. I look forward to meeting your daughters.' Todd smiled.

4

Davie

Loyalty counted for everything and was something that couldn't be bought.

'Hello Davie, long time no speak,' Larry said.

'Hello, mate. How's it going?'

Larry and I went back aeons. He ran a second-hand car lot at the back of Shoreditch High Street, and due to the unfavourable terms of his credit agreement, he regularly needed to avail himself of my services. My official line of work was that I ran a debt collection agency, where I pursued money owed by individuals or businesses. That kept the taxman sweet.

'Things will be a lot better when I get back the money I'm owed. The geezer's been messing me around for months on end now; I've had enough. It's time to send in the big guns.' Larry laughed.

I took that as my cue to get involved. 'How much are we talking?'

'Ten grand.'

I blew out a whistle for effect. 'That's a lot of dosh. I don't know if I'd be up for that. I'm a bit strapped for cash myself at the moment,' I lied and began reeling him in. I felt a smile spread across my face; my old mum always used to say I had the gift of the gab. God rest her soul.

'You're breaking my heart, Davie. I was relying on you to take it off my hands,' Larry bleated, hoping to gain sympathy.

'I'm sorry, mate, no can do.'

'You've gotta help me out; we've been friends for years.'

If somebody gave me a pound every time that old chestnut was thrown into the mix, I could give up work altogether and retire on the proceeds.

'I know we have, and believe me, if I could help, I would, but like I said, money is tight for me at the moment too.'

'I don't know who else I can turn to; you're the best in the business,' Larry continued, trying a different approach when he realised I wasn't taking pity on him by attempting to butter me up. 'I've got bills coming out of every sodding orifice at the moment.'

'Tell me about it. We're all victims of a bruised and battered economy.'

That wasn't strictly true. One man's pain was another man's pleasure. Thanks to the country being in the grip of recession, my business was booming.

'I don't know what the fuck I'm going to do.' I could hear the anguish in Larry's voice.

Larry was painting such a tragic scene, I almost got my imaginary violin out and started playing it. But you had to be tough in this game; everyone had a sob story.

'My heart bleeds for you, mate, really it does, but the most I could offer you is four grand.'

That was a cheeky offer, even by my standards. We'd soon find out how desperate Larry was for the money.

'You're killing me, Davie. I can't let the debt go for as little as that.'

'I understand, mate, but that's my final offer. Like I said, times are hard for all of us. I can't afford to pay you any more than that; believe me, if I could, I would.'

Larry let out a loud sigh. 'Thanks anyway,' he replied, and then he hung up.

I'd barely put my mobile down on my desk when it rang again.

'OK, I'll take the four grand. But I'm in a hurry for the dosh. Can you get it to me by the end of the day?'

'Of course,' I replied with a smug smile on my face. I could have gone right over with the cash; I had more than enough on the premises to cover the amount Larry wanted, but I knew from experience, it was never a good idea to look too keen. I'd make him wait for a while so he'd start to sweat.

As soon as I ended the call, I dialled Rio's number. He was my main man, and I never did business of this nature without him.

'I've just taken on a job. Come over to the house in a couple of hours and collect me.'

'No problem, boss,' Rio replied.

Rio de Souza and I had been friends since childhood. To look at him now, he was a mean fucker; well over six feet tall with biceps of steel, but when we were kids, he was a scrawny little lad who found himself at the mercy of the playground bullies on a daily basis until I took him under my wing. It was something he never forgot. Over the years, his loyalty had been tested on countless occasions, but it had been unwavering; he'd never let me down.

Rio parked my Jaguar on the private lane that led up to my house. He punched the four-digit PIN into the lock on the gate and let himself in. I was sitting behind the desk in my office space when he slid open the triple-glazed door. Rio was an imposing figure as he stood in the doorway, immaculately turned out in a dark-navy suit, crisp white shirt, and blue silk tie. He was a handsome, mixed-race man. Unlike myself, who had more lines than the National Grid, his caramel-coloured skin was as smooth as it had been twenty years ago when he was in his prime.

'So what's occurring?' Rio asked, flashing me his winning smile.

'Larry's in a spot of bother, and it needs sorting.'

I walked across to the family portrait hanging in the centre of the room that concealed my safe. Gripping the sides of the frame, I carefully lifted it down and placed it on the black tiled floor, leaning it back against the wall. I began turning the dial to the left and then to the right until the lock clicked open. I took out four bundles from the large stack of pre-counted fifty-pound notes and ran the pad of my thumb down the edges. Nothing beat the feeling of crisp notes against my skin.

If I'd been a man with a conscience, I might have felt guilty that I was offering a friend such a small amount to take the debt off his hands; it wasn't as though I couldn't afford to pay the full amount for it. But the game I was in was a risky business, which was why I got away with offering such unfavourable odds. There was no guarantee I would be able to recoup my money, so that's how I justified ripping off an old mate. It didn't play on my mind; I had no trouble sleeping at night. I had a wife and family to support. Taking on another person's debt was a gamble, but one in my experience that always paid off. I was a very persuasive person by nature; it wasn't in the debtor's best interest to say no to me. I wouldn't leave them alone or stop harassing them until I got what was mine.

Before Rio and I made tracks, I dialled Todd's number to pass on some instructions.

'I'm popping out for a while. Make sure you look after my girls,' I said before I ended the call.

'Don't worry, they're in good hands,' Todd replied.

'You ready?' I asked, turning towards my sharp-dressed friend as I tucked the wad of notes inside my jacket.

'Yes, boss,' Rio replied.

'Well, let's rock and roll then.'

I ran my hand over the gleaming metallic paintwork of my pride and joy. She was a beauty. Amanda had voiced her concerns when I'd shown her a picture of the Jaguar F-Type coupé in Velocity Blue I was going to buy.

'But it's only got two seats,' she'd said.

'It only needs two, one for me, one for Rio,' I replied. Her face had been a picture; it brought a smile to my face every time I thought about it.

I needed something to take my mind off the hellish journey. It shouldn't have taken us long to get here from my house in Bow, no more than ten minutes under normal conditions. But the traffic around Shoreditch High Street was gridlocked as usual; it had virtually ground to a halt on one of London's busiest roads. There wasn't much point in having a top-of-the-range car that could go from zero to sixty mph in three and a half seconds when we were crawling along bumper to bumper.

'Larry will have chewed his fingernails down to the quick by the time we arrive.' Rio laughed, and then he began drumming his long fingers on the leather steering wheel as we waited for the lights to change.

'Once we drop off the cash, we'll head back to my place, and I'll go through the details with you.'

Larry was pacing up and down outside his car lot like an expectant father when we arrived. He took one last drag on his cigarette and tossed it to the kerb before rushing over to my Jag. As soon as I stepped out, he covered my hand with both of his and started frantically shaking it. His mirror sunglasses matched the high-polished surface of my car and the shine of his forehead.

'You don't know how glad I am to see you. I wasn't sure you were going to make it,' Larry said.

'I gave you my word, didn't I?'

I made a mental note not to stay too long in Larry's company in case his desperation was contagious. I didn't want to catch it; the man was a total mess. We all had our share of worries at times, granted mine weren't financial, but I didn't need to take on anyone else's.

'Right, let's get down to business,' I said, walking towards the glorified shed at the back of the lot that Larry used as an office.

'Would you like to sit down, Davie?' Larry gestured to a hard plastic chair pushed under his desk, then swiped the pile of paperwork littering it to one side.

'No, thanks.'

I put my hand into the inside pocket of my grey checked sports jacket – I'd never been one for suits – and pulled out the cash. Larry rubbed his hands together at the sight of the fifty-pound notes. His eyes were fixed on them as I counted them out.

Larry handed me the paperwork detailing his bad payer's name and address along with the make, model, and registration of the car his customer was buying on credit. I worked differently to others in my field. Instead of pursuing the client's debt for a percentage, it was signed over to me, and I collected it for myself.

'Thanks, Davie, you're a lifesaver.' Larry beamed, shaking my hand.

I liked to think so.

5

Kelsey

My view on love was that it was something imagined, not real. But that didn't mean I shied away from the opposite sex. I just preferred to have casual flings more than anything deep and meaningful. Being a party animal at heart, I couldn't remember how many times I'd woken up after an event with a crippling hangover, vowing that I'd never drink again as I tried to piece together what happened the night before. Until the memories began to surface, I'd carry on with my day blissfully unaware that I'd probably hooked up with somebody or at the very least given them my number.

Mum, Mia and Scarlett were off doing good deeds, delivering presents to the local hospital for children unfortunate enough to be spending Christmas confined to a wing. Although it was a noble cause and it was the season of giving, it wasn't how I wanted to spend my Saturday afternoon.

It was also the time of year for celebrations and the

Christmas party season was in full swing, which was much more my style. Mum wasn't impressed that I was working instead of accompanying them. I was looking forward to spending a couple of hours swanning around with a glass of mulled wine clamped in my hand, so I told her I couldn't get out of it, but I'd volunteered to host the informal drinks party for some influencers. Mum tried her best to guilt-trip me into going with them, but I was having none of it. Todd was escorting me, and I'd been looking for an opportunity to be alone with our bodyguard since the first moment I'd set eyes on him.

'Let me get you a drink,' I said when Todd and I arrived at the venue ahead of the guests.

'No thanks. I got the impression your dad doesn't want me to drink while I'm working,' Todd replied.

'You leave Dad to me. I can wrap him around my little finger.' I flashed Todd a smile, then went behind the bar, opened a bottle of Stella and handed it to him.

'Cheers,' Todd said, fixing me with his eyes as he took a sip.

Influencers might yield a lot of power to a product or brand, but this particular group of people with a vast number of followers on their social networks weren't my cup of tea at all. They were so dull. It would have been more pleasurable enduring a full-body wax than hosting this event. I was beginning to wish I hadn't volunteered to work now as the time dragged by. There was only one thing for it. Todd was about to be on the receiving end of one of my optical orgasms. Eye fucking was a skill. Not everyone could do it, but I'd got it down to a fine art. I could write a guide on it.

Todd was standing by the entrance, back against the wall with his hands clamped one over the other in front of him, eyeing up the scantily clad women. He looked gorgeous, so I stared at him with lustful intent written all over my face. I wanted to make it very clear that I was interested in him and wasn't in the least put off by all the competition.

'I'm home,' I called into the echoey hallway. As expected, silence greeted me.

The weather had been horrendous on that day in mid-December as howling wind fired rain into our faces before we made it into the house. If I hadn't known better, I would have thought Mother Nature was behind all of this. She'd become my biggest ally, orchestrating the elements to produce the perfect scene. Thanks to the heavy downpour, Todd and I were soaked to the skin. I was just about to suggest putting his clothes in the tumble dryer when a clap of thunder directly above the house made me jump.

'That frightened the life out of me,' I said, clutching my hands over my heart.

'Don't be scared,' Todd said.

Before I had a chance to reply, I found myself in his muscular arms. My heart began pounding as I looked up at him. Todd lowered his face towards mine and planted a kiss on my lips; desire shot through my body like an electric current. I suddenly pulled away, realising we should go somewhere more private. I took hold of Todd's hand and, without saying a word, led him up the stairs. Our bodies cast shadows onto the walls as we walked; the natural light from the cold grey sky was weak as it came in through the landing windows. Once I closed my bedroom door behind us, I draped my arms around his neck and took matters into my own hands.

My lips found Todd's, and as we kissed, we began ripping each other's sodden clothes off. When I unzipped his bomber jacket and saw the way the fabric of his black T-shirt clung to his well-defined muscles, I knew I'd struggle to wait another minute. I wanted him so badly my body ached. I backed away towards the bed, pulling Todd along with me. I could see he was already hard in his boxer shorts, and when I pressed my body against his, he moaned a little.

Todd clambered onto the bed, his dark eyes never leaving mine. I stripped off his boxers, and as I mounted him and used my hand to slip his cock inside me, he closed his eyes. The sensation of his damp skin on mine as I slowly rotated my hips before we began to move together sent a rush of ecstasy around my body. I came first, but Todd wasn't far behind me. I wanted to do it all over again, but then I heard a car door slam, and I knew the moment was over. I opened my eyes and tilted my head towards the window. I could hear the rumble of thunder in the distance and female voices chattering below. Mum would go mental if she found me in bed with Todd. If we hadn't been interrupted, I'd have been begging for more.

'Oh shit, my mum and sisters are back.'

I jumped off the bed, tore across the room and flung open the door of my en-suite bathroom. I took two towelling robes off of the hooks on the wall and threw one of them to Todd before I slipped my arms into the sleeves of the other.

'Grab your clothes,' I said as I hurried out of the door,

along the corridor and down the stairs. Todd was hot on my heels.

We were sitting opposite each other at the kitchen table when Mum, Mia and Scarlett walked in. Mum's eyebrows rose, and her mouth dropped open when she saw us sitting there dressed in the white towelling robes. My heart was pounding. I was trying my best not to look breathless, but my face was already flushed from having sex, and that was before I'd had to charge through the house at breakneck speed.

'Todd's clothes are in the tumble dryer,' I volunteered before she had a chance to speak.

'We got caught in a torrential downpour and were soaked to the skin by the time we made it inside,' Todd added.

'I wondered what was going on.' Mum smiled.

She seemed to buy our explanation, but we'd almost been caught red-handed; we'd only made it to the kitchen by the skin of our teeth. It was just as well Todd's clothes were wet – he'd never have had time to dress.

'How did it go?' I asked, changing the subject. Not that I was interested, but I needed to divert the attention away from Todd and myself.

'Really well.' Mum smiled again, pulling out a chair and taking a seat at the table.

'I'll put the kettle on, and you can tell me all about it. Who wants tea?'

6

Davie

'We'll swing by the yard before we pay the wanker a visit,' I said.

'Yes, boss,' Rio replied as he fired up the engine, and my Jag came to life.

I employed a crew of enforcers and used a commercial property on an industrial estate as my firm's official HQ. It was ideally located, close to major A roads and motorway networks as my work often took me all over the country. I used different stages of intimidation; the first stage was verbal persuasion, constant phone calls and text messages. That was usually enough to get an average debtor to pay up. But for those proving more challenging to reel in, I upped the ante. I had a dog unit, which came in useful when extra intimidation was required. People weren't so lippy when they were faced with a couple of ferocious-looking Rotties.

I opened the glass door and stepped inside. Jack was sitting behind his desk, tapping away on a keyboard. 'How's it going?'

'Good,' he replied. 'I'm just looking over last month's figures so that I can do some financial forecasting and risk analysis.'

Like any good accountant, Jack was worth his weight in gold. He knew exactly what I could claim against my legitimate self-employed income and used every relief going to ensure I paid the least amount of tax legally possible. He was also a dab hand at washing the proceeds of my not so legitimate income. Accountants were required to report illegal activities to the authorities as deliberate fraud costs the taxpayer billions of pounds in evaded tax every year. But Jack turned a blind eye to the code of ethics and conduct he was obliged to follow.

'Where's Wes?'

'He's just exercising the dogs.'

Moments later, the door opened and in walked Wesley with the Rottweilers.

'Hello, boys,' I said as they bounded over to greet me, tails wagging. While I patted their glistening, short black coats, the rust-coloured markings over their brows moved around. 'Don't take their leads off – we've got some business to attend to.'

Wesley put the Rotties into the dog crates in the back of the black Transit emblazoned with 'Dog Security Unit'. I'd had the words painted in fluorescent yellow writing in case anyone was in any doubt of the van's purpose.

Rio climbed into the driver's seat and punched the address into the satnav as Wes and I sat side by side in silence. I glanced over at him on the journey to Kent; talk about dogs and their owners looking alike. Wesley had a full beard, a thick head of dark brown glossy hair and serious-looking peepers. He was tall and strong and emanated the fearlessness that mirrored his pups.

'According to the satnav, this is it,' Rio said when he pulled up in the slip road behind the high street.

I couldn't have pictured a more destitute suburban setting if I'd tried. The block of flats looked like a forgotten space. It was hard to imagine anybody could live in the properties; they were barely habitable. All of them had dingy curtains and showed signs of neglect; some looked unoccupied and had boarded-up windows. The place was a shithole if ever I saw one. I almost considered calling the whole thing off. I actually felt sorry for the bloke. The man who lived here truly was an unlucky soul.

After we stepped out of the van, Wesley retrieved the Rotties. They obediently sat side by side like furry bookends, gazing out from beneath their expressive brows, waiting for their master's instructions.

'Right, let's go and pay him a visit.'

I led the way across the pay-and-display car park, up the black metal stairs and along the open-air access path, stopping outside the shabby front door of number forty-seven. I rang the doorbell and gave the knocker a rap for good measure. The door cracked open several minutes later, so I rammed my foot inside to stop the occupant from closing it before I could say my bit.

'Kane Tyler,' I said to a man in his thirties who looked like he needed a wash and a square meal.

'Who wants to know?' was his reply.

I gestured with a nod of the head to Wesley, who forced the door open further with the aid of his steel-toe-capped boots.

'I don't like conducting business of this nature in public,' I replied as I stepped over his threshold.

Kane opened his mouth and was about to protest when he clocked the two Rottweilers. He wisely thought better of it and retreated towards the back of the property, which overlooked the high street. The inside of the flat was worse than the outside if that was possible. It was shambolic, to say the least.

'I'm sure you can guess why I'm here.'

'I haven't got a scooby-doo,' Kane replied as if he didn't know what I was talking about.

A rough-looking woman still wearing pyjamas was flicking through the channels on a dust-covered TV in the corner of the room. She stopped what she was doing and suddenly piped up. 'What's going on?'

I glanced over towards her, but she had already averted her eyes and gone back to channel surfing.

'I'm here to recover the money you owe Larry for a car you bought nine months ago. How do you intend to pay the fourteen grand you owe?'

I stood with my arms folded across my chest as he registered what I'd said. In my experience, people had a habit of maintaining they didn't know what you were going on about until you mentioned a different figure that was outstanding than the one they were expecting.

'I only owed Larry ten.' The defiance in his tone was apparent.

'But he sold the debt to me, which means the costs I incurred pass on to you.' I bought the debt for four thousand, so at least Larry got some of his money back, but now I was the one taking the risk. 'I'm not about to be out of pocket, so you need to cough up the full amount. In cash,' I added as an afterthought.

As Rio, Wesley and I walked back to the van in silence, I couldn't help thinking this could be one of those debts that might prove to be hard to recover. There was nothing of any value in the flat, and it was clear that the man didn't have a pot to piss in. If he had, he wouldn't have been residing in that dump. The smell had hit me as soon as he'd opened the front door.

It would be bad enough living above an ordinary shop, but a chippy, with the smell of frying fish wafting up your nostrils every day of the week, must be hell on earth. I couldn't see the attraction myself, but common sense told me it was a financial one.

'Did you see the state of his missus?' I laughed as Rio drove the van back to London.

'She had one hell of an underbite. The last time I saw a lower jaw like that was on an English bulldog.' Wesley chuckled.

I shook my head. 'She had saggy jowls and the lot. That's not a good look for a woman in anybody's book.'

'Poor bastard, imagine waking up with that face next to you on the pillow. It makes me glad I'm single,' Rio added.

'You looked stressed,' Amanda said when I walked in the door. 'Is everything OK?'

'Something tells me the debt I just bought from Larry is going to cause me no end of trouble.'

'What makes you say that?' Amanda tilted her head to one side and fixed me with her beautiful eyes.

'The bloke hasn't got a bean and everyone's short of

cash at this time of year, aren't they? I reckon I'd have more chance getting blood from a stone.' I laughed.

'Is there anything I can do to help?'

'Not this time, babe.'

Amanda was surprisingly good at helping me strategize. She'd developed quite a taste for the dirt and darkness associated with the underworld over the years but was able to hide behind her homemaker appearance so that nobody suspected. I liked her to pretend she knew nothing about my business to protect her from my rivals.

7

Davie

Christmas Eve

The sound of Christmas music was filling the house, and as I walked into the kitchen, Amanda had her back to me and was singing along to Mariah Carey's version of 'Santa Claus Is Comin' to Town'. When she turned around, peeler in one hand, potato in the other, I couldn't help smiling; she was wearing the apron she reserved for this time of year; the one with the bunch of mistletoe and 'kiss the cook' written across the front. I could see she was busy, but in her element. Preparations for the big day were well underway.

'Do you want a hand?' Mia offered, poking her head around the door.

'That would be lovely,' Amanda replied. 'Would you mind peeling some carrots?'

Christmas was steeped in tradition in our house, and I

wouldn't have it any other way. Even though my girls were all in their twenties, my wife still insisted on leaving a plate out with a mince pie and a glass of Hennessy XO for Santa, not forgetting a carrot for Rudolf.

'I have to pop out for a bit,' I said sheepishly. I knew that wasn't going to go down well.

Amanda put the potato and the peeler down on the pale grey granite work surface. 'But, Davie, it's Christmas Eve.'

'I know it is, but I've got an urgent bit of business that needs attending to.'

'Larry's debt? Surely that can wait a couple of days.'

I waltzed across the room, planted a kiss on my wife's cheek, then made a hasty retreat before she could protest any further.

'Ho, ho, ho, Merry Christmas,' I said when Kane Tyler opened the front door.

Instead of receiving a warm welcome, I saw his face drop to the floor. Call me a bastard for turning up unannounced on Christmas Eve, but I had a job to do and bills to pay. My girls cost me a small fortune at this time of year, so I'd like nothing more than Kane's cash to fund my festive season.

'Give me a break, man.'

'Sorry, Kane, no can do. Have you got the cash you owe me?'

Kane shook his head. 'I didn't know you'd be coming back today.'

'I'm not in the habit of making appointments. In my experience, if I do that, I usually find the property's empty when I arrive. I prefer to turn up at a time that suits me.'

'I've tried to raise the money, but I need more time. I'm at my wit's end,' Kane whined.

But he was wasting his time; I'd never been a sucker for a sob story.

'Anyone would think you had it in for me.'

I backed Kane into the hall and got up in his face. I didn't like his attitude. 'Whatever gave you that idea? I just want the money you owe me. Why should I fund your Christmas?'

I'd tried to recover my money without turning up the heat, but Kane was resisting. He needed to realise I wouldn't walk away from recouping the cash. For many people, the thought of a long, drawn-out court battle was too much to bear, so they were prepared to simply write off a debt. I wasn't one of them. I didn't use the official channels. There was no point; people like Kane didn't have a bean or any assets to seize legally. So why do things by the book? The menacing methods I used got results every time. It was all about job satisfaction for me. I did whatever it took to make the debtor cough up.

I glanced over at Rio before I fixed my eyes on Kane. 'We didn't drive all this way for a wasted journey. We're not leaving here empty-handed.'

The man had turned into a human jelly in front of my eyes, and now that I was starting to pile on the pressure, he was literally shaking in his shoes.

'I can't give you what I haven't got,' Kane said in a quavering voice.

December was full of extra expenses for all of us. I had to maintain sufficient cash flow to cover my outgoings the same as the next man, so an excuse like that didn't wash with me.

'That's a pity. I was hoping to avoid having to ask Rio to swing into action. Being a bare-knuckle fighter, he's a dab hand at rearranging a person's features.'

'Come back next week, and I'll have the cash,' Kane said.

The scrawny, pathetic excuse of a man was really starting to wind me up now. I noted the lack of please and thank you in his request. People normally resorted to grovelling when they were trying to negotiate extra time. Experiencing rudeness first-hand wasn't something I was accustomed to.

'Didn't your mother ever teach you any manners?' Silence followed my question. 'Luckily for you, Rio's here to show you what's expected in a situation like this. Over to you, mate,' I said, gesturing to my right-hand man with a flick of the head.

As I started to walk down the metal stairs, I could hear Kane cry out in pain before he began begging for mercy.

'Hold up, Davie,' Rio called as I walked across the pay-and-display car park to where my Jag was parked.

'That was quick.' I smiled.

'I didn't want to get blood on my new suit, so I just gave him a clump, a little taster of what's to come if he goes back on the agreement,' Rio replied.

When his face broke into a smile, he exposed his natural straight white teeth. No poxy veneers were needed here. Every inch of Rio was the real deal, highlighting the advantage of being mixed-race. His dad was Afro-Brazilian, and his mum was white; the result when they reproduced was phenomenal. You'd be hard pushed to find a man with a more handsome face or better physique. That's payback indeed to the racist bullies that terrorised him as a small child outside the school gates.

'I only landed a couple of punches, and they felled him like a tree,' Rio said, amazed at how easily he'd defeated his opponent.

That didn't surprise me one bit. Rio de Souza was well over six feet tall with bulging biceps and hands like a grizzly bear's paws. Even if he hadn't been an adept fighter, his sheer size would have ensured he could pack a punch, but when you added the fact that he was a seasoned boxer with the skill of a world champion into the mix, Kane's card was marked before Rio even raised a fist.

'Well, that will give the fucker something to think about when he chows down on his turkey dinner tomorrow.'

'That's if his jaw isn't out of action. We might need to pop back later with a packet of straws.' Rio grinned.

8

Mia

Christmas Day had to be my favourite day of the year, and from the collective squealing coming from my younger sisters as they ripped off wrapping paper, I wasn't the only one who thought so. Unlike a lot of people our age, and much to my parents' despair, there were no lie-ins until lunchtime. The three of us still woke early and piled into Mum and Dad's room like we'd done since we were small children.

'Doesn't it make your heart melt, seeing our girls looking so happy?' Dad said before planting a kiss on the top of Mum's head.

'Where have all the years gone, Davie? It seems like only yesterday they were tiny tots,' Mum replied, getting all nostalgic, dreaming of Christmases past.

Kelsey, Scarlett and I were gathered around the Christmas tree dressed in our pyjamas, working our way through the huge pile of colour co-ordinated presents Mum had arranged beneath it. Everything looked incredible; the wrapping was so beautiful, it was almost a shame to open it, I thought. My sisters didn't share my sentiment, enthusiastically ripping off the expensive paper Mum had spent hours perfecting in a matter of seconds, leaving it discarded in shreds on the floor. But she didn't seem the slightest bit bothered that her hard work was being annihilated; she sat on the sofa, her plush lilac dressing gown wrapped around her, with a smile spread over her face.

'Look what I got!' Scarlett looked delighted as she held up a Radley bag to add to her ever-growing collection.

My face broke into a beam, and I looked across at Mum. She smiled back at me. We'd chosen well when we'd opted to buy the Radley red zip-topped shoulder bag with the iconic Scotties wearing Fair Isle jumpers. Mum had also bought her the matching purse, but she hadn't got to that present yet. It was lost somewhere in the sea of gifts.

By the time everything was unwrapped, Kelsey, Scarlett and I were surrounded by blue Tiffany boxes, YSL makeup, Chanel perfume, hand-made chocolates, the list went on; there were too many things to mention. We'd been thoroughly spoiled as usual.

'Who's hungry?' Mum asked before she retreated into the kitchen to take on the role of domestic goddess.

We trailed along behind her like ducklings following their mother and took a seat around the large circular glass table that overlooked the garden and outdoor pool.

Mum looked up from her mixing bowl. 'Can you open a bottle of champagne, Davie? It's almost ready.'

Mum glided across the kitchen with two plates piled high, one with fluffy, American-style pancakes, the other with French toast. She placed them down on the pre-laid table and went back to get a large crystal bowl filled with fresh fruit salad and a platter of smoked salmon and cream cheese bagels.

'How many people are you expecting to feed?' Dad laughed.

Mum slapped him playfully on the arm, then picked up her fizz and held it out towards us. 'Merry Christmas,' she said before clinking glasses with us all.

I was just loading the dishwasher when the doorbell rang.

'I'll get it,' Dad said. He'd find any reason to excuse himself from helping to tidy up.

'Merry Christmas,' Jack said as he walked into the kitchen laden down with presents, his blue eyes sparkling.

'Merry Christmas,' we all replied.

Jack placed the gifts down on the table, then crossed the room and came to a stop behind me. When he slid his arms around my waist and planted a kiss on my cheek, I stopped what I was doing, spun around and threw my arms around his neck.

'You've just missed the most amazing breakfast,' I said.

'No, he hasn't. Take a seat, Jack, and I'll bring you some food.' Mum beamed.

I loved nothing more than spending some quality time together with my family and the morning flew by as we sat around the kitchen table while Mum effortlessly whipped up a feast with Dad's assistance. Surprisingly, the role of the trusty sous chef suited him down to the ground. He should try it more often.

Mum had transformed the dining room into a winter wonderland; the large table was a vision of silver and white, and lights twinkled from every corner of the room. After a stuffed mushroom starter, we tucked into a traditional Christmas dinner: turkey with stuffing, pigs in blankets, roast potatoes, a selection of vegetables, gravy, and cranberry sauce. Unable to squeeze in another bite, we took a break from the courses.

'Why don't we pull the crackers?' Mum suggested, picking hers up and holding it towards my dad.

Disillusioned with the shop-bought variety, Mum always hand-made ours with personalised gifts, and I looked forward to this every year. We took it in turns to pull the silver card tubes embossed with crystals and tied with organza ribbon so that we could see each other's gifts.

I thought nothing of it when all the pairs of eyes around the table fixed on me. Jack held the cracker towards me with a big smile on his handsome face. When the velvet box dropped onto the table, my brain froze. I picked it up and held it in my hand; I still hadn't realised what was going on until Jack dropped down onto his left knee and took the box from me. Holding it in his left hand, Jack lifted the lid with his right. My mouth dropped open as I took in the sight of the stunning pink diamond ring. My hands flew up and covered my trembling lips. I thought I was going to burst into tears.

'You're the love of my life. Will you marry me?' Jack asked.

'Yes,' I replied without a moment's hesitation. 'What took you so long?'

When Jack smiled and took hold of my left hand, sliding the ring onto my third finger, I thought I was going to burst with happiness. He couldn't have picked a more perfect time to pop the question. I loved the fact that all my family were gathered together and could share the special moment with us.

As Jack and I gazed into each other's eyes, Scarlett suddenly burst into song, belting out her version of 'Love Is in the Air', and the whole room erupted into laughter.

Dad walked over and threw his arms around me, then planted a kiss on the top of my head. After he released me, he shook Jack by the hand. 'You'd better take good care of my angel,' he said.

'You know I will,' Jack replied.

9

Davie

'Let's make one thing clear: non-payment is not an option,' I said as Kane's eyes bulged in response to the iron hold I had on his windpipe. 'It's time to cough up what you owe me unless you want to find yourself in A&E.'

I released my grip, and the scrawny fucker dropped to his knees on the stained carpet and began gasping for air. A smile played on my lips; I had to admit I got immense pleasure from another person's misery. There was no better feeling.

'I like to think I'm a reasonable man, and I've been extremely patient with you up to this point, but you're taking the piss if you think I'm leaving here again today empty-handed,' I said once Kane had caught his breath.

'I've tried to get my hands on the cash, but everywhere's been closed for Christmas,' Kane said.

'That's not my problem. I've got my reputation to think of, so I can't let you keep mugging off my firm. People like you never learn. If you don't want to get a knock on the door, don't buy things you can't afford. It's as simple as that.'

'I don't know what you want me to say,' Kane replied, looking up at me with wild eyes.

'How about, I'm sorry I messed you about, Mr Saunders; here's your money?' I prompted.

'I wish I could, but I haven't been able to raise it,' Kane said, lowering his eyes to the floor.

I sucked in a loud breath and watched him hug his knees into his chest as he cowered on the filthy carpet awaiting the beating he knew would follow his admission. But there was fuck all Kane could do about it. It wasn't as though he could call the police and tell them he felt like he was in danger and his safety had been threatened.

'Most people in your position would be desperate to sort this as quickly and as peacefully as possible.'

'Believe me, if I could, I would.'

'Get up,' I barked. When Kane stayed rooted to the spot, I gave Rio the nod. I'd brought him along to provide the muscle, so he gripped onto Kane's forearm and dragged him to his feet. 'That wasn't a request; it was an order,' I said, getting up in his face. 'You've wasted enough of my time. Get your wallet – we're going to the bank.'

'I've got fuck all in my account.' Kane threw his hands out.

'I'd like to see that for myself.'

Kane's English bulldog suddenly appeared in the hallway. Her short, bleached blonde hair was standing on end, and she had a grubby pale pink dressing gown wrapped around her shapeless body. You could see her saggy tits and gut dangling freely under the thin fabric, and I felt my stomach heave at the sight of her.

'We haven't got a penny,' she confirmed, but the statement fell on deaf ears.

'Let's go,' I said.

Rio caught hold of the sleeve of Kane's grey hoodie and frogmarched him out of the flat. Then he discreetly steered him along the walkway, down the stairs and through the alleyway underneath the flats that led to the high street.

'Put your card in the machine,' I said when we stopped outside the post office.

Kane pushed his Santander debit card into the slot, then entered one, nine, eight, nine with fumbling fingers.

I'd put money on the fact that his PIN was his date of birth and made a mental note of it. Kane pressed several buttons until his available balance appeared on the screen. The minus in front of the figures showed that he was overdrawn.

'Now, do you believe me?'

'I'll take that,' I said, confiscating the card once it had been released from the machine.

It was almost a pointless exercise seizing a card that had exceeded its spending limit, but it was a way of gaining control over the person who owed me cash. I often took hold of debtors passports, driving licences and bank cards when they didn't have any other valuable assets, to ensure I received repayment.

'You've got two days to come up with the cash. Otherwise, I'll let Rio go to work with the power tools.'

'Two days!' Kane echoed, a note of panic in his voice.

'That's correct,' I replied as I stepped away from the wall

I'd been leaning against. 'This is your final warning. Either you pay up or accept the consequences.'

Money was like a drug; the power it held over others intoxicated me. I couldn't get enough of it.

'We'll need to keep tabs on him to make sure the fucker doesn't go to ground,' I said as Rio and I walked back towards my Jag.

'I'll see to that, boss,' Rio replied.

I'd had enough of listening to Kane bleating on and on, trying every excuse in the book. I wasn't running a charity; in my eyes, what I provided was an essential service.

10

Davie

During a recession, most of the population suffered a loss to some degree, but I was glad to say I wasn't one of them. Business was booming; my bank account had never looked better.

As agreed, two days later, I rapped my knuckles on Kane's cheap PVC door. After a brief pause, his English bulldog opened it. Thankfully, she was dressed for once, albeit in a velour tracksuit, a staple item in any chav's wardrobe.

'Hello, Mrs Tyler. Is Kane in?' I asked. My old mum would have been proud of me; my manners were impeccable.

'Nah, he flew out to Barbados yesterday,' she replied, eyeballing me.

You had to admire the woman's bravery. Not all debt collectors were as good-natured as me, and a comment like that might get a lesser man's back up. Having said that, I had a limit to what I would take. If I was completely honest about it, I'd been a bit of a football hooligan in my younger days. Although I had to admit I'd mellowed with age, I still liked nothing more than a pub brawl or a street fight. I couldn't change the fact that I was a natural-born bully and had a passion for hitting people.

'I don't like conducting business on a person's doorstep. Can we come in, please?'

Kane's missus let out a loud sigh. 'If you must,' she said before she turned around and led the way along the narrow hallway.

My eyes were drawn to the word 'Juicy' emblazoned across her sizeable backside. The letters stretched in length and width as she waddled along. As we neared the front room, Kane came into view. He was sitting at the table with his head in his hands, looking like a broken man.

I wasn't that tall, five feet ten, but I was stocky, and I'd been told on many occasions that I had the kind of presence that said 'don't fuck with me, or you'll regret it'. I stood in front of Kane and fixed him with a glare. My grey eyes were cold, the colour of stone, and I had a heart to match where business was concerned.

'Have you got the cash?' I asked, folding my arms across my chest and adopting a stance with my legs apart.

'You only gave Kane two days. How was he meant to come up with the dosh as quickly as that? Did you expect him to pull it out of his arse?' Kane's missus piped up.

This tracksuit-clad woman really was a vile creature. I'm not sure I'd ever encountered a member of the fairer sex that was more vulgar than her. She had a mouth like a docker. My old mum would have threatened to wash it out with soap and water.

'It would be a sorry state of affairs if a person had to borrow from one loan shark to pay the other, wouldn't it?'

The English bulldog's lower jaw jutted out further than usual as she clamped her hands on her flabby hips and glared at me.

I felt myself bristle, so I turned to look at her. 'What did you just call me?'

I'd never been one to hit women, but this disgrace of the species was asking for a clatter. If she didn't shut her trap and wind her neck in, I was tempted to do it for her.

'You heard,' she replied.

I felt my blood pressure rising. 'Just so we're clear on this, I'm not a loan shark; I run a debt collection agency. There's a big difference between the two, and you'd do well to remember that. Do yourself a favour and sling your hook. Your hubby and I have got business to discuss.'

'You call it business, but I'd call it bullying.'

'And you'd know all about that, wouldn't you? I can see who wears the trousers in this relationship.'

A flash of anger crossed Kane's missus's face. She opened her big gob, about to give me an ear-bashing, but I didn't have time to deal with this crap, so I cut her off before she had a chance to speak.

'Get rid of her,' I said to Rio. The woman was doing my nut in.

'Come on, love,' Rio said, cupping her elbow in his large hand and steering her towards the hall. Rio stepped behind her and used the pads of his fingers to prod her in the small of her back as he guided her to the bedroom at the other side of the flat. 'Stay there until I tell you to come out.'

'Your wife's got a mouth on her, hasn't she?'

Amanda, on the other hand, was the height of discretion. She knew when and where to voice her opinion.

'Your missus offended me when she called me an illegal lender. My work involves the recovery of assets. I'd never target low-income families on benefits desperate for a pay-day loan. I go after people like you who try to be flash and buy motors they can't afford.'

Kane didn't reply but continued to cradle his head.

Why anybody would spend ten grand on a car when they lived in a shithole like this was beyond me. But men like Kane were ten a penny. Over the years, I'd become numb to the excuses I'd heard when I'd come to collect a debt. Every line known to mankind had been used in the past, so I was curious to know what Kane was going to come out with.

'Right, let's get down to the purpose of my visit. Have you got the fourteen grand?'

I was desperate to get out of the filthy flat before the smell of fish and chips penetrated every pore in my body and was fully expecting a bad case of verbal diarrhoea and pathetic excuses to spill from his mouth. So you could have knocked me down with a feather when Kane lifted his head and looked into my eyes. Then he picked up a carrier bag lying on the floor by the side of his chair and tipped the contents of it all over the table.

'There's your money,' he said with more than a hint of aggression in his voice.

'No offence, but you don't mind if I count it, do you?'

'Be my guest.' Kane's bloodshot eyes bored into mine.

I pulled out a high-backed wooden chair and took a seat. As I lowered myself onto it, my weight made the legs creak, and for one moment, I thought it was going to collapse beneath me.

'How did you come up with the cash so quickly? Did you rob a bank?' I laughed.

'I wish I'd thought of that.' Kane let out a loud sigh. 'I had no way of raising it, so I borrowed it from Barney Coleman.'

Taking a loan from a man like Barney wasn't a good idea, even if you felt you had no other options. It was a drastic measure and the behaviour of a desperate man. The action would be financial suicide at the very least. He was a complete nutter and brought misery and fear to everyone who had the misfortune of coming into contact with him. Barney didn't know when to call it a day. If anyone tried to have his firm over, they'd completely overreact. The punishment never fitted the crime. His dodgy practices made me look like a Boy Scout in comparison. My terms of business were extremely reasonable when you considered Barney Coleman's exorbitant interest rates. He also made a habit of adding other charges to loans whenever he felt like it and actively targeted people with poor credit histories.

'Good luck with that, son,' I replied, knowing that Kane would find it almost impossible to break free from the new debt.

I had a nose for trouble, and it told me that Kane had made a crucial mistake. If he didn't stick to the terms of their agreement, he could expect more than a bit of argy-bargy in return. But I wasn't going to dwell on the mess he'd got himself into; I wanted to recoup my cash and get out of the disgusting hovel he called home before I caught something.

Kane didn't take his eyes off me the whole time I was leafing through the piles of fifty-pound notes. As soon as

I'd counted the last bundle, I placed the money back in the carrier bag and pushed my chair back from the table.

'It was a pleasure doing business with you,' I said before I tucked the bag inside my jacket and turned away from the table.

Rio and I were walking down the stairs, side by side, when Mrs Tyler's dulcet tones bellowed after us. We stopped in our tracks at the sound of her voice.

'I hope you're happy now! You people are the scum of the earth. I don't know how you can sleep at night.'

At first, her words brought a smile to my face; I considered turning around and thanking her for the compliment, but the gentleman in me stopped me from rubbing salt in her wounds, and I decided to rise above it instead of openly gloating about their misfortune. But when I heard her snort back the contents of her nose and spit it at us, I felt fury rise within me. As I was about to turn on my heel, Rio grabbed hold of my arm and held me steady.

'Don't give her the satisfaction. Let it go, boss,' he said.

Rio was right; I'd got my money back, and that was all I cared about.

Amanda and my girls were gathered around the kitchen table when Rio and I walked in. I stood in the doorway for a moment drinking in the sight of them. Luckily for my daughters, my wife had been a model before we got hitched; she'd been a stunner and still was to this day. She'd passed her beauty on to them. The three of them shared their mother's delicate features, but each of them had different hair colouring. Mia was blonde like Amanda, Kelsey was dark-haired like I used to be, and Scarlett was a redhead. Talk about variety being the spice of life. We had every angle covered.

'I'll put the kettle on,' Amanda said when she looked up from the magazine spread between them on the table and noticed Rio and I standing in the doorway.

'Don't bother, love. After the day we've had, I think we need something stronger.'

The sound of my footsteps echoed as I walked across the tiles and pulled open the handle of the enormous American-style fridge-freezer. I took out two bottles of Birra Moretti, flipped off the lids, and handed one to Rio.

'Get that down your neck.'

'Thanks, boss,' Rio replied, holding the bottle up to his lip and taking a large swig from it.

'So you had a bad day,' Amanda said, fixing me with her beautiful blue peepers.

'I've had better.'

Although I was sure my wife was curious to know what had driven me to drink in the early afternoon, she knew better than to ask while we were in company and let the matter drop without pushing it. I liked to keep my girls out of the business, so we never discussed the finer details of my profession in front of them.

'How was your day?' I asked before I took a slug of lager.

'Good,' Amanda replied.

'What are you girls so engrossed in?' I asked. They were poring over the contents of a magazine with the same enthusiasm as a teenage boy let loose with his first porno mag. Their eyes had barely left the page.

'We're looking for ideas in these bridal magazines,' Mia

replied, pointing to the stack of glossy-covered publications littering the top of the table.

'Mia's going to start trying on wedding dresses soon.' Amanda beamed.

'Really? I bet she'll look beautiful in them.'

Mia spun around in her chair and smiled at me. 'Thanks, Dad.'

'There's so much to organise,' Amanda said.

'Shouldn't Jack be helping?' I laughed.

'He said he just wants to know the place, date and time, and he'll leave the rest to me,' Mia replied with a big smile on her face.

My firstborn seemed happy enough with the arrangement. Although I couldn't help thinking Jack was being a crafty little bugger, leaving Mia to do all the planning. But then again, who could blame him? He'd made the right decision as far as I was concerned. His input would be worthless in this situation anyway, so he was better off staying out of it and leaving it to the professionals. Women loved this kind of stuff. I only had to glance over at my wife and daughters to see how much they were enjoying themselves. Mia had plenty of help; Jack's opinion wouldn't be necessary when she decided which flowers she should choose and how she should have her hair styled on the big day.

Jack was a man after my own heart. I had a lot of time for him. He was proper old-school for a young man, which counted for a lot in my book. When he'd come to me and asked for my daughter's hand in marriage, I'd said yes without a moment's hesitation. Jack would be a welcome addition to our family. It also made good business sense to have my dodgy accountant tied by blood so that I could trust him completely with my money.

'So I take it you didn't get the money back?' Amanda asked once we were alone.

'I got every penny, but he only went and borrowed it from Barney Coleman.' I shook my head. For the life of me, I didn't understand why Kane had done that.

'Why does that matter?'

'Because sometimes a man just wants a quiet life, and I doubt I've heard the last of this.'

II

Davie

For want of a better word, Barney Coleman was a thug. I knew him from my days on the football terraces. He was an avid Millwall supporter and a member of F-Troop, which later became known as the Millwall Bushwackers. They were one of the most notorious hooligan gangs in England during the Seventies and Eighties.

Mine and Barney's paths first crossed in January 1988, when Millwall were knocked out of the FA Cup. I'd gone to Highbury to support my team but got caught up in the violent clash that followed when Millwall fans threw missiles onto Arsenal's pitch before running riot, pelting people with bricks and bottles.

Barney and I ended up in a brawl after he attacked the man standing next to me with a broken bottle. The guy hadn't been looking for trouble; he was an innocent bystander and had been trying to get out of the stadium when Coleman attacked him. As he dug the jagged glass into the bloke's cheek and slashed him from his ear to his mouth, the man let out a blood-curdling scream. I watched the horrific scene unfolding in front of my eyes, and a red mist descended over me. When the blood started spurting from the gash, I hurled myself towards Barney, knocking the improvised weapon out of his hand before bashing his face into a pulp with my bare hands.

'Davie... it's Kane,' the voice on the other end of the phone said.

I put down my mug of tea and let out a loud sigh; I knew this wasn't a social call. 'What can I do for you?'

'I hope you don't mind me phoning you.'

I responded by allowing a long pause to stretch out between us.

'I'm sorry to interrupt your afternoon, but I'm in real trouble.' Kane's voice wavered and quavered as he spoke.

I couldn't pretend to be surprised. When Kane had told me that he'd turned to Barney Coleman to bail him out, I could hardly believe what I was hearing. I was well aware that he had limited options, but he couldn't have picked a worse person to borrow money from. He'd bitten off more than he could chew by getting himself involved with a man like Coleman.

'Please, Davie, you've got to help me. I desperately need to borrow some money,' Kane begged.

He was sobbing down the phone, completely hysterical, like a toddler whose ice cream had just dropped onto the dirty pavement.

'You'll have to try somebody else, mate.'

'There's nobody else I can turn to. It's not as though I can ask the bank, is it? Please, Davie, you're my only hope.'

Kane could grovel all he liked, but that wasn't going to sway my judgement. It was nothing personal; it was purely a business decision. I couldn't extend Kane Tyler a line of credit when I knew he had no viable way of repaying it.

'Barney Coleman's giving me till the end of next week to come up with thirty grand.' When Kane spoke, panic coated his words.

'Thirty grand!' I felt my eyes widen. My interest rate was a bargain basement in comparison.

'If I don't come up with the dosh, Barney told me he's going to show me what the inside of a coffin looks like.'

Kane broke down in tears again, but I was unmoved by his plight even though I knew if Barney Coleman said he was going to kill you, it was no idle threat. Kane wouldn't be the first person who lost his life over an outstanding debt, and he wouldn't be the last. We live in a dog-eat-dog world. It's tough out there and only the strong survive. I couldn't help every Tom, Dick and Harry who came knocking on my door. I'd put myself out of business if I did. Men like Kane were a liability and bad for cash flow. That might sound harsh, but there were no two ways about it.

Kane was still blubbering when I ended the call. I put the phone down on my desk, leant back in my leather chair and gazed out of the windows at the huge garden beyond. My home was stunning; the acre plot was nestled in secluded countryside close to the banks of the River Lea, but just a stone's throw from Westfield, something that delighted the ladies in my life. We had it good, but I'd worked hard to provide us with this lifestyle, which was more than could be said for some people.

A couple of weeks later, Rio and I were cruising along the Thames in my Velocity Blue Jag on the way to my firm's official HQ when the news came on the radio. Three fire engines were attending a blaze at Frydays, a fish and chip shop on the high street in Rochester. The details of what started the fire in the early hours of the morning were sketchy at this stage as the crew were still in attendance tackling the huge inferno.

'Fuck me,' I said.

As we waited for the car in front to turn right, Rio turned towards me, and we locked eyes. No prizes for guessing what the fire crew were going to find in the flat above the chippy. People living above a restaurant was an insurance company's nightmare at the best of times, and that was before you threw a nutter like Barney Coleman into the mix.

12

Mia

'Wow, you look beautiful!' Scarlett clasped her hands together under her chin when I walked out of the changing room, followed by a billowing sea of ivory fabric.

My mum and sisters had been enlisted to help me choose the perfect dress for my upcoming wedding. 'What do you think?' I asked, resting my hands on the full tulle skirt.

'You look incredible,' Mum replied. 'We're going to have a difficult task on our hands. Being tall and statuesque, you've looked amazing in everything you've tried on.'

'Thank you,' I replied, looking up through my eyelashes.

Mum's compliment made me blush, and I felt myself retreat behind my hair. I liked to keep it long because it gave me something to hide behind when shyness got the better of me.

'Don't get all bashful on us. Give us a twirl,' Scarlett said.

I looked over my shoulder and smiled at her. As I moved, light bounced off the crystals decorating the fitted bodice. 'I'm so confused; I don't know which one I like best.'

'All the dresses have been beautiful, but this one's my favourite so far. It's exquisite,' Kelsey remarked.

'Don't feel pressured to choose one today,' Mum said, throwing the owner of the shop a warning look.

I had to stifle a laugh when I saw the look on the woman's face. Her jowls had been heading south when we'd walked in, but they were almost hitting the floor now.

'Mum's right; you've got plenty of time to make up your mind. It's such a big decision – at least sleep on it,' Kelsey agreed.

Seeing the pushy assistant baulk at the idea of allowing me to leave without making a purchase, my youngest sister decided it would be rude not to join in.

'Getting to try on the dresses is a perk of being a bride-to-be. If it was my wedding, I'd try on every dress in every shop in England!' Scarlett joked.

If looks could kill, she'd be a dead girl walking.

All the females in my family were gripped by wedding fever, and with the big day drawing closer, the plans were gathering pace. I decided to put dress shopping on hold for the moment. I wanted to wait until I'd booked the venue so that I could match the dress to the location.

Much to my dad's horror, Jack and I had decided to have a small, intimate wedding. Dad liked the idea of having a big, flashy, all-singing, all-dancing cockney knees-up. He wanted to splash the cash and invite everyone and anyone, but being an anxiety sufferer, that didn't suit my personality at all. I couldn't think of anything worse than spending my big day surrounded by hordes of people I'd never even met and would probably never see again.

I knew what my dad was like; he was a workaholic

and never missed an opportunity to network. As my intended was also employed by the firm, I didn't want our reception to turn into an oversized business meeting. Whether Dad liked it or not, a low-key ceremony was the way forward; I didn't want my wedding to turn into a three-ringed circus.

Ever since I'd been a little girl, I'd dreamt of getting married in a castle, and that was what I had my heart set on, so my mum and sisters accompanied me while I checked out the shortlist of venues Jack and I had compiled. Strawberry Hill House, an eighteenth-century Gothic castle in Twickenham, was the first one we looked at. It was undeniably beautiful, but something didn't feel right about it, so we moved on to the next on the list: Farnham Castle in Surrey. Again, this was a beautiful venue, but it was enormous, and I felt like we'd be rattling around in the immense space. I had everything crossed that Severndroog Castle, a small Gothic-style tower in Greenwich, would fit the bill, but our appointment was cancelled at the last minute and rescheduled for the following week, which was a nightmare as I was doing extra sessions at the sports centre to cover while one of my colleagues was on annual leave. Working around my busy schedule was going to be problematic, if not impossible.

'Cheer up, sweetheart,' Mum said as she parked her black Range Rover in the drive.

'I can't help it; I was looking forward to seeing Severndroog. I took this week off work to view the venues. I'm teaching back-to-back classes next week, so getting time off isn't going to be an option,' I replied, wiping away the tiny beads of sweat that had formed on my upper lip before I opened the passenger door and stepped out onto the gravel.

Mum prepared to write the wrongs by making tea while my sisters and I sat around the kitchen table, thumbing through wedding magazines. No wonder Jack had left the planning to me; it was proving to be almost impossible to cross anything off my ever-increasing list.

'I know you've already made your list, but what about this place?' Scarlett said. Her blue eyes were shining brightly as they scanned over the page before she turned it towards me.

Thistledown Castle stared back at me, and my heart skipped a beat. With its rose-pink sandstone walls and turrets, it was like something out of a fairy tale. It was spectacular; I couldn't believe Jack and I had overlooked it.

'It's absolutely perfect.' As my eyes drank in the sight of it, I tried to work out how I'd managed to miss it when I'd googled potential venues. When I began to read the article, the penny dropped. Thistledown Castle was located in the beautiful Highlands of Scotland. I let out a groan and allowed the magazine to slide from my hands onto the table.

'What's the matter, Mia?' Scarlett asked with the slightest hint of a pout. 'I thought you'd like it.'

'I do; I love it.'

'So, what's the problem?' Scarlett studied my face while she waited for me to reply.

'I'd book it in a heartbeat if it was six hundred miles closer to home,' I said, feeling more despondent by the minute. My scalp began to throb as a tension headache started.

My enthusiasm for wedding planning was at an all-time

low, and if things carried on the way things were going, I'd have to pull Jack to one side and suggest we forget the whole thing and elope instead. Instead of being enjoyable, the whole process was beginning to stress me out.

Mum brought a tray over and placed four bone china mugs down in front of us. She took a seat next to me and picked up the discarded bridal mag. After studying the full-page spread for a moment, she spoke.

'Scarlett's right; that venue looks perfect. Don't discount it just because it's in Scotland.'

I turned to look at my mum as a glimmer of hope began growing within me.

'I don't want to get my heart set on somewhere that Dad will never agree to; you know what he's like. He wants me to have a traditional East End wedding with pie and mash and jellied eels.' Wedding planning was so stressful.

'And he wanted the same thing when we tied the knot all those years ago, but he didn't get his wish. Just concentrate on what's right for you and Jack; leave your dad to me,' Mum said, flashing me a knowing smile.

I opened the lid of my laptop and typed the postcode of Thistledown Castle into Google Maps.

'Even if we could get an appointment, we'll never be able to view it; it's so far away. It's almost a ten-hour drive from here,' I said, letting out a loud sigh.

'Who said anything about driving?' Mum replied as she scrolled through the advert. 'It says here the castle is a short drive from Inverness Airport.' Mum tapped the glossy paper with her slender finger. We can fly up and hire a car. It'll be fun.'

Without waiting for me to reply, Mum picked up her phone and called the castle, scheduling an appointment for the day after tomorrow.

'All we need to do now is book some flights.' Mum beamed.

Mum, Scarlett and I sat side by side on the one-hour forty-minute flight. Kelsey had volunteered to sit in the row behind us with Todd, under the pretence that she wanted to discuss the best way to deal with the threats she kept receiving on social media from jealous internet trolls. Mum seemed to buy it, but if Kelsey expected me to believe that, she didn't know me very well. My younger sister might think she was being subtle, trying to hide her true feelings from my parents, but it was obvious she had a crush on Todd. I could see it a mile off. I just hoped for her sake Dad didn't get wind of it, or there'd be hell to pay.

Todd had been hired as our bodyguard, so Dad wouldn't be impressed to know his mind wasn't on the job because he was allowing my raven-haired temptress of a sister to distract him from his duties. Even though our minder ticked all the right boxes in the looks department, I couldn't help thinking my sister might not have been as fixated with him if he hadn't been off-limits. Kelsey had always been a rule breaker.

Our flight took off on time, and before we knew it, we were coming in to land. I'd never been to Scotland before, so I craned my neck and stared out at the fantastic scenery as lochs and mountains glided past the window.

'It's beautiful, isn't it?' I felt my lips stretch into a wide smile.

Mum squeezed my hand. 'It's absolutely stunning,' she agreed.

13

Davie

I glanced down at my Breitling watch and realised it was time for our daily ritual, so I walked over to the sideboard, took out the cut-glass decanter and two tumblers and poured a generous measure of single malt for Rio and myself. I didn't like my employees drinking while they were on duty, but Rio didn't fall under the same umbrella; he was like family to me. After handing him a glass, I picked up the remote control and switched on the TV. Rio took a seat next to me on the sofa, and we sipped our drinks in silence as we caught up with the day's events.

According to the report on the six o'clock news, an investigation had been launched following the blaze that destroyed Frydays fish and chip shop and the flat above it. The police and the fire and rescue service were still working to determine the events that led up to the fire. They were appealing for witnesses to come forward as the cause at this stage was unknown.

'Three crews attended the address in Rochester in

response to a series of 999 calls after smoke was seen billowing out of the premises in the early hours of the morning. Wearing breathing apparatus and using hose-reel jets and water from a nearby hydrant, firefighters attempted to bring the blaze under control. They tackled the fire throughout the night, but despite their valiant efforts, there was no way of preventing severe destruction at the fish and chip shop, and it was destroyed in the blaze. The brigade's fire investigators believe the fire started in the ground-floor kitchen before spreading up to the residential flat. They haven't ruled out arson at this early stage of the inquiry as preliminary investigations indicate the fire might have been started deliberately. The restaurant had been closed for at least six hours when the blaze broke out, and staff were no longer on the premises,' the newsreader said.

'Now there's a surprise,' I said, not taking my eyes off of the screen.

'People living in the block reported that the building's fire alarms didn't go off, and frantic neighbours were left to alert each other, banging on doors to let residents know they were in danger. A woman, who asked not to be named, said there was a strong smell of petrol in the air. The police confirmed two bodies had been recovered from the extensively damaged residence above the ill-fated chippy. The charred remains were believed to be that of the husband and wife who rented the flat. They were the only casualties. The other residents managed to evacuate their homes. When interviewed by the press, an eyewitness said they'd thought the flat destroyed by the blaze was unoccupied at the time because nobody could have slept through the commotion that was going on outside. Another added that bystanders were shocked to learn the couple had remained inside despite desperate efforts from their neighbours to alert them to the fire,' the newsreader continued.

'Poor bastards. What a way to go,' Rio said, shaking his head.

'The police have not named the occupants of the flat at this stage. Autopsies will be conducted to formally identify the victims. More than a dozen police officers remain on the scene as the investigation into the suspected arson attack continues,' the newsreader concluded.

The grim report ended with a clip of white-clad forensic scientists sifting through the rubble with shovels. I picked up the remote control and turned off the TV.

'There's no love lost between myself and Barney Coleman, so I'm seriously tempted to drop his name in the frame,' I said, turning to face Rio.

'It would serve him right if you grassed him up,' Rio replied.

I wouldn't normally consider ratting someone out, but the man had lower morals than I'd given him credit for. Although we were in a similar line of business, we used completely different methods when it came to retrieving money that was owed to us. I might be guilty of roughing my debtors up to encourage them to pay up promptly, and I have been known to deliver verbal threats to their family members to help speed the process up. But that was all.

I couldn't deny I had a reputation as a mean fucker with a heart of stone, but Coleman and I were poles apart when it came to the business tactics we used. Barney had set a new precedent when he'd set fire to a couple asleep in their bed. But I wasn't going to follow his lead.

Although the cause of the blaze was still under investigation, there was no doubt in my mind that Barney was responsible. He'd killed the Tylers in cold blood. They were the only people in the block who hadn't managed to escape the inferno; multiple witnesses had given accounts that their neighbours had repeatedly tried to raise the alarm, but there had been no response. I wasn't claiming to be a hotshot detective, but it was glaringly obvious that something untoward had happened to Kane and his missus inside the flat before it had been set ablaze. Otherwise, they would have escaped unscathed like the people in the neighbouring properties. Being overcome by smoke might have led to their deaths, but my money would be on the fact that Coleman had either drugged them, restrained them, or used some other method to prevent them from leaving the flat.

It seemed like a bizarre business practice for a debt collector to have adopted but killing off a late payer served two purposes at once for Barney. It acted as a deterrent to other debtors while providing the warped individual with entertainment, feeding his sick appetite for inflicting pain and suffering.

Barney enjoyed torturing people to such an extent that, on some occasions, he was prepared to write off the debt and not recoup his money. He didn't need the cash. Killing people was like a sport to him. He was like one of those bloodthirsty big-game hunters that go on an African safari. They shell out huge sums for an expedition to bag a lion, elephant, rhino, or any of the other big-game animals ripe for stalking. The only difference was Barney's victims were human.

Barney had no intention of issuing Kane with another warning. He'd given him an ultimatum, and when the poor bastard failed to deliver the thirty grand, Coleman carried out his threat.

'Barney's one sick individual,' Rio pointed out before lifting his glass to his lips and finishing his drink.

'Ain't that the truth,' I agreed.

'What are you going to do, boss?'

I let out a sigh. 'Now I'm faced with a dilemma: to squeal or not to squeal, that is the question.'

14

Mia

Todd took the wheel of the BMW X5 when we left Inverness Airport for the short drive to Thistledown Castle. The moment we approached the rose-pink, sandstone building with its fairy-tale turrets and hand-carved, twisted chimneys via a long tree-lined driveway, I knew I'd found the perfect venue. I sat in the back of the car, my heartbeat pounding with my eyes glued to the exterior; this was everything I wanted and more. The castle looked even better than it had on paper. I was glad I'd let Mum talk me into checking it out now.

My family were so confident that I was going to like it that Mum booked an overnight stay so that we could give the food and rooms a trial run ahead of the big day. Dad had insisted that Todd tagged along to make sure we were protected. I wasn't sure what trouble he was expecting us to get into while we were away. The castle was situated in a remote location, surrounded by one hundred hectares of picturesque Scottish countryside. We'd barely passed another vehicle on the journey from the airport. We were more likely to be pecked to death by the local grouse or trampled by the Highland cattle we'd seen grazing in the fields by the side of the road than encounter problems that would require Todd's military prowess to be called into action. But that was Dad for you; he was fiercely protective of the ladies in his life.

Todd parked the BMW at the base of the stone steps. As we clambered out of the car, a young, auburn-haired woman dressed in a dark-navy suit appeared in the doorway. She waved to get our attention, then began walking towards us with a warm smile pasted across her face. As she grew closer, she extended her right hand towards my mum.

'Welcome to Thistledown Castle. You must be Mrs Saunders,' she said. 'My name's Isla, and I will be showing you around today.'

'Pleased to meet you,' Mum said, shaking the fair-skinned woman by the hand.

'Which one of you lovely ladies is the bride-to-be?' Isla asked, casting her eyes over my sisters and I.

'That would be me,' I replied. 'I'm Mia.'

Isla shook my hand and then turned her attention towards Todd. 'So you must be the lucky man?'

Kelsey and Scarlett couldn't contain their laughter. The colour rushed to Isla's pale freckle-dusted cheeks, and my heart went out to her.

'Unfortunately, my fiancé couldn't accompany us; he had work commitments,' I replied, flashing my sisters a warning look. Even though we were close in age, they could be so immature at times, egging each other on where mischief was concerned. I often felt like I was middle-aged in comparison.

'Oh, I'm so sorry, my mistake. That's the first rule of wedding planning: you should never make assumptions; it can get you into all sorts of trouble. I have to confess, I'm new to the job,' Isla apologised, clearly hoping the ground would open up and swallow her.

I admired her honesty. There was something really nice about her. Isla's light-hearted manner made a refreshing change from the overly formal staff we'd encountered up until now.

'Todd drew the short straw as I wanted to get a man's perspective on the venue,' I said as I didn't want to tell Isla the real reason he was here.

'I should have known better; during my induction, a colleague told me they'd thought the bride's husband-to-be was her father. The couple were so horrified by the faux pas they decided not to hold their wedding here after all!' Isla bit down on her lip. 'I hope I haven't put you off.'

'Absolutely not!' I beamed.

So far, Thistledown Castle was ticking all the boxes even though I was doing my best to find problems with it. Why were humans programmed to find themselves drawn to the thing they were trying the hardest to resist? I wasn't the first person to battle with my conscience; it was an age-old dilemma.

'Would you like me to organise some refreshments before we begin?' Isla tilted her head to the side and smiled. As she did, her thick auburn hair tumbled over her shoulder.

'No, thank you,' I replied without consulting the others. I was keen to look around as soon as possible.

'As the rain's holding off, I think we should start with a tour of the grounds,' Isla said.

We followed behind as she led the way past the formal gardens in front of the castle, pointing out woodland walks to the left and walled gardens to the right. Isla stopped outside a small, granite-walled building with a slate roof, which was situated in a wooded area, surrounded by mature gardens, at the far edge of the grounds. She waited for the others to catch up with her as Kelsey, Scarlett and Todd were lagging behind.

'This is the chapel,' Isla said, walking around to the front of the building perched dramatically on the cliff-top.

'Wow,' I said, turning to smile at Mum before we went inside.

Isla turned the black metal handle and pushed open the arched wooden door with elaborate metal hinge plates down one side. As we stepped inside, the sun came out from behind a cloud, and its rays bounced off the stained glass windows, casting colours onto the whitewashed walls.

I stood in front of the huge stone altar that dominated the space, listening to the sound of the waves crashing on the rocks far below. This was everything I'd always dreamed of and more. Everything about Thistledown felt right. As I pictured myself walking up the aisle on my dad's arm, a tear rolled down my cheek.

'Are you all right, Miss Saunders?' Isla asked.

The sound of her lilting Scottish accent brought me back to reality, and I dabbed at my face with my fingertips.

'I'm fine, thank you. Just feeling a bit emotional.' I smiled.

That's to be expected,' Isla replied. 'Are you ready for a tour of the castle?

'Yes.'

Leaving the hidden gem behind us, we walked back in the

direction of the main building. After climbing up the stone stairs, we walked over the threshold and into the grand entrance hall hung with large crystal chandeliers. The walls and floors were covered with the same rose-pink sandstone, but unlike on the outside of the building, the interior slabs were polished to a high shine, giving the spacious area a warm, homely feel. Thistledown wasn't like a typical castle; there wasn't a scrap of dark panelled wood or a single gaudy portrait of yesteryear's ancestors like some of the others we'd viewed. Even though it was centuries old, it had a modern feel to it, which I loved.

Isla led the way through a series of interconnecting rooms, each with its own open fire roaring away until she came to a space that spanned the width of the castle.

'We normally set up the wedding breakfast in here, but all our events are bespoke, so we can tailor them to meet your needs and individual requirements.'

'This is perfect,' I said, looking around the bright, airy, whitewashed room, with just a hint of natural stone poking through. It had a vaulted ceiling and tall narrow windows and would be an impressive space in which to wine and dine our guests.

'Rest assured your every whim can be catered for. Our team of in-house chefs will be able to create a menu to suit any taste,' Isla said, grinning from ear to ear.

I smiled back as I considered asking her if they would be able to rustle up pie and mash and jellied eels to keep my dad happy, but I thought better of it, deciding to keep the inside joke to myself.

'The doors open out onto a cocktail terrace. Your evening reception can spill out here if you like. Some guests choose to round off their celebrations with a cannon fire salute and fireworks.'

Being of a nervous disposition, I wasn't sure how much I liked that idea, but I smiled warmly all the same. Isla was going out of her way to be helpful, so I gave her some friendly encouragement as she was new to the job.

'Let me show you the bedrooms,' Isla said, weaving her way through the warren-like interior and back to the main hall.

The staircase, easily wide enough for four people to stand side by side, beckoned us towards it, and our footsteps echoed as we walked up to a landing that split into two upper flights – one to the left and one to the right. Isla turned left and breezed along the corridor.

'Every bedroom has been individually designed; no two are the same,' she said, opening each of the doors as we walked past so that we could glimpse inside. 'But I'm sure this is the one you'll be most interested in.' Isla grinned.

My mouth dropped open as I stepped into the bridal suite. It was out of this world, a vision of ivory and aquamarine. A huge four-poster with floor-length curtains stood against the back wall with a pair of swans made out of bath towels perched on the end. A velvet chaise longue rested along the bottom of the bed, positioned so that it could make the most of the panoramic views. A door off to the left housed the nicest en suite I'd ever seen. The room was centred around a large rainfall shower set in the middle with double sinks and a free-standing roll-top bath.

'There's just one final feature I need to show you,' Isla said.

I had to confess I didn't think she'd be able to top what

I'd seen, but that was before she opened up the floor-to-ceiling windows and stepped outside. The turreted bedroom had its own private terrace and hot tub with a set of stairs in the corner that led down to the gardens.

'I'm speechless,' I said as I looked around and noticed the dining area, loungers, fire pit and bar area. 'It's so beautiful here; we'll never want to leave.' I sighed, knowing my heart was well and truly set on this venue.

'As you can see, Thistledown Castle's set on a headland with far-reaching views.' Isla paused so that we could take in the scenery. 'If you choose to have your wedding here, you'll have a unique location for your photos.'

Isla didn't need to try and sell it to me; I was already sold.

Isla checked the time on her watch. 'The restaurant's open now, so I'll take you down to meet the chef. Once you've had lunch, we'll get you checked in and then you'll be free to enjoy the beautiful surroundings for the duration of your stay.'

'Thank you,' I replied as I attempted to memorise every detail of the castle so that I could tell Jack about it later.

15

Kelsey

I heard a gentle rap on the door, so I opened it; my face broke into a huge grin when I saw Todd standing on the other side. He smiled back at me, and without waiting to be invited in, he stepped over the threshold. Todd planted his tattooed arms on my waist and pushed me back against the wall, kicking the door closed behind him. I began to giggle when he started kissing the side of my neck, so he silenced me by plunging his tongue deep into my mouth. Todd ground himself against me, leaving me in no doubt what was on his mind.

'Every time I'm near you, I'm in a constant state of horniness,' Todd whispered in my ear.

'Wait,' I said, wriggling free from his embrace.

Todd stared at me with a look of bemusement on his face.

'If this is going to become a regular thing, I think we need to know we're on the same page,' I said. 'My dad will lose his shit if he finds out we're sleeping together.'

'Who's going to tell him?' Todd replied, pulling me towards him before clamping his hands at the base of my back.

I put my hands on his chest to put some distance between us. 'Seriously, Todd, which would be more important to you in the long run: your job or a relationship?'

'That's a bit heavy, isn't it?' Todd loosened his grip on me. My question appeared to have put the wind up him.

'Maybe.' I shrugged.

We didn't have a lot in common aside from physical attraction, but I wanted him to acknowledge there would be consequences for both of us if we got caught.

'What's with the ultimatum?' Todd's brow furrowed. 'I prefer to keep my love life uncomplicated; free and easy works best for me.'

I snorted. 'I don't like being tied down either, but I'm your boss's daughter. Do you seriously think you could stay in your job if this doesn't work out?'

'I hadn't really given it much thought.'

'Well, you should. There are a lot of attractive girls out there who aren't related to the man you work for.'

'That's true. I'm sure I saw one of the waitresses giving me the eye earlier. Perhaps I should take the sensible path and hook up with her instead.' Todd smirked.

I could see he was trying to get a rise out of me, but he was wasting his time. There were plenty more fish in the sea.

'Be my guest. It's your loss.'

I reached for the door handle, and Todd covered my hand with his. Talk about giving me mixed signals.

'Come on, Kelsey, where's your sense of humour?'

Was this banter or a battle of wills? The last thing I wanted was to get caught up in a power struggle. A relationship like that was too exhausting for words.

'I know what's at stake, and I think it's worth it. Let's just make sure we don't get caught.' Todd smiled at me with a twinkle in his eye.

Then he pulled me towards him and started kissing the side of my neck. I knew what we were about to do was risky as my mum's room was next door to mine, but I was powerless to stop myself; Todd's pull right now was magnetic, too great for me to resist. I didn't try to stop him as he began stripping off my clothes.

My heart started to pound as my fingers found the hem of his fitted black T-shirt. I gripped onto it, and we momentarily unlocked lips so that I could pull his top over his head. Todd had an amazing physique. I ran my fingers down his hair-free chest and well-defined stomach, then I traced the nail of my index finger along the waistband of his black combat trousers.

Todd unbuttoned my stonewashed skinny jeans and peeled them down my legs, taking my underwear with them. Then he slipped his fingers into me. I fumbled to undo his combats, but when I finally managed to, I dropped onto my knees and took him into my mouth. Todd let out a moan, and his head rocked back in ecstasy. I felt his body tighten as I moved my head backwards and forwards.

Todd helped me to my feet, lifted my top over my head and unclasped my bra before he backed me onto the bed. Lifting my arms above my head, he pinned me down; one of his hands encircled both of my wrists, so he was fully in control. My back arched, and I lifted my hips when I felt him inside me. I closed my eyes; pleasure began rising as he pounded into me. Todd let go of my arms; then he pulled out to tease me. My eyes sprang open. I wanted him so badly.

I reached down with my right hand and closed it around him, letting my fingers glide up and down his length before I guided him back inside me. I tingled with excitement as he pushed faster and deeper. Once I'd come, he speeded up and cupped my buttocks as he prepared to let go completely. I felt Todd shudder as he released everything he'd been holding back.

'Kelsey, it's me,' I heard Mum call as she knocked loudly on the door.

Todd and I froze; we'd almost been caught in the act. But instead of fretting about it, I was buzzing; I thrived on excitement and never did what was expected. I'd always been a bit of a rebel.

Mum began knocking again, louder than before. 'Kelsey, Kelsey,' she called.

I knew I was going to have to answer the door, so I scooted out from underneath my bodyguard, grabbed a towel from the bathroom and wrapped it around myself.

'You'd better find somewhere to hide,' I whispered as I rushed past Todd. 'Just a minute,' I called before I flung open the door.

Mum looked startled to see me standing in front of her in a semi-naked state. I noticed her crane her neck as she tried to look over my shoulder, and I had to stifle a laugh.

'I didn't have time to have a shower before we left this morning, so I was freshening up,' I said to explain away the fact that I was undressed.

Mum seemed to buy my excuse, and I saw a look of relief spread over her face.

'I'm sorry, I didn't mean to interrupt; I just wanted to let you know we're going to head down to dinner in ten minutes,' Mum said, checking the time on her watch.

'Perfect. I'll throw some clothes on and give you a shout as soon as I'm ready.'

Once I'd closed the door, I leant back against it and smiled. After all the exertion, I'd built up quite an appetite.

16

Davie

Due to the heavy-handed approach some of my competitors used, enforcers were often referred to as leg-breakers. It was a derogatory term that didn't sit easily with me. I liked to think I was a reasonable man and only used force in some instances where low-level intimidation had failed to reap the correct result. I was good at my job; I could be very persuasive, so I didn't often need to resort to extreme violence. Barney Coleman, on the other hand, didn't know when to quit; sticking the boot in one last time was his signature move.

While Amanda and my girls were away in Scotland, I'd happily adopted the role of a bachelor; eating takeaways straight out of the box had become my latest pastime. My wife's hair would be standing on end if she'd seen what I'd been eating. Nobody kept a closer eye on my high blood pressure and cholesterol than she did. My dad had died young. He'd suffered a massive fatal heart attack when he was forty-six, and Amanda was determined the same wouldn't happen to me. She was going to make sure I lived until I was a ripe old age. But a man had to cut loose and enjoy life every once in a while, didn't he? Although Amanda had left the fridge stocked with home-cooked healthy options, I'd thrown my regular meal plan out of the window now that I'd been given the opportunity to fend for myself.

Being a former model, Amanda looked after herself both inside and out, so junk food was always off-limits. Not just for herself, for the rest of the family too. I knew she had our best interests at heart and wanted us to be a better version of our current selves. But to a man who'd been raised on cheap cuts of meat and stodgy puddings, it was proving to be a hard habit to break. Good nutrition and a balanced diet help to keep a person fit; that was a fact. Ever since our children had been little, Amanda strove to be the best role model she could be in that department. She'd done a brilliant job; that was undisputed.

My wife was a magician in the kitchen. She could conjure up a feast at the drop of a hat and always ensured we had our five a day, no matter how much we protested. Don't get me wrong, I knew what she was doing was a good thing, but occasionally I had to overrule her for the good of our insides. I'd like to think I'd done us all a favour when I'd officially banned kale and broccoli smoothies from the breakfast menu. My issue was this clean living was all very well, but having unclogged arteries wouldn't do you any good if you got flattened by a bus when you were crossing the road.

'Do you want me to get that?' Rio asked when the doorbell rang, signalling the arrival of our takeaway.

'Yes, mate,' I replied before cracking open a couple of cans of Stella.

Rio appeared a couple of minutes later carrying a brown paper bag stained with oil, and I knew we were in for a treat. Sometimes a person could develop a craving that only a calorie-laden curry swimming in grease could satisfy. The Taj Mahal never let me down on that front.

'Have you had any more thoughts about Barney?' Rio asked as he tucked into his lamb bhuna.

'I've thought about nothing else,' I admitted shovelling chicken korma into my gob as though my life depended on it. 'But being a grass doesn't come naturally to me. I'll have to do something, though. A man like Barney gets older, not wiser. He needs taking down a peg or two. The geezer's getting too big for his boots.'

'Ain't that the truth,' Rio agreed.

'Let's talk about this later, or it'll put me off my food.'

I put all thoughts of Barney Coleman out of my head so that I could enjoy my freedom before my girls returned. Not that I wouldn't be glad to see them, but I'd be lying if I said I hadn't enjoyed the peace and quiet while they'd been away, not to mention the twice-daily takeaway. It had been fun while it had lasted, but all good things had to come to an end sooner or later. If I continued eating the way I was, it would be disastrous for my health. You won't hear the waistband on my trousers complaining; they would be glad to see the back of my full-fat blowout. Since I'd turned forty, I seemed to put on weight just looking at food and every year older I got, the problem was only getting worse.

17

Mia

'So how was bonny Scotland?' Dad asked when Mum, Kelsey, Scarlett, and I walked through the front door.

'It was amazing. Thistledown Castle was out of this world,' I replied as I followed Mum into the kitchen.

'I'm surprised you haven't faded away,' Mum joked when she clocked all the uneaten food in the fridge.

'I'll be back in a minute; I need to make a phone call,' Dad said, rushing out of the door, so he didn't have to endure the inquisition.

'I swear your father thinks I'm stupid, but I know exactly what he's been up to while we've been away; he's been on one of his junk-food binges. But that's going to work in our favour.' Mum smiled.

'How come?' I wasn't sure what that had to do with anything.

'He'll feel guilty that he didn't eat the food I cooked for him, so he'll be desperate to please me, which will give me the perfect opportunity to tell him you've chosen your venue and it isn't a London one.'

'Good luck with that,' I replied.

My mum was an incredibly skilled manipulator where Dad was concerned, but she had her work cut out for her on this occasion. The words 'watch and learn' sprung to mind.

'Dad's not going to be happy that the wedding's being arranged in a castle six hundred miles from home!'

'He'll come around to the idea, and anyway, it will do him good to have some time off from work for once, even if it is only for a couple of days.'

'I'm just going to phone Jack and let him know we're back,' I said, sliding open the glass door that led out into the garden. I took a seat at the cast-iron table nestled in a sheltered spot on the patio to make the call.

'So Mum tells me you've got your heart set on the Scottish place,' Dad said, fixing me with expressionless eyes when I walked back into the kitchen.

A pang of guilt stabbed me and made my insides twist; I could see the disappointment in his face. He didn't need to voice his opinion; if I chose Thistledown Castle, I'd be going against my dad's wishes.

'I know you were hoping the wedding would be in London, but it's in a different league to the other venues I've looked at...' Dad cut me off with a wave of his hand, and I let out a sigh.

I could feel my anxiety start to build, but I had a technique I used as a coping strategy, and it seemed to work very well. If I forced myself to focus on tiny details, I could stop myself from freaking out when I was stressing about something. So

I slowed my breathing and began to concentrate on the fine lines in the travertine wall tiles until the sound of Dad's voice brought me back to reality.

'Listen, Mia, your happiness is the most important thing in the world to me.' Dad reached forward and squeezed my hand.

'Thank you. That's such a lovely thing to say.'

'I mean it; whatever my daughter wants, she gets.' Dad smiled. 'So if I have to drag my arse up to the Scottish Highlands for a couple of days, you won't hear me complaining. Well, not much anyway.' He winked.

I felt my eyes widen as my brain registered what Dad had just said. I hadn't expected him to back down so easily; he was paying the bill, after all, so you would expect him to have some say in the matter. Dad might have had a reputation for being a bit of a tyrant when it came to business, but he was a big softie where the family were concerned.

'You seem a bit underwhelmed. I was expecting a bit more of a response than that.' Dad laughed.

'Sorry, I'm just trying to let it sink in.' I threw my arms around his neck. 'Thanks, Dad, you're the best.'

'I aim to please. As long as you're happy, I'm happy,' Dad replied, planting a kiss on the side of my head.

I looked up at my dad and grinned. 'Now who's being underwhelmed? Happy isn't a big enough word to describe how I'm feeling. I'm absolutely ecstatic!'

My dad truly was one in a million. My fiancé, Jack, had a hard act to follow; Dad had set the bar high.

'I'm so glad you're all right about the wedding being in Scotland. I don't mind admitting, I wasn't sure how to break it to you.' Thank God my mum had volunteered to do that particular task.

'You didn't need to say a word; I could see it in your face.' Dad ran his fingertips down the side of my cheek. 'I'm more than happy to go along with whatever you choose. I don't want you to start stressing out over the arrangements; that's the last thing you need.'

I should have realised I'd given the game away. I wasn't very good at hiding my feelings; I wore my heart on my sleeve. Dad was right; keeping my anxiety in check should be my top priority. But it was always a struggle. I had to remind myself on a daily basis not to stress about the little things that were unimportant.

'I think you're going to love it, Dad. Not only has the castle got superb views across the sea, it's also got its very own chapel. It's a magical place; it cast a spell on me the moment we entered the grounds.'

'Todd was impressed with the venue as well. One of the reasons I wanted him to tag along was to give him the opportunity to carry out a recce before the big day,' Dad said.

Why did that not surprise me? Dad never left anything to chance.

'I'm sure I don't need to tell you, I've acquired a fair few enemies over the years, and the last thing I need is for you to get hitched somewhere that might compromise our security,' Dad said.

'I didn't even think of that.'

My mind had been on other things. I was fully immersed in the exciting stage of wedding planning, but I had to confess there was more to it than met the eye, and I was beginning to find the whole thing daunting.

'If it puts your mind at ease, Thistledown Castle's set on a headland in a very remote location, and we'll have exclusive use of the twenty bedrooms, reception rooms and the extensive grounds.'

Apart from the obvious beauty of the place, that was a major selling point for me. Unlike some venues, we'd have sole use of the facilities, which would give us total privacy and guaranteed that our celebration would be uninterrupted by other events.

'That's good to know, babe. Like I said, if you're happy, I'm happy. Just don't ask me to wear a kilt. I haven't got the legs for it!' Dad smirked.

18

Davie

Easter Sunday

I was just about to sit down to roast lamb with all the trimmings that my good lady wife had cooked for our family when my mobile began to ring.

'I'll be back in two ticks,' I said, jumping out of my seat and heading out of the door before Amanda had a chance to protest.

'Sorry to disturb you, boss,' Rio said, knowing how strongly I felt about having time with my loved ones disrupted. 'But I thought you'd want to know what your old mate's been up to.'

My right-hand man had to be talking about Barney Coleman.

'What's the prick done now?'

'Word has reached me that he frogmarched a geezer out of his home this morning while his kids were tucking into their Easter eggs. He drove him to a deserted location, locked the bloke in a container, poured petrol over it, then set it alight.'

'What the fuck?' I could hardly believe what I was hearing. What Rio had just described sounded like a scene from a movie. 'Did your info come from a reliable source?' It sounded too far-fetched to be true.

'Yes, my guy put me in touch with the man's widow. I've just put the phone down from her. She was bawling her eyes out, Davie.'

'Fuck me, so the bloke's dead then?'

'Yes, there's no doubt about that. Nothing left but a pile of ash.'

Barney Coleman seemed to have developed a fascination with fire. This was the second incident in a matter of months where he'd callously burned his victim to death. I wished I hadn't talked myself out of dobbing him in to the cops now after Kane and his missus perished in the chippy blaze. Even though I'd been sorely tempted to stitch him up, I hadn't liked the idea of being a grass – it wasn't part of the criminal code – so I'd let the opportunity pass me by. Big regret. But hindsight was a wonderful thing, wasn't it?

'What do you want me to do, boss?'

'Phone her back and tell her we'll call over later. Come and pick me up in an hour. That'll give me time to eat my dinner and pacify the wife.'

Amanda wasn't going to be happy when I broke the news, but what could I do? Business had a habit of calling at the most inappropriate moments sometimes.

'Really, Davie? It's Easter Sunday,' Amanda said as she cut into the three-tier chocolate cake she'd made.

'I know, babe. I promise I won't be long.'

Amanda let out a loud sigh. 'We haven't even finished eating yet.'

She didn't need to tell me that! Nobody was more disappointed than I was to be missing out on the towering gateau covered with chocolate shavings and Lindor mini eggs. It looked delicious; my mouth was watering at the sight of it. Amanda rarely allowed me to indulge in anything so decadent, so I was gutted to be missing out on the opportunity.

'Save me a piece, will you?'

I fixed my eyes on Amanda, but she didn't reply or look up. She continued offering the cake around the table, so I took that as my cue to leave.

As Rio parked my Jag outside a scruffy-looking block of council flats in Tower Hamlets, I was beginning to wish we'd brought the van instead. I gazed up at the balconies cluttered with personal effects and gained an insight into the people who lived there. Bikes and children's toys lay discarded on some, and others had washing strung out on them, flapping back and forth in the breeze. I couldn't imagine living like this. The whole place looked an eyesore.

'Let's keep this brief; I'm not sure my motor will be safe here,' I said as Rio and I walked across the soulless space and into the foyer.

Rio pressed the button for the lift, and I tapped my leather shoe on the ground while we waited for it to arrive. A loud clanging sound punctuated the silence as it trundled towards us then juddered to a halt. When the doors started to squeak open, the smell of stagnant piss hit me full force in the face.

'Let's walk,' I said. There was no way I was going to confine myself in a tiny metal space that smelt like a rhino's cage, especially as the lift sounded like it was about to break down.

Rio pushed open the heavy fire door that led to the concrete staircase, which incidentally emitted the same foul aroma as the lift. I clamped my hand over my mouth as we started to ascend the stairs two at a time.

'For fuck's sake. Don't these people have shitters in their flats?' I said when we came out of the stairwell, and it was safe to take a breath.

'You'd think not,' Rio replied as we began making our way along the communal landing. 'It's this one, boss,' Rio said, stopping outside number thirty.

I rapped on the door with my knuckles, and almost instantly, a man in his sixties wearing a deathly pallor opened it.

'Is Pauline here?' I asked.

'Who wants to know?' the man replied.

I could feel my temper start to rise. I hadn't popped over for a social visit; I'd come to help the woman out. 'Davie Saunders,' I said through gritted teeth.

'It's OK, Dad, let him in,' I heard a woman say.

The man stepped back from the doorway, and Rio and I walked in. 'She's in the front room,' he said, pointing down the hall.

Pauline was sitting on the sofa next to an older lady who was cradling a small child on her lap.

'Can you take the kids out of here, Mum?' Pauline asked. The woman nodded and got to her feet. 'Come on, sweetheart,' she said to the little girl, taking hold of her hand.

'But I want to stay with Mummy.'

'I know you do, but Mummy's got something to do, so be a good girl and come with Nanny.'

The child did as she was told, but not before she stared up at me with her bottom lip jutting out.

'Go with Nanny, boys,' Pauline said to the two little tykes sprawled across the carpet, building a structure out of Lego.

'Who wants to help me make some cupcakes?' Pauline's mum said as she led the little girl out of the room.

The boys scrambled to their feet, forgetting all about the Lego. 'We do, Nanny,' they called, racing after her.

What was it with males and food? The obsession clearly started from an early age, I thought, and if the circumstances of our visit hadn't been so tragic, it would have brought a smile to my face.

Pauline sat perched on the edge of the sofa, wringing her hands in her lap. The woman looked like she'd gone to hell and back; her face was blotchy, and her eyes red-rimmed from the buckets of tears she'd shed.

'Thank you for coming,' Pauline said when she heard the kitchen door click closed. 'Sorry about the mess,' she continued, pointing to the toys and chocolate wrappers strewn around the floor.

'It's fine,' I replied. The poor cow had enough on her plate without worrying about a bit of mess.

'Would you like to sit down?' Pauline asked.

'No thanks.' I was conscious that my Jag was probably receiving some unwanted attention and was keen to get back to it as soon as possible. 'Do you feel up to talking about what happened with Barney Coleman?'

Pauline covered her face with her hands; I could see her body visibly shaking as she plucked up the courage to speak. Then after a moment, she let out a deep breath and steepled her fingers in front of her mouth while she gathered her thoughts.

'Barney burst in here this morning and demanded the two of us go with him. It's just as well my mum and dad are staying with us, or the kids would have been left alone. How could we have left three little ones under five unattended?' Fresh tears began sliding down Pauline's cheeks.

'What happened after that?' I pressed.

'One of Barney's men drove us down to the port, and they made Owen get into one of the containers.' Pauline's voice broke as she relived the experience, and she began sobbing again.

I felt bad coaxing the story out of her, but I needed to get the details clear in my head before I could confront my old enemy. I wasn't going to press her on what Barney did to her old man after that; Rio had already told me the bastard had poured petrol over the container, then set it alight.

'Do you know which port he took you to?'

'Tilbury,' Pauline replied after composing herself. 'There was nothing I could do. The place was deserted, so nobody came to help. I can't get the sound of Owen's screams out of my head.' Pauline covered her ears with her hands. 'He was banging on the metal with his fists and trying to kick the door out before the fire took hold. But then it must have got too hot for him to touch, and he just started begging for his life over and over again before everything went quiet.' Pauline pulled the cuffs of her hoodie over her hands, wrapped her arms around herself and started rocking backwards and forwards like a psychiatric patient in need of a top-up of meds.

'You've been very brave, love. Don't you worry, I'm going to make the fucker pay for what he's done.'

Amanda looked up when I walked into the conservatory. She had her back to the view of the garden, and when I took a seat opposite her, she put the magazine she was reading down on the coffee table positioned between us.

'I'm sorry I had to skip out,' I said.

'I know how much you love your food and family time, so it must have been something important,' Amanda replied.

'It was. Barney Coleman killed a man in front of his missus. The poor woman's beside herself. I'm going to have to sort that bastard out once and for all.'

A look of fear swept over Amanda's face. 'Don't do anything hasty, Davie. You're going to start a war if you're not careful.' Amanda's eyes were pleading.

'I know. But what can I do? Somebody's got to stand up to the fucker. He's running amok. Don't worry, babe, I'm not going to do anything stupid,' I replied, hoping to put my wife's mind at rest.

19

Scarlett

'What are you doing?' Kelsey asked, poking her head around my bedroom door before she stepped inside without being invited.

'Getting ready for rehearsal.' The opening night for my end-of-year performance was growing closer by the day.

'I need you to cover for me,' Kelsey said.

I lowered the mascara wand away from my eyelashes and put it back in the tube. Then I spun around on my dressing table chair so that I was facing my older sister and folded my arms across my chest before tapping my lips with my forefinger.

'Let me guess; you're sneaking off to hook up with Mr Muscle again.'

'No shit, Sherlock. And I wish you wouldn't keep calling Todd that,' Kelsey replied, rolling her eyes at me.

'Why not?' It described our burly bodyguard perfectly.

Kelsey and Todd's love affair was being conducted as an undercover operation, which undoubtedly added an element of excitement to the whole thing. My sister never took the easy option; the riskier something was, the more she liked it. But she got bored with things quickly once the novelty wore off and the thrill started to decline.

'Todd and I never get to wake up together, so I was wondering if you'd be up for staying somewhere overnight. We could go away for the weekend. What do you think?'

'Hell no,' I replied.

Kelsey did my head in sometimes. My uni schedule was full-on at the moment, so I had little time for anything else. The last thing I wanted to do with the precious downtime I had was play the third wheel for an entire weekend so that my sister could enjoy a hotel for a bunk-up.

Kelsey carefully planned every detail of her secret trysts to coincide with when she was working to make sure she covered her tracks. So far, she seemed to be getting away with it; my parents hadn't suspected a thing. But if she upped the ante and started pushing the boundaries, she might end up tripping herself up. If that happened, she'd take me down with her. I retired from being her scapegoat a long time ago. When we were little, Kelsey always threw me under the bus if we got caught doing something we shouldn't be, under the pretence that because I was the baby of the family, I could get away with murder.

'You're going to get caught if you're not careful.'

'You know me; I can't help being a rebel. Rules are meant to be broken.' Kelsey laughed.

'It's not funny. Dad will go ballistic if he finds out.'

'When did you suddenly become middle-aged? What have you done with the fun-loving girl who used to be my partner in crime?' Kelsey questioned.

'She's still here,' I replied, but my tone was flat.

Since Todd had been on the scene, Kelsey and I hadn't spent much time together; we used to be like each other's shadows and did everything together. I felt a bit miffed that she'd dropped me when she'd got a better offer. Now she was attempting to manipulate me into going away with them, not because she was craving my company, but because it would provide them with the perfect cover. Kelsey was unbelievable at times; she was using me, and that hurt.

Kelsey had always been carefree. Dad reckoned she was a tearaway from the moment she could walk. And once she'd entered her teenage years, she'd ramped things up a notch when she'd discovered she possessed seductive powers that turned the opposite sex to putty in her hands. Rather than being overwhelmed by the wolf whistles and leery glares that followed her every move, Kelsey threw herself in headfirst and embraced the experience. But this time, she was playing with fire, and if she wasn't very careful, she was going to get burned.

'Come on, Scarlett, it'll be a laugh. I'll even let you choose where we go,' Kelsey said, batting her eyelashes at me.

'You can't ask me to do this. It'll be torture having to spend days confined to my room while you two are doing the horizontal tango. What would I do all day?'

'You could practise your lines!'

I reached towards my bed, picked up a cushion and threw it at my sister.

'If you don't come with me, I'll have to invent an old school friend and say I'm going to visit them,' Kelsey said, hands on hips, trying to pressure me.

That sounded like a great idea. 'Why don't you do that?'

I saw a flash of anger spread across Kelsey's face. 'I can't believe you won't help me out. You're so bloody selfish sometimes!'

That was rich coming from her. 'I'm selfish? Get out of my room,' I yelled, hurling another cushion in her direction. I didn't appreciate being taken on a guilt trip.

Kelsey glared at me then slammed the door shut behind her. I was surprised she was still interested in Todd. I thought she would have bored of him by now. She didn't usually like to tie herself down; variety was the spice of life. The saying the grass was always greener on the other side of the fence pretty much summed Kelsey up.

20

Davie

October

I couldn't get my head around the fact that Barney Coleman had made Pauline watch while he murdered her husband, and now she was left to bring up those three little kiddies alone. He was a sick bastard; there was no doubt about that, but he was becoming more warped with each passing day. I had to put a stop to his reign of terror before another family was made to suffer.

I'd put the feelers out, and a very reliable source had told me that my old sparring partner had migrated from London some years ago. The former East Ender had taken up residence in the neighbouring county of Essex.

'It's time to pay that wanker a visit,' I said to Rio. 'But first, we'll swing by the yard and pick up the dogs.'

Wesley followed Rio and I out of the commercial property and put the Rotties into their crates in the back of the black

Dog Security Unit van. My source had assured me that these days, Barney liked to play a round of golf before he dined in style at the club's restaurant, so Rio and I were going to travel in my Jag while Wes followed behind in the Transit. He would keep a discreet distance until the moment was right. I didn't want to give Barney the heads-up that I had something unpleasant in store for him.

Rio slipped off the main road and drove the gleaming Jag up to the main entrance of Grays Hall Golf and Country Club while Wesley parked up in the mouth of the turning. By the looks of it, the swish venue was more used to welcoming A-list footballers and celebrities through the doors than glorified thugs like Barney. As we walked into the posh foyer and were greeted with a warm welcome, I was surprised the bouncers allowed Coleman across the threshold. Unless he'd gone through a dramatic transformation, the man I remembered wouldn't fit in with the clientele.

'Well, well, well, Mr Coleman,' I said, pretending to be surprised to see him. I approached Barney while he was propping up the bar with a pint of bitter clamped in his hand. He looked over his shoulder, following the sound of my voice. 'It's been years since I had the pleasure. You haven't changed a bit.'

'Likewise,' Barney replied.

That wasn't strictly true. Barney's forehead was deeply furrowed now, and his crew cut had turned grey and was receding, but apart from that, he had the same hard-nosed appearance that he'd always had. I was trying to butter him up, so I didn't think he'd appreciate me telling him that he was still an ugly fucker and had the sort of face only a mother could love. A bit of flattery never did any harm, did it?

'What brings you to this part of town?' I asked.

'This and that,' Barney replied, not giving anything away. It wasn't like him to be so measured and cautious. 'How about you?'

'A bit of business,' I said with a smile on my face, being economical with the truth.

'Have you been playing golf?' I asked, stating the obvious as my eyes scanned over his pale blue diamond-patterned Pringle jumper and his black and white two-tone shoes that looked like the type of footwear a 1940s gangster would wear if the soles hadn't had cleats all over them.

'Yes,' Barney replied, eyeing me suspiciously.

'That's a bit of a change from your days on the terraces.' I laughed.

He might like to think of himself as a country squire, but if you asked me, he wasn't fooling anyone. You can take the man out of the East End, but you can't take the East End out of the man. He'd need more than some fancy threads to disguise the fact that he'd been a football hooligan in a past life.

Barney knocked back the dregs of his glass, then checked the time on his watch. 'I'll have to love you and leave you. I'm running late,' he said.

As I watched his stocky frame exit the building, I dialled Wesley's mobile to give him the heads-up. Rio and I waited for a few minutes before we took our leave.

'I think our presence in his new stomping ground might have spooked the old bastard.' I laughed. 'Instead of lording it up in the restaurant like he usually does, he's decided to cut and run. If he's not careful, that sizeable beer gut of his will disappear to nothing.'

'I don't think there's any fear of that happening any time soon, boss.' Rio chuckled.

'Which way did he go?' I asked when Wesley answered the phone.

'He threw a left, and he's heading along the A13 towards Stanford-le-Hope. I'm tailing him, but I'm hanging back,' Wesley replied.

Rio put his foot down once we were out on the open road, and we soon had the transit van in our sights.

Seeing the empty stretch of road in front of us, I called Wesley back. 'It's time to put the plan into action.'

Rio slowed down to create some distance between us as Wesley slammed his foot onto the accelerator and closed the gap between himself and Barney.

'That would have hurt.' I laughed when the sound of the two vehicles colliding reached us.

Barney stopped his BMW 7 Series Saloon and jumped out of the driver's seat. He paced red-faced and arms flailing over to the driver's side of the van. Wesley flung the door open when Barney began pounding on the glass with his fist. As Rio stopped my Jag behind them, I turned to him, and a huge smile spread across my face.

'If I'd known we were going to have ringside seats, I'd have brought us a couple of beers and some popcorn. This is going to be very entertaining.'

Wesley squared up to his opponent, then he landed a headbutt right on the bridge of Barney's nose, which left him looking shell-shocked.

'Go on, my son,' I cheered from the passenger seat, egging Wesley on.

Blood spirited out of Barney's nostrils all over his hideous, pale-blue sweater. He tried to cover the flow with his hands. Before he had a chance to retaliate, Wesley grabbed him by the scruff of his neck and welted Barney's forehead off the side panel of the van. When he staggered backwards, tears of laughter began rolling down my cheeks.

'It's like a scene from one of the old *Tom And Jerry* cartoons, where the character has stars rotating around their head.' I chuckled.

Barney looked like a drunk sailor on shore leave as he tried to stand up straight on jelly legs. Before he had a chance to keel over, Wes manhandled him into the back of the van. The Rottweilers were nicely riled up by the commotion, so I was sure it would be an interesting journey for the three of them cooped up in the back of the van together. Barney should count himself lucky that my furry intimidators were contained within their crates. Otherwise, he'd have had more than a sore head and a bloody nose to worry about.

Wesley put the van into gear and drove around Barney's smashed-up BMW.

'Dear, dear, dear,' I said, shaking my head when we passed the wreckage, and I was able to inspect the damage close up.

The whole boot was crushed from being hit full force, but fretting over the state of his motor would be the least of his worries when Barney finally found out what I'd got in store for him.

'Head across to East Tilbury,' I said, knowing that the

further downstream we travelled from London, the more secluded the areas became. And the last thing I wanted to attract was an audience.

Unluckily for Barney, I was very familiar with this stretch of the river. My mum and dad often used to bring my sister and I down here when we were nippers. Visiting Coalhouse Fort was a regular Sunday outing for us. The creepy building had a long, ghoulish history attached to it. There was a reason it was a popular ghost-hunting location; people had reported hearing footsteps following them from room to room when there was nobody there. And it was easy to become disorientated once you were deep within the maze of twisting tunnels, especially at night when everything was pitch-black. Each to their own, but I preferred being out in the fresh air than traipsing around a decaying building in search of an apparition.

One of my favourite pastimes was scavenging on the nearby beach, a treasure trove of broken bits of the past. We used to park up at the fort and follow the Thames Estuary path west towards Bottle Beach. As the name implied, it was littered with shards of Victorian-era pottery, china and glass, a stark reminder that London's rubbish was dumped in landfill sites along this barren stretch of shoreline for centuries. And if that wasn't bad enough when the old cemeteries of the City were excavated, people's remains were also dumped here, so it wasn't unheard of to find human bones while beachcombing, which made the whole place slightly eerie but incredibly exciting to a child. I think visiting places like this with a dark history from an early age shaped my character.

'Go straight over the roundabout onto Princess Margaret

Road and then follow us,' I said when I called Wesley on his mobile.

Once we'd driven over the level crossing, Rio overtook the transit at the first opportunity. We'd recently done a recce of the area and had spotted a disused landfill site between East Tilbury and the shoreline, which would be perfect for what I had in mind. We passed a tyre warehouse, then a junkyard.

'Slow down a bit; it should be coming up any time soon on the left,' I said.

A few moments later, 'Keep Out' signs came into view. The former gravel quarry, which was closed after it started to become eroded by the tide, was surrounded by a perimeter fence more than four miles long to stop unwanted trespassers from entering, but we knew a way around the problem. We drove past the mouth of the entry road until we came to an unmarked turning. The slip road, close to the banks of the river, led to the site's now redundant car park.

We parked in a bay outside the locked-up site, and Wesley pulled in next to us. As predicted, the place was deserted. Rio and I stepped out of my Jag and walked over to the Transit.

'You were brilliant, mate,' I congratulated, slapping my employee on the back. 'I was splitting my sides watching you give the wanker a pasting. He didn't know what had hit him when you smashed his head off the side of the van. It was a class move. Now let's not keep the bugger in suspense any longer.'

I walked around to the back of the van and waited while Wesley did the honours and opened the double doors.

Barney was crouched on the floor with a dazed expression on his face.

'What happened to you? You've got claret all over the front of your lovely jumper.' It was just as well; he wouldn't be needing it again. His missus would never be able to get the bloodstains out.

Barney narrowed his eyes and scowled at me. It amused me to think he was still trying to play the tough guy. He was a pathetic sight. The crotch of his light blue golfing trousers was several shades darker where he'd clearly pissed himself. I shook my head slowly from side to side as my eyes scanned over him.

'You've got worse manners than my Rotties. They wouldn't dream of emptying their bladders in the back of my van, and neither would you if you knew what was good for you.' I grabbed a fistful of his lairy jumper and pulled him out the back door.

When Barney landed in a heap on the floor, he jutted his jaw out in a last-minute show of defiance. He should save his energy rather than trying to muster a half-hearted attempt at bravado. It wasn't going to help him now.

'Do you want me to bring the dogs, Davie?' Their contrasting facial markings moved around as they studied me.

'Why not. I'm sure they'd love to stretch their legs.' Not that I thought we'd need their assistance, but if we did, they were trained to spring into action at a moment's notice.

Barney's face was a picture; his features were paralysed by fear. Wesley controlled the dogs with his left hand and gripped Barney's arm with his free hand. After taking a canister of petrol from the back of the van, Rio took hold of the other side, and together they steered Barney out of the car park. I led the way through the flat, scrubby floodplain crisscrossed with footpaths.

As we walked, I thought about what I was about to do, but it didn't prick my conscience. I hadn't rushed into anything; I'd taken my time and made a considered decision. Six months had passed since that fateful day when Barney Coleman had robbed three innocent children of their father. I'd given the police an opportunity to bring him to justice, but when they'd failed to do so, I was left with no option. I had to take matters into my own hands. I'd given Pauline my word that I'd make him suffer, so I wouldn't go back on that. I wasn't going to let him off easily; he was going to die screaming. A thug like Barney deserved to be tortured for hours for what he'd done, but time wasn't on my side, so I'd have to get on with the grisly deed.

'This should do nicely,' I said when we came to a secluded location far away from the road. It was hidden from view by piles of rubbish, old clothes, bits of electrical equipment and general detritus stretched skywards in enormous, man-made mounds.

Rio undid the canister after I gave him the nod and began pouring the petrol over Barney, who by now had the eyes of a madman; his irises were like pinholes in a sea of white.

'What the fuck do you think you're doing?' Barney yelled as he tried to break free from Wesley's grip.

Wes used the dogs to get Coleman back under control so that Rio could apply some restraints. By the time he'd finished, Barney was trussed up like an oven-ready chicken. Then Rio taped his mouth closed.

'What goes around, comes around,' I said as I lit the match and threw it toward him.

Unable to do anything else, Barney let out a guttural groan as he went up like a rocket on Guy Fawkes night. I was glad we'd taped his mouth shut; otherwise, I didn't doubt a blood-curdling scream would have escaped from his lips. Barney rolled on the ground as he tried desperately to put the flames out, but they licked around him. He was writhing in agony; Rio had doused him in enough petrol to fuel a jumbo jet on a long-haul flight, so nothing he could do would extinguish the flames. Until he lost consciousness, he was going to be in agony. Burning to death could be the worst possible way to die. Barney had more body fat than most people, which would act as a fuel source, but it would still be a slow and painful process.

Barney's corpse continued to burn; the extreme heat was making his skin blister and split while his muscles, bone and organs shrank; it was a gruesome way to die. Exactly what he deserved. I gazed at the long since closed Bata shoe factory as it towered out of the windswept marshlands, a shadow of its former self, looking like a ghostly figure watching over the proceedings.

'We'll be here all night at this stage,' I said. 'Throw some more petrol on him, Rio, to speed things up a bit.' I was keen to get away from the scene as soon as possible.

I led the others a short distance along a path towards the water. The tide was out, so the saltmarsh creeks and water channels in the mudflats were dotted with small birds hoping to find their next meal. We sat side by side on the sea wall mottled with yellow lichen, watching the smoke drift on the wind and mingle with that of the factory chimney stacks churning out a constant stream of air pollution along this industrial stretch of the Thames.

When it was all over, I glanced behind me to take in the view and noticed the container ships in the distance and the old timber pier still lying sideways at the top of Bottle Beach, the way it had all those years ago. This stretch of shoreline was seriously neglected, which was ideal for me but not so good for Barney.

'Right, lads, let's make sure we get every last piece of evidence. I'm not doing time for that fucker.' The saying 'no face, no case' sprang to mind.

Rio and Wesley headed towards the van with the Rotties and came back a couple of moments later with a drum of water, a shovel, two rakes and gloves. Rio poured the water over the flames then Wesley began raking through Barney's remains. Gone were the tattoo of the lion on his left shoulder, his deeply furrowed brow and grey receding crew cut. Not much was left of the former thug. Fire was a destructive force, but parts of the skeleton always survived. Pretty soon, his bone fragments would be a thing of the past, having found their way into a vat of acid.

21

Mia

Once Jack and I had booked the venue, everything else seemed to fall into place. The spring and summer had passed by in a blur of dress fittings, wine tasting and menu trials. Not that I was complaining; the day couldn't come around soon enough for my liking. I spun my pink diamond engagement ring around my finger, and thoughts of my gorgeous fiancé popped into my head. In a romantic gesture, he'd designed the ring himself. Then a jeweller had used the gold from my grandmother's wedding ring to craft it, making this token of love even more special and memorable than I'd thought possible. I couldn't be happier than I was at this moment in time.

The whole family had flown up to Scotland the day before the wedding, so we could spend time relaxing together at the castle, enjoying the facilities. I'd always wanted to get married in winter, but I hadn't anticipated how cold it would be in the Highlands. Being the end of November, there was a definite chill in the air. It felt at least ten degrees colder than it had been in London, which seemed positively balmy in comparison. A knot of anxiety formed in my stomach. Hosting our big day in a draughty old castle might not have been the smartest move. The walls were three or four feet thick, but I bet the damp and cold still penetrated them.

'Hello there. Welcome to Thistledown Castle,' Isla said as she greeted us at the door with a beaming smile.

Once we were inside the galleried entrance hall, I breathed a sigh of relief. A roaring fire was doing a brilliant job of keeping the chill at bay, and the spacious area felt warm and cosy, which was one less thing for me to worry about. As I peeled off my coat, I took in my surroundings. My eyes were drawn to the wide staircase. It looked amazing; groups of candles housed in clear votives stood on every step; their flames flickered against the river of ivy cascading down from the floor above, woven with thistles and black-centred anemones.

I'd initially been reluctant to get a wedding planner involved. I didn't want to hand over control, or my anxiety would go into overdrive. But Isla had such an easy way about her, it would have been stupid not to go down that route. As Jack and I dealt with last-minute preparations, I was glad I'd put my trust in her. She'd done a fantastic job; everything looked perfect.

I'd wanted the colour scheme to incorporate the rich tones of ripe berries, and Isla hadn't disappointed me. Huge floral displays dripping with calla lilies and acres of moss green foliage decorated every room. Twinkling fairy lights adorned every surface. It looked magical; even my dad was impressed with the venue, and he was a difficult man to please.

By early evening, the small party of wedding guests we'd invited had all arrived. They'd joined us for dinner in one of the castle's staterooms. After a delicious four-course meal, we had drinks alongside a roaring open fire. Everyone was in high spirits, but it was getting too much for me, so I'd decided to turn in for the night. I knew I probably wouldn't sleep much; I could feel nerves starting to build within me. The best way for me to deal with my anxiety was to have some time alone, away from all the excitement. I needed to be in a calm environment.

Having whispered my intentions to Jack, I'd stood up in front of my guests. 'Enjoy the rest of your evening, I'm going to turn in now.'

'You can't go yet. It's only early, and it's your last night as a single woman,' Kelsey replied.

The corners of my mouth lifted lazily. I'd mastered the art of giving a bland social smile necessary for such occasions years ago, and Kelsey was a frequent recipient of them. She'd tirelessly tried to encourage me to shed my inhibitions, but I always resisted, preferring to shy away from the limelight.

Kelsey was in her element, snuggling into a faux fur throw draped across a sofa, knocking back the signature fresh berry cocktails the chef had prepared to mark the occasion as if they were going out of fashion. My sister was twenty-two, only two years younger than me, but our personalities couldn't have been more different, although that didn't mean I didn't love her dearly. By Kelsey's own admission, I was more Monaco; she was more Magaluf. A never-ending happy hour and dancing the night away were her kind of heaven, my kind of hell.

Just as I was leaving the room, a sudden outburst of laughter made me glance towards my sisters. I sometimes envied the close bond Kelsey and Scarlett shared, but it made sense really; they both had a laid-back approach to life, whereas I worried enough for all of us. I wished I could cut loose and let my hair down like they did; they always had so much fun, but I lacked their confidence.

I was sitting on the bed with my back against the headboard, practising my deep breathing to calm my pre-wedding jitters, when peals of laughter broke the silence. Kelsey was in the corridor. I'd thought she was coming to see me, but I turned to face the adjoining wall after I heard her door open and close, then something thudded against it. I thought my sister had drunkenly stumbled and was about to go and see what was going on – it was far too early for Kelsey to be calling it a night – when I heard the unmistakable sound of grunting and moaning on the other side of the wall. The pounding sounds continued as I stood frozen to the spot. They weren't holding back. They were in the throes of passion.

I felt myself cringe when I heard a man's muffled voice say, 'You like it when I do that, don't you?' I made a mental note; the walls might be thick but sounds still managed to somehow travel into adjoining rooms. I would die of embarrassment if Kelsey overheard Jack and I on our wedding night, but if I told her about this tomorrow, she'd think it was hilarious.

'I'm coming,' Kelsey moaned, and the pounding against the wall speeded up.

From the sound of the animalistic panting coming from next door, her partner had too. When I heard her bedroom door open a few moments later, I couldn't resist sneaking a peek. I was curious to know whether my suspicions were correct. I turned the handle and inched open the door. Kelsey was walking along the corridor, holding hands with a man who looked very much like Todd from the back, if I wasn't mistaken. Just before they turned the corner, the man pulled her into his arms. Now that I could see him more clearly, it confirmed Kelsey's love interest was our bodyguard. What the hell was she thinking? Dad would go ballistic if he found out. My sister threw her arms around his neck as he kissed her passionately, grinding himself against her while cupping her buttocks, putting on a very public display of affection.

I covered my mouth with my hand when I saw my dad come into view. He stood watching them for several seconds with a look of fury on his face before his shout resonated around the high-ceilinged space. My heart leapt in response. I wouldn't want to be in Kelsey's shoes.

'What the fuck do you two think you're doing?' Dad roared at the top of his voice.

Kelsey and Todd sprang apart at the sound. Dad's arms were down by his sides, but I could see him clenching and unclenching his fists. It was clear he was ready to explode with rage. Dad put his hands on his hips and switched his glare between the two of them as he waited for an explanation that didn't come.

'I pay you to watch over my daughter; not put your grubby hands all over her arse and stick your tongue down her throat,' Dad fumed, squaring up to Todd. 'Haven't you ever heard of the phrase *don't shit where you eat*?'

I felt myself cringe and hoped all hell didn't break loose

on the eve of my wedding. But Dad had a point. Generally speaking, people should place a clear distinction between their business and personal lives. If you messed one up, it affected the other. That probably sounded hypocritical as my future husband also worked for my dad.

Jack had joined the firm straight after graduating. That was how we'd met. Dad liked to look after his loyal employees and often used to invite them over for barbeques and get-togethers. We'd been at the same gatherings countless times before Jack started dropping hints that he'd like to get to know me better. I'd known Jack for ages before he'd plucked up the courage to ask me out. We knew we'd be expected to take our relationship seriously. There was a lot riding on it. But that wasn't a problem; love blossomed slowly between us. My fiancé approached our romance the same way he approached everything; he'd set an unhurried, measured pace. By the time we'd started dating, we'd already developed strong feelings for each other. I doubted very much Kelsey and Todd could say the same thing. My sister had a casual attitude towards relationships. I'd put money on the fact that this was nothing more than a brief fling.

'I thought something was up when I realised both of you were missing. I'm glad I trusted my gut now. It was too much of a coincidence. Are you crazy?' Dad started jabbing the bulging vein in his temple with his finger as he eyeballed the two of them.

Kelsey had really gone and done it now. Dad was reaching boiling point. She needed to give him the apology he was waiting for or everyone was going to suffer. But she had a stubborn streak and was refusing to back down even though she was clearly in the wrong.

'So what's the story? Were you deliberately trying to piss me off, or were you just hoping to sabotage your sister's big day? You can't bear the thought of the focus not being on you for once, can you?' Dad wasn't holding back.

Kelsey looked like she'd been slapped around the face by Dad's words. She'd always been an attention-seeker, but I didn't believe she'd set out to ruin the wedding. Sometimes Kelsey didn't think of the consequences before she acted, and now that had come back to haunt her. I was willing her to just apologise, but sorry didn't often appear in her vocabulary.

Dad tore his eyes away from Kelsey, turned towards Todd and puffed out his chest.

'And as for you, you've crossed the line, son. I don't take kindly to an arsehole like you disrespecting my daughter.'

'Oh my God! We're not living in the Middle Ages.' Kelsey threw her hands up in the air. 'It might surprise you to know, you don't have ownership over my love life. I'm an adult, and I'll have a relationship with whoever I want.'

So much for smoothing over the situation. Kelsey had just escalated it. Some dads were really protective of their girls; my dad was more protective than most. He thought Todd was taking advantage of Kelsey, so he was trying to defend her honour. He was old-fashioned like that. He liked women to be treated with respect, and Todd grinding himself against his princess while cupping her buttocks in the middle of a hotel corridor was more than he could bear.

'Is that so? Having a relationship with your bodyguard is a serious conflict of interest,' Dad said to Kelsey before he turned his attention towards Todd. 'You've taken a fucking liberty and deserve a good hiding.'

'Let's not get carried away...'

Dad held his hand up to silence his employee. 'You've shown me zero respect, so I've a good mind to fire you on the spot. I don't want a man whose dick rules his brain in charge of my daughters' security. But I won't be able to replace you until I get back to London, so I'll have to let you stay on until I find a better option.'

'For God's sake, Dad, that's not fair,' Kelsey protested, her retort full of anger.

'Do yourself a favour and go to bed; you've caused enough trouble for one night.'

'But it's not even eleven o'clock.' Kelsey faced our dad with a look of defiance on her face.

'Bed, Kelsey.' Dad's eyes blazed, letting my sister know his request wasn't open to negotiation as he pointed down the hallway towards her room. 'I'll deal with you when we get back to London.'

Kelsey stood her ground for a moment before conceding defeat. Then she tossed her head and stomped along the corridor with a look of fury on her face, dark hair flying behind her like Batman's cape.

'I'm sorry, Davie. In hindsight getting involved with Kelsey probably wasn't a smart move,' Todd said.

'Save it,' Dad growled. 'I don't want to hear another word about it tonight. The last thing I want is for this to affect Mia's wedding. I had a bad feeling about you right from the start.' Dad jabbed his finger in Todd's face. 'Stay out of my way. You're on borrowed time, my son.'

As Kelsey got nearer, I slipped back inside my room and closed the door behind me.

22

Kelsey

I couldn't believe Dad had caught Todd and me snogging the faces off each other before he sent me packing with my tail between my legs. I should have felt bad leaving my bodyguard to deal with Dad's anger, but he was a big boy in more ways than one, so I was sure he could handle the situation. And rather him than me any day. Dad wasn't an easy man to placate once his feathers had been ruffled.

I stood with my back against the door, wondering how things were unfolding. I'd thought Todd and I were being so discreet. In hindsight, we probably should have waited until everyone had gone to bed before we took ourselves off to have a quickie. But the fresh berry cocktails had gone to my head, and I'd thought nobody would notice that we'd slipped out; passion had got the better of me.

The sexual tension between Todd and I was electric as usual; we didn't waste time with words. Our lips had already been clamped together when I'd opened the door, and we'd barely gone inside the room when we'd started to have sex. Todd had turned me around and bent me over the small table in the hallway. Still fully clothed, he'd ground his hips into mine. Todd had run his hands up and down the sides of my thighs before they'd delved under my silky red dress. With one smooth movement, he'd caught hold of my knickers and pulled them down to my ankles. Then he'd spread my legs without bothering to undress me. I'd gasped when he'd thrust his penis deep inside me while talking dirty in my ear. It was such a massive turn-on; I knew it wouldn't be long before he'd made me come. And when I had, Todd had rested his chin on my fully clothed shoulder as he released himself into me.

Just thinking about the experience made my body ache for him. Tempting as it was, I couldn't risk sneaking him into my room again tonight. Dad would be watching the two of us like a hawk from now on.

When a text came through from Scarlett, it brought me back to reality.

> What the hell's going on? Dad's stomping around with a face like thunder. Please tell me he didn't catch you and Todd together???
> He did!
> Oh my God. What are you going to do?
> There's not much I can do.

When I told Scarlett Todd and I were slipping out for a bit of action, she'd tried to talk me out of it; being headstrong and not easily restrained, I hadn't listened. But my dad wasn't a man to be crossed. He was absolutely livid; now we'd have to face the music. My relationship with Todd was meant to be a bit of fun, but our reckless behaviour had cost him his job. I'd have to try and work my magic to stop that from happening. Sometimes I could twist my dad around my finger and get away with murder. But it was going to be a tall order. Dad was furious, so I didn't rate my chances this time.

My thoughts turned to Mia; she was stressed enough without me adding to the drama. I hoped for all our sakes she didn't get wind of my antics. Despite what my dad had said, I hadn't set out to cause trouble and sabotage her big day. I hadn't given it that much thought. I'd acted in the moment without considering the consequences. I was a selfish, spoiled brat at times who did things without thinking and then ended up regretting my actions. When Todd and I had sloped off, I'd never expected to get caught. My hormones had run away with themselves, and I'd given in to temptation. It was as simple as that and not a premeditated manoeuvre like my dad suggested.

The last thing I wanted was for there to be an atmosphere tomorrow. If I could turn back the clock, I would. I'd been looking forward to the wedding; any excuse to let my hair down, but now I was dreading it. I could picture Dad eyeing Todd and I to make sure we weren't doing anything inappropriate. I just hoped the three of us wouldn't end up forming a triangle of unrest that ruined Mia's perfectly planned day.

With the wedding at the forefront of everyone's minds, hopefully – by the time the celebrations were over – Dad would have had time to calm down, and the situation would blow over.

Who was I trying to kid? This was a monumental fuck-up even by my standards and way too big to sweep under the carpet. I might be able to limit the damage by using my experience in hospitality to make sure everything ran smoothly and pandered to Mia's every need, making sure she wanted for nothing. If I pulled that off, maybe I could redeem myself.

> What the fuck am I supposed to do now? Your dad's going to fire me when we get back to London.

I let out a long sigh when I read Todd's text.

> I'll try and talk him around.

It was a genuine offer, but I wasn't sure I was going to be able to change Dad's mind.

> As if that's going to happen. I can't believe I've been so stupid. I've lost a well-paid job over a bunk-up with the boss's daughter.

What a bloody cheek! Who did Todd think he was? I was well aware that our relationship was purely physical and that he was only in it for sex, but nobody liked to see it pointed out in black and white. Todd was a commitment-phobe. We were clearly cut from the same cloth, but I wasn't going to let him get away with that comment, so I quickly typed a reply.

> How charming! I'm glad I meant so much to you.
> I didn't mean it like that. I'm just pissed off that I've been sacked.

Todd knew the risks when we'd decided to get involved. We both did. He knew he'd need to leave his job if my family found out. If there was zero chance of him wanting to do that, he shouldn't have started a relationship with me. I wasn't going to feel guilty about it.

23

Mia

November 29th

I'd woken up in the early hours of the morning on my wedding day with a stomach full of nerves that were refusing to budge. After getting out of bed, I tiptoed across to the windows that overlooked the gardens. Apart from the glow of low-level lighting dotted in and around the flower beds, it was pitch-black outside. It wasn't just dark like it would be in London; I'm talking about a can't-see-your-hand-in-front-of-your-face situation. I gazed up in wonder. Without the light pollution of an overcrowded city dulling the atmosphere, I was lucky enough to witness a proper Scottish Highland sky. I'd never seen so many stars. The sight of them seemed to ease my nerves, so I decided to go back to bed and try to rest.

I must have dropped off at some point because the next thing I knew, heavy rain was pelting the windowpanes. I lay back against the feather pillows listening to the sound. It was incredibly soothing, so I wasn't going to dwell on the fact that it had been a beautiful crisp, cold day yesterday with the bluest skies I'd seen in a long time; my favourite kind of weather by far.

Anyway, I was sure it was meant to be lucky if it rained on your wedding day and the ceremony was hours away yet. Hopefully, the wind howling outside the castle walls would pull the weather front out to sea. In the meantime, I needed to remind myself that whatever happened, the weather was out of my control, so I shouldn't be worrying about it. I knew when I booked the venue that we were unlikely to get good weather at the end of November in the Highlands, but that hadn't put me off. I was just grateful we were avoiding the midge season, one of the many benefits of not having a spring or summer wedding.

So far, Dad's discovery of Kelsey's secret tryst hadn't cast a shadow over the celebrations, and the early part of the day passed by in a flurry of excitement. My mum, sisters and future mother-in-law had all taken up residence with me in the dressing room the hotel had laid on for us to use. The champagne was flowing as the hairdressers and makeup artists got to work. My sisters and I were sitting in a row in matching white satin dressing gowns having our long hair curled in complementary styles, giggling like schoolgirls while Mum took photos on her iPhone.

After having neutral makeup applied, Kelsey and Scarlett went off to get changed and reappeared a short while later wearing their long-sleeved bridesmaid dresses, which were the colour of bramble wine.

'You both look stunning,' I said, jumping to my feet.

Kelsey ushered everyone out of the room apart from myself and Scarlett. 'Let's get you into your dress before Jack gets cold feet and does a runner.'

Everything was starting to come together. The rain had eased off, and the wind had dropped; even the sun was trying to put in an appearance. Weak rays pushed through the clouds and bounced off the mirror as I stared at my reflection in the full-length mirror. I turned my head away when I heard a gentle knock on the door.

'Can I come in?' Dad asked, poking his head around the door.

'Of course,' I replied, turning towards him.

'Wow, you all look stunning,' Dad said.

Dad cast his eyes over each of us in turn. My pulse speeded up as I watched him exchange a glance with Kelsey. To my relief, there was no awkwardness between them, and when my younger sister flashed him her winning smile, the corners of his mouth lifted ever so slightly in response. Even though Kelsey was skilled at manipulating him and she'd had years of practice, it didn't look like he'd forgiven her. But my dad was a man of his word, and he'd said he didn't want the incident to affect my wedding, so he must have decided to put his anger aside for the day.

Dad walked over to me and took my hands in his. 'You look absolutely beautiful; the sight of you has brought a tear to my eye,' Dad said, wiping his cheeks with the back of his hand.

My dad wasn't an emotional man, so I knew his comment was heartfelt. He had a tough exterior, but for those of us lucky enough to see beneath the surface, he could be a real softie. In business, Dad had a reputation for being unapproachable and cold, but if you were in his trusted inner circle and got to know him properly, you would discover that he had a warm, caring side, too, especially where the family was concerned. Mum was his queen, and if Jack and I ended up half as happy together as my parents were, we were in for a blissful marriage.

'So you approve then?' I asked, smoothing down the front of my ivory, lace, long-sleeve gown.

Dad's confidence boost was greatly appreciated. I was feeling the pressure to look my best on my wedding day. Every bride wanted to, didn't they? I couldn't be the only woman who'd experienced the big day stress, but other brides probably handled the pressure better than I did.

'Very much so. I've never seen you look better.'

'Aww, thanks, Dad.' My eyes threatened to well up, so I took a deep breath and held it.

'I mean it; you look stunning,' Dad replied before planting a kiss on my cheek.

'And you look very handsome too. You scrub up well.' I appreciated the effort he'd made.

'Thanks, but you know me, I'm not a lover of suits, and I hate wearing a tie; it makes me feel like I'm being strangled. I don't like the thought of standing out like a dog's balls; I prefer to blend into the background.' Dad laughed.

'Sorry to interrupt, but I think we should get going if you're ready,' Kelsey said, handing me the large, hand-tied, dark-pink and mulberry toned bouquet made up of black-centred anemones, roses, and sprigs of berries. Then she stepped behind me and picked up the small train on the back of my dress.

The chapel was lit entirely by candles, and as I walked

up the aisle on my dad's arm, I focused on the way they flickered to help calm my nerves. When I saw Jack beaming at me from the altar, the pre-wedding tension finally let me out of its grip. He looked so handsome, standing there in his black suit. My eyes scanned over his chiselled features, dusted with a light covering of stubble before I smiled back.

'Take good care of her,' Dad's said when we came to a stop beside my future husband.

'You know I will,' Jack replied, his blue eyes shining.

Jack and I pledged our love and commitment to each other and then exchanged our rings.

'It is my pleasure to pronounce you husband and wife. You may now kiss the bride,' the registrar said.

Jack leant in towards me, and as he planted his lips on mine, his honey-blond hair brushed the side of my cheek. I felt colour rush to my face when a cheer went up from the congregation, and for a moment, I wished my hair hadn't been pinned away from my face. I felt exposed without my security blanket. Jack had kissed me a thousand times before, but somehow this felt different. It was the first time my new husband and I had locked lips, and that felt exciting. We were about to spend the rest of our lives together, and I was floating on air; I'd never been so happy.

Jack and I stood gazing at each other while the photographer organised our family around us so that he could capture a group picture. We'd made it clear that we didn't want to spend hours being lined up for formal photographs, so I was sure he felt pressured to get this over and done with as soon as possible. Considering my mum was a former model, I was incredibly camera-shy. I hadn't inherited her ease in front of the lens.

As our family members stood in a line while the photographer began snapping away, I hoped the smile I was wearing looked more natural than it felt. My cheeks were aching from the effort. The opening bars of 'Girls On Film' popped into my head as the sound of the camera's shutter filled the silence.

'I have to say, you're a very photogenic group. I think I'm about ready to wrap this up and then we'll focus on the bridal party,' the photographer said.

But as the words left his mouth, a different noise penetrated the room. It took me a moment to realise that I'd just heard gunshots ring out around the chapel.

24

Kelsey

I'd leant towards Dad and was about to whisper a heartfelt apology in his ear when the sound of gunfire and my mum's screams made the smile slide from my face. I turned my head to the side to look at her, and that was when I noticed my dad falling backwards. He'd been standing between Mia and me in the line-up. I didn't know what was going on at first; everything happened so fast. One minute the photographer was clicking away, promising us that he was nearly finished, and the next, somebody had opened fire. For a moment, it felt like time had stopped.

'Get down,' Todd shouted as more shots rang out.

Todd jumped out of the pew, pulling a weapon out of the inside pocket of his suit jacket, then he took off after the marksman. We all fell to the floor and covered our heads with our hands. Panic broke out among the guests as plaster and debris rained down on us. When I took a tentative look out from under my arm, I saw Rio pace across the stone floor of the chapel. Mum had abandoned her position and was leaning over my dad, trying to rouse him.

'Somebody call an ambulance,' Rio said when he dropped down beside them.

'Davie, Davie, can you hear me?' Mum repeated over and over again while gently shaking Dad's shoulder.

'Leave this to me, Amanda,' Rio said. Mum sat back on her haunches as he assessed my dad's injuries.

I heard Scarlett on the phone to the emergency services. Thank God she'd managed to get through. The castle was in such a remote location, the mobile coverage was flaky. I glanced over at her; she was crouched on the floor with her phone pressed to her ear, trying to get her words out over the sound of Mia wailing. The bride was hysterical, but Jack was trying his best to calm her down, so I didn't intervene. When I looked back in my dad's direction, I noticed my mum was trembling like a leaf, so I went to comfort her. She fell into my arms, and I rocked her backwards and forwards as we sat huddled together on the altar's steps.

'He will be all right, won't he, Kelsey?' Mum asked, but I couldn't answer her question.

I looked over my shoulder. Rio was still checking my dad's pulse, but it was obvious there wasn't going to be a good outcome. Although multiple shots were fired, Dad only had a single bullet wound on his forehead, which didn't appear to be too big a deal from the front. He wasn't bleeding from the entry wound, but he was lying in a pool of dark red blood. As it continued to seep out of him, I felt completely helpless watching his life ebb away. There was nothing any of us could do to save him. Judging by the amount of gore that was splattered over the pink sandstone behind Dad, it would be a miracle if Rio was able to detect any signs of life. The slug had blown his brains out the back of his head. The sight was horrific. When my stomach began to churn, I had to look away.

Everything felt like it was happening in slow motion; it was difficult to explain, but I felt like I was having an out-of-body experience. I was taking in every detail of the scene, but it was as though I was watching a film and the unfolding events were happening to somebody else. Time was almost standing still; the seconds felt like hours while we waited for the paramedics to arrive. I wasn't sure why I was clinging to hope; it was clear that Dad was beyond medical intervention.

'Hold on, boss, the ambulance is coming,' Rio said, his voice cracking with emotion.

So I wasn't the only one refusing to accept the obvious even though the evidence was compelling.

'I'm so sorry the emergency services haven't arrived yet, Mrs Saunders, but we're in quite a remote location,' Isla said, averting her eyes from the gruesome sight.

Mum didn't reply. She wasn't being rude; she was in shock. I tightened my grip on her before I stole another look over my shoulder. The pool of blood was larger now and surrounded Dad's body like a halo. Rio was still crouched down by his side, willing him to hold on. As the minutes rolled by, I couldn't help wondering if Dad's chances of survival would have been better if Mia had hosted her wedding in London, but then I pushed the thought from my mind. Some injuries just weren't survivable, even if a medical team had been on hand.

The deafening sound of a helicopter landing filled the room moments before the chapel door opened. A sudden gust of wind almost ripped it from its hinges. I felt my pulse quicken when I saw a member of staff rushing towards us with two members of the HEMS crew dressed in red boiler suits with reflective strips. Even though I knew it was too late to save my dad, their presence gave me a small glimmer of hope. I didn't want to accept we'd lost him as nobody official had confirmed it. Being in denial was the only way to get through the situation. I had to be strong for Mum's sake. If I allowed myself to face the truth, I knew I'd fall to pieces.

The hotel employee peeled off to the side, and the man and woman hurried past Mum and I with bags of equipment slung over their shoulders. The woman dropped down on her knees and placed two gloved fingers on the side of Dad's neck to check for a pulse even though it was pretty clear he was dead. His skin was drained of colour, and he hadn't moved a muscle since he'd fallen; his grey eyes were still open and unblinking. As I watched the woman checking my dad over, a thought suddenly occurred to me. Did she really think we'd all be standing around doing nothing if we'd thought there was a chance we could have brought him back to life?

As soon as we realised he'd been shot, we'd sprung into action. But there was little we could do. Dad's brains had been blown out and were currently decorating the back wall of the chapel and surrounding area. Rio had stayed by his side, loyal to the end, while Todd had taken off after the gunman. As yet, he hadn't reappeared. I didn't want to think about what that might mean. Although I wanted

Todd to catch up with my dad's murderer, I wouldn't allow myself to consider the danger my lover was now in as he tried to track down the killer.

The woman leant towards Rio and whispered something in his ear, but it was impossible to hear what she'd said; her tone was too low. Rio didn't reply but pointed over towards Mum and I.

'Hello, I'm Doctor Campbell,' the woman said in a Scottish accent.

'Hello,' I replied. Mum was too shocked to speak.

The man she'd arrived with was a paramedic according to the embroidered badge on his boilersuit, but he didn't introduce himself.

'I'm afraid there's no easy way to say this, but Davie is dead; there was nothing we could do to save him. I'm so sorry for your loss.' Dr Campbell looked mum in the eye as she spoke.

There it was: the confirmation I'd been dreading. I felt a shiver run down the entire length of my body. Compassion coated the doctor's words, but they brought little comfort. They hovered in the air around me as all the what-ifs began bombarding my brain at once.

Mum pulled out of my embrace and looked around the chapel. She seemed lost and confused as she scanned the faces in front of her. Then a flash of anger crossed her face, and she fixed her eyes on the doctor who had just broken the bad news.

'What are you talking about?' Mum struggled to her feet and stood in front of the doctor. 'How can Davie be dead? Our daughter's only just got married, and he was alive and well when he gave her away.'

Mum directed her anger at the doctor, but the medic handled her outburst like a true professional.

'I understand this must be very distressing for you, Mrs Saunders, but when the bullet entered your husband's head, it caused catastrophic damage, and he has died from his injuries,' Dr Campbell said.

Mum turned towards me and fixed me with a look of panic in her eyes before she focused her attention back on the doctor. 'There must be something you can do.'

'Your husband was too badly injured. There was nothing I could do to save him,' Dr Campbell reiterated.

Mum was struggling to wrap her head around the news; the shock was so numbing she'd gone into complete denial. A sudden wave of guilt swept over me. I'd been trying to protect her by shielding her from the sight of my dad bleeding out on the chapel's steps, but now she didn't believe that he hadn't made it no matter how many times the doctor patiently told her.

'There was nothing anyone could do to help Dad,' I echoed.

Mum's eyes were still searching mine, questioning what I'd just said. 'Nothing?'

I shook my head. I tried to repeat it again, but the words were stuck in my throat.

'He can't be dead. I didn't get a chance to say goodbye or tell him I loved him.' Mum stood clinging to me as she processed what had happened. 'I need to see him.' Mum tried to turn around, but I held her steady, knowing the sight would haunt her for the rest of her life.

'I'm Detective Inspector Stewart, and this is Detective Sergeant Murray,' a brown-haired woman said in a high-pitched, sing-song accent as she walked towards us.

The sound of the woman's voice caught our attention. I hadn't noticed the police officers arrive; I'd been focused on the doctor. They must have been hanging back at a discreet distance until Mum mentioned going to see Dad.

'I'd like to extend my deepest sympathy to you and your family, Mrs Saunders. Losing a loved one in such tragic circumstances must be a terrible shock to all of you.'

I wasn't sure what part of the country the detective hailed from as I wasn't skilled enough to appreciate the regional differences, but she had a very different accent from the doctor and the hotel staff.

Mum stared at the detective with unblinking eyes before she turned to face the doctor. 'Can I see Davie now?'

'I'm afraid that won't be possible. I'm going to need to ask you all to leave,' the detective cut in before Doctor Campbell had a chance to reply. 'We need to establish a crime scene,' Detective Inspector Stewart continued after glancing behind Mum and I. It was clear she was trying to prevent Mum from viewing the carnage.

'I'm not going anywhere without my husband.' Mum was doing her best to stand her ground.

'I'm sure you understand time is of the essence, and we have to act as quickly as we can to help minimise the amount of evidence that could be lost,' Detective Inspector Stewart went on.

Then she signalled to some hotel staff to get their attention. They were halfway down the chapel, attending to my sisters and other wedding guests.

'The first hour after a crime is the most important,' Detective Sergeant Murray said in a deep-toned Scottish accent somewhat different from his high-pitched colleague's.

Mum looked up at the Detective Sergeant with pleading eyes. 'I can't leave Davie here on his own.' As she spoke, her voice broke with emotion.

'I know this is very distressing for you, but I'm afraid you can't stay,' DI Stewart said. Even if she'd wanted to bend the rules, she couldn't; she had a job to do. 'Excuse me a moment, please,' the DI said when the crime scene investigation team arrived.

'The coroner's office will make arrangements to move your husband to the mortuary in due course. In the meantime, we need to secure the scene to preserve any evidence,' Detective Sergeant Murray said, gesturing to the door with his outstretched limb.

Rio appeared behind Mum and I, looking like a broken man, with blood covering his white shirt. He slung an arm around each of our waists then squeezed us tightly.

'What do we know so far?' one of the white-clad investigating team asked.

I didn't hear the response as we were being ushered out of the chapel. The whole wedding party shuffled along the narrow aisle in silence, each one of us numb to the core.

25

Scarlett

Isla and other members of staff escorted us from the chapel over to the castle under huge umbrellas in an attempt to shield us from the elements as the rain had started again. She must have rounded up every member of the team to attend to us; the wedding party was greatly outnumbered as the hotel employees made every effort to help us in any way they could.

We'd been ushered into the room that should have been hosting the wedding reception. The waitresses were handing out china cups filled with hot sweet tea to give us some comfort and warmth. For those of us, myself included, who needed something stronger, tumblers of single malt whisky were passed around to help calm our frazzled nerves as we came to terms with the shocking situation. They had even called a local doctor who was busy doing the rounds administering sedatives to those in need.

This wasn't the way things were meant to pan out. We should have been sitting down to a five-course meal in the beautifully decorated room. Mia had spent months perfecting every tiny detail so that her reception would be incredible and one that people would always remember. I doubted very much that anyone would forget this day in a hurry, but it would be etched in their memories for entirely different reasons than my older sister had intended when she'd organised the day.

Losing a parent was a difficult thing to accept under any circumstances, but when it happened on your wedding day, the aftermath was going to be twice as tragic, totally devastating. I looked over to where Mia was sitting slumped in a chair, her face red and swollen from all the tears she'd shed, and I wondered if she was going to be strong enough to cope.

Instead of laughter, there was a quiet hum of conversation going on in the room, and I'd unintentionally found myself floating around the periphery like a spare part. Jack was still trying his best to comfort Mia, and Kelsey was busy supporting Mum; everyone else was huddled in small groups. Feeling out on a limb, I drifted across to Jack's family and was gratefully accepting their show of sympathy when I saw Todd enter the room and walk across to Rio. I immediately switched off from what those around me were saying and trained my ears on the men's conversation.

'How's Davie?' Todd asked.

Rio didn't answer, but he shook his head from side to side.

'Oh no, you're not serious. For fuck's sake,' Todd replied, and I saw him immediately glance over in Kelsey's direction. My sister didn't notice; she was too busy helping my mum.

'Any sign of the shooter?' Rio asked.

'No, mate. I scoured the grounds the best I could, but the place is huge, so there was a lot to cover. This wasn't a random drive-by; it was planned, so whoever was responsible would have had an escape route well and truly sorted.'

I saw Kelsey glance over her shoulder. When she spotted Todd at the back of the room, the corners of her lips lifted ever so slightly. It must have been a relief for her knowing that he hadn't come to any harm, and not being able to go to him at a time like this must have been torture for her. But there'd been enough drama for one day without her adding to it.

'Who do you think is behind this?' Todd asked as he helped himself to a whisky offered to him from a silver tray.

'My money would have to be on the Coleman crew; either they shot him themselves, or they paid someone to do it,' Rio replied.

That surname seemed familiar. I'd heard my dad mention it before in passing, but I had no idea how they knew each other or what their connection could be. It wasn't the right time to start grilling my mum, so I'd have to store the information away for now. Who knows? It might come in handy at a later stage.

'Excuse me a moment, I'm going to check on Mum,' I said, having zoned out of the conversation.

26

Kelsey

The beautiful room, where my sister's wedding should have been in full swing, was a hive of activity. The staff were fussing around us like worker bees; nothing was too much trouble as they tried to compensate for the tragic events that had just happened, as though they were in some way responsible.

Scarlett and I were sitting like sentries on either side of Mum, surrounded by huge displays of flowers; fuchsia anemones and ruby-hued calla lilies were nestled in amongst heirloom roses, peppered with pinecones and berries. I didn't know why, but the close proximity of the blooms made me feel safe. It was as though they were standing guard over us.

I could hear Mia start to sob behind us again; I'd thought she'd cried herself dry at this stage, but I was mistaken. Jack was doing his best to comfort his new wife, but she was inconsolable; her heart was breaking, so there was nothing anyone could do or say to make her feel any better. We were all suffering in our own way, but Mia was a sensitive soul and more in tune with her emotions than the rest of us. I was too shocked to cry, too bewildered to think straight. Everyone dealt with grief differently; there was no wrong or right way to mourn.

I'd been staring out of the window as the rain pelted against it, focused on nothing in particular when some movement in the distance caught my eye. I could see the two detectives and the other members of the team making their way towards us. Dad was with them, now enclosed in a black body bag; he was being wheeled on a trolley after them. I felt myself gasp; it was a shocking sight. Mum reached her hand towards the rain-splattered window and pressed her fingertips onto the pane of glass as though she was trying to touch her husband one last time. Tears streamed down her face as she watched the procession disappear out of sight.

'I'm sorry to disturb you. How are you feeling, Mrs Saunders?' the DI asked with a look of concern on her face.

Scarlett, Mum and I were staring at the empty space that my dad's black shrouded body had filled moments earlier.

'I have to say, I've had better days,' Mum replied.

The DI looked a bit taken aback, but you couldn't really blame Mum for the abrupt response. She'd just lost her husband of twenty-six years. How did the woman think she'd be feeling?

'I know this is a difficult time, but I'll need to take statements from everyone in attendance to make sure we have all the facts.' The detective inspector crossed her arms while she waited for one of us to reply.

None of us were particularly forthcoming. We were all still trying to comprehend that we were never going to see my dad again. He was a larger-than-life character, and he'd left big shoes to fill. Up until now, my sisters and I had believed our family was invincible. Death was a foreign concept to us. Our grandparents had all died before we were born, so this was our first real experience of handling grief. But now, we'd become members of a club we'd never wanted to join.

'I'm not trying to be insensitive, but we need to piece together a picture of the lead-up to your husband's murder to help with our investigation,' Detective Inspector Stewart said, bringing us back to reality.

The police officer's words rang in my ears. That was easy for her to say; she dealt with situations like this all the time. But I wasn't sure I'd ever accept the fact that somebody had deliberately taken my dad's life.

'It's best to do this while the memory is still clear,' Detective Sergeant Murray added.

Who was he trying to kid? Did he seriously think any of us would be able to erase the events of today from our minds even if we wanted to? But I suppose they were just trying to do their job, even if it did feel like an invasion of privacy at an incredibly difficult time. We wanted to be left alone, not made to relive the horrific details of what should have been a perfect day.

'I'll start with yourself, Mrs Saunders. Can you tell me what you remember?' DI Stewart asked.

Both of the officers had taken a seat by us, and Detective Sergeant Murray had pulled out a notebook and pen and was poised, ready to take notes as soon as Mum began to give her account.

'It all happened so fast. When the first shot rang out,

I wasn't sure what was happening, so I turned to look at Davie. He was staring straight ahead with his eyes wide open. Then his legs gave way, and he slumped back onto the steps. I reached out to try to stop him from falling, but I couldn't; he was too far away. One minute he was standing there, and the next, it was too late to say goodbye.' Mum's voice broke, so she paused to clear her throat before she continued. 'I'm sorry, but I can't remember anything else.'

Mum had held it together remarkably well, but it was clear to see she was trembling like unset jelly.

'You've had a terrible shock. The death of someone you love is one of the most traumatic events in a person's life, especially when it's unexpected,' the DI replied. 'Have you any idea why somebody would murder your husband?'

Mum looked into the detective's face and shook her head.

'To your knowledge, does anyone hold a grudge against your husband?' the DI asked.

Mum shook her head again.

'What did Davie do for a living?'

The probing questions went on and on. She seemed oblivious to the distress she was causing my mum.

'There's a team of officers searching the grounds. I want to assure you we're focused on catching the person responsible, and we'll do everything in our power to bring the perpetrator to justice. The first twenty-four hours of any investigation are crucial, so we'll pull out all the stops and leave no stone unturned. We'll be in touch as soon as we have any updates,' the DI said.

Each member of the wedding party was questioned in turn, and we all had similar accounts. Nothing seemed untoward or out of place in the moments before the gunman opened fire. That was the most frustrating thing; none of us had seen anything or anyone to arouse our suspicions. Whoever had pulled the trigger had blended in perfectly, making me wonder if Dad's murderer was somebody we knew, but all the guests were accounted for, so that couldn't be the case, could it?

27

Mia

It was two o'clock in the morning, and I was still wide awake. Jack was lying on his side facing me. I watched his eyelashes gently fluttering for a couple of moments before I slipped out of bed and walked across the honeymoon suite. I stood gazing out of the window at the private terrace and hot tub, which I'd expected to use on our wedding night. The turreted bedroom would have been the stuff of dreams if our special day hadn't turned into a nightmare. The rain was still pelting off the glass as I stared past the terrace at the huge expanse of gardens beyond.

I looked over my shoulder; Jack wasn't stirring, so I grabbed my dressing gown from the chaise longue at the end of the bed, and after slipping my arms into the silky sleeves, I carefully opened the patio door and stepped outside. I wrapped my fingers around the wrought-iron railing to steady myself as the wind howled around me. I hoped it would blow my troubles away.

With my dressing gown pulled around me, I put my chin

down and battled against the gale, inching towards the set of stairs in the corner of the terrace that led down to the gardens. I headed out into the grounds, trying not to be blown off balance. As I walked, the driving rain stung my face as it lashed against me; the grass was chilling my bare feet to the bone. In my haste to go outside, I hadn't thought to put shoes on. Once I'd reached the outer perimeter of the castle grounds, my toes became like flesh tent pegs, digging into the soft ground as I tried to stabilise myself on the cliff edge. I stared out into the darkness; I could hear the ocean roaring far below me. My eyes were drawn to a waning moon reflected on the choppy water. As I stood wavering on the edge, I contemplated jumping from the cliff so that I could end the pain and suffering I was going through. I imagined what it would feel like to let the black sea claim me, wondering if I would put up a struggle when I was sucked down into the depths.

I let out a howl of pain that had been bottled up inside me; my heart was breaking. How could my dad be dead? I tried to block the memory out; it was too painful to deal with, but it was impossible; his last moments were stuck on a continuous loop in my head. One minute everyone was smiling, and the next, the sound of gunfire drowned out people's laughter. Everyone was screaming and diving for cover. Jack had thrown himself on top of me to protect me. I wasn't sure what was going on. When the sound of spraying bullets stopped, I looked around me, and that was when I saw my dad. He was lying face up, and his body was lifeless. As long as I live, I will never forget the way my dad looked sprawled out on the steps of the altar like a sacrificial offering; his grey eyes were wide open, such was the shock of the single bullet that penetrated his head. I hope for his sake he died instantly.

When we'd booked this beautiful venue all those months ago, I'd never dreamed that something I'd been so looking forward to would end in tragedy. My wedding day would forever be tarnished by the memory of my dad's murder. No matter how much I wanted to, I would never be able to erase that, but I wasn't sure I was strong enough to be able to live with the knowledge either. Instead of being a day to remember, one of the happiest of my life, it was one I was desperate to forget.

'Mia, what the hell are you doing?'

I froze. The sound of Jack's muffled voice behind me shocked me back to reality. I hadn't heard him approaching; his footsteps had been drowned out by the torrential rain and the noise of the wind screeching through the treetops. I tried to turn towards him, but I was being buffeted around. Jack reached forward and wrapped his arms around me, then pulled me back from the edge. As he did, I came to my senses. What the hell was I thinking? As if my family hadn't experienced enough pain for one day without me adding to it. I was soaked to the skin, and as the reality of what I'd almost done hit me, I began to shiver uncontrollably.

'Are you OK?' Jack held me at arm's length now that we were at a safe distance from the sheer drop, and his eyes scanned over me.

'I couldn't sleep, so I thought I'd come out here and get some fresh air,' I replied, offering him an explanation.

'On a night like this?'

I could tell Jack didn't believe me, and if truth be known,

I didn't really know what had drawn me to the cliff; I hadn't made a conscious decision to come here.

'When I saw you teetering on the edge, it frightened the life out of me. For one awful minute, I thought you were going to jump,' Jack said, blowing out a breath before he pulled me back into his arms.

'I'm sorry; I didn't mean to scare you,' I said, burying my face into Jack's broad chest.

'It's OK; at least you hadn't come to any harm.'

I didn't dare tell him that was what I'd been considering. It seemed such a cowardly, selfish way out now I was looking into his face, etched with worry. But as I'd stood on the cliff edge, my mind had zoned out of the present and taken me to a place where the pain, threatening to tear me in two, had stopped. For a brief moment, I hadn't been thinking straight; I was consumed by grief.

'When I woke up and realised you weren't next to me, I wasn't sure where you'd gone.'

'What made you check outside?' Jack was right; it wasn't exactly a nice evening for a stroll.

'You didn't close the door properly, and the draught woke me up. I went out onto the terrace, but there was no sign of you anywhere. So I decided to see if you'd gone down to the gardens.'

As the reality started to sink in, I clung to my husband, feeling thankful that he'd arrived when he had. Jack was the only one who could have reached me and dragged me back from the dark place I'd unwillingly visited in my mind. If he hadn't woken and realised I was missing, there could have been a very different outcome.

'The grounds are huge. How did you know where to look?' I asked.

'When I got to the bottom of the staircase, I spotted some footprints on the grass and decided to follow them.'

'I'm glad you did,' I said, standing on my tiptoes so that I could plant a kiss on my husband's lips.

'Let's get you back to the room. You're soaked to the skin, and you'll end up with pneumonia if we don't get you into some dry clothes soon.'

Jack threw his arm over my shoulder and guided me back towards the hotel. Once we'd battled the elements and made it to the safety of the bridal suite, we lay awake, staring into each other's faces, wrapped in each other's arms. We were so comfortable together that we didn't feel the need to talk. This was our first night as a married couple, and I hadn't expected to get much sleep, but I'd thought we'd be making love until the sun came up. It didn't seem appropriate under the circumstances, so instead, we clung to each other like moss on a rock waiting for daylight to put in an appearance.

28

Scarlett

The festivities were meant to be continuing tomorrow, but nobody felt like celebrating, so Mia and Jack cancelled the rest of their reception. The police investigation was well underway. In the weeks leading up to Dad's death, they believed the murderer tracked his movements, choosing to open fire in the chapel because it wasn't covered by CCTV cameras. With nothing else to do but sit and wait for news, we were advised to head home to London. The journey back to Bow seemed to be endless; I hadn't noticed the time drag like that on the way to Scotland, but we'd all been in high spirits when we'd set off for the wedding.

I couldn't wait to get home, but the mood in the house was sombre. My whole family had intended to spend four days celebrating what should have been a happy occasion, but everything was turned on its head when tragedy struck, and one of us hadn't returned. Life as we knew it was never going to be the same again. We were all suffering from shock and trying to deal with things the best we could.

I didn't know whether it was my twenty-year-old mind processing things differently from everyone else, but I was finding the doom and gloom challenging to deal with, even though it was to be expected. We couldn't change what had happened. What was done was done; I needed to focus on something more productive than weeping and wailing for my own sanity. Mia was doing enough of that for all of us.

Mum was always so poised, but my dad's death had floored her. She was lost without him. In the blink of an eye, her life had been blown off course and taken a new direction. She was consumed by grief, so Kelsey and I were doing our best to support her, helping her through the dark days, but comforting Mum while we were dealing with our own loss was a hard thing to do. It felt so unnatural; Mum was the one who gave us unconditional love and support. It was as though we'd swapped roles with her. It was distressing watching her struggling to cope. She was usually so organised and on top of things. Because Dad had died unexpectedly, none of us had had a chance to say goodbye. Mum was finding that especially difficult to grasp.

I hadn't thought a lot about how death consumed physical space until I'd witnessed my mum imagining my dad was still here on one occasion. She'd glanced out onto the driveway, saw his car, and uttered, 'Dad's home,' before she realised what she'd said and then continued, 'Of course he isn't. Dad's not coming home again, he's dead.' Mum looked horrified that she'd vocalised her thoughts, but a person's mind went to crazy places and played tricks on them when they were under an insane amount of stress.

I was suddenly glad my dad hadn't died at home. We'd been spared picturing his body every time we walked into a particular room. We wouldn't have to avoid the space because we didn't want to be overwhelmed by the image of him lying motionlessly where he'd fallen.

I had no idea how much work was created by somebody's death. Mum needed help planning my dad's funeral, and I was determined to shoulder a lot of responsibilities and prove I was more grown-up than any of my family gave me credit for.

As I'd broken up from uni for the Christmas break, I had time on my hands. I couldn't deny I was more comfortable being the class clown, but it was time to step up to the mark and give her some support. Because Dad was still in Scotland, we had to arrange to bring his body back. All the red tape she would inevitably have to wade through was going to place additional emotional strain on Mum. It was a complicated procedure, so I wanted to do everything possible to take the burden from her. While I was filling in the paperwork, her mobile began to ring.

'Hello,' Mum said, putting the call on speakerphone before placing it down on the kitchen counter.

'Mrs Saunders, it's DI Stewart. We're still trying to piece together why your husband was murdered at such a remote location, and I wondered if you could shed some light on things. Who would have known that your daughter's wedding was being held there?'

'Only the guests who were invited,' Mum replied.

'We're still trying to work out why your husband was targeted. Can you think of anyone who would want to see your husband dead?'

'No.'

'Have you any idea what motive would have been behind the crime?'

'I'm afraid not, Detective.'

'Please get in touch if you remember anything else, even if it seems insignificant,' the DI replied before ending the call.

'Why do the police keep asking you who killed dad? Surely it's their job to work that out,' I said, but Mum didn't answer me.

None of us had been expecting to lay my dad to rest the week before Christmas. We were shocked and numb, still trying to come to terms with the tragedy when the day of the funeral arrived. I fixed my eyes on the spray of red roses covering the top of the golden oak coffin as the pallbearers lowered it from their shoulders, and my mind drifted back to a year ago. Who would have thought that was the last time the three of us would pile into Mum and Dad's room before we went downstairs to open our presents.

My grief had taken on many forms. I'd experienced a jumble of contradictory emotions since my dad had died: anger, guilt, regret and sadness jostled inside of me, but I was doing my best to keep them in check. Kelsey and I were sitting on either side of Mum at the front of the tiny church. Mia and Jack were in the pew behind, along with Rio and Todd. Every seat was taken, and a sea of people had gathered outside to listen to the service being played on a loudspeaker.

Mum seemed to be taking some comfort from the large turnout and appeared to have pulled herself together. But as everyone huddled together under umbrellas around the graveside while we watched the casket being slowly lowered into the ground, I couldn't help wishing she'd opted to have a private burial. I didn't want to share something so personal with hordes of people, and there was still the wake to get through.

Kelsey, Mia and I didn't feel much like joining in when we got to the wake. We'd taken ourselves out of the dining room, where pictures of Dad were being cast onto the wall as a slideshow while people sat around telling funny stories about him. Mum was busying herself, refilling everyone's glasses and offering around plates of food, making laps of the room on autopilot. I'd considered giving her a hand, but she seemed to have it covered and to tell the truth, I couldn't face the wave of sympathy that threatened to smother her every time she approached a mourner she hadn't yet spoken to.

Mum was trying so hard to be strong for all of us and show everybody how resilient and tough she was. But I couldn't help feeling she was putting on an act. Her sudden transformation seemed to have come from nowhere. Yesterday she was a lost soul, and today she was a picture of composed elegance.

I could tell she was pushing the pain below the surface so that nobody would see how much she was suffering. I wanted to reach out to her and tell her it was OK to let go of her emotions and have an outburst. She'd just buried her husband, so she was entitled to fall apart. The pain wouldn't vanish overnight. But something stopped me. Mum wouldn't want me to expose the front she was putting on as she'd made such a valiant effort to pull herself together. There was no returning to life as we knew it. Dad was no longer here, and nothing would change that fact. We all had to deal with his death in our own way and learn to live with the huge hole left behind. If Mum wanted to pretend she was coping, I had no right to reveal her vulnerability to all the people she'd chosen to hide it from.

We were taking one day at a time. That was all we could do. Nobody had any idea what we were going through when they told us they were sorry for our loss. It was a conditioned response, but I hated that phrase; I'd heard it over and over, and every time somebody uttered it, I wanted to scream. I tried to remind myself their words were coming from a good place. People didn't know what else to say to show their sympathy.

Death was a tough subject. It made many people awkward and uncomfortable. People felt the need to express their condolences, but sometimes, words weren't necessary. Saying nothing at all was better than saying the wrong thing.

I'd thought I'd been doing so well handling my emotions, but once the preparations were complete and I had more time on my hands, negative feelings had started to surface. I was sure it was part of the process, one of the phases, the next stop on the grief timeline. I wanted to lash out and blame anyone and anything for what we were going through. Dad's death had been unexpected, so there was no time to prepare for it, which somehow made it more difficult to adjust to the loss. It was hard to second-guess the feelings of others, but I couldn't wait for the day to be over, and I was pretty sure my sisters felt the same way.

29

Kelsey

Todd had more than proved his loyalty to Dad since he'd been gunned down at Mia's wedding. Even though my dad had threatened to terminate our bodyguard's employment for stepping over the line, nothing had come of it. If my mum knew about our liaison and Dad's wishes, she'd turned a blind eye.

Rio's devotion to my dad hadn't wavered either. Now that the boss was no longer with us, he was doing his best to keep the business my dad had worked so hard to build up running, knowing that my mum's heart wasn't really in it. But as the days turned into weeks, I felt enough time had passed to float an idea.

'Mum, have you got a minute?' I asked when I saw her sitting alone at the kitchen table, pushing her cereal around the bowl.

Mum looked up at me. Her lavender-blue eyes were misted with tears, and I wondered whether I should abandon the chat and leave it to another time when she was feeling better.

'Of course,' Mum replied, pasting a smile onto her beautiful face.

'I've been thinking about Dad's firm,' I said, telling her what was on my mind. It was the perfect opportunity; we were the only two up, so I knew we weren't about to be disturbed.

'What about it?' Mum replied, loosening the grip on her spoon and allowing it to rest back in the bowl.

'Dad was a self-made man. He worked all his life on making his business a success.'

'That's true,' Mum agreed.

'I know Rio has been keeping an eye on things, and don't get me wrong; he's doing a brilliant job. But surely that's just a short-term solution.'

'To be honest with you, I haven't really given it much thought. I've had other things on my mind,' Mum replied before sweeping her blonde hair out of her eyes with a well-manicured finger.

'I know Rio could manage the firm permanently, but if you'd had three sons instead of three daughters, it would have fallen to Dad's heirs to take over the reins, wouldn't you agree?'

'I suppose you're right,' Mum replied.

'Well, I was thinking, what's to stop Mia, Scarlett and myself stepping up to the challenge?'

Mum's mouth dropped open, and her perfectly arched eyebrows rose several inches. 'You can't be serious?'

'I am. I've never felt more serious about anything.'

I felt guilty that Dad had died with bad blood between us and that our last words were exchanged in anger. Not that I'd ever admit that to anyone. It was eating away at me, and I was desperate to do something to ease my conscience. Carrying on Dad's legacy would be a good start.

'I can tell you now, your dad wouldn't be happy about that. He never wanted you girls involved.'

'That's such an outdated idea.' I let out a loud sigh. 'Times have changed; it's not a man's world any more.'

'Maybe it isn't, but your dad was old-fashioned and held traditional values close to his heart. Do you remember when Mia wanted to study accountancy?'

'Yes.'

'She wanted to run the financial side of your dad's business, but he wouldn't hear of it. Poor Mia was so disappointed. But you know what your dad was like; once he made his mind up about something, there was no changing it. Dad had very firm views on women in the workplace. He insisted I gave up my career when we got married because he wanted to be the sole provider. It made him feel good about himself. He loved taking care of us.' The sound of Mum's voice brought me back to reality.

No disrespect intended, but although Mum was a model in her younger days, she'd never hit the big time. To her credit, she'd appeared on the cover of countless knitting patterns sporting chunky knit jumpers and the like, but I would hardly say she'd sacrificed her calling in life in return for marital bliss.

'Your dad would turn in his grave if he thought I'd allowed the three of you to step into his shoes.'

'Why?' I threw my palms up. Mum exasperated me sometimes. 'Surely he'd want to see the business he started from scratch grow and thrive.'

'And you seem to have conveniently forgotten that Scarlett's still at uni. Your dad wouldn't want her to drop out.'

My parents had insisted that we all go into further education after leaving school. Mia was the brains of the family and a straight-A student. She was a high achiever, but Dad pulled the plug on her chosen profession, and she wasn't strong enough to stand up to him. I didn't understand his reasoning, but it was as though intelligent women posed a threat and were dangerous somehow.

Dad was adamant that we should study something that interested us rather than enrolling on a course that offered great career prospects. Was he trying to control us by stopping us from reaching our full potential? Or was there another reason? I was capable of so much more.

Thanks to my dad, my sisters and I were in a privileged position. So many people spent their entire lives working just to put food on the table with no other reward, raising their families and trying to provide them with a better life than they had. Dad had set out to achieve this and had passed the test with flying colours. We'd never wanted for anything, but he wasn't around to top up our wages now. We couldn't just assume the money would keep rolling in and go about our lives as we did before.

'There's nothing to stop Mia and I from running the firm though,' I said after a long pause. I was determined to keep the pressure on.

'Please don't put me in an awkward position and ask me to go against your dad's wishes.'

'I'm not trying to; I want to continue where he left off, so his business flourishes for generations to come,' I said, putting my heart and soul into my sales patter as though I was pitching my idea to the multimillionaires on *Dragons' Den*.

'Don't take offence, Kelsey, but it's a ridiculous idea,' Mum replied.

I could see she was going to be tough to negotiate with and difficult to win over, but I was my father's daughter, and if he taught me one thing, it was that persistence paid off, so I wasn't about to limp off and lick my wounds. It was time to try a different approach.

I let out a laugh. 'I don't think it is.'

'You don't know the first thing about running a business; you studied party planning,' Mum pointed out.

'Creative Events Management, actually,' I replied, using the official title.

Being paid to do what I loved best should have been a dream job, but I never used to dream about working. I used to dream about sipping cocktails while stretched out on a palm-fringed tropical beach. But I suddenly felt the need to prove myself. I wanted to run the family firm, and the more Mum tried to put me off, the more I wanted to do it.

'Dressing your course up with a fancy title doesn't change the fact that you haven't got any experience in Dad's line of work,' Mum replied.

I wasn't going to back down. 'There's only one way to get that, isn't there?'

'You don't have the faintest idea what you'd be taking on. Running a firm is harder than you think.'

It was time to show Mum I wasn't a one-trick pony.

'Dad's business revolved around controlling lines of credit given to customers, a bit like a bank. Sometimes he bought the debt outright, and other times he lent cash to people who had difficulty securing a loan from the usual channels. How hard can it be? I honestly think it would be good for us. It would take our minds off things. All the grieving has been draining.'

'You don't need to tell me that. Nobody knows more than I do what a massive void your dad's death has left. Life can be tough, and I've felt so lost and alone without him by my side.' Mum cast her eyes to the table so that I wouldn't notice the tears that had suddenly begun glistening.

I reached across and covered her hand with mine. 'I'm not trying to upset you, but please think about what I've said.'

'I don't know, Kelsey. Dad wanted you to enjoy the fruits of his labour. He never intended for you and your sisters to get involved in the family business.' Mum let out a long sigh. 'I never thought I'd be in this position. Sometimes life exceeds all expectations, and sometimes it doesn't. Things don't always turn out the way we think they will.'

'I know, but we have to try and make the best of this. We can't change what's happened. Dad wouldn't want to see us all moping around. It's not good for any of us, especially Mia. I'm really worried about her mental state.' I knew that would get Mum's attention.

'I am too. She looks so pale and drawn,' Mum agreed, taking the bait. Now all I had to do was reel her in.

Mia was suffering the most of all of us; she was literally going out of her mind with grief. As the weeks passed, her mental health had deteriorated. Mum needed to take control and put an end to her agony. Mia's depression was a destructive force, and it would eat away at her if she didn't try to fight it.

'If Mia had an active role in the family business, it would give her a purpose in life again.' I decided to throw in for good measure before I let go of Mum's hand and pushed my chair back from the table. I wasn't going to give up on this. I needed to focus on something, anything other than reality.

'Wait, Kelsey,' Mum said. She looked into the middle distance as she drummed her fingers on the kitchen table while she considered what I'd said. 'Keep all of this to yourself for the minute and let me think about it, will you?'

'No problem.'

At least Mum was mulling over my suggestion, and hopefully, once she'd had time to digest it, she'd realise I was right. My parents were wealthy, but how long would the money last before it ran out? We could end up losing everything. A place like ours must cost a fortune in upkeep. I had no idea what kind of overheads running a house entailed; I'd never paid a bill in my life. I just used my credit card to buy what I wanted, and my parents picked up the tab at the end of the month. The same went for my sisters. What I earned, I spent on myself. I'd never taken work seriously before; I'd never had to. But now that Dad was no longer on the scene, I was beginning to realise there was more to life than partying.

30

Mia

Despite being married now, Jack and I were staying with my mum for the time being. I was finding it hard to deal with Dad's death and wanted my family around me. I needed to be close to my siblings and Mum, so we'd put moving into our new house on hold for the moment. If that bothered Jack, he wasn't letting it show.

I'd lost direction and felt like I'd been hit by an avalanche, buried under metres of snow, waiting to be rescued. Everything was collapsing around me. None of it made sense. How could this have happened? How could my dad be dead? The unanswered questions rolled around on a continuous loop in my head.

My first real experience of grief was harrowing, and the journey was only just beginning. I had no idea how I would make it through the pain of losing my dad. Nothing could have prepared me for this. I couldn't motivate myself to do anything. Time seemed to be standing still while I tried to ride out the emotions that had taken over my life.

Gentle knocking on my bedroom door brought me back to reality, away from the place where my thoughts could roam freely. I watched the handle move before the door opened a fraction and a few wisps of blonde hair and a blue eye came into view.

'Can I come in?' Mum asked.

'Of course,' I replied, throwing back the quilt and swinging my legs out of bed.

'I didn't wake you, did I?'

As if. I hadn't had a decent night's sleep since before Dad was murdered, but I didn't want to worry Mum. She had enough on her plate.

'No,' I replied.

'This isn't healthy, Mia. It's nearly lunchtime, and you're still in your pyjamas. It's not good to spend your whole day moping around.' Mum's concern-filled eyes scanned over me.

'I know, but I can't make sense of what's happened.' Tears flowed down my cheeks.

The memory of my dad taking his last breath at my wedding was too vivid to ignore. But the thoughts were holding me captive in the past. I'd retreated deep within myself, hiding away from everyone that cared about me while keeping my new husband at arm's length. My grief was having a devastating impact on my relationships.

I'd tried meditating and mindful breathing to cope with the overwhelming feelings of anxiety. Dad had thought that kind of thing was a load of mumbo jumbo, but he'd always encouraged me to follow my heart. In an attempt to declutter my innermost thoughts, I'd started writing daily diary entries, but nothing seemed to be helping. I was a

trained yoga instructor, but I still found it was all too easy
to slip into a negative mindset. It was a destructive force
and played havoc with my emotions.

'I'm so worried about you, darling. You've become this
pale, ghostly figure, and the weight has dropped off you,'
Mum said, reaching for my hands.

She was right. I didn't need to weigh myself to know
that – I could feel my clothes were looser, but I'd lost my
appetite and was having to force myself to eat. Food didn't
interest me in the slightest. Grief was a powerful thing;
it didn't just affect your mind, it also ravaged your body.
Losing my dad had been stressful, and stress impaired the
immune system. I was completely exhausted and ached all
over from doing nothing.

'I know you're struggling to cope with your dad's death,
but staying healthy will help your body handle the stress.
You need plenty of rest, but you also need good food and
exercise. Maybe it's time you saw a doctor,' Mum suggested.

I didn't need a doctor to tell me what was wrong with
me. For as long as I could remember, I'd been highly
strung, crippled with anxiety and self-doubt. There was
such a stigma surrounding mental illness that facing up to
it was hard, so despite Mum's good intentions, her words
went over my head; I wasn't listening. I knew my negative
thinking was impacting my life, but talking to a mental
health professional wasn't going to happen. I found it hard
to share my thoughts, especially with a stranger. I didn't
want to be labelled a basket case or be given drugs to block
out the pain, which would undoubtedly make me feel like
a zombie.

'I know you're concerned, but I need to deal with things

my own way. Now, if you don't mind, I'd like to be left on my own.'

'Sort yourself out! You're driving all of us nuts,' Kelsey said when we were gathered around the table.

The words tripped off her tongue without any regard for my feelings. I'd been hiding behind my hair, my eyes glued to the tiny portion of dinner Mum had dished up for me as I pushed it around the plate while I tried to psych up the enthusiasm to eat it. As my sister continued to talk, I zoned out from the one-sided conversation and stared at the plate with the fork gripped in my hand. The only thing my brain could focus on was the sound of her voice resonating on a loop in my head. Sort. Yourself. Out. Three words, but they held so much power. I kept hearing them over and over again as they continued to echo in my head. If only it was that simple. I'd hit a wall and felt like I was trapped in my body with only my destructive thoughts for company.

Talk about tough love. But what did I expect? Despite the best attempts from the people closest to me to help me through the nightmare, I'd allowed myself to turn into a blubbering mess, unable to leave the house without bursting into tears at the slightest thing. I felt as if my life had collapsed. I'd allowed grief to suck the life out of me.

Negativity spread like a disease if you let it. I'd always had very fragile emotions and a harsh inner critic and wrestled with low self-esteem on a regular basis even before my dad died. But I'd hit an all-time low; going through every emotion under the sun was exhausting, as was fighting the internal battle I didn't appear to be winning. Kelsey's words had hit me like a slap around the face, but her no-nonsense approach had given me a much-needed wake-up call.

I put down my fork and raised my eyes from the plate to meet my sister's.

'I'm sorry I've been driving you mad.' I tore my eyes off Kelsey, then looked at Mum and Scarlett in turn.

'It's OK, darling,' Mum replied.

'Stop mollycoddling her, Mum. It's not OK; she's been a complete pain in the arse, hasn't she, Scarlett?' Kelsey wasn't holding back.

Scarlett declined to answer and offered me a half-smile instead.

'That's enough, Kelsey,' Mum said before she turned her attention to me. 'Dad wouldn't want to see you like this. He wouldn't want you to give up. You've got your whole life in front of you.'

Mum's words brought a tear to my eye. They seemed to hit the right note and gave me the strength to crawl out of the dark place that had been holding me a prisoner for so long. Mum was right; Dad wouldn't want me to be like this. Destructive emotions bred and multiplied all the time if you didn't control them. I had to turn things around and cultivate the inner peace I knew was lurking deep within me. I was fed up with being plagued by my demons. It was time to change and shut out the voices in my head.

I would always miss my dad. I would always love him, and a part of me would always grieve the fact that he was no longer part of my life. But it was time to accept the loss and the gaping hole he'd left behind and move on from it; I couldn't allow myself to be consumed by grief any longer. I wanted to make my dad proud.

31

Kelsey

'Now that we've dealt with the elephant in the room, I want to run something past you,' I said to Mia.

Mum shot me a warning look. I could tell she wanted me to tone things down so that I didn't upset Mia, but we had a different approach to dealing with my sister's issues. Mum was a wrap-things-up-in-cotton-wool type of person, whereas I was more gung ho and not as cautious about her jagged nerve endings. I'd proved earlier that sometimes the best way to help Mia was to stop holding her hand and jolt her back to reality.

'Mum and I have been talking about us potentially running Dad's business now that he's not here to do it himself. He started it from scratch, so I think we owe it to him to make sure it grows and thrives.'

Scarlett's mouth dropped open, and Mia turned her angelic face to one side and fixed me with her blue eyes.

'What about me?' Scarlett asked before she crossed

her arms over her chest. 'Why do I always get left out of everything?'

My younger sister was in her final year at drama school. Unlike some students who spent their mornings in bed before an afternoon lecture a couple of times a week, Scarlett's course was full-on and left little time for anything else.

'Nothing's been decided yet, so you're not being left out of anything,' Mum said.

'I'm ready to step up to the challenge,' I added, then I directed a question at my older sister. 'What about you?'

I glanced over at Mum; she was digging her teeth into her bottom lip while she waited for my sister to reply.

'I think it's a great idea,' Mia replied after a long pause, and then the corners of her lips lifted into a smile, which took us all by surprise.

'Well, I don't,' Scarlett replied, throwing me a scowl. 'Why am I being shut out of the business?'

'Nobody's shutting you out, but you need to finish uni first,' Mum said.

'I don't want to. I want to help Mia and Kelsey run the firm.'

When Scarlett put her hands on her hips, I couldn't help rolling my eyes. She was digging her heels in and getting ready to throw one of her well-practised tantrums.

'Like I said, once you finish uni, you can do whatever you like, but until then, it's not up for discussion.' It was good to see Mum stand her ground.

'Why do you suddenly want to pack in your course? What happened to your burning desire to be a West End sensation? I thought you were desperate to tread the boards?' I probably should have kept my mouth shut, but I couldn't resist stirring the pot.

'A person's entitled to change their mind, aren't they?' Scarlett retorted.

'That's enough, girls. I don't want to listen to you squabbling over this.' Mum said.

'Kelsey started it!' Scarlett replied before she stormed off in a huff.

'So that's sorted then. Mia and I are going to run the firm.' Don't you just love it when a plan comes together?

'Hold on a minute, Kelsey, you're getting ahead of yourself. I'm still considering your suggestion. I'm not convinced it's a good idea,' Mum said.

'But I thought we'd agreed? We've both handed in our notice.' Mum was driving me nuts; she kept blowing hot and cold.

'You should have spoken to me before you did that. But if you're hell-bent on getting involved, I need to tell you the truth about what you're taking on. I'm not sure either of you have the skills to manage the firm,' Mum said.

Mia and I exchanged a glance.

'Your dad wanted me to pretend I knew nothing about the business to protect me from his rivals. He upset a lot of people and had countless enemies. I'm going to tell you how he really made a living, and then you can decide if you still want to get involved.'

Whatever Mum was about to divulge sounded juicy; I was eager to hear what she had to say. Mia, on the other hand, seemed to have shrunk several inches as she tried to retreat within herself.

'You know your dad ran a debt collection agency, which involved the recovery of assets,' Mum began.

Mia and I both nodded.

'He was also involved in money laundering; there was a dark side to his work. You're going to be breaking the law if you follow in his footsteps. Your dad didn't like to do things by the book, so he didn't use official channels to recoup his money.'

'What exactly do you mean by that?' I asked.

'He'd do whatever it took to make the debtor pay up. He had to threaten people and used violence sometimes.' Mum bit down on her lip as her eyes flicked backwards and forwards between Mia and I. 'More than sometimes. Things used to turn nasty most of the time. I accepted this a long time ago, but I know it's come as a shock to you.'

There was a lot to take in. I glanced over at Mia; she was deathly pale, staring straight ahead with a horrified look on her face. I wasn't sure how I felt about the way Dad made his living. But Mum had always known that the money was illegal, and she seemed untroubled by the fact, so why should I concern myself? Mum had the right idea, so I'd take a leaf out of her book and shrug it off. That was the best option. Overthinking things always complicated a situation.

'You'll have to be prepared to use force if you want to succeed and command respect from people. Now, do you understand why he didn't want you involved? It's a dangerous line of work. I want you to go away and think about what I've told you. You need to know what you'll be taking on if you get involved in the business. Everyone will underestimate you,' Mum said.

'Never underestimate the female thought process,' I replied with a smile on my face.

There had to be a way to move forward with the plan. What if we could find a different way to run the business? Bringing a new perspective to the table would be like a breath of fresh air, wouldn't it? I appreciated Mum's honesty, but I wasn't about to be put off; I was ready to run the firm. I was my father's daughter, and it was time to take hold of the reins. I'd bring Mia along for the ride, but I wasn't convinced she was cut out for the role. It was going to get dark, and she was a sensitive soul. A confident person needed to be at the helm. Mum's reluctance to let us get involved only made me more determined to prove I had what it took to succeed in Dad's arena. I couldn't wait to get started; I fancied myself as a kick-arse businesswoman. And I'd have Rio and Todd by my side if things got heavy.

Mum had got used to her way of living, and I was sure she wouldn't want to give it up any time soon. In fact, all of us were guilty of loving the good life. We'd been a conduit through which Dad funnelled cash, so we'd been spoilt rotten, and I wasn't sure any of us would want to have to manage on a regular income or buy our clothes from discount stores. We were used to certain standards; we'd never known any different. Dad had liked lavishing us with designer dresses and anything with an expensive price tag. Whatever we wanted, we got; he was happy to pick up the tab. I couldn't imagine what it would be like if we lost everything after Dad had worked so hard to achieve it. That wasn't an option as far as I was concerned.

32

Mia

I was still reeling from Mum's confession and the fact that she'd always known our dad was a crime boss. She might have tolerated it, but it bothered me to know that everything we had came off the backs of people who'd got into trouble with money. I was stunned that Dad's work centred around illegal activities, violence and intimidation. The revelation wasn't going to be easy to overcome, especially because Jack had been involved in it behind my back.

No wonder my dad had been bitterly opposed to the route I'd originally chosen and wouldn't hear of me joining the family firm. He knew I'd discover the skeleton hiding in the cupboard. My heart had been set on a career in accountancy. Dad had other ideas. He thought I wouldn't be able to handle the stress and discouraged me from having a proper job with responsibilities. Now I was questioning his motives. I'd been pressured into following a different path, but numbers were my first love. It was something that Jack and I had in common.

Jack had been my dad's accountant for years. Well, at least that's what I'd thought. I'd always known my dad respected my husband, but I hadn't realised that Jack's role in the company was pivotal. I couldn't believe the man I'd married was involved in shady money laundering. And to think people assumed accountants were boring. I loved Jack with all my heart, but now I wasn't sure if I really knew him. I hated the thought that he'd been lying to me. It was time to find out how far he'd go to cover up the truth.

'I don't think you have any idea what you're getting yourself involved in,' Jack said when I told him that Kelsey and I were going to take over the day-to-day running of Dad's firm.

'Maybe you'd care to elaborate.' I willed Jack to open up and be honest with me.

'Davie used to deal with some dodgy people, and Rio's doing a great job, so you should leave him to it.' Jack ran his strong fingers through his honey-blond hair.

Disappointment threatened to crush me when Jack failed to fill me in. 'Well, it's too late to back out now; I've already accepted the challenge.'

Jack ran his hand over his golden stubble, deep in thought before he fixed me with his eyes and began to speak.

'Take it from me; there's more to money lending than meets the eye.'

'Like what?' I questioned, hoping that he'd spill the beans. When he didn't answer, I pressed on. 'Are you worried that I'll be cramping your style?'

I fixed my eyes on Jack, but he didn't notice; he was staring into the middle distance with a scowl on his face. He clearly had a lot on his mind.

'Be honest with me, don't you like the idea of your wife being your new boss?'

Jack let out a long sigh. 'That's got nothing to do with it.'

'So, what's the problem?'

'Sometimes things get messy at the firm, and there are risks involved. You don't know what you're letting yourself in for. You're going to be catapulted into uncharted territory. I think you're making...' I could hear the frustration in Jack's voice; he didn't try to hide it from me.

'I was hoping you were going to support me on this,' I replied, cutting Jack off mid-flow.

Jack fixed me with a glare. 'If you'll let me finish my sentence, I was about to say, I think you're making a huge mistake.'

'I'm sorry you feel that way, but that just makes me even more determined to prove I have what it takes to run the company.'

'I can't let you do this, Mia. What kind of a husband would I be if I didn't try and stop you from wading in unprepared? I had a lot of respect for your dad, but he wasn't as squeaky clean as you think. Your dad's business is far from legitimate. I have to break the law every single day to cover his tracks: converting cash the firm gains through illicit means into legitimate forms, creating explanations for the source of the assets without attracting the attention of the authorities. It's a delicate operation; large cash transactions are meant to be reported and can't float around without waving red flags,' Jack confessed.

Jack's brow furrowed; I could see he was stressed. He'd been reluctant to come clean and confide in me and didn't own up until I'd backed him into a corner. Why didn't he feel like he could trust me? I was his wife, for God's sake.

'I can't believe you've been lying to me. I deserved to know the truth. Why didn't you tell me this before?'

'I'm sorry, I should have told you, but I was trying to protect you. Davie was adamant that details of the firm should stay behind closed doors, and I was ashamed of what I'd been doing. I never wanted you to find out I'd been cooking the books,' Jack replied. 'But I didn't have a choice; only a stupid person would cross your dad.'

'What's that supposed to mean?'

Jack's eyes searched mine as though he was trying to find the right words. Then he decided against it and walked off without answering my question, leaving me to form my own conclusion.

33

Scarlett

It was so obvious that Mum, Mia and Kelsey were talking business when I walked into the kitchen because they immediately stopped the conversation they were having and changed the subject. It made me feel resentful, and I was about to storm off in a huff when Mum caught hold of my arm.

'Can you two give me a minute, please? I want to have a chat with Scarlett.'

Mia and Kelsey pushed back their chairs, got up from the table and walked out of the room without saying a word, which only added extra tension to the situation.

'Are you OK?' Mum asked.

Hunger had got the better of me. I couldn't ignore the rumbling coming from my stomach any longer, so I'd forced myself to venture out of my room.

'What do you think?' I spat the words into Mum's face.

I was already annoyed at the way she'd spoken to me earlier, and that was before I'd witnessed the reaction when I'd walked in on my mum and sisters' top-secret meeting. Anyone would think they were world leaders attending a highly important G7 summit the way they were acting.

'I don't know, Scarlett, that's why I asked you.'

There was no sign of Mum's patient tone; her voice was laced with irritation, which did nothing to smooth over the awkwardness between us.

'Why did you storm off earlier?' Mum tilted her head to one side while she waited for me to reply.

'Because you took Kelsey's side.'

'I didn't take anyone's side. I'd just asked you both to stop squabbling,' Mum said. 'Don't you think you overreacted?'

'Maybe I did, but I resented the fact that you told me I couldn't give up my course to run the business with Mia and Kelsey. How do you think that made me feel? They're a team, and I'm the odd one out.' I crossed my arms over my chest, and as I did, I felt my bottom lip jut out, so I consciously sucked it back in.

'I wasn't trying to upset you or make you feel left out.'

'Really?' I threw my arms up in the air. Who was she trying to kid? 'So why did you all stop talking when I walked into the room?'

Mum answered my question with a long sigh. 'Your sisters haven't even decided whether they want to run the business or not yet, so I don't know why you're getting so het up about it.'

'Because it's bringing back painful memories. When we were young, playtime was always unfair. I never had any say over which games we played, and that was on the rare occasion they let me join in. Most of the time, I was too little to play their games. It used to make me feel left out, and it's happening all over again.'

'Don't be so dramatic, Scarlett,' Mum said.

I felt tears stab at my eyes. Thoughts of my empty stomach were a thing of the past. I had to get out of the room; it suddenly felt stifling. Being the baby of the family sucked. I hated it. I always got treated like a child even though I was an adult. The pattern just kept repeating itself no matter how old I got, and it was doing my head in.

34

Mia

'I want you to go into this with your eyes wide open,' Mum said.

Once Scarlett had left for uni, she summoned Kelsey and I into the dining room. Rio and Todd were already sitting around the table.

'The girls want to take a more active role in Davie's firm, but I'd like to hear your thoughts on the matter first,' Mum said.

Rio's eyebrows rose a couple of inches. 'With all due respect, Amanda, I don't think that's a good idea. I know it's not really my place to speak up, but I'm not sure Davie would be happy about that. Why don't you leave things as they are? I'm happy to continue running things.'

'I know you are, and I appreciate that, but the girls want to front the business. They're both smart and will be a real asset to the firm. They have hidden depths that their dad ignored; now's their chance to prove themselves.' Mum was doing her best to win Rio over.

'You know how dangerous this line of work can be. I can't pretend the business is something it's not,' Rio replied.

'I don't want you to; tell it like it is and don't hold back. I want the girls to know what they'd be taking on before they make a decision.'

'But you've already dropped the bombshell,' Kelsey interrupted. 'We know we'll be breaking the law if we follow in Dad's footsteps, but we want to be at the helm.'

Kelsey appeared unbothered about the morality of our dad's business. I sometimes wished I had her water-off-a duck'- back attitude.

'Could I speak to you in private, Amanda?' Rio asked.

'Of course,' Mum replied. 'But if it's business-related, feel free to talk in front of the girls.'

The whites of Rio's dark eyes grew wider as he fixed them on Mum.

'Has it ever occurred to you what the motive for Davie's murder was?' Rio's dark eyes scanned each one of us in turn.

'Of course it has. My husband upset a lot of people over the years and had countless enemies. I presumed one of them was responsible. The police don't seem to be able to track the killer down, which pretty much confirms it was a professional hit,' Mum replied.

'It's an absolute certainty that Davie's work got him killed, so it's too dangerous for Mia and Kelsey to even consider getting involved. Do you want your daughters to be next?'

Rio's words sent a chill down my spine.

'Anyone would think you're trying to put us off,' Kelsey replied.

'Is it working?' Rio questioned before he fixed his eyes on Kelsey.

I was tempted to jump up and say, 'Yes, let's forget all about it; it was a stupid idea,' but something stopped me from speaking up. So I stayed quiet and let Kelsey answer the question.

'No, it's not putting me off,' Kelsey replied.

I had a feeling that was going to be her response. I had to admit I was seriously getting cold feet. I let my eyes wander to the vase of flowers in the centre of the table and concentrated on one of the heads in an attempt to slow my pounding pulse.

'We're serious about running the business, aren't we, Mia?'

My head sprang up at the sound of Kelsey's voice, but my mouth was too dry to be able to produce an answer.

'I won't stand by and let you go into this blindly. You're being naïve about what it will take to fill your dad's shoes and how dangerous it's going to be. Barney Coleman's no longer on the scene, but back in the day, he and Davie were rivals. They'd had beef from day dot. It's a certainty that it was the Colemans who took out the hit on Davie. If one of them didn't shoot him, they paid someone to do it,' Rio said, and his gaze flicked towards my mum.

Mum gasped. 'What makes you so sure?'

'The Colemans had a real grudge against him. There was a lot of bad blood between them.' Rio stared into Mum's eyes as though they were the only two people in the room.

'Lots of people had a grudge against Davie,' Mum replied.

'That's true, but Davie started a war when he went after Barney Coleman.'

'The man was a monster,' Mum said.

'I know he was, and he needed to be stopped.' Rio paused and began chewing the side of his thumbnail. Then he dropped his hand down by his side and straightened his posture. 'There's something I need to tell you. It's important you understand what you're getting involved in; I don't want you to be in over your heads and end up hurt or worse. Davie did away with Barney so that he couldn't torture any more innocent people, which is why his family wanted to get revenge.' Rio looked gutted that he'd broken my dad's trust.

Mum's hands flew up to cover her mouth, and she looked at Rio with tears in her eyes.

'I'm sorry I didn't tell you about Barney. Davie didn't want you to know.'

Mum wiped the tears that were flowing down her cheeks away with the back of her hand. 'And Davie could always rely on your loyalty. It breaks my heart to think he was targeted because he was being a good guy, ridding the world of a psychopath who tortured and murdered people.'

'Why don't we tell the police the Colemans had a grudge against Dad?' That seemed like the obvious thing to do.

Rio pushed his chair back and stood up from the table. 'Davie would want us to get our own kind of justice. I'm sure I've given you food for thought. Please reconsider your decision. I don't want to see you girls come to any harm.'

Rio gestured to Todd then he gave Kelsey and me a weak smile before they filed out of the dining room.

'DI Stewart said to get in touch if we remembered anything else. Surely it couldn't help to drop the name Coleman in the frame,' I said.

'Rio's right. Being put behind bars isn't enough punishment for scum like that. Rather than shy away from this, we owe it to your dad's memory to escalate the situation with the Colemans.'

There was a lot to absorb, and my mum and sister's presence suddenly felt intrusive. I needed to be on my own, so I could process all the information. Now that I knew what lay behind Dad being murdered, I was scared to get involved in his murky world. Rio's warning had shocked me to the core. But Mum was relying on Kelsey and I to step into Dad's shoes. I didn't want to let her down and desperately wanted to take up the challenge; I just wasn't sure I'd be able to overcome my fear. I knew from experience the invisible battles within myself were the hardest ones to win.

I'd come to a fork in the road. I didn't want to continue to live with my issues; they would consume me if I let them. I needed to conquer them by overcoming the things that were holding me back; negative thinking was my biggest enemy. I had to try to replace it with optimism and hope. I either did something about it or resigned myself to this way of living. Kelsey's suggestion had blown my mind, especially now that we knew the reality of Dad's business. If I could pluck up the courage to take the leap of faith, this could be just what I needed to pull myself out of the dark place I was stuck in. It was time to channel the inner warrior lurking inside me.

For people who had never experienced an anxiety attack or the overwhelming feelings of stress or panic that had plagued me for years, it was difficult for them to understand what I'd been going through. I was sure my sisters thought

I was being self-indulgent as I'd struggled to come to terms with Dad's death. After all, they'd lost a parent too. But I was determined to show them what I was made of and overcome my demons.

My dad was a hero and had lost his life because he stood up to the bad guys. If we hadn't been miles away from civilisation in a location without CCTV footage, it might never have happened. I'd given his marksman the green light to gun him down and escape without being brought to justice, and I'd have to live with that fact. But I was determined to use that knowledge to drive myself to work harder to leave my anxieties behind and step up to run the business.

A desire to succeed had surfaced within me, and I had no intention of suppressing it. I wanted to start a new journey, one that would no doubt take me to highs, lows and everything in between. Breaking free from the shackles holding me a prisoner would be liberating; I was no longer prepared to surrender my free will. I'd wasted enough time allowing things to drag me down. Life was too short to let opportunities pass me by.

'I'm going to tell Mum and Kelsey that I want to help run the firm,' I said when Jack came into the bedroom.

'Really? After everything I said? I thought I'd scared you off when I told you the truth. Is this a wind-up?' A flash of anger spread across Jack's handsome face.

'No, it's not a wind-up; I'm deadly serious. Mum's right. Rather than shy away from the business, we owe it to Dad's memory to get back at the Colemans.'

Jack's response had blindsided me. He was normally so supportive and dependable, standing beside me when

I needed him while giving me space to roam free and grow as a person.

'To attempt that would be a suicidal move. You and Kelsey are incapable of doing that.' Jack shook his head from side to side. 'Listen to me, Mia, you might be the next in line to the throne, but that doesn't mean you need to accept the position.'

'Please don't underestimate me. You know I hate it when people write me off without giving me a chance to prove myself. I thought you'd be happy that I was doing something proactive for once.'

I was the quiet one of the family and much more reserved than my two sisters, so people made a habit of assuming things about me. Just because I tended to blend into the background, it didn't mean I was a weak link.

'I'm happy that you're in a better headspace and feel ready to face the world again.' Jack paused, took hold of my hands and looked deeply into my eyes. 'What can I do to make you change your mind? This is madness, Mia.'

I knew Jack's words had come from a place of genuine concern. My husband was my rock and had the ability to be strong and stay calm when I couldn't. He knew better than anyone how I dealt with pressure. But if I prepared myself mentally and emotionally, I was sure I'd become more resilient in time. Kelsey was going to run the firm with or without me. I wasn't going to let her take over and push me out. I had just as much right to take my place as she did.

Although I'd been shocked by Kelsey's directness, when she'd told me I was driving everyone nuts, in the long run, she'd done me a huge favour by giving me a kick up the backside. She was right; Mum tended to spoon-feed me and build me up with motivational speeches, which, don't get me wrong, I appreciated, but sometimes the tough-love approach was needed.

35

Mia

The sun was pushing its way through the grey clouds, making the weather better than it had been for the last few days. I filled my lungs with the cool spring air as I stepped outside and made my way along the path to Dad's office space at the bottom of the garden. I slid open the triple-glazed door and stood in the opening before I plucked up the courage to go inside.

It was the first time I'd been in here since Dad was murdered, and memories of him suddenly hit me like a tsunami; I didn't see them coming. But I was drowning in a sea of self-doubt, so it was easy to fall prey to negative thinking. A full-blown panic attack threatened to pull me into its clutches if I didn't get a grip. I was struggling to breathe, so I tried to focus on my mum's words, which were burned into my brain. 'Dad wouldn't want to see you like this,' she'd said. The moment was just passing when I heard Mum and Kelsey's voices getting closer. I inhaled a deep breath and held it for ten seconds, and when I let it go, I painted on a smile.

'Somebody's keen,' Mum said when she joined me in the office space.

'I wanted to make a good impression. It wouldn't look good if I was late on my first day,' I replied.

I was grateful that my mum and sister hadn't arrived any earlier. The last thing I wanted was for my family to think I wasn't up to the job.

'Sorry we're late; the traffic was a nightmare. Don't you just hate long commutes?' Kelsey joked.

'Take a seat, girls,' Mum said, gesturing to the black leather sofa.

I wasn't sure I would be able to focus on work in this space – which had previously been Dad's haven – if I was permanently surrounded by his possessions and things that reminded me of him. Kelsey and I might need to consider giving the place a makeover to tone things down a bit without stripping away the heart and soul.

Rio slid open the glass door and stepped into the office space.

'Now that Rio's here, let's get started. Actually, just hold fire for a minute,' Mum said, getting up from behind the desk.

She walked across to where Rio was standing, stuck her head out of the glass partition and called over to Todd. He was busy surveying the grounds, checking that everything was as it should be when Mum beckoned our bodyguard towards her. Moments later, Todd walked through the door, notebook in hand.

'Mia and Kelsey have come to a decision; they're going

to be handling the day-to-day running from now on,' Mum said as she sat back down behind the desk.

Rio looked at us with an expression of utter bewilderment on his face. 'I have to say I'm stunned after everything I told you.'

'We know the risks, but nothing's changed; we want to run the business in Dad's honour,' Kelsey said.

'The girls will never be able to do it without you. I can advise them, but you were Davie's right-hand man, so you should be the one teaching them the ropes.'

'Please don't ask me to do that. If anything happened to them, I'd never forgive myself.' Rio bowed his head.

'I can see you're reluctant, but I think we should respect their wishes. They're young and have fresh ideas. Kelsey's a problem solver and is used to dealing with impossible people. And Mia has a head for numbers and an analytical mind. Don't write them off without giving them a chance. I'm hoping I can count on you to support and assist them.' Mum smiled. 'Do it for Davie,' she threw in for good measure.

Rio straightened his posture and pushed his broad shoulders back as he trained his eyes on my mum. 'I know when I'm beat,' he said after a long pause. 'For the record, I still think this is a bad idea, but I can't let the girls go into it blindly.'

Rio de Souza and Dad had been childhood friends and next-door neighbours, and even though my dad was no longer with us, his loyalty was still unwavering. He was prepared to do anything for his former boss even though he had serious reservations.

'I take it you're on board too, Todd,' Mum said.

'As a security professional, I'd have to advise against this. Your daughters will have to face violence and threats on a daily basis.'

'If you won't watch over them, we'll have to take on somebody who will,' Mum replied.

'I didn't say I wouldn't do it; I just said I'd advise against it. Your daughters' safety is paramount. Rest assured, they'll be in good hands with me.' Todd flashed Kelsey a sly grin.

It was subtly done, but I saw how his eye contact dropped to her lips and lingered there. Mum didn't appear to notice the tell-tale signs that showed our minder had a vested interest in one of her daughters.

'That's all for now. You can go back to what you were doing, Todd,' Mum said.

The bodyguard cast his eyes over Kelsey once more before he turned on his heel and went back out to check the perimeter fencing. My younger sister was an absolute stunner and an expert at arousing sexual interest. Her pale skin, gleaming dark brown hair and bright blue eyes were a winning combination, so she'd never been short of admirers. She loved to play the part of the seductress; leading others astray was her favourite pastime.

'Let's get down to business. Can you get us up to speed on what's happening?' Mum asked, craning her neck to look up at Rio.

'I had a call from Larry yesterday. He's got a large debt that he wants us to buy. He feels out of his depth with it.'

'So, what's the problem? We do a lot of business with him.' Mum rested her elbows on the desk then steepled her fingers.

Rio shrugged. 'I've just got a bad feeling about this debt.'

'How come?' Mum asked. 'Surely, every deal carries risks. I know Davie had a better track record for recovering outstanding money than most, but there are never any guarantees in this business.'

'That's true, but I think even Davie would have been wary about this one.'

'Maybe you could put Larry and Davie's relationship into context so that Mia and Kelsey understand the background,' Mum said.

Rio's eyes bored into my mum's as if he was trying to read her mind. It was clear he was hesitant to open up to us.

'If the girls are going to run the business, they need to know the history,' Mum said, urging him to continue.

Rio turned towards Kelsey and I. 'Larry runs a second-hand car lot at the back of Shoreditch High Street. His customers often find the terms of his credit agreement difficult to stick to; when they stop paying the instalments, Larry doesn't want the hassle involved in taking them to court. You go to all that trouble, and then the person ends up declaring themselves bankrupt. Selling the debt works out cheaper and quicker in the long run than hiring a solicitor to fight the case. Davie used to buy the debt from Larry and then recoup it at a profit.'

'If the customer's having trouble managing the repayments, how would transferring the debt to another party help them?' I asked.

A wry smile spread across Rio's handsome face. 'It doesn't. That's why defaulting on repayments sometimes turns nasty, and we have to use threats and violence to get the money back or take away the person's bank cards as security.'

The contents of my stomach did a backward flip.

'To get back to what I was saying earlier. Larry's got a large debt that he wants us to buy, which wouldn't normally be an issue, but the people who owe the money are bad news.'

'Anyone, I know?' Mum asked, leaning back in her chair.

'The Colemans,' Rio replied.

After Rio's words left his mouth, you could cut the atmosphere with a knife. The mention of that name made my blood run cold, and my pulse went into overdrive. A flash of anger spread across Mum's face. Her expression changed in an instant; she tightened her lips, and a frown settled on her forehead.

'Barney's brother Victor and his nephew Craig are running the firm now. They've been kicking up a whole heap of shit in the last couple of weeks and are getting really out of hand now that Davie's not around to keep them in their place,' Rio said.

'We owe it to Davie to sort them out,' Mum replied.

'I think it would be a bad idea to take on this debt. Given the history, it might be a trap. The Colemans would have known Larry's first port of call would be the Saunders firm. And he didn't disappoint them.'

Mum froze and stared at Rio with wide eyes. 'No wonder you were hesitant to take this on,' she said after collecting her thoughts.

'It's a tough call. Larry was begging for help. I know what Davie would have done, but now that he's not around, I think it's too risky.'

Rio's eyes flicked towards Kelsey and I. We were the

reason he was holding back, but we never going to succeed if we baulked at the first sign of trouble.

'How would Dad have handled this?' I asked.

Rio glanced over at my mum, and she nodded to give him the go-ahead.

'Davie never shied away from anything. He would have given Larry the money and gone after the Colemans to recoup his debt,' Rio replied. 'But I'm not suggesting we do that. Larry will have to find somebody else to take this on.'

'How much do the Colemans owe?' Mum asked, wringing her hands together.

'Around one hundred grand,' Rio replied.

Mum's mouth dropped open. 'What the hell did they buy, a fleet of cars?'

Rio shook his head. 'Larry had taken possession of some top-of-the-range Audis he'd acquired from another car dealer who'd recently gone bankrupt. He got badgered into giving Victor and Craig two of them on a try-before-you-buy agreement. But so far, the men have failed to either return or pay for the cars. Larry reckons they are easily worth fifty grand apiece.'

'That's a lot of money,' Mum said.

'It is, but we can't just walk away from this. Dad lost his life because of this family. It's up to us to redress the balance,' I said, and Kelsey's eyes nearly popped out of her head.

'I'll leave you ladies to decide what you want to do,' Rio said as he headed for the door.

36

Kelsey

I trained my eyes on Mia when Rio closed the door behind him. She was talking the talk, but who was she trying to kid? I wasn't buying it. She might think she'd suddenly become a crime boss badass, but she was perched on the edge of her seat, balling her fists in her lap as her right knee bobbed up and down. The only person she was scaring was herself.

Our first day in the office had been an eye-opener, and if we were hoping for a gentle start, we were going to be bitterly disappointed. The words 'baptism of fire' suddenly sprang into my head.

Mum got out of the leather chair and walked around to the front of the desk. Her black, silk, palazzo pants swayed as she moved. When she took a seat on the edge, she wrapped her arms around the front of her chest. The tips of her manicured fingers dug into the soft cashmere jumper she was wearing as her eyes shifted between Mia and I.

'Be honest with me, now that you know what's really

involved, do you still want to run your dad's firm? Mum asked, biting down on the side of her lip.

Mia nodded, but she seemed lost for words.

I'd watched my older sister's expression and body language change when Rio began to divulge the trouble the Colemans were causing. She'd seemed shocked by the information he'd given us, and as she'd absorbed his words, Mia had retreated back into the chair and let her golden hair fall over her face, hiding behind it like a curtain with one blue eye peeping out. Where was Edward Scissorhands when you needed him?

Mia had put a lot of focus on debt management and appeared particularly troubled when Rio had explained that defaulting on repayments meant things turned nasty sometimes. She'd asked questions to deepen her understanding of how things worked, but I couldn't help feeling she was desperate to justify why Dad would sanction violent behaviour. Mia had always put my dad on a pedestal, so she probably didn't want to think about him doing anything underhand.

There were plenty of words you could use to describe my dad; he was a typical cockney geezer, a lovable rogue, a rough diamond, but he wasn't a strait-laced businessman. Threatening violence to get his money back or taking away a person's bank cards as security until they coughed up what they owed was just another day at the office for him, by all accounts.

I wanted to explore a different approach and pit grey matter against muscle, brains versus brawn, in the hope that we could use our wits to outsmart our rivals. I considered myself a natural leader who thrived at influencing and manipulating others. But if my powers of persuasion failed, and we had to turn the thumbscrews to get back our investment, then so be it. I'd always courted danger, and my desire for vengeance against the family that killed my dad was at an all-time high.

'What about you, Kelsey? Do you still want to run the business?' Mum asked.

I nodded. 'Mia's right; we need to redress the balance.'

Mum smiled at me and then turned her attention to Mia. 'Are you sure you're going to be able to handle this?'

'Yes,' Mia replied, pushing back her slumped shoulders. 'I'm a determined character, and although your dad was a great provider, I've found living in a gilded cage frustrating. Now that I'm able to spread my wings, I want something to sink my teeth into. It's going to be dangerous, but I want us to get even with the men that robbed me of my husband.'

'I know Rio has his reservations, but I think we should take on Larry's debt. Dad wouldn't have shied away from it, and neither should we,' Mia said.

Mum and I glanced at each other; Mia's words had taken us by surprise.

'We need to consider this carefully. I don't want to risk your safety. The Colemans are dangerous people,' Mum said.

'Larry has asked for help, and if we do nothing, we're going to give everyone the wrong signals. People will write us off before we have a chance to prove ourselves,' Mia pointed out.

Mum and I both fixed our eyes on Mia. She appeared to be transforming in front of our eyes, shedding the protective armour she'd been shielding behind. She seemed different, stronger than she'd ever been. I never hid behind anything or anybody. I had nerves of steel. Maybe that was starting to rub off on her. Were we going to make a good team, or was this going to cause friction between us?

Mia sat bolt upright, swept her long, flaxen hair over her shoulders and tucked it behind her ears. I was so used to my sister hiding behind her hair, that gesture was a breakthrough in itself. I could see there was an alter ego in there somewhere, but it would take a lot of courage to let that person out.

'I'm not saying it's going to be easy, but we need to develop a strategy to deal with the Colemans,' Mia said. 'I get the impression that a woman has to be twice as smart as a man in this business.'

Mum wiped a tear away with her index finger, then she leant forward and took hold of Mia's hands. 'I'd been so worried that this would be too much for you, but it looks like you're going to prove me wrong. You're like a different person,' Mum said, and her lavender-blue eyes glistened with tears.

'I'm getting there; it feels good to have a purpose,' Mia replied.

She didn't need to try and convince me; I could see my sister meant what she'd said.

'Grit and determination are key traits all models must have, and it looks like both of you have inherited that.' Mum smiled, then she picked up her mobile. 'Can you join us for a minute, please?' she said before she ended the call.

Moments later, Rio walked into the room.

'We've decided we're going to help Larry. What do you think he'll accept?' Mum asked.

'I think you're making a huge mistake,' Rio replied.

'If we don't stand up to the Colemans, they're going to walk all over us. They'll have no competition, and that can only be a bad thing. Correct me if I'm wrong, but you said Victor and Craig were getting out of hand now that Davie wasn't around to keep them in their place,' Mum said.

'They are, but the girls will be walking into the middle of a violent turf war. I can't let them do that,' Rio said.

'The Colemans have taken my husband's life; they're not taking his business too. Are you going to help us or not?' Mum put her hands on her hips and fixed Rio with a glare.

Rio let out a loud breath. He knew when he was beaten. 'Larry told me the cars are worth around one hundred thousand pounds. Davie would never have paid him the full amount; he would have made him an offer instead. Taking on the debt has risks attached, so Davie would have expected to pay less than the cars were worth.'

'I bet Larry needs the deal much more than we do. Why don't we offer him half?' Mia suggested like a true accountant, ready and poised to save the firm money.

Mum and I both laughed.

'I'm serious,' Mia insisted.

'You're more like your dad than I thought. That's the sort of cheeky offer he'd make, but he had the gift of the gab, so he could pull it off. I'm not sure Larry will accept such a low amount from the two of you,' Rio said, giving us his honest opinion.

'There's a lot riding on this; it's the first time we've dabbled in this line of business, and we don't know if we're going to be able to get the money back, do we?' Mia continued.

'I know what you're saying, and I agree with you, but

I can't imagine Larry will go for that. He's a second-hand car salesman, so he's a skilled wheeler-dealer. It goes with the territory,' Rio replied.

I rubbed my hand across my chin while I mulled over Mia's suggestion. 'Let's give it a try. What have we got to lose? If Larry doesn't like it, he can always make a counteroffer, and if he accepts, think of the profit we'll make,' I said.

Haggling was an art form, but it was a necessary job requirement. The key to our success would be learning the back-and-forth dance.

'Kelsey's right. We're talking about a lot of money. There can't be too many people out there who would be able to buy a debt of this size from him.' Mia folded her arms over her chest, then tilted her head to the side as if she was considering what she'd just said.

'That's true,' Mum agreed.

'Which one of you's going to do the deal?' Rio asked.

'I'm happy to give it a go,' Mia said.

'Fine by me,' I replied. I didn't want to be the one to fall flat on my face first.

'Larry's as slippery as an eel. He'll run rings around you and end up with the upper hand if you're not careful,' Rio warned.

Mum offered some words of wisdom. 'Let me pass on some advice. My agent told me when she used to agree the terms of my contracts, she stuck to a golden rule: if she didn't like the way things were heading, she was prepared to walk away.'

'I'll keep that in mind, but I might end up surprising you and wiping the floor with Larry.' Mia laughed.

Who knew what Mia was hiding beneath her meek, mild exterior?

'Hi Larry, I'm Mia Saunders, Davie's daughter.'

Mia had put the call on speakerphone so that Mum, Rio and I could listen in.

'Hi, Mia, I don't think we've ever had the pleasure before,' Larry began.

He sounded like a prize sleazeball if you asked me, and I was glad Mia was dealing with him.

'What can I do for you, love?' Larry continued.

'Nothing, but from what Rio tells me, you need my help,' Mia replied, putting Larry firmly in his place.

I had to stop myself from whooping with delight.

'I'm prepared to offer you fifty thousand for the Audis.'

We heard Larry suck in a loud breath. 'I can't let them go for that, love. We're talking about two top-quality cars, not a couple of handbags.'

I saw Mia bristle and had to stifle a laugh.

'I'm well aware of that. But when you buy in multiples, you expect to get a better price.'

'Sorry, no can do, love,' Larry replied.

'OK, fair enough, but that's my final offer. I can't afford to pay you any more than that.'

Mia was doing a great job. I wasn't sure how I felt about that. I'd been expecting to run the show with her taking a supporting role, but she was really stepping up to the mark, and I felt a bit threatened by that.

Mia might not have had Larry eating out of the palm of her hand from the start, but she had a clear sense of when to walk away. That was coming across loud and clear. If she held her ground and stuck to her terms, where would that leave Larry?

'I can't let them go for a penny less than seventy-five grand,' Larry countered.

'I understand. In that case, I'll have to bow out,' Mia replied. 'Enjoy the rest of your day.'

'Hold on a minute, love,' Larry said as Mia was about to end the call. 'Will you go to sixty? There's still a lot of profit to be made.'

I had a feeling Larry's sales pitch was falling on deaf ears.

'I'm afraid I can't pay more than fifty.' Mia wasn't going to budge. 'Maybe you should try one of your other contacts,' she suggested, calling his bluff.

'OK, OK, I'll take it, but I'm in a hurry for the dosh. Can you get it to me by the end of the day?'

Mia looked over at Mum, who nodded.

'Yes,' Mia replied.

'Your old man taught you well. I'd like to say it's a pleasure doing business with you, but you've just broken my balls just like he used to,' Larry said before he ended the call.

'That's my girl,' Mum said, planting a kiss on Mia's cheek. 'You were fantastic. On the surface, you have such an unassuming manner, but you've inherited your dad's ability to drive a hard bargain. There's no question about that. You've broken out of your shell and found your voice. I don't mind telling you it was empowering to watch.'

Somebody pass the bucket. Mia had been incredible, but Mum was being ridiculously over the top, blowing hot air up her arse. She was clucking around her like a mother hen, and it was doing my head in. Sealing the deal had really boosted Mia's confidence, and the room felt buzzy and full of energy, but I didn't feel a part of it. Was this how it was going to be from now on?

37

Mia

I always seemed to encounter more stumbling blocks in life than most, which challenged me on a daily basis and defeated me over and over again. I had a strong inner critic who believed that if I was hard on myself and judged myself relentlessly, nobody else could make me feel worse than I already did. Today had been like a breath of fresh air. Instead of going through the motions like I usually did, I'd switched my focus and turned off autopilot. Learning to navigate life's difficulties while keeping my emotions in check would take time, but I felt like I was making real progress.

Nobody in my family really understood what made me tick or the way my mind processed things differently from theirs. But we were all unique and had our own personal qualities. If you'd told me a week ago that I'd be brave enough to pick up the phone to one of my dad's business associates and negotiate a very favourable deal for the firm, I wouldn't have believed you. Trying something new and succeeding where I'd thought I might fail had given me a much-needed confidence boost. I felt like I'd found my niche.

I'd broken out of the box, and now, I had a spring in my step, which made a refreshing change. I was usually tired and drained, weighed down by the things that troubled me. The experience had been liberating. What had happened to me? I'd spent my entire life being the one with the low self-esteem who just wanted to disappear. Even though we had an unbreakable bond, I was constantly overshadowed by my younger sisters. I was naturally reclusive and tended to keep people at arm's length. I spent too much time in my own head, putting myself down, thinking the worst of myself.

I'd been scared when I'd jumped in feet first and suggested we bought the debt off of Larry. I'd been testing the waters to see how Mum and Kelsey responded, and I'd been pleasantly surprised by their reaction. They seemed genuinely pleased that I was taking the initiative for once. I made a habit of opting for safe choices instead of courageous ones, constantly second-guessing my ability to do things.

I was glad I'd stepped out of my comfort zone and made a bold move, a brave move. I'd been so worried that I'd let people down and feel like a failure if I couldn't step up to the mark that I'd almost thrown the towel in without even trying. But I'd taken a gamble, and it had paid off. I wanted to shed my old skin and reveal a new, tougher one. One that I hoped wouldn't be so easily offended.

I was a cautious and calculated person. I didn't do things that made me scared. I would never usually take a leap into the unknown. I didn't think I had it in me, but I'd proved myself wrong. Believing I could succeed had changed my outlook, and now I felt driven, focused, determined. This was a defining moment. I was still scared, but I wasn't going to let that fear stop me or hold me back any more. Having confidence in myself would be a powerful driving force, and if I harnessed it, there would be no end to what I could achieve. I couldn't wait to rise to my full potential now that my dad wasn't around to suppress it.

'So, how was your day?' Jack asked when he walked into the bedroom.

I was sitting Lycra-clad on a mat in the middle of the bedroom floor, cross-legged with my eyes closed and my hands on my knees, palms up, forming a circle with my index finger and thumb while my other three fingers pointed directly outwards.

I'd just entered a male-dominated world full of testosterone, and it would take some getting used to. I'd had a successful first day, so I'd decided to meditate to harness the joy I felt and build up my confidence like an underdeveloped muscle. I opened my eyes at the sound of my husband's voice. Things were still frosty between us. Even though he'd apologised for keeping me in the dark, I hated the thought that he'd been lying to me for years. And I hadn't appreciated the comment he'd made about not crossing my dad. That was causing a bit of tension between us, aside from the fact that the dynamic of our marriage had shifted now that I was technically his boss. But I didn't want our falling-out to do lasting damage to an otherwise perfect relationship.

'It was great,' I replied, letting my hands drop to the floor.

'I'm glad to hear it,' Jack said, flashing me a beaming smile that looked genuine. He fixed his blue eyes on mine as he sat on the edge of our bed and began loosening his tie. 'Tell me all about it then.'

Living and working together meant we couldn't separate our personal lives from our professional. The potential for conflict to spill over the borders of both areas was inevitable if we didn't manage our disagreements correctly. Jack was making a huge effort, so I should at least try to meet him halfway. I was so buoyed up by my achievement; I was desperate to share it with him.

'You're never going to believe this, but I bought my first debt for the company. You're now looking at a fully-fledged businesswoman.'

Jack finished unbuttoning his pure white shirt, got to his feet, then held his hand out towards me. I smiled up at my husband as he pulled me up from the ground.

Jack pulled me into his arms. He slid his hands over the silky fabric covering my buttocks before he continued speaking. 'You don't look much like a businesswoman in that outfit,' he said, casting his eyes over the aqua blue floral bra top and leggings I was wearing. 'I'm glad we don't work in the same office; I'd never get any work done.' Jack interlocked his fingers at the base of my back, then planted a kiss on my lips. 'So, who did you buy the debt from?'

'Larry.'

'You bought the Audis? No easing yourself in gently then – that was a huge amount.'

'I know, but I haggled him down to half price.' I laughed. 'Larry said I'd broken his balls like Dad used to.'

Jack released his grip on me, and the smile slid from his face. 'It's not funny, Mia. I need to have serious words with Rio. He should have steered you away from that particular debt.'

'He tried to,' I replied. 'But it's not up to Rio to choose which areas of the business I get involved in. The same goes for you. I don't want to be butting heads with you every time I make a decision you don't like.'

'Open your eyes, Mia. Recovering that debt will be nigh on impossible. I take it you know you'll have to go after Victor and Craig Coleman to get the money back,' Jack said.

'I know that.'

'I'm trying to be supportive, but I'm worried about you. There was a lot of bad blood between the Colemans and your dad. They would have known Larry would go to Davie's firm for help, so there's probably a lot more to this than meets the eye.'

'Thanks for your insight, but we've got it all under control,' I bluffed, but my husband knew me better than that; he could see I was putting on a front for his benefit.

'I'm not trying to interfere, but you're my wife, and I don't want to see you come to any harm.' Jack's features softened.

'I thought you'd be happy for me. I felt on top of the world when I made the deal with Larry.'

I could feel tears stabbing at my eyes, so I blinked them away before they had a chance to form.

'I am happy that you had a good day, but you should leave the face-to-face visit to Rio. Don't get involved. He knows what he's doing, and it's likely to be dangerous,' Jack said, giving me a half-smile.

'Thanks for the advice, but I can handle it. Please don't underestimate me. The Colemans were responsible for Dad's murder, and that's driving me to get back at them. I have to make my mark. I won't gain anyone's respect if I shy away from things.'

'Seriously, Mia, you can't walk up and ask nicely and expect the Colemans to hand over the cash; it doesn't work like that,' Jack said, putting his hands on his hips and glaring at me.

Admittedly, running a company was new to me, but did my husband really think I was that stupid? I always followed my mum's example and chose my battles wisely. And as I hadn't come up with a strategy to deal with the Colemans yet, I didn't have the ammunition to fight this one, so I let the moment pass.

38

Kelsey

Todd and I had dropped Scarlett off for a spot of retail therapy at Bluewater while we got down and dirty at the Holiday Inn a few miles away. It wasn't exactly a luxurious, romantic option, but we were only checking in for one thing, so it didn't warrant wasting money on a quick bunk-up. We'd been here so many times before; we were almost on first-name terms with the hotel staff.

Todd opened the door of the soulless room that we'd booked, and I stepped over the threshold. When I turned around, I found his dark, brooding eyes intently staring at me, then he pushed me back against the wall and entwined the fingers of one hand into my hair. As his tongue began to explore my mouth, his other hand disappeared under my top.

I reached forward and undid his black combat trousers. When my hand slipped inside his boxers, Todd's mouth left mine, and he let out a muffled moan. His cock sprang into life as I trailed my fingertips along its length. Todd responded by coiling his fingers tighter into my long dark brown hair. Already aroused, he walked me backwards to the bed, then gently lowered me onto it, and my head sank into the pillow. Todd stripped off, and as my eyes scanned over his muscular, tattooed frame, my heartbeat speeded up.

Todd climbed onto the bed, straddling me, placing his long legs on either side of me. He pulled my long-sleeved T-shirt over my head and unclipped my red lacy bra, slipping my nipple into his mouth. Then he took off my Converse and trackies and slid my red satin knickers slowly down my legs, sending tingles through me.

Todd trapped my body between his and the cotton sheets, his face inches from mine, holding his weight over me, pausing before he placed his mouth on mine and kissed me again. His strong hands stroked me while his lips and tongue worked their magic. Todd nudged my legs further apart and pushed himself into me, making me draw in a sharp breath. I pulled him towards me, and my fingers dug into the skin on his back. Todd took the backs of my thighs in his hands, adjusting my legs around his waist. We moved as one, slowly at first and then quicker and deeper. I was almost there, almost there, agonisingly close, then suddenly, we were both there, and afterwards, we fell back exhausted, lying together with our limbs entwined.

'I love your tattoos,' I said, propping myself up on my elbow.

'Thanks, they tell the story of my life.'

Todd had just piqued my interest. He was a closed book and never told me much about himself. I'd put that down to the fact that he didn't want me to know about the things that made him vulnerable in case I ended up breaking his heart. He wouldn't be the first man I'd done that to; this arrangement was working fine as far as I was concerned. I never seemed to be able to connect with him on any level except a sexual one anyway, but that didn't mean I wasn't interested in hearing about his time in the forces. Being a Royal Marine must have been a pure adrenaline ride.

'Please feel free to elaborate.' I smiled.

'Some of these commemorate tours I was on, and this needs no explanation,' Todd replied, pointing out a large red poppy on his upper arm.

'What about this one?' I asked.

Todd had a tattoo with the initial M over his heart. He paused for a moment before he replied.

'It stands for all the things I love. My mum, the marines and the military. We should probably think about making tracks,' Todd said.

Todd suddenly clammed up. He seemed keen to stop discussing his inkings. I couldn't help wondering if I'd unintentionally dredged up painful memories, but now wasn't the time to probe deeper.

'I'm just going to have a quick shower,' I said, untangling myself from Todd.

When I returned from the bathroom, Todd was leaning back on the pillows with his arms folded behind his mop of dark hair and a satisfied look on his gorgeous face. His eyes followed me as I sat on the edge of the bed and began drying myself on the towel, taking my time purely for his benefit.

When I dropped the towel and went to put on my underwear and quick-release shagging outfit, he reached towards me and traced his fingertips across my lower back.

Then he got onto his knees, and his hands cupped my breasts as he attempted to pull me back into bed.

'We can't,' I protested.

'Why not?' Todd trailed kisses up and down the side of my neck. He didn't seem bothered about making tracks now.

'We've got to pick up Scarlett, remember?'

I knew I had to resist Todd's attempt to seduce me back into his arms. Leaving her hanging around outside the shopping centre wasn't an option unless I wanted to witness her throwing a tantrum in the middle of the car park.

'We'll make it quick. I promise,' Todd said, and as he pressed his erection into my back, I felt my resolve waver.

'Not too quick.' I laughed with a glint in my eye as I scooted back onto the bed.

We were going to be late if we didn't leave now, but suddenly I didn't care about my sister. It was all about me, and I wanted to feel Todd inside me again. I couldn't get enough of him. We'd been sleeping together for over a year now, but the passion hadn't died. We couldn't keep our hands off of each other. Dad had been furious when he'd discovered our affair. I felt terrible that we'd fallen out over it. But if Todd and I turned our fling into something meaningful and we made a go of things, it might make all the aggro our relationship caused worthwhile. Then maybe it would ease my guilt.

Todd flipped me over onto my stomach, and I didn't put up the slightest resistance. I gripped the pillow in my fists as he stretched his warm body over mine. He pinned me down as he pumped slowly and rotated his hips in circles. Every minute was more blissful than the last. When Todd's breath started becoming more rapid behind me, I arched my back like a cat stretching, pushing back on him. I turned my head to the side when I felt him start to shudder so that I could see his face; Todd's eyes were closed, and his lips had stretched into an involuntary smile.

My timekeeping was appalling; always had been and always would be. Scarlett knew what I was like. I was a free spirit and lived for the moment, changing my mind on a whim if I got a better offer. As I scrambled to put on my clothes and make myself look half presentable, the faintest glimmer of guilt endeavoured to prod my conscience, but I batted it away. What was the point in being the older sibling if you couldn't abuse the position? That was a perk of being born first; you were able to pull rank. So if Scarlett challenged me about being late, I'd put her firmly in her place.

39

Scarlett

I was sitting outside Lakeside shopping centre waiting for Kelsey and Todd to collect me when I noticed a hot guy take a seat on the bench closest to me. I tilted my head to one side and casually pulled my long red hair over one shoulder before adjusting my Sunday Somewhere cat-eye sunglasses so that I could get a closer look at him. The dark-haired man was leaning against the seat with his tanned arm stretched along the back of the bench. It was a sunny spring day, but there was a gusty wind, so he either didn't feel the cold or was brave to be wearing just a T-shirt.

'Have you been stood up as well?' he said, turning his face towards mine.

The man's smile grew wider, revealing straight, white teeth. His comment took me by surprise. When I first heard him speak, I looked over my shoulder to see if anybody was behind me. We were the only two people around, so I knew he must have been talking to me. While he waited for me to reply, he took off his Ray-Bans and fixed me with his dark brown eyes. I felt myself blush; then, I pressed my back against the metal bench as I retreated into it. It wasn't like me to be so shy, but the man was so good-looking, he was making me flustered. My heart was pounding in my chest, and I felt beads of sweat break out on my upper lip as I tried to compose myself, but it was hard with butterflies fluttering around in my stomach.

'I'm actually waiting for my sister,' I replied. Thankfully my voice remained steady and didn't come out in a high-pitched squeak.

I should have known better than to accept a lift from Kelsey. She had a habit of being unreliable, especially when she was hooking up with Todd for a marathon sex session. Her time management had only got worse now that my dad wasn't around to voice his objections. She was so selfish sometimes; everything revolved around her.

'So, who stood you up?' I asked, suddenly feeling brave. I couldn't imagine anyone would be stupid enough to do that.

'My friend. He's never been good on time,' the dark-haired man replied. 'Do you mind if I keep you company while we wait?'

Did I mind? What kind of question was that? Of course, I didn't. I would be delighted, but I had to get a grip of myself and not come across too keen. I didn't want to scare him off before I had a chance to get to know him. I suddenly pictured myself as the emoji with heart-shaped eyes. That wasn't a good look. I needed to tone things down and play it cool. But it was hard to suppress the giggling schoolgirl that kept threatening to surface. I was twenty now and had been trying to ditch my other persona for years; the problem was she didn't like to be parted from me and was like my evil twin, putting in an appearance at the most inconvenient moment.

'Why not,' I replied, grinning at him.

It would have been nice if my sister had dropped me a text to let me know she was running late, but that wasn't her style. At first, I was a bit miffed that she thought her time was more important than mine, but in the long run, she'd done me a favour. I could think of worse things to be doing than chatting to a gorgeous guy while I waited for my wayward sister to return. Now that I was getting to know the hot guy on the bench next to mine, I wanted to stop the clock and spend more time with him. The longer they took to show up, the better. It was weird, but I felt completely in tune with him even though we'd only just met.

'I'm CJ, by the way.'

'I'm Scarlett,' I replied, shaking CJ by the hand. My heartbeat speeded up when his touch lingered a little longer than necessary.

'Don't look so worried; I'm not a serial killer scouting out my next victim,' CJ said as his lips stretched into a broad smile.

I laughed, but his comment made me feel uneasy. I'd only just met him, and gorgeous as he was, he *could* be a mass murderer for all I knew. My head was telling me to proceed with caution, but when he suggested we go and get coffee while we were waiting, my heart had other ideas. When I saw Todd's BMW approaching, my mind started racing.

I didn't want our chance encounter to end. If Todd's car hadn't pulled up at that moment, I might have gone off with him.

'My lift's arrived,' I said when the BMW came to a stop by the kerb.

'Can I have your number?' CJ asked as I stood up.

When the words left his mouth, my heart had skipped a beat. Half an hour ago, he'd been a total stranger, but now we had an opportunity to make something out of being thrown together by circumstances. I had an overwhelming feeling that this could be the start of something good.

'I don't see why not,' I replied, trying my best to sound unbothered by his request. My stomach did a flip before I took the handset he was holding towards me; our fingers brushed during the exchange. I began punching my mobile digits into it and had to stop myself from whooping with joy.

CJ flashed me a set of straight, white teeth before putting the phone in his pocket. Then he stretched both arms along the back of the bench.

I felt my cheeks turn the colour of my name as he gave me the once-over. I wondered how he was rating me and whether I was moving up or down the attractiveness scale. I had the distinct impression he was undressing me with his eyes. He had that way about him. CJ was self-assured, confident, but I liked that in a prospective partner.

'Who was that?' Kelsey asked when I climbed into the back of the black BMW.

She seemed a bit put out that I hadn't been inconvenienced by the fact that she was half an hour late, and by giving me a grilling I guessed she was hoping to take the focus away from her timekeeping; but for once, I wasn't bothered.

'His name's CJ,' I replied. The smile on my face was making my cheeks ache, but I couldn't stop grinning.

'Did you just give him your number?' Kelsey swivelled around in her seat and fixed me with her blue eyes.

'Maybe.' My lips stretched into a huge grin.

Kelsey scowled then shook her head from side to side. 'I can't leave you alone for five minutes, can I?'

Why was she so bothered that I'd given CJ my number? A faint smile played on my lips; maybe she was jealous. Men always lusted after Kelsey, and by the look on her face, she couldn't bear the fact that a hot guy was interested in me for a change. To make matters worse, he knocked spots off Todd in the looks department.

'He seems cocky if you ask me,' Todd remarked before making eye contact with me in the rear-view mirror.

'That's rich coming from you!'

I glared back at him, and as I did, I felt my bottom lip jut out. You'd have to go a long way to find anyone more arrogant than the former Royal Marine behind the wheel of the car. I was tempted to let rip and give him a piece of my mind. I had a lot of pent-up anger inside me, but I decided to let Todd's comment float away on the tide. I wouldn't give him the satisfaction of seeing me react, and anyway, I was in too good a mood to get into an argument with him.

'But seriously, Scarlett, it's not a good idea to give your number out to any Tom, Dick or Harry,' Todd pressed on, continuing to eyeball me in the mirror.

'You didn't give my safety a second thought while you were at the Holiday Inn getting your end away with Kelsey, so spare me the lecture.'

Todd and Kelsey exchanged a glance. 'What the hell's got into you?'

Kelsey turned around in her seat with a look of thunder on her face.

'I'm fed up with the way you've been treating me since he's been on the scene,' I gestured towards Todd with a flick of my head.

Kelsey tossed her hair and turned away without replying.

I could feel Todd's eyes boring into me from the rear-view mirror, so I threw him a look of contempt, then turned my face towards the window as the scenery raced past. I had no intention of enduring one of his personal protection speeches, especially as he was talking to me like I was a child. I wished he'd pay more attention to the road and lose interest in me so that I could bask in the warm, fuzzy feeling currently surrounding me.

I didn't use to believe in love at first sight, but I couldn't deny there had been an overwhelming jolt when my eyes had first met CJ's. My heart had begun galloping in my chest, and I'd felt a bit giddy and light-headed when we'd started talking. There'd been an undeniable connection between us. Every time his dark gaze had settled on me, I'd wanted to clap my hands together and burst out laughing. I was a perpetual giggler. Laughter alleviated stress and social tension, and I'd felt nervous in CJ's presence, but it was a childish habit I needed to break.

'You're behaving like a five-year-old, Scarlett. It's no

wonder Mum doesn't want you involved in the business,' Kelsey suddenly piped up.

Her words brought me back to reality like a slap around the face.

'Oh, here we go, you always have to go for the low blow, don't you?' I said through gritted teeth. 'You can't help yourself, can you?'

Kelsey was a dirty fighter; she couldn't resist taking a cheap shot. We hadn't even been arguing about the firm, but her comment was designed to hurt me, and it had. I wanted to live up to my dad's legacy too and resented my mum and sisters for keeping me out of the loop. I had a right to know what was going on.

'Shut up, Scarlett. Save it for someone who gives a shit,' Kelsey fired back before she turned the volume up on the radio to silence me. She always had to have the last word.

I wanted to retaliate, but I felt my lip begin to quiver and didn't trust myself to speak. So I bit down on it and hoped the moment would pass. It would only add fuel to the fire if I burst into tears, and I couldn't face seeing Kelsey gloat, knowing that she'd burst my bubble. I'd been floating on air before I got in the car.

I sat in the back of the car with my arms folded across my chest, stewing about the way Kelsey had cut me down to size with one lash of her tongue. This was the story of my life. Nothing I did or said was ever seen as important. Nobody took me seriously. My opinion didn't matter, and that was hard to accept. Kelsey had been in my position once upon a time until I'd come along and dethroned her. No matter my age, I would never lose the title of being the baby and would forever be overlooked by my siblings. I wished Mum and Dad hadn't stopped at three, then I wouldn't have been last in the pecking order.

40

Mia

Raising her family had been Mum's mission in life. Blessed with height and long limbs, she'd enjoyed success as a model before she'd married my dad. But all of that changed once the ring was on her finger. My parents had a traditional marriage; Dad worked while Mum stayed at home with the children. He'd wanted it that way, and my mum didn't begrudge picking her family over her career. Being a full-time mum was one of the most challenging jobs in the world, but she'd thrown everything into the role and had excelled at it. She was patient, kind and incredibly loving. My sisters and I had a strong bond with her. She was one in a million.

I know Mum was amazed by my transformation, but that worked both ways. I'd seen a different side of her, too, since my dad had died. She'd allowed herself to become dependent on Dad, both financially and emotionally, and was suddenly having to find her own way again. But she wasn't a naturally needy person and was adjusting well to life without her other half, even though her grief was still raw.

'This situation is driving me crazy. Nobody's been arrested and charged with Davie's murder, even though we know the Colemans were responsible,' Mum said.

'I feel the same way,' I replied. 'Although the police investigation's still ongoing, no suspects are in the frame.'

'It's not right. Dad's killer is free to roam the streets when he should be behind bars,' Kelsey added.

'I want to get justice for Davie.' Mum's eyes glistened with tears.

'We all do.' Rio nodded.

'I know Davie started a war when he went after Barney Coleman, so he brought a fair bit of trouble to his own door. But he didn't deserve to die.' Mum's words broke with emotion. 'He did the world a favour by getting rid of a maniac who tortured and murdered people as a pastime.'

'Don't worry, Amanda, we're going to get the Colemans back for what they did to Davie,' Rio replied.

Rio had dropped off fifty thousand pounds in cash to Larry. That was the easy part of the deal; the next stage would be far more complicated. The Saunders and the Colemans had old scores to settle, so buying the debt was going to kick-start the cycle of revenge. The idea of that terrified me.

'Now that we've paid Larry, we need to set up a meeting with the Colemans and see what they have to say about the situation,' Rio said, realising that Kelsey and I were clueless about the way things worked.

'OK, great. Let me know when that's been arranged,' I said in a breezy manner, not really knowing how to respond.

I pasted a smile on my face when I looked at Rio to hide the nervousness that was building inside me. It was crawling up from the pit of my stomach into the back of my throat, threatening to break out of my mouth and show itself as a scream any minute now. I stood grinning, hoping nobody would notice the battle I was having to swallow it back down. I held my breath and counted to ten until the moment passed.

'Davie would have gone in hard and made a stand. Your dad was tough and never took any prisoners. He was a force to be reckoned with and adopted a "don't fuck with me" attitude that served him well.'

I couldn't help feeling that wasn't quite true. Dad had clearly collected his fair share of enemies along the way as he'd been gunned down in cold blood on my wedding day. But Rio had known him longer than any of us, and it was interesting to hear how Dad conducted himself inside the business arena. The insight was invaluable to a couple of rookies.

'Davie used to add what he'd paid Larry on to the price of the original debt, so the costs he incurred passed on. You bought the debt for fifty thousand. Larry got some of his money back, but now you're the ones taking the risk.' Rio's dark brown eyes fixed on Kelsey and I in turn.

I was beginning to wish I hadn't taken on such a large job as our first venture into business. It would be bad enough trying to recoup the amount we'd paid Larry, but adding that onto what the Colemans already owed would be a tall order.

'That's how Davie made such a good living; he was never

out of pocket. The full amount had to be paid in cash, or else...' Rio's words trailed off.

The heavy hand of doubt was closing its grip around me, trying to squeeze out every trace of confidence and self-belief I'd mustered. Not for the first time, I wondered if Kelsey and I had bitten off more than we could chew.

'Wesley, Todd and I will obviously go with you as backup if that's what you want, but I would highly recommend that you and Kelsey stay away from the meet and keep yourself anonymous for your own protection,' Rio said.

'Really? I was expecting Mia to lead the negotiations,' Kelsey questioned with a wry smile on her face.

I couldn't help feeling she was setting me up to fail, but I didn't want her to think I wasn't up for the job.

'I'd been happy to,' I replied, hoping I sounded more confident than I felt.

Taking on the role of chief haggler when I'd phoned Larry to make an offer on the debt he'd wanted us to buy was an entirely different situation; the ball had been firmly in my court. Trying to persuade two of my dad's competitors to part with one hundred and fifty thousand pounds was going to be almost impossible, and I could feel my recently acquired can-do attitude floating away like the evening tide. Optimism and positivity were hard things to master; I felt like I was losing my grip, and they were slipping through my fingers.

'Are you sure you want to do that?' Rio quizzed.

I nodded in reply. I didn't trust myself to speak in case my voice betrayed me and gave away how apprehensive I felt about the situation.

'You're the boss, so I'm not going to get into an argument over it,' Rio replied, but I could tell he wasn't happy.

'Actually, we're both the boss,' Kelsey corrected, with a sour expression pasted on her face.

I wasn't looking forward to breaking the news to Jack. I knew without even running it past him that he would disagree with what Kelsey had proposed. I was beginning to wish we'd left Rio to run the show and taken a background role instead. If something wasn't broken, you didn't need to fix it, did you?

41

Kelsey

Mia and I sat side by side in the back of the black Range Rover. Rio was behind the wheel, and Todd was sitting in the front passenger seat. None of us were speaking as we travelled along the A13. I glanced over my shoulder and saw Wesley gripping the steering wheel of the black Dog Security Unit van as we stop-started in the heavy traffic. Once again, we'd slowed to a crawl and were now stationary. Minutes later, the build-up of vehicles began to move, and before we knew it, we were travelling at full speed. It was frustrating beyond belief. There didn't appear to be any reason for the hold-up. There were no roadworks, which was a miracle in itself, no sign of an accident or any other possible explanation for the traffic. No doubt somebody up ahead had been dabbing their brakes, setting off a chain reaction that disrupted the flow of traffic.

We couldn't arrive soon enough for my liking. I had better things to do with my time than waste it sitting in congestion. It was a beautiful day, the sun was high in the sky, and I was gagging for a glass of cold, white wine. We were meeting the Colemans at Grays Hall Golf and Country Club. Rio suggested the safest option for Mia and I was to be introduced somewhere public where there would be plenty of people milling around. He wanted the meet to be on their turf, and by all accounts, the club was the Colemans' playground.

'Just so you girls know the background, Barney and Victor were former East Enders who moved out to Essex some years ago. Once upon a time, villains like them used to stick to the areas where they were brought up, but sadly that's not the case any more, so we'll have to endure being stuck on the A13 for the time being.'

'Why are we travelling to see them? Couldn't they have come to Bow?' Mia asked, wringing her hands in her lap.

'They wouldn't have turned up. If we want to meet them, we're the ones who need to do the travelling and put in the hard graft. It's the way things work,' Rio replied, keeping his eyes fixed on the fluctuating tailback.

Todd pulled down the sun visor, lifted his aviators and glanced at me in the mirror. He looked so sexy in his uniform, black combats, crew-neck T-shirt and bomber jacket. It was all I could do not to leap over the seat and rip his clothes off; that would have to wait until later, I thought with a smile on my face. Todd lowered his sunglasses and flipped the mirror back into place, training his eyes back on the road.

Rio turned off the dual carriageway, and the car snaked its way along a country lane for a couple of minutes before he pulled into the extensive, well-maintained grounds of the members-only country club. The freshly planted avenues stretched away to infinity in every direction. He dropped his speed as the Range Rover's thick tyres crunched over the gravel driveway. The Transit hung back while trailing us, keeping a discreet distance. When Rio parked up, Wesley found a space on the other side of the large car park.

Rio twisted around in his seat and smiled at Mia and I. 'It's not too late to back out, ladies.'

'I'm still in,' I replied.

I glanced over at Mia. Her blue eyes were fixed on something unidentified in the distance. She'd zoned out of the conversation and seemed like she was miles away. By the looks of it, Mia had lost her nerve, which was what I'd been expecting to happen. This was my opportunity to swoop in and save the day. I was determined to prove myself and my value to the firm. I had a lot of experience in dealing with difficult, demanding customers. I was sure those skills would come in handy when negotiating with the Colemans.

Mia suddenly fixed her eyes on Rio. 'Let's do this,' she said.

My mouth fell open. You could have knocked me down with a feather.

We climbed out of the car and filed up the steps of the country club in a procession behind our tall broad-shouldered mentor. The main building housed a bar, restaurant and leisure facilities, and once we were inside the grand foyer, we were greeted with a warm welcome by the sharp-suited doorman.

'Can I help you, sir?' he asked Rio. His role was to make sure only the right people entered the high-profile premises.

'Mr Coleman is expecting us,' Rio replied.

The doorman began walking towards the reception desk

and gestured to us to follow him. 'Paige, can you escort these people over to Mr Coleman?' the doorman asked an attractive female employee.

'Certainly,' Paige replied, nodding her bleached-blonde extensions, then her glossy red lips stretched into a smile. 'If you'd like to come with me, I'll take you over to his table.'

Even though I didn't want to admit it, I felt a sharp stab of jealousy prod me in the stomach when I saw Todd's eyes sweep over her, lingering on her well-endowed chest before he looked away. The sting stayed with me long after my lover's actions faded. I wasn't Todd's official girlfriend, but we were having a sexual relationship, so that didn't give him the right to look at other women, especially while he was with me. He hadn't just glanced at Paige, he seemed to be lusting after her, and the thought of that made my blood boil. I was absolutely fuming; I could feel my eyes blazing as we followed her pert backside across the tiled floor.

Todd was testing me. He was trying to see how far he could go by pushing the boundaries, but he was walking on very thin ice. I had a very low tolerance for his kind of behaviour. It was the biggest form of disrespect that a man could show a woman, and I wanted to rip his head off. Todd had just proved to me he would treat me badly if I allowed him to get away with it, no questions asked. If I didn't challenge him over this, I was basically giving him the green light and telling him he could do whatever he wanted. I would be to blame if I let it slide, but I'd have to keep a lid on my temper for the time being. Mia and I had business to attend to. As we neared the table, my eyes fixed on a handsome young man; time to give Todd a dose of his own medicine, I decided, channelling my inner minx.

The older man, clutching a tumbler containing a dark spirit, poured over ice, stood up when we approached. He was a creepy-looking guy with white hair and round eyes like snooker balls. I could feel his tiny pupils boring into me.

'Hi, Victor,' Rio said, shaking the man with the Trappist monk's haircut by the hand. 'I'd like to introduce you to Davie's daughters, Mia and Kelsey,' he continued, gesturing to us both.

Victor nodded, and as he did, my eyes fixed on quite possibly the worst head of hair I'd ever seen. It was like one of those comedy wigs; a huge bald patch was surrounded by a semi-circle of thinning strands that fell in a pageboy beneath the expanse of skin. If you asked me, it needed shaving off. Victor scrutinised both of us, then sat back down at the head of the table, opposite a young dark-haired man. An almost full pint sat on the table in front of him.

'This is my accountant, Freddie,' Victor said, flicking his serial killer eyes towards him.

'Your accountant? Where's your son?' Rio questioned.

'He couldn't make it; something more important came up,' Victor replied, and I saw Rio bristle at the disrespect being shown.

'The pleasures all mine, ladies,' Freddie said, treating us both to a double-handed handshake. It was clear his ego was bigger than his veneered grin.

I maintained eye contact with him and offered him a coy smile in return. Once I knew I had his attention, I lowered my gaze to the table, tilting my head to one side. Then I glanced back up so that I could continue making flirty eye contact with him. Todd was sitting next to Mia, on the opposite side of the table, so I purposely avoided looking in his direction.

'Let me order some drinks.' Rio gestured to a waiter.

A couple of minutes later, the waiter returned with a large brandy for Victor, a pint of Birra Moretti for Freddie, a glass of orange juice for Mia, a large glass of Sauvignon Blanc for me and two diet Cokes for Rio and Todd.

'We understand from Larry that he gave you two top-of-the-range Audis on a try-before-you-buy agreement. But so far, you've failed to either return or pay for the cars,' Mia said.

She'd wasted no time getting straight to the point and had a tone of no-nonsense in her voice I'd never heard before. My guess was she was worried she might lose her nerve if she didn't get down to business immediately. I felt a bit miffed that she was doing such a great job. I hated it when the attention wasn't on me.

Victor raised the tumbler to his lips and studied Mia with his shifty eyes while he contemplated what she'd just said.

'What's that got to do with you, missy? The agreement we have is with Larry.'

'Was with Larry,' Mia corrected, straightening her posture. 'We've bought the debt from him, so now we need to establish how you're going to pay us back. We are out of pocket to the tune of one hundred and fifty thousand pounds.'

My eyes fixed on Mia. She was doing brilliantly. I would never have thought she had it in her. I was struggling to deal with the fact that my shy, quiet dormouse sister had totally stepped up to the plate and was taking control of the company. I hated to admit it, but she was smashing it. My confidence had taken a knock, and now I was questioning my role and my future within the firm. I was a leader, not a follower. I couldn't help feeling turbulent times were ahead and not just with the Colemans.

'I'm not giving you a penny. If Larry reckons they're worth seventy-five grand apiece, he's deluded. I tell you what; you can take the cars back. We've decided we don't want them,' Victor replied before knocking back his drink.

'I'm afraid it's too late for that. Our firm doesn't deal in second-hand cars; we only accept cash,' Mia said like the true boss lady she was shaping up to be.

Victor narrowed his eyes before fixing them on Mia.

I felt a shiver run down my spine, but Mia didn't flinch; she stood her ground. Where was she finding the strength?

'Do us all a favour and go back to playing with your dolls.' Victor laughed.

Mia didn't look impressed, but she carried on undeterred by Victor's slur. 'We'll be back here the same time next week to collect the cash.'

Victor slammed his empty glass down on the table. Then he stood up and gripped onto the edge as his face turned several shades darker and a curly vein pulsed in his temple. 'It's a free country so you can come here if you like. But I won't be waiting for you, and neither will the money.'

Victor gave Freddie a nod, and both men marched out of the bar with their heads held high and their chests puffed out like two prize cockerels strutting around a farmyard, asserting themselves.

I couldn't say I was surprised the meeting had become a train wreck before we'd even finished our drinks. But Mia had done a sterling job at stepping up to the mark. I wasn't sure I could have handled the situation any better.

'Was it something I said?' Mia laughed as Victor and Freddie's backs disappeared out of sight.

'Maybe he's late for his appointment at the barber's.' I smiled.

'Have you got the hump with me?' Todd asked later that day. He caught hold of my hand as I went to take a bottle of mineral water out of the fridge.

I pulled my fingers out of his grasp and glared at him, my eyes blazing. 'I'm so bloody angry with you I can hardly bear to look at you.' I fired my words into his face.

'What have I done?' Todd asked, turning his palms upwards, trying to act all innocent.

'As if you don't know. You were eyeing up Paige with your tongue hanging out; you practically had your head down her top at one stage.'

Todd laughed. 'We seem to have a little green-eyed monster in the room,' he said, clearly delighted that he'd made me jealous.

I was annoyed with myself for reacting, but I couldn't help it. I felt like he was playing me, and I didn't like it.

'Is that why you tried to pull that stunt with Freddie?' Todd asked with the faintest smile playing on his lips. He folded his arms across his chest while he waited for me to reply.

'I don't know what you're talking about,' I replied, taking a bottle of water off the shelf.

'I must have been mistaken, but I could have sworn you

were fluttering your eyelashes and doing your best to flirt with him,' Todd said, and his face broke into a huge smile. 'Just for the record; I'm not the jealous type, but it was very amusing watching you trying to wind me up.'

I gritted my teeth when I twisted the plastic top off the bottle. I almost threw it across the room in a temper, but I didn't want to make the situation worse. 'Thanks for sharing that with me,' I said, sarcasm coating my words in a thick layer before I stomped out of the kitchen and ran up the stairs two at a time.

I stood behind the door in my bedroom, panting, for several seconds and then I jumped onto the bed and started pounding my fists into the mattress to get rid of some of my pent-up aggression. Once my rage had subsided, I lay on my back, looking up at the ceiling. After a couple of minutes passed, I heard a text come through on my phone.

Do you fancy going down to the river?

Our family home in Bow was situated in a beautiful spot, a stone's throw from the banks of the River Lea.

'Come here,' Todd said, flashing me a wide smile once we were out of sight of the house.

He attempted to pull me towards him, but I was having none of it. Todd thought he could click his finger and I'd come running, but he was going to be disappointed. I had more self-respect than that. If he wanted to play games, bring it on. I'd give him a run for his money. I wasn't used to losing a power struggle.

As it was such a beautiful evening, I'd changed into a semi-sheer floaty dress that buttoned down the front and I made sure I'd undone just enough of the fastenings to make things interesting. Todd's eyes scanned over me, and I knew what was on his mind. He was desperate to get into my pants. He might not want a committed relationship, but he was quite happy to keep coming back to me for sex. Todd had a lot to learn. I didn't take shit from anyone, so if he thought he could disrespect me and get away with it, he had another thing coming.

I had enough on my plate at the moment with Mia transforming herself into her crime boss alter ego in front of my eyes without Todd acting up as well. There was only so much I could take. My position within the family was really important to me, and that trumped whatever was going on with Todd. He was very much replaceable, and if he didn't start playing by my rules, he was going to find himself left out in the cold. My identity had been called into question now that Mia had stepped up, and I needed to figure out who I was. Todd could go to hell for all I cared.

'Where are you going?' Todd called as I started walking away. The smug smile he'd been wearing slid from his face.

He hadn't even bothered to apologise, so I didn't reward him with an answer. As I strolled along the waterway, taking advantage of the spring sunshine, I felt my spirits lift. The power had most definitely shifted in my direction. It was time to draw a line in the sand to establish a boundary. Obviously, I wouldn't tell Todd about the line, but if he crossed it one more time, he'd be history. There was only room for one of us to play games in our relationship, and it wasn't going to be Todd.

42

Scarlett

Where the hell was Kelsey? I'd looked all over the house for her, but she'd disappeared into thin air. She must have slipped out somewhere with Todd, which was just my luck. I was desperate to share my news with her. Kelsey wasn't just my sister; she was my best friend. But at this moment in time, I would have settled for anyone. I'd have been happy to strike up a conversation with next door's pet hamster if I'd thought it would hear me out and listen to what I had to say. Where was everyone? The whole house was deserted, and I was about to burst. Exciting things like this didn't happen to me every day of the week. I switched on my phone, opened the text and reread it.

Do you fancy going out for a drink?

I'd tried to play it cool and not reply instantly, but my fingers felt like they were electrically charged as they hovered over the keys, so it was all I could do to wait two minutes before I responded. I made myself do laps of my bedroom to pass the time, but I didn't want to make CJ wait too long in case he thought I wasn't interested.

I'd love to.

I tapped out my reply and hit send. Then flung open my cupboard and started rifling through my clothes, deciding what to wear. I had a tendency to read into everything and was already trying to weigh up how much CJ liked me based on the amount of time it took him to reply to my message. I'd only just began to consider some outfits when the sound of a text brought my phone back to life. That was a good sign, wasn't it?

Text me your address, and I'll pick you up in half an hour.

I felt my eyes widen and my heartbeat speed up; half an hour barely gave me enough time to pick my clothes. There was no way I'd have time to shower, wash my hair and apply fresh makeup. I couldn't allow first-date jitters to get the better of me. I had to focus and use the time I had wisely; damage limitation was my only option.

Grabbing some clean underwear, my favourite pair of stonewashed skinny jeans, a royal blue blouse, nude strappy sandals and a matching clutch bag, I took off in the direction of my en-suite bathroom. Although I would have appreciated longer to get ready, it was probably for the best and would help keep my pre-date anxiety at bay. The more notice CJ had given me, the more nervous

I would have become. I was only twenty, so I didn't have a lot of romantic experience under my belt. My dad used to be a prospective partner's worst nightmare. He was very protective of all his girls, Mum included.

I was having one last look at myself in the full-length mirror when a text came through on my phone. The palms of my hands broke into a sweat in response to the sound. I opened my phone and smiled at the screen.

I'm outside.

The pads of my thumbs raced over my screen to type a reply.

I'll be with you in a minute.

My heart was pounding as I walked down the stairs. I crossed the tiled hallway and stepped out of the front door. Strappy sandals weren't the best choice of footwear on gravel, so I took my time walking across the driveway and out of the side gate. The last thing I wanted was to get into the car with a host of pebbles wedged between my toes.

CJ's car was parked in the lane outside our house. He was sitting behind the wheel of a shiny black BMW with the driver's window open and his elbow resting on the door rim.

'You look great,' CJ said, turning to look at me.

My face broke into a huge grin. 'Thank you,' I replied, hoping my cheeks didn't look as flushed as they felt.

The conversation flowed between us as CJ drove us towards the River Thames. He parked up, then led me towards an unassuming ground-level entrance in the shadow of London Bridge.

'This is it,' CJ said, ushering me through the door. 'Don't look so horrified; I'm sure you're going to love it.'

I sincerely hoped he was right, but if first impressions counted for anything, I wasn't sold on the idea. Because of my background in dance, I would consider myself physically fit, but my legs were on the verge of turning to jelly by the time we'd climbed up six flights of stairs. This better be worth the effort, I thought, smiling through the pain of my aching muscles.

CJ threw open the door, and we stepped over the threshold of the Three Sisters.

'When I realised what this place was called, I couldn't resist bringing you,' CJ said.

The venue was an eclectic mix; pastel-coloured decking and matching rustic picnic benches gave the space a beach bar feel while blending seamlessly with the ultra-modern glass bar area. We took a seat at a bench closest to the edge of the sophisticated rooftop cocktail bar so that we could make the most of the spectacular three-hundred-and-sixty-degree panoramic view of London's skyline.

'Wow,' I said as I took in the sights of the Shard, Borough Market, Southwark Cathedral, St Paul's Cathedral, the London Eye, and the Tower of London. 'This place is incredible. The views are stunning. It was definitely worth the climb.' I laughed.

CJ picked up the drinks menu, angling it between us. 'What do you fancy?'

CJ was top of that list, so I almost replied *you*, but I managed to resist the urge. He looked gorgeous, dressed in a grey T-shirt and dark denim jeans, and he smelt divine. The aroma of his aftershave kept wafting towards me on the breeze, so I was having trouble concentrating on anything else.

'Don't tell me, you're spoiled for choice,' CJ said when I didn't respond to his question.

The sound of his voice made me refocus on the menu. 'I am. There's such a huge selection.'

After some more deliberation of the tropical-themed cocktails, I settled for a glass of Tiki Punch. It sounded delicious: vodka, pineapple juice, lime juice and mint. It was billed as a real thirst quencher, which was just what I needed after the unexpected hike in high heels.

'I can't get over how lovely this place is,' I said, tearing my eyes away from the London sights.

I couldn't picture a better setting to go for a date. Artificial grass covered the ground, and palm trees were dotted around the interior; fronds and trailing flowers dangled from the pergola above us, giving the place a jungly rainforest feel. A DJ was playing Balearic anthems and salsa music, which added to the ambience. If it hadn't been for the view of the Shard, I would have thought I'd been transported to the middle of the ocean and deposited on an exotic island.

'Have you been here before?' I asked before taking a sip of the Tiki Punch that tasted like heaven in my mouth.

'No, it's a brand-new venue; it only opened last week,' CJ replied. 'So tell me about yourself.'

'I'm a final-year drama student. I love my course, but sometimes it takes over my life. The hours are much longer than I was expecting, which was a bit of a shock to the system. I don't enjoy the early starts. They play havoc with your social life.' I smiled, taking another sip of my drink. 'What about you? Are you working or studying?' I asked. I wasn't sure how old CJ was. If I had to guess, I would say early to mid-twenties.

'Working. I couldn't wait to leave school,' CJ replied.

'So what do you do for a living?'

'I work for my dad's firm as a general dogsbody.' CJ laughed, then he stood up. 'I'll get some more drinks in; same again?'

'Let me get this round,' I said, picking up my clutch bag. I might be a student, but I had a generous allowance, so I was able to pay my way even in a place like this where the drinks came with hefty price tags.

'No way,' CJ replied.

CJ came back to the table just as daylight started to fade and the colours of a beautiful sunset were spreading across the sky. Thick orange, yellow and purple bands stretched out in front of us while the strings of fairy lights entwined around the lush foliage above us came to life, bathing the canopy in a warm glow.

'I'll probably have to call it a night soon,' I said.

CJ checked the time on his watch. 'It's ten past eight. You're a real live wire, Scarlett Saunders, aren't you?' He laughed.

I hated being a killjoy. Nobody enjoyed having fun more than I did, but I had an early class tomorrow, which would involve a rigorous warm-up, body stretches and vocal exercises. There was no way I'd get through it if I was hungover and functioning on hardly any sleep.

'I'm really sorry, but we're rehearsing for our end-of-year

performance, and I'm already going to struggle after having a few of these,' I said, holding up my cocktail.

'And I thought our date was going well...' CJ smiled, running his fingers through his dark brown hair.

'I've had a fantastic time; I'm gutted I can't stay out later.'

I hoped I'd said enough to convince CJ that I wasn't making up excuses so that I could bail on him.

'In that case, when can I take you out again?' CJ asked with a twinkle in his dark brown eyes.

'Where the hell have you been?' Kelsey asked when I closed the front door behind me. 'We've been worried sick.'

I spotted Mia and my mum hovering in the hallway behind her. A wave of guilt washed over me as three pairs of worried eyes scanned my face.

'I didn't mean to worry you. I only went out for a drink.'

I couldn't help feeling my family were overreacting; it wasn't even nine o'clock. I was hardly rolling in at dawn. And anyway, Kelsey was a fine one to talk. She'd disappeared into thin air earlier; if I'd have been able to find her, I would have told her where I was going. But I couldn't bring that up now without throwing her under the bus.

'Todd really should be escorting you when you go anywhere other than uni. Do me a favour, darling, next time, let somebody know what your plans are,' Mum said, ever the diplomat.

'I would have done, but it was all a bit last minute, and I couldn't find any of you.'

'I sent you a text asking where you'd gone. Why didn't you reply to it?' Kelsey glared at me.

I wasn't sure why she was so bothered by my absence.

'I didn't see it. And in my defence, I've only been out for a couple of hours, so I wasn't expecting you to be organising a search party.'

'I think we're all a bit edgy after what happened to your dad,' Mum said, trying to keep the peace. 'Anyway, there's no harm done. You're home now, and I'm glad to see you're in one piece.' Mum flashed me her winning smile.

I was just getting into my pyjamas when I heard gentle rapping on my bedroom door.

'Come in,' I said.

Kelsey opened the door, closed it behind her, then walked across to where I was standing. 'So where were you?' she threw her hands up and fixed me with a glare.

What was her problem?

'I was out on a date if you must know.' I smiled. My feet hadn't touched the ground since I'd agreed to meet up with CJ.

'Please tell me it wasn't with the guy you met outside the shopping centre.' Kelsey placed her hands on her hips while she waited for me to reply.

I'd been hoping I'd be able to go over the post-date debrief with her. I'd expected her to be as excited as I was. It was clear that wasn't the case.

'His name's CJ, and he took me to a rooftop bar overlooking the Thames for cocktails,' I said, thinking my sister would be seriously impressed by the grand gesture.

I was about to elaborate on every single detail of our first date, from how nice he dressed to the divine smell of his aftershave to the number of drinks we had when Kelsey interrupted me.

'You can't go out with him again, Scarlett,' Kelsey said.

The directness of her words took me by surprise. Who did my sister think she was?

'You can't tell me what to do or how to live my life. And for what it's worth, we've already arranged our next date,' I replied with a tone of defiance in my voice.

'Well, cancel it! You don't know this bloke from Adam. He could be a serial killer for all you know. I've had plenty of unwanted attention from weirdos, and take it from me, they're not easy to swerve.'

Kelsey marched across the floor, flung the door open then disappeared out of sight as her words tumbled around in my head.

I was making a packed lunch when Mum walked into the kitchen.

'I'm just about to get going. We're running through some of the tricky dance routines today, so I'll probably end up finishing late. I'll grab something to eat with my friends before I head back,' I said.

I didn't want to have to lie to Mum, but I was going out with CJ tonight, and I didn't want her to suggest Todd escorted me on the date.

'What time will you be home?' Mum asked.

'I'm not sure. Maybe around eleven; it's hard to say. I'd better get going; I don't want to be late.'

I made a hasty exit before Mum could quiz me any further. She was keeping me out of the loop where the business was concerned, so she couldn't really expect me to spill the beans on my personal life, could she?

CJ picked me up from uni, and after we'd been out, he took me back to his flat. The top-floor, new-build apartment in Canary Wharf was amazing. Everything was newly fitted, and it had been kitted out to a high spec; the sparklingly clean kitchen had dove-grey, handle-free cupboards and cream stone work surfaces. It didn't look like it had ever been used.

'You must really hate living here,' I joked when he led me across the spacious dual-aspect living area to the bi-fold doors that opened out onto an L-shaped terrace.

'Yeah, it can be tough sometimes. Take a seat, and I'll fix us a drink.'

I walked across to the chrome railing and rested my elbows on it. The view from the balcony was incredible; the twinkling lights of London's skyline stretched out before me as far as the eye could see.

CJ slid his arm around my waist when he reappeared, having put the drinks down on a glass-topped wicker table. I leant my head against his shoulder as I continued to admire the view.

'It's so beautiful,' I said.

'It's one of the best things about the place. The moment the estate agent showed me the balcony, I was ready to sign on the dotted line, and that was before he'd told me about the other facilities. There's a state-of-the-art gym and a swimming pool that overlooks the South Dock. You wouldn't have to leave the building if you didn't want to,' CJ said.

'That's awesome, but I'm glad you ventured out; otherwise, we would never have met.' I smiled.

I was glad to say the first-date jitters I'd experienced when

CJ took me to the Three Sisters were no longer an issue, and our fledgling relationship was going from strength to strength.

'It's really weird; I know we only met recently, but I'm so comfortable with you; I feel like I've known you for years,' I said as CJ and I gazed into each other's eyes.

'Likewise,' CJ replied before kissing me on the lips.

The riverside balcony of CJ's penthouse was a secluded oasis, surrounded by the shadowy foliage of swaying palms and rustling bamboo. We sat side by side, sharing a bottle of pink Moët & Chandon. I wasn't usually a big drinker, and I'd already had several cocktails with our dinner, so once we started on the bubbles, they went to my head as quickly as they were rising to the surface of the glass. I could feel them fizzing inside me, lowering my inhibitions a little bit more with every sip that I took.

We'd had a magical evening; warm spring sunshine had faded into a cloudless night. Things didn't get much better than this, I thought, as I swung in a wicker bucket chair made for two with CJ's arm draped over my shoulder as we watched the bright city lights dance on the surface of the water. I knew Kelsey was concerned about me getting involved with a stranger; I couldn't help feeling she was worrying about nothing. My sister had formed an opinion of CJ without even meeting him. If she gave him a chance, she'd realise how lovely he was.

CJ shifted his position and leant in for a kiss. My body started to tingle in response. Without saying a word, he took the champagne flute out of my hand and placed it down on the glass-topped table. CJ took hold of my hand and stood up. Then he led me back into his swanky bachelor pad. I trailed behind him as he walked across the open-plan space, down the corridor and through his bedroom door.

A huge, black, leather bed dominated the minimal space, and I felt my pulse rate speed up at the sight of it. CJ stopped walking when he reached it. He looked deeply into my eyes as he unzipped the back of my dress, then he gently pushed it over my shoulders, and it dropped to the floor. I thought my heart was going to jump out of my chest when he undid my white lace bra and then slid off my matching knickers, leaving me naked.

I wasn't a virgin, but I hadn't tried every position in the *Kama Sutra* either. Who was I trying to kid? I'd had a few teenage fumbles with my previous boyfriend, but he wouldn't win any prizes for his performance, and I was sure the same could be said about me. We'd been like the blind leading the blind!

As I began to undo the buttons of CJ's pale grey shirt, I noticed he had an intricately patterned black and grey tattoo across his chest. My eyes were drawn to it and his muscular, gym-honed torso. While I was distracted by his ink work, he'd slipped out of his jeans and boxers.

CJ gently lowered me back onto the bed, then climbed on top of me. He watched me as he pushed his fingers all the way inside me; as he did, I closed my eyes, arching my neck into the feather pillows. My mouth opened, but I didn't make a sound. CJ pulled his fingers almost out; then, he sank them in again. This time I moaned with pleasure and trailed my fingers along the length of his shaft. CJ removed his skilful fingers and eased himself inside.

As I started to come, I opened my eyes and saw his muscular back spasm as he released himself inside me. Not that I'd had a lot of experiences to compare it to, but I hadn't realised sex could feel as incredible as that. CJ was clearly more worldly than I was in that department, he'd been so gentle with me, and thankfully he'd taken the lead. I didn't care what my friends thought; missionary had to be one of the most underrated positions.

Rolling onto his back, CJ pulled me with him. A smile spread across his face as he held me against his toned chest. He lowered his head and pressed his soft lips on my neck, then kissed the side of my face, and I let out a sigh before burrowing my face into his skin. That was a great way to end a perfect date.

43

Mia

Rio was running over the details of today's meeting with Kelsey and I when Scarlett pirouetted into the room in a leotard and ballet shoes.

'We should probably hit the road, ladies,' Rio said, putting an end to our conversation.

'Why do you always change the subject when I'm around?' Scarlett yelled before she turned on her heel and ran off in a huff; her red hair flapped behind her, licking at her back like fiery flames.

We weren't trying to hurt her feelings; we were just trying to shield her from the ugly truth. Scarlett didn't understand that because she had no idea how Dad really made his living, and we weren't in a position to explain without involving her, so it all seemed unfair to her.

My mind began wandering on the journey to Essex. I hadn't appreciated it when Victor had told me to go back to playing with my dolls. He'd been trying to undermine me and make me look stupid. But I wasn't going to let him get to me. I had a job to do, so it was time to toughen up and stop being offended by the slightest thing. I needed to develop a thick skin if I was going to survive in this industry, and there was no time like the present.

Victor's words rang in my head when Kelsey, Rio, Todd and myself turned up at Grays Hall Golf and Country Club a week later. *It's a free country so you can come here if you like. But I won't be waiting for you, and neither will the money*, he'd said.

Kelsey and Todd dropped back a little as we walked up the steps towards the entrance.

'Try not to drool all over Paige and her ginormous plastic tits if she's working today,' I heard Kelsey say. 'You're being paid to protect us, so keep your mind out of your pants and on your job. We don't want a repeat performance of what happened to Dad.'

My eyes welled up at the mention of my dad but I had to blink the tears away and refocus my mind. I'd need all my wits about me for our meeting with Victor Coleman.

'We're here to see Mr Coleman,' I said as sunlight flooded into the entire reception area through the atrium windows.

Paige's heavily sculpted eyebrows knitted together, and she tilted her head to one side. 'I'm afraid Mr Coleman isn't here.'

'Would it be possible to wait for him in the bar?'

'One moment please,' Paige said. She wiggled the mouse on the desk in front of her and brought her computer to life. Then her Barbie-pink, extra-long nails clattered across the keyboard. 'I've just checked the reservations, and I'm afraid Mr Coleman isn't due in today.'

I had to refrain from letting out a long sigh and settled for drumming my fingers on the edge of the polished wood counter in an attempt to vent my frustration.

'Come to think of it; I haven't seen him for a couple of days.' Paige went back to looking at the screen. 'In fact, the last time he was here was this time last week.' Paige looked at me, her enhanced glossy lips pouting.

Although she was quite determined that Victor hadn't been to the club since our meeting, I needed a little more reassurance. I'd hoped Victor was bluffing when he'd insisted he wasn't going to show or give me a penny, suggesting we take the cars back instead. But it looked like I was wrong.

'Are you one hundred per cent sure about that?'

Paige nodded, and the light bounced off her bright pink gloss. 'Yes. All our members and their guests have to sign in when they arrive.'

'Thanks for your help,' I said, finally admitting defeat.

Rio, Todd, Kelsey and I crossed the polished-tiled lobby and walked out of the exit.

'As predicted, Victor Coleman was a no-show. No disrespect, ladies, but you're both new to the game, so he wasn't likely to cough up a large amount of money without putting you through your paces.' Rio turned his attention back to the road.

'What do you think we should do?' I asked.

Rio had years of experience under his belt when it came to dealing with things like this. He looked into the rear-view mirror and fixed me with his dark brown eyes.

'You've done things by the book until now, but now we

need to pile the pressure on. We'll pay them a visit and make sure they understand what will happen if they mess you ladies around. Everything in life comes with consequences, but sometimes people need reminding about them,' Rio replied.

I inhaled a loud breath. I could handle the negotiating side of the business. In fact, I'd go as far as to say I enjoyed a bit of haggling, but I had a horrible feeling Rio was proposing an entirely different scenario. Sending in the big guns to issue a warning could turn ugly.

'What would that entail?' I asked, dreading the answer to my question.

'Most people freeze in the face of cold-blooded violence. A swift slap around the chops is all that's needed to get the point across, but we're not dealing with run-of-the-mill debtors. The Colemans might need a bit more force to push them outside their comfort zone, but they need to know you mean business and won't back down. Then you'll be in a powerful position,' Rio said.

I felt myself inwardly groan as his words registered in my brain. 'I was hoping we wouldn't have to go down that route.'

'Get a grip, Mia. Knocking on his door and asking nicely isn't going to make Vic pay up, is it? He's taking us for fools, and I'm not putting up with it.'

Kelsey turned to glare at me. She'd clearly inherited a lot of our dad's toughness.

I wished I'd kept my comment to myself now. I felt my cheeks flush. I hadn't expected Kelsey to publicly challenge me, and I didn't know how to respond. I'd come this far, so I wasn't going to let her overshadow me. I didn't want to compete against her for status or power in the family firm. But I supposed, if we were working together, the issue of internal politics would rear its ugly head from time to time. It was unavoidable.

Up until now, Kelsey had been taking a back seat to give me an opportunity to shine, but I should have realised it was too good to last. My sister was confident and outspoken and wasn't afraid to voice her opinion. I just wished she'd waited until we were alone to discuss it with me. If a power struggle broke out between us, it might prevent us from pulling together and winning the battle with Victor.

I felt uneasy about Rio's suggestion, but that didn't mean I was going to ignore his advice. We were being played as part of a much bigger game, and we needed to establish a reputation worthy of my dad's memory. Victor Coleman was underestimating us, but he needed to start taking us seriously.

44

Kelsey

Scarlett was sitting on the end of her bed, holding an A4 booklet in her hands, when I'd pushed open her door.

'What are you up to?' I asked.

'Learning my lines for the end-of-year performance,' my sister replied with a frostiness in her tone as she looked up from her script.

Scarlett seemed to be growing more bitter and discontented by the day; things were strained between us, which surprised me. Up until recently, we'd had a brilliant relationship; Scarlett usually went along with everything I said. It was a perk of being older; I had a higher priority in the pack. Every family had a ranking system. The youngest sibling was the last one to the party, so the structure was already in place by the time they arrived, which meant they didn't get a say in the matter. That never used to bother Scarlett; she was only too pleased to be included. But something had changed.

'Do you need a hand?' I said, offering my little sister an olive branch.

'No, thanks,' she replied, looking back down at her script.

'In that case, I'll leave you to it,' I replied, closing the door behind me.

I could take a hint, especially an unsubtle one. I wasn't about to grovel for forgiveness; I'd done nothing wrong. I was trying to be nice to her, and she'd thrown it back in my face. Scarlett could be such a stroppy little bitch at times, but the cold-shoulder treatment didn't work with me. She should realise that by now.

We'd called an emergency meeting to discuss our next step. When I slid open the glass door of the office nestled at the back of our garden, Rio, Todd, Mum and Mia were waiting for me to arrive.

'Sorry I'm late.' I smiled.

Todd exhaled a slow breath out of his nostrils as he scribbled something down in his notebook. Then he discreetly shook his head. It was like being back at school, having a red mark put beside your name on the register if you turned up after the teacher had called you. I knew my poor timekeeping wound him up; coming from a military background, punctuality was essential to him. But he was my family's employee, so it wasn't his place to give me a disapproving look.

'Not to worry; now that you're here, let's get started and decide the best course of action,' Mum said.

'If Davie was still with us, he'd tell us to strike while the iron's hot.' Rio glanced across at Mum and offered her a half-smile, which I was glad to see she returned. 'Men like the Colemans will take liberties if they're left unchecked. We've been finding out as much as we can about them so that we're fully prepared before we make our next move.'

'I'm glad to hear that,' Mum said.

'Davie taught us well, Amanda. Intimidation isn't just about violence and sending in the heavies. If you get hold of personal information about somebody, you can threaten them with it and use it to your advantage. Todd and I have been working behind the scenes for a while now, haven't we, mate?' Rio said.

'Yes,' Todd replied, leafing back through his notebook. 'We've been monitoring their every movement. So far, we've established that Victor lives with his wife Lorraine in a detached house in a quiet turning about five minutes' drive from the country club.' Todd paused and turned over the page in his notebook before he continued speaking. 'Although Craig officially lives in a swanky bachelor pad, he seems to spend a lot of his time back at Mum and Dad's.'

'How did you find all of this out?' Mia asked; her blue eyes were wide with curiosity.

'We've had them under surveillance for a little while now. It's always good to get the low-down on people we cross paths with,' Rio replied.

'So what are you proposing we do?' Mia asked.

'As they've snubbed our attempt to recoup the money, we'll need to pay them a visit on their turf and make sure they understand the terms and conditions of our business and the consequences they face if they choose to ignore them,' Rio said.

I glanced over at Mia. She was putting on a brave face,

but her skin seemed to have drained of all its colour and appeared to be a couple of shades paler than it was a minute ago, which was pretty good going as her complexion was milky white to begin with. As I watched, her shoulders rounded, and she retreated behind her hair as if to shield herself from what was about to happen.

I knew my sister hated confrontation, but in some circumstances, it was necessary. Preparing for a violent clash was the only sensible option. We had to be tough to succeed. There was a big difference between buying a debt and assaulting people, but Rio and Todd had that side of the business covered. They knew how and when to escalate the situation.

We all wanted revenge, so I was glad Mia wasn't challenging Rio even though I'd put money on the fact that she would have taken an entirely different approach if it had been left up to her to decide. Mia would probably prefer we held a peaceful demonstration at the end of Victor's driveway, arming ourselves with 'please, can you pay us back' placards like a bunch of wacko activists exercising our right to freedom of speech. But that was never going to happen. There was more chance Victor would appear on the cover of the *Hairdressers Journal*.

'Victor's house will be the ideal place to deliver the ultimatum as Craig spends most of his time there anyway. We'll have to go in firm-handed because we don't know what we're going to be up against. The Colemans owe you a lot of money, so if they can't or won't pay, they should be expecting to get a slap at the very least,' Rio continued.

'I'll do some more digging and gather other personal

information we can use against them,' Todd said, jotting down notes.

'We have to make a stand and establish who's the boss in this situation so they know they can't mess with us. Don't look so worried, Mia; Todd and I will be the ones enforcing the message,' Rio said.

He was trying his best to reassure Mia that this was a necessary step, so the Colemans knew who was in the driving seat. Rio's scare tactics were psychological at this stage; he would only use violence as a last resort.

When we came back into the house, Scarlett had gone out. She'd left a note on the kitchen table saying she was meeting up with friends, but she hadn't mentioned that to me earlier. I had a sinking feeling, she'd gone out with CJ. I was pretty sure they were dating in secret, but I couldn't say anything because of my situation with Todd. We'd always shared a close bond, but since we'd fallen out, she was keeping me in the dark.

If that was the way she wanted it, so be it; I had more important things to worry about than my sister slipping out to see a guy she barely knew. The showdown with the Colemans was looming, and right now, that was at the forefront of my mind, preoccupying all my thoughts.

45

Scarlett

'What are you up to?' CJ said.

My face broke into a huge grin at the sound of his voice. 'Nothing much; just learning my lines for the performance,' I replied.

'Do you fancy going out?' CJ asked.

'What sort of question is that? Of course I do.'

'I'll pick you up in an hour.'

'At the risk of sounding extremely keen, could you be here in half an hour?' I laughed.

'No worries,' CJ replied before ending the call.

A little while ago, I'd walked in on Mum, Mia and Kelsey talking about Victor and Craig Coleman. They were obviously discussing something business-related they didn't want to include me in, so they'd taken themselves off and were now closeted away in Dad's office so that they could continue their conversation in private. That suited me fine as it gave me an ideal opportunity to slip out. But I had no idea how long the coast would be clear for, and if I wanted to avoid answering any awkward questions, it would be better if I'd gone before they came back. I'd adopted this strategy since CJ and I had had our first date, and it seemed to be working well. Kelsey was suspicious of every move I made, probably because she was also sneaking around, so I knew she'd start interrogating me about where I was going and who I was going with if I didn't make myself scarce.

As I rushed around my bedroom, selecting something suitable to wear, I couldn't help feeling there was a pattern emerging here. Every time I went out on a date with CJ, I had to get ready in record time. I hadn't once been able to languish in the bath before washing my hair and carefully applying my makeup. I just about had time for a quick shower and change of clothes before I'd have to head out of the door.

I was standing outside the side gate, cleaning gravel dust off of my white high-heeled sandals with a Kleenex, when CJ's car pulled up alongside me.

'Have you been waiting long?' CJ asked, turning his dark brown gaze on me.

'No, just a minute or two,' I replied as I fastened my seatbelt.

'You look gorgeous,' CJ said.

'Thank you,' I replied as a smile spread across my face.

I was glad CJ approved. I thought I'd scrubbed up quite well under the circumstances. Because I'd been short on time, I'd pulled my long hair into a high ponytail and grabbed a long-sleeve white chiffon playsuit with a wrap-over front as it didn't need ironing, pairing it with a 3D floral clutch bag that was every colour under the sun. When I'd bought it, Mum had pointed out that it went with everything and nothing.

'So, where are you taking me?' I asked, turning to look at my handsome date, whose eyes were fixed on the road.

'I don't want to spoil the surprise,' CJ replied, flashing me a row of straight, white teeth.

A few moments later, CJ parked his BMW in a side street, and we walked the short distance to the swoon-worthy haunt, hand in hand.

'Eat your heart out, Casanova, I'm seriously impressed,' I said when CJ pushed open the door to the most amazing little bistro with a dark, broody interior.

The intimate space was a haven for love-struck couples; two-seater semi-circular wrap-around booths strung with twinkly fairy lights and a candlelit table set the scene for a romantic evening. The way the plush velvet seating had been designed made you feel like you were the only two people in the tiny restaurant.

The menu was full of classic delicacies, from pie and mash to roast rib of beef and Yorkshire pudding. I wasn't sure I'd ever eaten in a restaurant that only served traditional British food before.

'What are you having to start with?' CJ asked, fixing his eyes on me.

'Asparagus, I think.' I didn't want to tell CJ that I'd been drawn to the dish because it was served with Gladys-May's duck eggs and imagining the eggs came from a duck called Gladys-May appealed to my childish sense of humour. 'What about you?'

'Beer-battered monkfish scampi,' CJ replied. 'Do you want wine or cocktails, or both?'

'Don't make out I'm some kind of lush!' I replied, pretending to be horrified by his suggestion.

'Both it is then.' CJ smiled, handing me a drinks menu.

'Please don't order both, or I'll be crawling out of here on my hands and knees.' I laughed.

Kelsey was the party animal in our family. I was a lightweight in comparison. My eyes scanned over the cocktail list and settled on the section inspired by the Zodiac calendar. I found my star sign and corresponding drink: Cranberry Daiquiri. It was made with spiced rum, which according to the menu, complemented the fiery, passionate character Leos possessed, so I couldn't resist ordering one. CJ settled for a pint of Amstel. We both picked the same main course: filet steak and hand-cut chips served with a trio of sauces – mushroom, peppercorn, and Béarnaise.

'You're very good at picking venues,' I said while we waited for our drinks and starters to arrive. 'I don't ever think I've seen such a quirky cocktail list before.'

'Feel free to have more than one,' CJ replied.

'Anyone would think you're trying to get me drunk so you can take advantage of me.'

Dinner had been amazing, and I was completely stuffed, so I wasn't going to have a pudding until I spotted dark chocolate fondant, served with hazelnut ice cream and candied orange, on the menu. CJ opted for the artisan cheese board with malt loaf and assorted chutneys.

When the waitress brought over the bill, I tried to get to it first, but CJ pounced on it like a hungry cat on a mouse.

'It's my turn to pay,' I protested.

'No way,' CJ insisted, displaying the kind of old-fashioned

chivalry Mum would be impressed by. 'Do you want to come back to my flat?' CJ asked once the waitress had left the table.

Kelsey's words started swimming around in my head, but I chose to ignore them. CJ had just taken me out for a candlelit dinner, and I was having a ball, so I didn't want to put an end to the evening any time soon. And besides that, since I'd met him outside Bluewater Shopping Centre, I'd been wearing a smile that wouldn't leave my face.

'That would be lovely. I haven't got to be in early tomorrow,' I replied.

'How are the rehearsals going?' CJ asked as we walked hand in hand back to his BMW.

'It's been a punishing schedule. I'll be glad when it's all over. I never thought I get bored listening to the soundtrack of *Mamma Mia!*, but I only have to hear the opening bars of "Dancing Queen" now, and I find myself reaching for my noise-cancelling headphones,' I laughed.

'It's easy to tell you're a dancer,' CJ said.

'Really?' I was intrigued to know why. I didn't think I was a natural choice as I was quite tall, five feet seven, so I didn't fit the elfin stereotype like the rest of my classmates. I was all arms and legs, like a baby giraffe.

'You've got great legs.' CJ stopped walking, and as his eyes slowly made their way up my bare skin, I felt my heart begin pounding in my chest.

I looked up at him through my lashes, shyness suddenly getting the better of me, then I started fanning myself with my hand to try and make light of my embarrassment.

'Why, thank you,' I said, fluttering my eyelashes at CJ.

My heart started pounding at the thought of his hands on my body.

A short time later, I was naked on CJ's bed, arching my body like a cat stretching as waves of passion built up inside me. I wished we could stay like this forever, I thought as we lay side by side, exhausted.

'It's pretty late now; why don't you stay?' CJ suggested. He placed a kiss on the top of my head, then wrapped his arms around me.

I knew that wasn't an option. 'I can't stay tonight, but maybe tomorrow.'

I looked over my shoulder while I put my clothes back on to gauge his reaction and was delighted to see CJ's dark eyes light up.

Tomorrow was Friday, so it wouldn't seem odd if I stayed away overnight, and it would give me time to come up with an excuse. Turning around, I wrapped my arms around his neck and kissed him. He made one last attempt to pull me back into bed.

'I've got to go. Can you call me a cab?'

CJ nodded. 'Do you want me to go with you to make sure you get home OK?'

'No, I'll be fine.' I smiled. Despite his bad-boy exterior, CJ was a real gentleman. A definite keeper, no matter what Kelsey thought.

'Are you sure you don't want me to go with you?' CJ asked, looking deeply into my eyes when my cab arrived outside.

'I'm positive.'

I appreciated the offer, but it would only complicate things if one of my family saw him dropping me off.

'Text me when you get home,' CJ said.

'I will,' I replied, enjoying one last lingering kiss before I headed out of the door.

46

Mia

Rio knew the business like the back of his hand, so we'd left him to come up with the best course of action, and he'd decided using the element of surprise was the best way forward. Victor's face was a picture when he opened the front door and saw Rio, Todd, Kelsey and me standing there.

I'd rehearsed my lines over and over on the journey, but that didn't stop a wave of nerves building inside me before washing over me as I climbed out of Rio's Range Rover. I stood on the pavement, trying to compose myself and looking up at the impressive neo-Georgian house, which was part of a new development. The red-brick walls, white columns and portico certainly had kerb appeal, but we hadn't come here to admire his perfectly symmetrical house, so I led the way down the block-paved driveway and rang his doorbell. The sooner we got this over with, the better.

'What the fuck are you doing here?' Victor asked through gritted teeth.

The hairs on the back of my neck stood up at the sight of him. 'As you failed to show up to our meeting, you left us no alternative but to come to you...' I let my sentence trail off.

Rio was right; the element of surprise worked like a charm at intimidating people. Anyone could see that our unannounced visit had rattled Victor.

'How did you find out where I lived?' Victor jabbed his finger in my direction before he narrowed his eyes and glared at me.

I wasn't about to elaborate and give away all of our trade secrets. Rio and Todd had done a brilliant job gathering information on the Colemans in recent weeks, so we now had a pretty clear picture of their movements.

'Aren't you going to invite us in?' Rio asked.

I looked over my shoulder at the tall, broad, man who was standing with his feet slightly apart. Rio's hands were in the front of his body, his left fingers clasped around his right wrist.

'No,' Victor snarled, looking thoroughly pissed off by our unexpected arrival.

'That's not very hospitable of you, but it's your prerogative.' Rio laughed. 'We're more than happy to conduct your private business in public, aren't we, ladies?' Rio stepped between us and flashed Kelsey and I a smile before he turned his attention back to Victor. 'I'm sure it will be very entertaining for your neighbours to see you get battered.'

I could see Victor's face change shape as he clenched his jaw before his cold, calculating, cue-ball eyes scanned the adjoining houses as he checked for curtain twitchers. 'You'd better come in,' he said, stepping back from the doorway.

Acres of glossy timber panelling and shiny marble floors opened up before us as he led the way into a spacious lounge at the front of the property. It overlooked the garden and flower beds, which were tended by hands unseen and never by the owner would be my guess. The room was either an interior design masterpiece or a testament to the Colemans' gaudy taste. Either way, the shocking colour palette wasn't easy on the eye.

The heady scent of flowers hit me when I walked into the huge space, even before I saw the massive bouquet sitting in the centre of a gilt table next to a baby grand piano. I'd put money on the fact that nobody in the family was musical. It was just another show of wealth.

'If someone owes our firm money and they refuse to pay it back, they have to expect a home visit,' I said, pushing my shoulders back and standing tall when I suddenly remembered what Rio had told me about acting with confidence.

Kelsey and I had to earn our reputation before men like Victor would take us seriously. We had Rio to guide us, and he knew his stuff, so we needed to listen to his advice and follow it closely.

Victor stood glaring at me while I examined the micro-expressions he was making so that I could try and read the situation and pre-empt his reaction. But he was giving off mixed signals. A prominent vein was throbbing in his neck, which indicated he was either nervous or angry.

'How do you intend to pay us back?' I continued when he didn't reply.

'I told you, we've decided we don't want the cars.' Victor's chin jutted forward as he spoke.

'And I told you returning them wasn't an option,' I replied, standing my ground.

Victor turned his balding head towards the door and bellowed, 'Lorraine, get your arse in here and bring me the keys to those fucking motors.'

Moments later, Mrs Coleman arrived; her musky perfume wafted into the room before she did. Lorraine was wearing a plunge-fronted, leopard-print, wrap dress, which did nothing to flatter her portly figure. The jersey fabric clung to all the wrong places. She was wearing fake tan, dangly earrings and bright pink lipstick and looked like a brunette version of Pat Butcher.

Victor held his hand out as she walked towards him. She scowled, then dropped two sets of keys into his palm and walked back out of the room without saying a word.

'There you go,' Victor said, dangling the keys in front of me with a smug look on his face.

I could see Rio bristle out of the corner of my eye. He was clearly annoyed that Victor was taking no notice of me, and I was sure he was itching to step in and put the older man in his place. But like the great mentor that he was, Rio hung back and gave me the opportunity to deal with the situation. Being thrown in at the deep end was the fastest way to find out whether I'd sink or swim. I was determined it would be the latter.

'As I already told you, we don't accept returns,' I reiterated with an undertone of annoyance in my voice that I didn't try to hide. Victor was pushing the boundaries, so I had to take a firm stand. 'At this stage, you've already exceeded the deadline I gave you, so when do you intend to pay?' I crossed my arms over my chest and fixed my eyes on him while I waited for a reply.

'On the twelfth of never,' Victor said, then he threw his head back and started braying like a donkey.

He was deliberately trying to wind me up, but I intended to stay professional no matter what.

'If you're refusing to settle the outstanding amount, we'll have to take a different course of action.' I had bucketloads of patience, but Victor was testing my resolve.

'Larry's valuation is way off the mark; there's no way the Audis are worth seventy-five grand apiece,' Victor said.

'I haven't come here to haggle with you. I just want to collect one hundred and fifty thousand pounds, and we'll be out of your way. If you can't or won't pay, we'll be forced to start removing assets to the same value,' I said, casting my eyes over Victor's expensive but lairy possessions.

'You can't do that. If you think I'm going to let you walk into my house and start stripping the contents, you've got another thing coming,' Victor fumed, getting up in my face and jabbing his index finger towards me.

Rio closed the gap between us in a heartbeat. 'Get out of her face right now and back it up, or you're going to witness first-hand how quickly I can turn into your worst nightmare,' he said, expanding his chest and squaring up for a fight.

The speed and ferocity with which Rio delivered his threat caught Victor off guard, and I watched him well up with fear while he did his level best to act the hard man. Victor might have been on home turf, but he was outnumbered, so he knew his options were limited.

I sauntered over to the baby grand piano and ran my fingertips across the shiny, lacquered surface, which got Victor's attention.

'I can't just pull cash like that out of thin air,' Victor said with an undertone of desperation in his voice.

I was glad to see he'd suddenly come around to my way of thinking, and I had to suppress a smile that threatened to spread over my face. The power shift between us was palpable.

'I appreciate that, but my sister and I aren't running a charity, and you've already exceeded the deadline I gave you. We can continue to extend you a line of credit, that's not a problem, but you should know there will be financial implications if we do.'

Victor's face turned purple as he glared at me with his fists clenched. 'Give me a fucking break, will you?'

'I wish I could, but we have to charge interest if a customer fails to make a payment on time. That's how we make a living.'

Victor's eyes started darting around the room like I'd said something shocking, but I wasn't sure what he was expecting me to say.

'I'm sure you understand.' I tilted my head to the side. I was tempted to pat him on the back of the hand in a condescending manner, but I just about managed to resist the urge.

I'd have to wait until I heard Rio's feedback for confirmation, but I felt like I'd done a good job handling Victor, considering I was winging it.

'If you agree to give me a couple more days and not add any more interest, I'll get the money for you,' Victor said.

I glanced over at Kelsey and Rio to gauge their reactions, and they both gave me a subtle nod, so I agreed to Victor's request. It was Thursday today; he could have until the end of the weekend. 'Fair enough, but we'll be back on Monday, and you'd better have the cash.'

I couldn't take the credit for Victor's change of heart. If Rio hadn't been right behind me, Victor would have tried to run rings around me. From the way he treated his wife, he clearly had no respect for women. But it was amazing how a few well-chosen words and a little gentle persuasion from a huge muscular guy could turn the tables on an otherwise problematic situation. I was glad Rio was on our side. He wasn't a man you wanted to cross.

All in all, the meeting had gone better than expected. Kelsey and I were still finding our feet in the new world we were inhabiting, but we would prove, in time, we had what it took to run our dad's firm.

Victor, like his mock-Georgian, three-storey house, appeared to be something that he wasn't. Both offered a veneer of traditional respectability on the surface – Victor with his clean-shaven face and expensive suits, and his home by displaying its powerful pediments, lavish stone mouldings and sash windows. But both were hiding behind a façade. Dressing the part and owning a lavish mansion in a suburban street didn't mean a person had reached the upper echelons of society. It took more than the trappings of wealth to gain social respectability. When you scratched beneath the surface, Victor was still as rough as they come. He might be living the high life, but he spat on the values of respect, dignity and trust to get there.

'You were fantastic, Mia, and I'm not trying to burst your

bubble, but Victor's not going to hand over a big wedge of dough just like that; he has his reputation to think of,' Rio said once we were back in the car.

'So why did he ask us to give him more time?' I asked, confused by the rules of the back-and-forth game we were playing.

'Because he wanted to get rid of us. Victor's giving us the run-around to buy himself some time. He didn't hand over the money; he gave us a promise of it. That's not the same thing. I can guarantee the Colemans will be formulating a plan as we speak. They had no intention of buying those cars, not from Larry and not from us,' Rio replied.

My temples began pounding, signalling the start of a tension headache. Kelsey and I were in way over our heads, and the thought of that terrified me. I had to keep reminding myself what led us to be in this position to find the strength to carry on. Dad lost his life because of these people; we owed it to his memory to stand up to them.

The whole episode had been draining, and the thought of coming back here to repeat it on Monday was going to cast a shadow over the weekend. But this was what Kelsey and I had signed up for, so there was no point whinging about it. I just had to suck it up and get on with it.

47

Scarlett

'You're in a good mood,' Mum said as I pushed the trolley around Waitrose.

Mum wasn't my favourite person at the moment so I'd thought twice about going to the supermarket with her. But I knew if I forced myself, I'd be able to pick up loads of goodies she wouldn't think to buy, so it was worth the sacrifice.

'I love Fridays.' I beamed.

That was true, but it wasn't the only reason I was feeling on top of the world.

'So what have you got planned for the weekend? Are you going out tonight?' Mum smiled.

Things had been frosty between us since she'd said I couldn't give up uni, but she seemed to be making a real effort, so I wasn't going to throw it back in her face.

'Yes, I'm catching up with friends. We're going out for a few drinks and something to eat.'

'Ooh, drinks and a meal – that sounds lovely,' Mum said as she unloaded the weekly shop onto the conveyor belt.

I didn't want to say that I was going out with CJ, so I decided to lie; being an aspiring actress, the words tripped off my tongue. Playing a part came naturally to me. I felt guilty keeping the truth from my mum, but if I told her I was seeing someone, she'd leap into overprotective mode. Now that Dad wasn't here to do it for her, she'd taken over that role. And there was no way I wanted Todd babysitting me while I was out on a date.

Tomorrow couldn't come soon enough for my liking. To celebrate our one-month anniversary, CJ was taking me to the Aqua Shard Bar. I couldn't wait; I'd always wanted to go to London's most iconic skyscraper. The view from the thirty-first floor was legendary.

'So I take it you won't want any dinner?' Mum queried.

'Whatever gave you that idea?' I laughed. I was a self-proclaimed dustbin, but in my defence, my course was a very active one, so I burned off a lot of calories.

'I don't know where you put it.' Mum laughed and shook her head. 'To be young and slim again.' She sighed.

Now it was my turn to shake my head. I really didn't know what my mum saw when she looked in the mirror. She had this insane notion that she'd lost her figure after having three children, and she spent a small fortune on expensive face creams to hold back the years and keep her imaginary wrinkles at bay. I knew she wasn't fishing for compliments; she didn't think she wasn't ageing well.

'If I look half as good as you when I'm fifty, I'll be a happy bunny,' I replied while loading groceries into our bags for life.

Mum turned to face me, her jaw slack. 'I'm forty-eight, Scarlett. I won't be fifty for years, and you'd do well to remember that,' she replied in a barely audible whisper.

I couldn't help but smile. I'd tried to pay her a compliment, but I'd inadvertently hit a nerve.

With my earlier faux pas forgotten, Mum and I were chatting away as she drove the car towards home when suddenly, a massive bang halted our conversation. We'd been jolted from behind by a heavy force that made us lurch forwards until our seatbelts stopped the momentum. Then we were thrown back into the leather upholstery, and it felt like everything was happening in slow motion.

'What the hell was that?'

I swivelled around in my chair and looked out of the back windscreen. A black van with tinted windows had gone into the back of us, which seemed really odd. It wasn't as though we were stationary or caught up in slow-moving traffic; we were travelling at around thirty miles an hour.

'How did that idiot manage to hit us while we were moving?' I turned my head to look at Mum, but she was staring into the rear-view mirror, trying to make sense of everything.

'Maybe the driver's been drinking,' Mum replied before she glanced over at me.

I couldn't help noticing her knuckles had turned white as she gripped the steering wheel with both hands. Before we had time to process what was going on, two men dressed all in black with balaclavas covering their features jumped out of the van and ran towards our car. My heart started hammering in my chest. Mum and I both froze with fear when one of the men hit the back windscreen with a crowbar, shattering it into thousands of tiny pieces. The sound in the car was deafening as the bang ricocheted around the interior.

We were still reeling from the shock when one of the men appeared at the driver's door. He knocked on the glass with the barrel of a gun before pointing it at Mum through the window.

'Get out of the car,' he ordered before he opened the door.

'Stay here,' Mum whispered as she battled to undo her seatbelt with trembling fingers.

'Hurry up; we haven't got all fucking day,' the man boomed, waving the gun around.

Mum was tall, but she looked tiny as she craned her neck to look up at the giant of a man. He pushed Mum back against the passenger door with one gloved hand while he pointed the barrel of the gun under her chin with the other. I felt my blood run cold. I'd already witnessed one of my parents being murdered; I didn't want to have a front-row seat at another execution. I was too busy watching what was going on to notice the other man opening my door, and when I felt the fresh air flood into the car, a yelp escaped from my lips.

The man unclipped my seatbelt, grabbed hold of my arm and pulled me onto my feet. 'Shut the fuck up. Don't do anything stupid unless you want to end up like your dad,' he said.

It must have been the confusion of the situation, but his voice sounded strangely familiar until terror quickly chased that thought out of my head. He stood inches away from me, wielding the iron bar that broke the back windscreen while glaring at me. I felt my pulse rate soar as his dark eyes bored into mine.

'I've got a message from Victor Coleman,' the other man said, diverting my attention from the man in front of me. 'We're keeping the cars, but we're not paying for them. You either drop this matter right now, or he'll be forced to take things much further.' The man pushed the gun right under Mum's chin, and I saw her flinch before she closed her eyes.

I inhaled a long breath to try and steady my nerves, but it didn't help. My fear was palpable. My situation was bad enough, but Mum was facing a much greater threat. I felt completely useless. All I could do was stand by and watch as the man held a gun to her head. There was nothing I could do to try and help her. I felt bile turn over in my stomach, and I thought I was going to be sick. The man must be a heartless bastard to put an innocent woman through an ordeal like this. Anyone could see she was suffering. My beautiful, gentle mum, who wouldn't hurt a fly, looked absolutely terrified. He didn't need to eke this out any longer. I was so scared he was going to pull the trigger; I didn't want to watch, but I couldn't seem to look away. My eyes were glued to the scene as it unfolded before me.

'Do I make myself clear?' the man said.

'Yes,' Mum replied, her voice breaking with emotion.

As fast as the men arrived, they were gone, reversing at high speed into a turning before swinging the van around and speeding off in the opposite direction. Mum and I stood rooted to the spot for several seconds before either of us dared to move. Mum walked around the bonnet of the car towards me. She reached forwards and took hold of both of my hands.

'Are you all right, Scarlett?' Mum spoke in a steady voice, but I could see her eyes were glistening with unshed tears.

I nodded my head. I couldn't find the words to answer; my mouth was so dry. I'd never known this stretch of road to be so deserted before, but that was typical, wasn't it? There was never a passing stranger around when you needed help.

Mum let go of one of my hands so that she could stroke my hair. Then she pulled me towards her and wrapped her arms around me. We held each other in a wordless embrace for what felt like the longest moment before we pulled apart.

'Let's get out of here in case they come back,' Mum said before getting back behind the wheel. She was shaken to the core. I could see her physically trembling as she started the engine and tried to concentrate on the road ahead.

We were both too shocked to speak. The light-hearted conversation we were having earlier was a million miles away now. I stared out of the windscreen, trying to process what had just happened as my fingers gripped onto the seat.

'Don't be scared. We'll be home in a minute, sweetheart,' Mum said, glancing across at me with worry etched across her face.

48

Mia

Mum was visibly shaking when she walked into the kitchen. Her creamy complexion had turned ashen, and her hands were trembling so much, the bags of shopping she was holding were quaking. Kelsey and I had been dissecting the details of our meeting with Victor, but our conversation stopped in mid-flow at the sight of her. We both sprang out of our chairs and went to help her.

'What's the matter?' I asked. 'You look like you've seen a ghost.'

Mum was in such a state, my initial thought was that she'd had some news from the detectives investigating my dad's murder. They seemed to be going around in circles and weren't any closer to catching his killer all these months later.

Kelsey took the shopping from her as I began guiding her across to a chair. Mum's legs started to buckle when Scarlett came into view. It was obvious my sister had been crying; her bloodshot eyes and tear-stained cheeks were a dead giveaway. I thought they'd had an argument and looked from one to the other, trying to work out what was going on.

Kelsey placed a glass of water in front of Mum, but she didn't attempt to drink from it; she gripped onto the side of the table instead.

'What on earth's happened? I asked, but neither of them responded.

My mum and younger sister sat across the table from each other, staring into the middle distance in a trance-like state. It was really bizarre. I'd never seen Scarlett so lost for words or withdrawn before, not even after our dad died. She was usually a ball of energy, but she looked like the life had been sucked out of her. She was also deathly pale. Something serious was up. My eyes found Kelsey's, and we exchanged a look.

'I'm worried about the two of you. Do you want me to phone the doctor?' I asked when Mum and Scarlett continued to stare into space.

Mum shook her head. ' No,' she replied.

'What's going on?' I pressed. I wasn't about to be fobbed off.

'We had a run-in with two of the Colemans' men on the way back from the supermarket,' Mum blurted out. '

I pulled out a chair at the head of the table and sat down facing the two of them. 'Oh my God, are you hurt?' I asked as a wave of panic started to build inside me.

'We're not injured, just shocked. I'm sorry if we worried you.' Tears glistened in Mum's eyes.

'What happened? Kelsey asked before she walked across the kitchen, filled the kettle and switched it on. The sound of the water boiling seemed louder than usual and dominated the silence.

Mum paused while she composed herself. 'My Range Rover was rammed by a black van when we were driving back from Waitrose.'

'What the hell!' Kelsey said as the kettle switch flicked off.

Mum swallowed hard before she spoke. 'It was terrifying. The van came from nowhere and smashed into the back of us, then two men jumped out, and one of them shattered the back windscreen with a crowbar.'

'You must have been petrified,' I said, leaning over the table and taking hold of my mum's and sister's hands.

Mum nodded, but Scarlett continued to stare straight ahead with a glazed-over expression on her beautiful face.

'The other man banged on the window with the barrel of a gun, then he ordered me to get out of the car.' Mum was struggling to hold back her tears.

'Jesus,' Kelsey said, shaking her head from side to side. 'I'm surprised you got out of the car.'

'I didn't want to, but I thought he was going to shoot me in the driver's seat, and I was scared Scarlett might get caught in the crossfire, so I did as he said. I definitely thought my life was over when he held the gun under my chin,' Mum continued. Her voice wavered as she recounted her ordeal.

The sound of Scarlett's sobs changed the focus of my attention, and I swivelled in my chair to look directly at her. She pulled her hand free of my grip and buried her face behind her long, slender fingers.

'It's OK, sweetheart, we're safe now,' Mum soothed.

Reaching over the table, she rubbed the skin on the back of Scarlett's lily-white hand.

My heart went out to my younger sister. She was only twenty, and she'd already experienced so much.

Kelsey abandoned making the tea. She crossed the kitchen tiles until she was standing behind Scarlett. Kelsey stooped forward and threw her arms around our sister's shoulders before resting her chin on Scarlett's collarbone.

'You must have been terrified,' I said, turning my attention back to my mum.

I felt like my heart would break when I saw two tracks of tears running over her beautiful complexion. Hadn't our family suffered enough without this happening? There was no denying it was a cruel world we lived in.

'I don't get it. Why did they target you and Scarlett?' Kelsey's sculpted eyebrows knitted together.

'They had a message from Victor. He said he's keeping the cars, but he's not paying for them, and we need to drop the matter right now. Otherwise, he'll be forced to take things further.' Mum covered her face with her hands and began to cry.

When I saw her shoulders begin to jerk up and down, I pushed back my chair, crouched down on the floor beside her and threw my arms around her neck.

'Don't cry; it will be OK,' I said, kissing Mum on the top of her head.

Kelsey and I exchanged a look, and then I turned my focus back to Mum. The whole episode sounded like a complete nightmare. It was no surprise she was suffering from the after-effects and was visibly shaken by the experience.

'I think we should phone Rio,' Kelsey said.

I nodded in agreement.

Rio burst into the kitchen a short while later and rushed over to Mum's side. 'Are you hurt, Amanda?'

Mum shook her head as she tried to paint on a smile, but the half-hearted attempt didn't look convincing and wasn't fooling any of us.

'How about you, Scarlett?' Rio's dark eyes scanned every inch of my sister's haunted face.

Scarlett shrugged her slender shoulders. 'I'm not hurt, but it was terrifying. I thought the guy was going to shoot Mum right in front of me, and it's brought back terrible memories of the day Dad died.' Scarlett broke down in tears.

I felt myself jolt as concern for my mum and sister suddenly got pushed out of the frame by an overwhelming wave of sadness. A sudden flashback to the graveyard and that miserable, wet December day when we laid my dad to rest was taking centre stage. The sensory overload threatened to floor me. Their ordeal had caused my grief to return, and it had come back with a vengeance. I felt like I was trapped in a confined space that was filling up with water, and there was no way out. I could feel myself going into meltdown. My hands started trembling, and my legs turned to jelly as I pictured the scene of carnage on my wedding day.

I'd expected Dad's birthday or times when the family would all be together like at Christmas to trigger moments of despair. It was natural for your thoughts to drift to the person missing. I'd never expected my sister to be faced with a situation like this; she'd thought Mum was going to be executed in front of her. Words couldn't describe how I felt as I tried to get my head around what they'd been through. It was too awful to process.

'The man's a fucking coward.'

The sound of Rio's voice brought me back to reality, so I pushed the painful memory from my thoughts. Dwelling on it wasn't going to help anyone, least of all my mum and sister. They needed me to be strong, and I wasn't about to let them down. I'd have to learn to live with moments like this. The future would be full of them. We'd have good days and bad days, so we'd have to help each other navigate the rough patches and sidestep the landmine of grief triggers that threatened to blow our family to pieces.

'If Victor had harmed a hair on either of your heads, I can assure you I would have torn the bastard limb from limb with my bare hands.' Rio clenched his hands into fists as he spoke, and a flash of anger spread across his face.

I didn't think my opinion of Victor could sink any lower, but it had. The man was lowlife scum and had worse morals than I'd given him credit for.

'Do you think we should back off?' I asked.

I didn't want to lose another family member for the sake of recovering a debt. Money wasn't important in the grand scheme of things. As far as I was concerned, if you didn't have your family by your side, you had nothing.

'No way.' Rio put his hands on his hips and shook his head. 'Caving in to Victor's demands is the last thing we should be doing. We have to make a stand. We can't let him get away with this; otherwise, he'll think he's got the upper hand. We have to fight back.'

'I agree. Being held at gunpoint was terrifying. I'll never

be made to feel so vulnerable again. I'm more determined than ever to get justice for Davie,' Mum said, showing her feisty side.

'We're right behind you,' Rio said, casting his eye over all of us.

'We need a change of tactics. Mia's right; I think we should involve the police. DI Stewart asked me if I could think of anyone who would want to see Davie dead. I said, no, at the time, but I'm going to phone her and tell her it's come to light that Victor Coleman had a grudge against him.' Mum smiled.

The fact that forensics officers couldn't find any evidence to prove who was responsible for Dad's horrific murder didn't stop my family from thinking the Colemans were guilty of doing the deed or ordering the hit. And the desire to get even with the men was growing stronger by the day.

Rio paused for a moment while he considered what Mum had said. 'Throwing Victor under the bus is going to ramp things up a gear. But if that's what you want…'

'I'm scared to escalate things; I think it's too risky.' My heart started pounding in my chest. We were reaching the point of no return.

'It will take time for the police to act on that information, so we'll take matters into our own hands in the meantime. I'll get Wesley to come over with the dogs and keep watch over you and Scarlett,' Rio said to Mum. 'We'll go and pay Victor's lovely wife Lorraine a surprise visit and see how he likes it.' Rio's eyes flicked between Kelsey and I as he spoke.

I bit down hard on the side of my lip as I mulled over what Rio had said. Even though Victor deserved what was coming to him, I felt a bit uneasy about giving him a taste of his own medicine. But I only had to look at the state of my mum and sister to know it had to be done.

After my dad was murdered, I'd struggled to come to terms with things. It had taken a super-human effort on my part to build a stable enough foundation beneath my feet so that I could get out of bed in the morning without the rising tide of my emotions washing me away. I couldn't let Victor undo all the progress I'd made. Rio was right. We had to fight back; if Victor thought he was the more dominant player in the game, this would just be the start of more to come.

Rio looked at his watch. 'In about half an hour, Mrs Coleman should be leaving the health club.'

My eyes settled on Mum first, then Scarlett. They looked completely traumatised, which helped me justify what was about to happen.

'Lorraine goes to Aphrodite's every Friday with her friend. They swim and have a sauna, but neither of them has achieved the body of a Greek goddess as yet.' Rio couldn't resist getting a sly dig in, and Kelsey laughed in response. He smiled back at her before rechecking the time. 'If we hurry, we'll be able to catch her before she leaves.'

'I don't even want to think about how you know all this information,' I said, blowing out a slow breath.

'We have ways and means of finding things out and making people talk,' Rio joked, raising his eyebrows up and down.

I cast my mind back to the reruns of a sitcom that my parents used to watch called 'Allo 'Allo. It was the worst comedy ever made if you asked me, but they seemed to love it. And if I closed my eyes, I bet I could still hear my dad laughing at the situations René used to get himself involved in. You would never expect a tough cookie like Dad to enjoy a programme about a café owner's life during the German occupation of France. But he had a passion for anything involving the Second World War and didn't discriminate. *Dad's Army* was another one of his favourites. I felt myself shudder at the memory of Captain Mainwaring and his troop of Home Guards.

'What do you think, Mia?' the sound of Rio's voice brought me back to reality.

'I'm sorry; I was miles away. I didn't hear what you just said.'

'So we don't lose any more time, Todd's going to stay here and watch over your mum and Scarlett so we can get on the road as we're cutting it fine. As soon as Wesley arrives, Todd will make his way towards us in case things don't go to plan and we need extra backup.'

'Do you really think that will be necessary?'

I wasn't sure how much muscle power was required to intimidate a lady of advanced years. I couldn't imagine Mrs Coleman would put up much of a fight or give Rio any trouble. Much as he was a big softie, Rio de Souza was a formidable-looking character – six feet two with biceps of steel. I didn't fancy Lorraine's chances if she tried to stand up to him.

'You can never be too careful in these situations. Remember what happened to your mum and Scarlett earlier? Don't you think that was a bit over the top?'

Rio had made a valid point, and I felt my cheeks flush. I was embarrassed that I was showing Victor's wife so much consideration under the circumstances, and any concerns I might have had for Lorraine went straight out of the window. Victor hadn't shown my mum or sister any compassion when he'd ordered his henchmen to deliver his threat. He'd used scare tactics and terrified my family to achieve the maximum effect. But in doing so, he'd thrown down the gauntlet.

'You two wait here,' Rio said after he parked the Range Rover in a shady corner of the car park. 'If there's any sign of trouble, get yourself out of here. Don't wait for me; I can take care of myself.'

I was in the front passenger seat, so I looked over my shoulder to where my sister was sitting in the back behind Rio. Kelsey and I exchanged a glance, but neither of us said a word. Rio climbed out of the car and began walking towards the main entrance. Kelsey immediately jumped out of the back and got into the driver's seat.

'What are you doing?' I asked when she began adjusting the seat.

'I just want to be prepared in case we need to make a quick getaway,' Kelsey replied, tilting the rear-view mirror downward.

I didn't try to talk her out of it; my sister handled pressure better than I did, so if one of us needed to drive away at speed, she was the better qualified of the two of us.

Rio took up position a short distance from the glass-fronted foyer. He was doing his best to be discreet, but he had the kind of memorable frame that made him stand out from the crowd, so blending into the background was a difficult feat at the best of times, aside from the fact that Aphrodite's was a female-only health club. It wasn't as though he could have just arrived for a spa treatment.

I hoped for our sake, nobody spotted him loitering outside.

Lorraine came into view with another well-groomed lady in her fifties; both of them were dressed in hideous head-to-toe matching Gucci outfits. Their tracksuits had an all-over monogram print displaying the brand's logo, and their high wedge-heeled trainers were also emblazoned with the iconic interlocking GG.

Lorraine pushed open the door and stood chatting in full view of the reception for several minutes. Rio had his phone pressed to his ear and was walking backwards and forwards as though he was engrossed in conversation, but I'd put money on the fact that there was nobody on the other end of the line. It was part of his cover story. He was primed and ready to spring into action at a moment's notice.

Kelsey and I sat in silence, observing the scene through the front windscreen. Mrs Coleman threw her head back and laughed at something her friend had just said. Then her friend checked the time on her watch, planted a kiss on each of Lorraine's cheeks before she darted off and jumped into her car. It was parked in one of the disabled bays in front of the building. I was fully aware that not all disabilities were visible, but I very much doubted that Lorraine's friend had a genuine reason to use the space. She started the engine of her white convertible Bentley and sped off with gravel flying from her tyres as though the police were in hot pursuit.

Once Mrs Coleman and her friend had parted company, Rio sprang into action. My heart began pounding as I watched Rio close in on her. He was like a panther sneaking up on an unsuspecting animal, opting for an ambush approach like any good predator. Mrs Coleman was oblivious to his presence as she placed her gym bag into the boot of her red convertible BMW.

Kelsey dropped the window so that we could hear their conversation.

'Excuse me, love, can I ask you a quick question?' Rio said before his lips stretched into a wide smile.

The boot was still open when she turned around and looked up at Rio, which provided him with some much-needed cover. Her eyes scanned over the fine specimen of a man in front of her, and she flashed him a bright smile.

'You can ask me anything you like, darling,' Lorraine flirted. Her voice had a cockney lilt to it.

The element of surprise had worked to Rio's advantage. Lorraine didn't seem to recognise him. I'd been worried that she might put two and two together and realise he was the same man that who stood in her front room yesterday, as we'd tried to extract money from her husband. Either she wasn't that bright, or it happened so frequently that she didn't bother paying any attention.

I felt a shiver run down my spine when I saw Rio point the gun at her and could only imagine what my mum and sister had gone through. Lorraine's smile slid from her face, and her jaw slackened. With her eyes fixed firmly on Rio, she placed the palms of her hand out in front of her then backed herself up against the BMW's boot. My eyes swept around the car park to check for passers-by and potential witnesses, but thankfully the place was deserted.

'Give your old man a message from my firm. If he thinks he can pull a stunt like that without any comeback, he can think again. Now do yourself a favour, close your mouth, keep it shut and get into your motor before I make an example out of you.' Rio waved the barrel of the gun at the petrified woman before lowering it. He put the gun into the waistband of his trousers and took several paces back. 'I'll be watching you, so don't try any funny business.'

Lorraine reached up with trembling fingers and pulled down the boot. As she rushed around to the driver's seat, she glanced over her shoulder to check if Rio was still there. He was rooted to the spot with his arms folded over his broad chest. As Lorraine's BMW exited the car park at breakneck speed, Kelsey started the Range Rover and drove across to collect Rio. Leaving my sister behind the wheel, he jumped into the back seat.

'I don't like having to scare women, but sometimes it's part of the job description.'

Although Rio had intimidated Lorraine, he hadn't gone overboard like Victor's two heavies who'd terrorised Mum and Scarlett.

'I think Lorraine got off lightly under the circumstances. You just did enough to send the message home to Victor loud and clear that if he wants to play dirty, we're up for a fight,' Kelsey said, glancing at Rio in the rear-view mirror.

'Victor needs to know he's not the only one who has information about family members' movements. Once you have that, you have collateral,' Rio said.

There was a lot to take in, and my temples began throbbing. I could feel a tension headache starting as Kelsey sped along the road towards home. The minute we walked through the front door, I knew something was wrong.

'Some backup you turned out to be,' Rio said to Todd when we stepped into the kitchen.

'I know; I'm sorry, mate,' Todd replied.

'Just as well, Mrs C didn't give me any lip. How come you bailed on me?' Rio crossed his arms in front of his chest and drummed his fingers on his biceps.

'Wesley's dealing with a problem at the yard, so he couldn't get away, and I didn't think I should leave Amanda and Scarlett on their own,' Todd said.

Rio shrugged his massive shoulders. 'Fair enough.'

'Anyway, how did it go?' Todd asked.

'I think I made myself clear.' Rio gave Todd a half-smile.

'Where's Scarlett?' Kelsey asked.

That was the first time Mum had looked up from the table since we'd entered the room.

'She's gone out with her friends,' Todd replied.

As Todd's words registered, Rio stared at him with dead eyes. 'And it didn't occur to you to try and stop her?' Rio shook his head and pursed his lips. His voice had a sarcastic edge to it.

'It's not Todd's fault; I told him to let her go. It will do her good to have some fun and take her mind off things,' Mum said.

49

Scarlett

I couldn't face sitting opposite Mum any longer. She'd had her hands clamped around a stone-cold mug of tea for the last half an hour while she'd stared into space, her mind no doubt fixed on what had happened earlier. But I didn't want to think about it, and the only way to stop the memory running on a continuous loop in my head was to get out of the house and focus on something different.

Todd was making me anxious. The way he kept pacing backwards and forwards in front of the full-length windows, craning his neck in every direction to check for intruders or something out of the ordinary was giving me the jitters. I needed some normality to try and take my mind off things. Otherwise, today's traumatic experience would end up haunting me for some time to come.

Mum didn't even look up from her mug when I pushed my chair back from the table and stood up. Todd glanced over at me, but I pretended not to see him as I made a hasty exit out of the kitchen. I ran up the stairs two at a time and crossed the landing before closing my bedroom door behind me.

After a quick shower, I changed into an emerald green, thigh-skimming, silk, shirt dress and black, barely-there stilettos. I applied some minimal eye makeup, and a slick of coral-coloured gloss, before grabbing a black evening bag out of my chest of drawers. Then I headed out of my room and down the stairs. Once I picked up my keys from the mosaic dish on the sideboard in the hall, I stuck my head around the kitchen door. It was as though Mum and Todd had been frozen in time. They were still in the same positions as when I left.

'I'm going to meet my friends. I won't be late,' I called, not bothering to wait for a reply before I turned on my heel.

'That's a terrible idea. I'll stop her,' Todd said.

When I heard his footsteps pace across the kitchen floor, my heart started hammering in my chest.

'No, let her go and have some fun,' I heard Mum reply before I disappeared out of the front door.

I walked down the lane and waited until I was some distance from home before I called an Uber. While I waited for it to arrive, I phoned CJ.

'I know we weren't meant to be seeing each other until later, but do you fancy meeting up now?' I asked.

'I can't at the moment; I'm at my mum and dad's,' CJ replied.

That wasn't what I wanted to hear. I was all dressed up with nowhere to go. The easiest thing to do was cancel the Uber and go back inside, but I couldn't face the doom and gloom, so instead, I got in the car and headed to CJ's apartment.

'I'm meeting my boyfriend for a drink, but I'm a bit early. Would it be possible to wait for him in the bar? He lives in one of the apartments in the complex,' I said to the receptionist at the exclusive members' club. All residents automatically became members when they bought a property.

I couldn't for the life of me remember which number CJ lived at, so I hoped the woman didn't ask. I'd only been to his bachelor pad a couple of times before, and I'd had more important things on my mind than memorising his address.

'That's fine,' the receptionist said, ushering me through to the Residents' Club Lounge.

The eighteenth-floor bar had a large terrace that offered panoramic views of Canary Wharf, the Thames, and the city skyline. I walked up to the bar without feeling self-conscious. I was on my own as the place was deserted. But then again, it was four o'clock in the afternoon, so most of the residents would still be at work, I reasoned.

'What can I get you?' the bartender asked.

'I'll have an Aperol Spritz, please.'

I took my drink out onto the terrace so that I could enjoy the heat but decided to sit under the shade of a parasol. Being a redhead, I only had to look at the sun and my pale skin burnt to a crisp. After the first couple of sips, I started to feel queasy and out of sorts. The Prosecco bubbles fizzed inside me, making the contents of my stomach cartwheel. What did I expect after the day I'd had? My nerves were in tatters, and I'd thought a drink might help to settle them, but it was having the opposite effect. I put the glass down on the table and walked across the terrace to the railing when something far below caught my eye. CJ had just stepped out of the back passenger seat of a car and was heading towards the building.

'CJ,' I called at the top of my voice while I waved my arm backwards and forwards.

I was trying to get his attention, but he couldn't hear me; the sound of London's traffic drowned out my voice. My heart began pounding at the sight of him. Leaving my drink unfinished on the table, I picked up my bag and rushed out of the members' club.

'Thanks for letting me wait in the bar; my boyfriend's just arrived,' I said to the receptionist before I paced over to the lifts.

I pressed the up arrow repeatedly while I waited for it to arrive, then got inside before the doors had fully opened and hit the button for the twenty-second floor. I couldn't wait to feel CJ's lips on mine and his strong arms wrapped around me.

'Surprise!' I grinned when the doors opened, and CJ stepped out onto the landing a few moments later.

I was delighted that I'd managed to beat him to the top floor. But he didn't look too pleased to see me, and for one awful moment, I thought I was going to burst into tears. It had been such a stressful day, and everything was getting on top of me.

'What are you doing here?' CJ asked.

'I had to get out of the house,' I replied, trying to pull myself together. I'd been hoping he would throw his arms around me and smother me with kisses, but he didn't do either.

'How come?' CJ looked over his shoulder at me as he put his key in the lock.

'It's such a beautiful day. I was going stir-crazy being cooped up inside.'

I didn't want to tell CJ the real reason I wanted to get out of the house because it might put him off having a relationship with me. I would think twice about getting involved with somebody who got held up by a masked gunman on the way back from the supermarket. Come to think of it, I'd go one step further and run a mile. Nobody in their right mind would want to get mixed up in the sort of drama my family had been through in recent months.

'What happened to your car?' I asked once we were inside.

CJ's eyebrows knitted together, and his dark eyes bored into mine before he replied, 'What do you mean?'

'I was on the terrace in the Residents' Club Lounge, and I saw you getting out of the back of a silver car.'

The look of confusion slid from CJ's face. 'So you've been spying on me, have you?'

'Hardly,' I replied, putting my bag down on the cream stone work surface. 'I was just about to take some photos of the view when I spotted you arriving.'

I'd come over to CJ's apartment hoping to take my mind off things, but he obviously wasn't happy that I'd turned up uninvited, and there was a tense atmosphere between us.

CJ ran his fingers through his dark hair, then he opened the fridge and got himself a bottle of Beck's. 'Do you want a glass of wine?'

'No thanks.'

My last sip of alcohol hadn't sat well in my stomach, so I didn't want to risk being sick all over his new flat if it didn't agree with me.

'Suit yourself,' CJ replied in a surly tone.

Since I'd been on my course, I'd been trying to develop a thick skin; performing arts tutors weren't known for their tact or diplomacy and didn't massage their students' egos or give out needless compliments. They gave you the cold, hard facts, nothing more, nothing less. But it was easier said than done. I had to admit I was finding that side of things difficult to handle; I was used to being wrapped in cotton wool, and any form of rejection had a sting in its tail.

'Is something the matter?' I asked, then braced myself for CJ's reply. He seemed very off with me, and I suddenly wished I hadn't paid him a surprise visit.

'No.'

CJ's one-word answer did nothing to put my mind at rest or thaw the frosty atmosphere that was stretching out between us. I could take a hint and wasn't about to stay where I wasn't welcome.

'I've obviously caught you at a bad time, so I'll leave you to it.'

I picked my bag up, and as I began walking towards the front door, CJ caught hold of my arm and pulled me around to face him.

'Don't go. I'm sorry, I'm being an arsehole, but I had a stressful day at work, and I wasn't expecting you to be waiting outside my apartment,' CJ said.

Although it was probably unintentional, he'd made me feel like some kind of deranged stalker and that suddenly made me doubt if his feelings towards me were genuine. I'd thought he liked me as much as I liked him, but now I wasn't so sure. Up until this moment, CJ had been saying all the things I wanted to hear; I'd thought we were on the same page and had a bright future ahead of us. Now he'd gone cold. It was like he'd suddenly hit the brakes and veered off in a different direction. I couldn't work it out. Maybe it was too much, too soon. Then again, it was a common conception that men were from Mars and women were from Venus; both sexes were programmed very differently. Wasn't that the truth?

'You never did say what happened to your car,' I said when we stepped out onto the balcony.

'It was a company car. My dad's traded it in, but the new one hasn't arrived as yet,' CJ replied. 'We'll have to rely on taxis for the time being to get around.'

That wouldn't be a problem. CJ's apartment was in a central location; everything was on his doorstep.

'I'm really looking forward to going to the Shard tomorrow. I'm literally counting the hours,' I said, not that I was wishing my life away.

'Me too,' CJ replied.

Kelsey was on the other side of the front door when I opened it. I nearly jumped out of my skin at the sight of her. 'You scared the life out of me,' I said, covering my pounding heart with my hand.

'Where have you been?' Kelsey asked in the manner of an outraged parent.

'I went out for a drink,' I replied.

'With CJ?' Kelsey probed.

'No.'

I wasn't going to feel guilty that I'd just lied to my sister. She was being such a bitch to me recently, and I was fed up with her meddling in my personal life. I didn't try and tell her what to do, so she should show me the same courtesy.

A rift had opened up between me, my mum, and my sisters since they'd cut me out of the family business. They were keeping me in the dark about everything, which was infuriating, so I'd decided to adopt the same tactic. If you can't beat them, join them.

To be fair, Mum was paving the way to ease the tension, doing her best to smooth things over with me. She was a peacemaker with years of practice under her belt. Defusing awkward situations was her forte. My sisters and I had such different personalities, and we squabbled endlessly when we were children.

What was Kelsey's problem? Since when did she decide what I could do in my free time? Although Todd had advised against it and had tried to stop me, Mum had let me go out, so Kelsey should mind her own business and wind her neck in. Even though I was sure Mum had been concerned for my safety, she hadn't wanted to rock the boat, so she'd overruled Todd. I'd had her blessing; I hadn't done anything wrong. Kelsey would do well to remember that.

Mia always had the good sense to stay out of the beef, but Kelsey couldn't help herself. She was the instigator and kept wading in with her opinions whether I asked for them or not. I was sick of it; it was driving a wedge between us. By the way she was carrying on, our argument wouldn't be resolved any time soon.

50

Mia

After I got into bed, I reached over and kissed my long-suffering husband. Today's events had shaken me to the core and made me appreciate the important things in life. The things I too often took for granted.

'I know I don't tell you often enough just how much you mean to me,' I said, resting my head on Jack's bare chest. 'But I love you with all my heart.'

'I love you too,' Jack replied.

The strength of our marriage had been tested when I'd found out that Jack had been lying to me. Discovering the truth about the firm and the way Dad made his money had shaken me to the core and had sent shock waves through our relationship. But Jack had been there for me through thick and thin and was my rock. I wasn't happy about it, but I understood why he'd kept the details from me; he'd been trying to shield me from the situation.

I'd been neglecting our relationship recently; focusing on the firm was taking up all my free time and every ounce of my energy. I'd thrown myself into the challenge hoping it would give me a welcome distraction from the grieving process, but in an effort to suppress my feelings, I couldn't help wondering if I'd taken on too much too soon. Now that the war with the Colemans was escalating, I found facing the dark side of the business daunting.

'Your mum and Scarlett had a lucky escape today. Now do you understand why I'm not happy about you being involved in your dad's firm? You could be the next one in the firing line,' Jack said before he tightened his arms around me.

Jack took his role of protector seriously. He promised my dad he'd take good care of me on my wedding day, and he hadn't let him down. But Jack couldn't guard me entirely from the threats, risks, and problems that life threw in my path every day of the week. Even though I valued his support more than I could say, I had to stand on my own two feet.

'I know you're worried about me, but Rio's got everything under control.'

'Seriously, Mia, you're kidding yourself if you think that; you've landed yourself right in the middle of a turf war. It was no accident your dad was killed in cold blood,' Jack said.

I felt myself freeze, and tears stabbed at my eyes. I was well aware of that, so I didn't know why Jack felt the need to point it out. Dad's murder was a sensitive subject and not one I talked about willingly.

'I'm not trying to upset you, but I want you to face facts. Davie had a lot of enemies, and the people he did business with weren't nice individuals; they were shady characters.

Doorstep loans and money laundering are illegal practices,' Jack said, wriggling out from under me and turning onto his side. His blue eyes bored into mine as he gauged my reaction. 'Trying to carry on the firm where your dad left off is a bad idea. You should get out while you still can. You and Kelsey are no match for the Colemans. Men like that routinely beat up, shoot and torture their rivals. If Victor had given a different order today, your mum and Scarlett wouldn't have walked away.'

Tears started rolling down my cheeks as Jack's words hit home. Life was fragile, and all of us were vulnerable. I'd listened to what he had to say and taken his advice on board; he had my best interests at heart. But Rio had said caving in to Victor's demands was the last thing we should do. If we didn't make a stand, he'd think he'd got the upper hand. I didn't know what to do; two conflicting opinions complicated the situation instead of making it clearer.

'Please think about what I've said. You've got nothing to prove, Mia. Walk away from the firm before it's too late,' Jack said, then he planted a kiss on the top of my head.

'I appreciate what you're trying to do, but I'm going into this with my eyes wide open.'

Deep down, I knew the only way to win the war with the Colemans was to take them on. Discovering the truth behind Dad's murder had given me the drive to fight for justice instead of crumbling into a heap. The feud wasn't really about recovering the money; it was about getting even with the men who'd robbed my family of the person we all loved dearly.

51

Scarlett

CJ opened his front door and pulled me over the threshold. We were meant to be going to the Shard this evening, but I couldn't wait, so I phoned him and told him I needed to see him urgently.

'What's up? You look like you've been crying. Is everything OK?' CJ asked.

I was balling my hands in the fabric of my summer dress in CJ's hallway, trying to pluck up the courage to tell him what was going on. CJ took hold of my hand and led me through to the living area. He took a seat on the black leather sofa then pulled me down onto his lap. I stared into his handsome face for several seconds before I managed to speak.

'I've just found out that I'm pregnant,' I blurted out before bursting into tears.

I didn't know if it was my hormones or the pressure of the situation, but either way, I had no control over my emotions and started sobbing my heart out.

'Don't cry, Scarlett.' CJ pulled me towards him and wrapped his arms around me.

We'd only been together for four weeks, so the timing couldn't be worse. Mine and CJ's brand-new relationship had been about fun and spontaneity. I was gobsmacked when I found out I was expecting his baby; the unexpected news shook me to the core.

'I'm not trying to trap you. I didn't plan this,' I said, not knowing what was going through CJ's mind.

'I know that.'

I'd been shitting myself about dropping the bombshell, but so far, CJ was handling it well. Far better than me, in fact. The news was life changing; it would end my plans to work on the West End stage, at least in the short term.

'This might be a stupid question, but are you sure?' CJ stepped back and held me at arm's length as he looked deeply into my eyes.

I'd been in such a hurry to share my secret with somebody that I'd forgotten to fill CJ in on the background.

'Sorry, I should have explained. Last night I realised that my period was late. My boobs were incredibly tender, so I'd thought it was about to start. When nothing had happened by this morning, I decided to buy a pregnancy test.'

I'd been feeling incredibly nauseous and out of sorts yesterday, but I'd thought that was due to the ordeal Mum and I had been through. It only struck me later on that my period was late. I never expected the test would turn out to be positive. I just wanted to rule it out and quash the niggling doubts that had started entering my head.

'I peed on the stick and followed the instructions to the letter, pacing around the bathroom, waiting for the time to be up. When I glanced at the test, I couldn't believe what I was seeing. Two blue lines were staring back at me.'

'So that means you're pregnant, right?'

I nodded.

'I'm not trying to be insensitive by asking this, but do you think there's any chance the test could be wrong?' CJ stared at me while he waited for me to reply.

I shook my head. I didn't think CJ was being insensitive. He was being incredibly level-headed, which was more than could be said for me. I was in a blind panic.

'I thought the very same thing. I was sure I'd done something wrong, and the result must have been a mistake, so I hot-footed it back down to Boots and bought five more tests. I got a few strange looks from the man who served me, but it was none of his business. I nearly gave him a mouthful, but I didn't want to draw attention to myself.'

'Why don't you do another test so that we know for sure?' CJ suggested.

'I already have. All five of them were positive. I still didn't want to believe it, so I phoned the doctor to make an emergency appointment.'

It was at moments like this that I was glad Dad had taken out expensive private healthcare for us. Who knows how long I would have waited to get an NHS appointment?

'I phoned you as soon as I came out of the doctor's office. She was really lovely about it, but she confirmed what I already knew. I felt a bit embarrassed when I went to see her with red-rimmed eyes. It was obvious I'd been crying. But she sat me down and explained that home pregnancy testing kits are so accurate these days the doctor doesn't usually bother to test a patient themselves. I told her I really needed to hear confirmation from somebody official. So she did another one just to put my mind at rest. And guess what? It was positive.'

I let out a groan as I dabbed at my eyes with a soggy tissue. CJ squeezed my hand in a show of support, which was just what I needed.

'The doctor said there's no doubt about it. I'm six weeks pregnant.'

I saw a look of confusion pass over CJ's face as he digested my words. My pulse rate went into overdrive; I was scared he didn't believe me.

'I know what you're thinking; I thought the very same thing – something doesn't add up. We've only been together for a month, so that would be impossible. The doctor told me they calculate the due date from the first day of your last period rather than from conception.'

CJ blew out a breath. 'You must have got pregnant straight away.'

'I didn't know how I was going to break the news to you. I wasn't sure how you'd react. But I knew I had to do it sooner rather than later. I'm sorry I've ruined our day.'

'You haven't. You're pregnant, Scarlett. You haven't got a terminal illness.' CJ smiled.

I ran a protective hand over my stomach as the realisation started to sink in. We'd only been a couple for a month, so being thrown together into a situation like this would either help us get to know each other quickly or scare the father of my child off completely. Whether CJ decided to stick around or not, I was going through with the pregnancy. At the back of my mind, I knew I had to be prepared that things between us could change. Having a baby would impact our relationship massively, and the relationship might not survive, so I might have to go it alone.

'I don't know whether you're prepared to stand by me or not, but either way, I'm going to have the baby. You can leave if you want to. I won't hold it against you.'

The last part of the sentence came out as a long sob as my emotions got the better of me. On the way over to CJ's apartment, I'd worked out exactly how I was going to tell him. I'd decided to be rational and not put pressure on him, but all of that went out the window when it came to it. So much for not pressuring CJ into staying with me.

'Don't be so stupid; I'm not going anywhere,' CJ reassured, pulling me towards him and planting a kiss on the side of my head. 'I have to admit I'm a bit shocked, but I'm not unhappy about the news. Everything will be all right.'

In the hours that followed, I had a few wobbles about my pregnancy and had become a tiny bit unhinged, to say the least, mainly to do with what other people would say. CJ was endlessly patient and kept reassuring me that he was happy about the baby and wanted us to stay together, which was one less thing for me to worry about.

'Do you mind if I stay here tonight? I can't face going home at the moment.'

'No worries. Stay as long as you like.'

That was music to my ears. If one of my family clapped eyes on me, they would know something was wrong. I knew I wouldn't be able to hide it. Mum wasn't expecting me back anyway. I'd told her I was going out to celebrate the end of my course with my uni friends and would be back sometime tomorrow.

'We might need to reschedule going to the Shard. I'm not really dressed for the occasion.' I glanced down at the baggy white T-shirt, pale pink jeans and flat pointed slingbacks I was wearing.

CJ disappeared out of the living area and reappeared a few minutes later, holding the black strings of a floral cardboard carrier bag. 'I was going to give you this later, but you might as well have it now.'

I peered inside, then took out the bright pink tissue paper parcel and tore the wrapper off. 'Oh my God, it's beautiful,' I said when I spotted the fabulous dress.

'Happy anniversary,' CJ said. 'I hope you like it.'

'I love it!' The white mini dress had a high neck with a keyhole back and colourful wildflower embroidery all over it.

'I bought it from a little boutique on the King's Road.' CJ smiled.

Dinner at the Aqua Shard didn't disappoint. CJ and I both chose the same thing; either that was a coincidence, or it proved the point that we were incredibly in tune with each other. We ate Cornish mackerel with red chilli marmalade, roasted English lamb saddle, caramelised onions and new potatoes, followed by apricot almond tart with apricot sorbet. I'd swapped champagne and cocktails for mocktails but hadn't missed the taste of the alcohol at all. In fact, when I'd taken a sip yesterday, it had made my stomach cartwheel. I'd thought it was because my nerves were in tatters, but I knew differently now. I placed my hands over my full-to-burst stomach and imagined what it would be like when instead of food, a developing baby was making my skin stretch.

I looked over the table, and CJ smiled at me before taking hold of my hand.

'You look beautiful. Are you happy?' he asked.

'I'm ecstatic,' I replied, and my face broke into a cheek-aching grin.

To think this morning I'd thought being pregnant was the end of the world and life as I knew it was over for good. CJ had been incredible – such a calming influence. He was going to make a fantastic dad. He'd taken everything in his stride, unlike myself who was terrified by the whole prospect of motherhood. I'd felt too young and unprepared when I'd first tried to get my head around the fact and was close to having a full-blown panic attack when the doctor confirmed the news. It had required more courage than I'd ever had to summon to tell CJ what had happened. Opening-night nerves paled into insignificance by comparison. But he'd taken me by surprise when he'd shown a level of maturity I hadn't managed to muster and been the loving, supportive partner I desperately needed him to be. In the space of just a day, my future seemed so much clearer, and I couldn't be happier that CJ wanted to be part of it.

There were no guarantees in life. Just because we hadn't been together very long didn't mean we couldn't make our relationship last. Most people, I was sure, would predict disaster would strike under the circumstances. But nobody knew where having a child together might lead us. I hoped we were going to live happily ever after.

'What would you like to do now?' CJ asked after he settled the eye-watering bill.

Being active by nature, I fancied taking a stroll to walk off some of the food we'd eaten. 'Why don't we head down to

Tower Millennium Pier and see if we can get on one of the evening cruises? They're great. I've been on one before. They take you down the River Thames, and you get to see all the sights of London from the water.'

'Sounds like a great idea. Just give me a minute. I need to make a quick phone call.'

CJ got up from the table and walked away before I could reply. I wondered why he couldn't have just made the call from the table, but I wasn't about to dwell on it. After a bumpy start, the day had turned out to be fantastic, and it wasn't over yet. I loved being on the water, so rounding off the day with a river cruise was the perfect way to end the evening. This would be the first time I got to spend the whole night with CJ and wake up in his arms.

'Are you ready to make tracks?' CJ asked when he reappeared.

It was a beautiful evening. Dusk was falling, but it was still warm from the day's heat. CJ and I were strolling hand in hand towards the river and had just turned onto Hay's Lane when he stopped walking, turned to face me and slid his arms around my waist. I closed my eyes and got lost in the moment as he kissed me.

My eyes sprang open, and I pulled away from CJ as two motorbikes roared into the road. A rider and passenger were on the first bike, and just a single person was on the second. CJ had his back to them as they sped towards us, mounted the pavement, and without even slowing down, the passenger leant over, grabbed hold of the strap of my white leather bag and attempted to pull it off my shoulder. My heart pounded against my ribs as I instinctively clung to it with both hands. The passenger wouldn't let go either, and I was dragged along behind the bike for several seconds before the man managed to wrench it out of my grip. The second bike was zig-zagging behind us and swerved right next to me before accelerating away.

CJ took off in hot pursuit as I stood on the pavement shell-shocked. 'Call the police,' he shouted over his shoulder as he disappeared around the corner and out of sight.

'Are you OK?' a lady asked.

I didn't reply; I was in shock and felt like I was having an out-of-body experience. Everything seemed to be happening in slow motion. I began shaking, probably an effect of the adrenaline rush.

'I need an ambulance and the police, please,' her partner said when he made the 999 call.

I wondered why the man had asked for an ambulance, then I felt a dull ache starting to pulsate and this warm sensation running down my right side. 'Oh my, God!' I started screaming when I saw the blood seeping across the fabric of my beautiful white dress, but I wasn't sure what had happened. Then I felt a pain, which quickly started to intensify and suddenly ramped up to a red-hot, burning sensation like somebody had set fire to my insides.

'There were three men on motorbikes. The men on the first bike stole the lady's handbag, and then the driver of the second bike stabbed her in the stomach with a long-bladed knife,' I heard the man say.

Every ounce of energy seeped out of me. I started to feel faint, then my legs buckled under my weight, and I collapsed on the pavement. The man had told the operator I'd been stabbed, but it took a moment for that to register because I hadn't felt the knife going in.

Passers-by gathered around me. As I lay on my side, I clamped my hands over my stomach to try and protect my unborn baby. The first lady on the scene crouched down next to me, placed her cardigan over my wound, and began putting pressure on it to try and stem the flow. She didn't seem to care that she was ruining her clothes.

'There's so much blood,' I wept as it started to cover my hands and drip through my fingers, leaving a pool on the paving slabs. I thought of my dad lying on the altar on Mia's wedding day and wondered if I was going to bleed out on the pavement. Then I began wavering in and out of consciousness.

'You're going to be OK. Stay with me.'

I opened my eyes and saw the lady patting my hand.

'Try and stay awake. The ambulance is on its way,' the lady said, doing her best to reassure me.

'I'm pregnant,' I sobbed as I stared into the face of this kind stranger. Then my vision blurred, and I had trouble focusing.

'Hold on; help is on the way,' she said.

I heard the sirens growing closer, but then my hearing started to fade, and everything went black.

52

Mia

Mum, Jack, and I were in the living room watching *Meet Joe Black*, a brilliant film I'd seen on countless occasions. Well, to be more accurate, I was sitting in the same room as the others, but I was staring blankly at the huge TV screen when the knock on the door came.

'I'll get it,' Jack said, getting up from the sofa we were lounging side by side on.

I could hear muffled voices in the hallway, but I couldn't make out what they were saying. When Jack returned to the living room a few moments later, accompanied by two uniformed police officers, my blood ran cold. They either had some news about my dad's case, or something had happened to one of my siblings. Kelsey was hosting an event for some reality TV stars, but Todd was accompanying her, so she should have been in safe hands. Scarlett was at more risk; she was out celebrating the end of her course with her uni friends. Students had a habit of throwing caution to the wind.

I got a sick feeling in my stomach when Jack sat down next to me and took hold of my hand. Instinct was telling me the officers hadn't come here to talk about the murder investigation. My heart began pounding in my chest as I watched the younger policeman shift from foot to foot. I glanced over to where my mum was sitting with her long legs stretched out in front of her, crossed at the ankles. She seemed confused by their presence but didn't seem concerned by the unexpected visit. She wasn't thinking straight. After yesterday's events, her mind was all over the place.

'There is no easy way to say this other than directly,' the older policeman said, and I felt my breath catch in my throat. 'Earlier this evening, your daughter, Scarlett, was mugged and stabbed with a large-bladed knife.'

Mum was out of her seat in an instant, as the penny finally dropped that something was wrong.

'Oh my God!' Mum's hands flew up and covered her mouth. 'Is she de...' Mum couldn't finish the sentence, but it was obvious what she was trying to ask.

The policeman shook his head slowly. I knew there was going to be a but; there was always a but in a situation like this. A knot twisted in my stomach as fear washed over me.

'Is she going to be OK?' Mum rephrased her sentence, steadying herself on the arm of the grey velvet chair while she waited for the officer's reply.

'It's too early to say. Scarlett was stabbed in the stomach and has lost a lot of blood. She's been taken to hospital and is currently undergoing lifesaving surgery.' The policeman bowed his head, pausing to allow us to absorb the information.

I knew the officers were here to deliver the facts, but I

sometimes wished they would sugar-coat the truth. The harsh reality was difficult to swallow. How could my twenty-year-old sister be on the brink of death? The thought was too awful to process. Why didn't one of her friends phone us?

'You said Scarlett was mugged. Do you know what happened?' I asked, suddenly finding my voice.

'According to witnesses, she was walking along Hay's Lane, heading towards the Thames with a young man when two motorbikes came up behind them and mounted the pavement. One of the men tried to snatch Scarlett's bag, but she resisted, so the rider on the second bike produced a large-bladed knife and plunged it into her stomach.'

'Oh, dear God,' Mum said as silent tears ran in rivers down her cheeks.

I was too numb to cry, but I felt myself shaking uncontrollably.

'Which hospital did they take her to?' Mum asked. The colour had drained from her face, and she looked like she might keel over any second.

'St Thomas's,' the older police officer replied.

Without hearing any more details, I knew my sister wasn't a random victim of crime. There was more to it. I was certain this was the Colemans' payback. Her encounter with Rio had rattled Lorraine, and Victor wouldn't want to lose face, so he'd retaliated. But by hurting Scarlett, he'd notched things up a gear.

The room fell into silence as we all became lost in our thoughts. The news was so unexpected and shocking we were completely unprepared to hear it, let alone believe it was possible. Five minutes ago, we were watching the

Saturday night film on TV, and now we were having to come to terms with the fact that my youngest sister had been stabbed. My eyes fixed on the two officers standing side by side. Although I was sure they'd been in this situation many times before, they looked uncomfortable to be here. It must be a horrible part of their job, but from the family's point of view, it was better that the bad news was delivered in person than received in a phone call from a faceless voice.

'Have you caught the people responsible?' Jack asked.

'Not yet, but a team of officers from the Serious Crime Unit are gathering information regarding the incident via CCTV, and we'll be appealing for witnesses to come forward.'

The policeman's words didn't fill me with confidence. The investigation into my dad's murder was going nowhere. Even after all this time, they were still no closer to catching the person responsible for his death.

'Can we see her?' I asked, suddenly feeling the need to be close to my sister.

'She's in surgery at the moment, but we can take you to the hospital. The doctors will want to speak to you,' the older officer replied.

'I'll phone Kelsey and let her know what's going on,' I said as Jack went to lock up the house. Mum stood by the chair, looking dazed in a world of her own. I let out a sigh of frustration when my call connected to Kelsey's voicemail. 'Phone me as soon as you get this message.'

'I'll get hold of Rio and tell him what's going on,' Jack said as we were preparing to leave the house.

'I'd appreciate that,' Mum said as she battled to regain her composure.

'Consider it done,' Jack offered Mum a half-smile before making the call. 'I don't want to go into details over the phone, but Scarlett has been stabbed, and she's in a bad way. They've taken her to St Thomas's Hospital. Can you meet us there? Bring Todd with you and get Wesley over here to keep watch on the house.'

Jack spoke with confidence; he was a good person to have around in a crisis, and his analytical mind had gone into overdrive. Problem-solving and decision-making came naturally to him, so he'd taken control of the situation. Mum and I were in a trance-like state and in no condition to think straight. I was proud of my husband. He'd stepped up to the mark and organised everything.

Jack ended the call, and a few moments later, we were in the back of a squad car being driven to St Thomas's Hospital. We sat shoulder to shoulder on the journey in complete silence, lost in our thoughts. There had been no build-up to the policemen's visit, so we'd had no time to prepare mentally or emotionally. As I gripped my husband's hand, anxiety started building up inside me, twisting itself into knots in the pit of my stomach. I was trying my best to remain hopeful, but not knowing what we'd be faced with when we got to the hospital made it a harrowing journey. All the time, I kept thinking, *Please don't die on the operating table, Scarlett.*

The police car dropped us at the entrance of St Thomas's Hospital. Rio had arrived before us and was waiting outside, pacing backwards and forwards in front of the building.

'Where's Todd?' Jack asked.

'He's with Kelsey, but he didn't pick up when I tried to call him, so I've left him a message,' Rio replied.

As Kelsey's phone had gone straight to voicemail too, for a split second, I wondered if something had happened to them. Then I remembered the event they were attending was at an undisclosed location; she'd been very cagey about where they were spending the evening when she'd left the house, which seemed suspicious the more I thought about it. One of Kelsey's favourite pastimes was bragging about the star-studded parties she hosted at prestigious venues. She loved to name-drop and wouldn't usually miss an opportunity to share all the details with anyone willing to listen.

'I'm so sorry, Amanda,' Rio said as Mum approached. 'We've let Davie down.' Rio bowed his head in shame.

Mum reached forward and squeezed his forearm. 'No, you haven't. You've been a tower of strength to all of us since he died, so I don't want to hear you talking like that again.' Mum gave him a weak smile before she turned to look at her son-in-law.

Jack walked into the foyer first, and I filed in behind him, with Mum and Rio bringing up the rear. The smell of disinfectant hit me smack in the face the moment the automatic door slid open, assaulting my olfactory system. I knew it was necessary; hospitals were full of germs and pathogens that needed keeping at bay for everyone's safety. But entering the sterile environment with undertones of artificial chemical scents triggered involuntary memories of negative childhood events. It used to terrify me if we went to visit someone who was sick enough to be admitted to a ward. I hated stepping over the threshold of a hospital at the best of times because I associated it with sickness and death. Now that I had to face the prospect of losing my youngest sister, it made this particular visit even more traumatic.

Jack walked up to the reception and gave Scarlett's name. The woman behind the desk got up and escorted us into a side room. We still didn't know if my sister was alive or dead. All of us were in a state of shock. The news had numbed us to the core. Everything seemed surreal like it was happening to somebody else, and we were just spectators.

'Take a seat in here. One of the doctors will come and see you shortly,' the receptionist said before she left.

The worst thing about being in the room apart from the harsh fluorescent lighting was that we didn't know what was happening. The waiting was a new kind of torture. It seemed to go on forever. Eventually, the door opened and a white-coated doctor appeared. As he approached us, I tried to pre-empt what he was about to say by the expression on his face.

'Your daughter has sustained severe, life-threatening injuries,' the doctor said.

'Please don't let Scarlett die. You have to save her,' Mum begged.

'The surgeons are doing everything they can to stabilise her. I'll update you as soon as I have more news, but prepare yourself for a long night,' the doctor said before leaving us alone.

Umpteen cups of barely palatable coffee later, I got to my feet. I needed some air. 'I'm going to try to get hold of Kelsey again,' I said.

But I wasn't very hopeful; she wasn't answering her phone. I'd left her countless messages at this stage and was preparing to leave another when to my surprise, she picked up the call.

'You've left me a gazillion cryptic messages. What's the problem?' Kelsey asked, clearly annoyed that I was disturbing her Saturday night.

'More champagne?' I heard a man's voice utter in the background.

'As if you need to ask. Fill her up.' Kelsey laughed before two glasses clinked together. 'Well, what's so important that you had to call me twenty times on a Saturday night?' Kelsey asked.

I inhaled a deep breath and held it for a moment as I tried to compose myself. Now that I was faced with it, I was scared to give her the dreadful news. Once I said it out loud, it would force me to believe it was true.

'Scarlett's been stabbed,' I blurted out as tears began streaming down my cheeks.

'Jesus, is she OK?'

'No, she's being operated on at the moment, but it's touch and go. She's fighting for her life,' I sobbed.

'Which hospital did they take her to?' Kelsey's voice wavered as her jovial mood took a nosedive.

'St Thomas's.'

53

Kelsey

'Come back to bed. I haven't finished with you yet,' Todd said as I ended the call to Mia.

I stood in the centre of the hotel room in a state of shock, gripping my mobile in one hand and my glass of champagne in the other.

'Kelsey, What's up?' Todd asked.

Realising that something was wrong, he'd thrown back the covers and jumped out of bed and was now standing in front of me as naked as the day he was born. Todd held on to my forearms, trying to get my attention, but I couldn't seem to focus on what he was saying. Thoughts were whirring around in my head at a million miles an hour.

Todd prised the glass out of my hand. 'What's the matter, Kelsey? I can't help you if you don't tell me what's going on.'

I looked up into his handsome face. 'It's Scarlett,' I said. The words caught in my throat then I felt my eyes fill up with tears before they started rolling down my cheeks.

'What's happened?' Todd asked with a sense of urgency in his voice.

'She's been stabbed,' I blurted out.

'Is she OK?' Todd's dark brown eyes fixed on mine, but I didn't need to reply to him. He could see from my expression that things were far from good.

My face crumpled, and I began to sob.

Todd pulled me into his arms and placed a kiss on the side of my head before he walked over to the bedside cabinet and picked up his mobile.

'Rio, what's going on? Kelsey said Scarlett's been stabbed.'

I couldn't work out what Rio was saying as Todd had the phone clamped to his ear while he paced around the hotel room, but I could hear he was shouting.

'Get dressed, Kelsey; we need to go to St Thomas's straight away,' Todd said, reverting to military mode at the flick of an internal switch.

Todd threw his clothes on in record time, but I couldn't seem to manage the simple task. Todd had to dress me like I was a small child; my fingers were shaking uncontrollably, making the trivial job of fastening buttons completely impossible.

Todd checked around the room to make sure we had all our belongings, then he began pacing along the landing, trailing me behind him. Once we got to the car, he fastened my seatbelt before we made the short journey to the hospital. Rio was waiting outside to meet us. Todd let go of my hand when he spotted the unmistakable frame of my dad's right-hand man in the distance.

'Why the fuck weren't you answering your phone?' Rio

squared up to Todd. 'You know you need to be contactable at all times when you're on duty.'

Todd chewed on the inside of his cheek as he faced Rio; to my relief, he didn't offer an explanation as to why his phone had been switched off this evening.

Rio's words hit me like a freight train. Todd wasn't the only guilty party. My phone had been switched off too. It was the first time we'd hooked up since we'd fallen out, and we didn't want to be disturbed. How were we to know something like this would happen? A pang of guilt stabbed at my conscience. While everyone was gathered at the hospital anxiously waiting for news, I was living it up, totally oblivious to the fact that Scarlett was hovering between life and death.

'You'd better have a good reason for not answering my calls,' Rio said. I felt my pulse rate speed up as Todd's lips parted as though he was preparing to speak. But thankfully, Rio put his hand out to silence him. 'I don't want to hear your lame excuses now; save them till later.'

'The party I hosted tonight was for some very high-profile celebs. All members of staff had to have their phones switched off; that's why neither of us were able to pick up,' I said, feeling the need to speak up. I'd been put on the spot, and that was the most feasible answer I could think of in the time frame.

'That's a real problem, Kelsey, but now isn't the right time to discuss it,' Rio replied.

Todd shook his head. 'We should have known something like this would happen. Scarlett shouldn't have been out without a security presence, especially at a time like this, but I can't be in two places at once, and Davie said to treat Kelsey as the priority.'

Todd was trying to justify why my sister was out in central London without protection, but I hadn't been working tonight, so he could have gone with her if I hadn't booked us into a hotel. The whole thing was a mess. None of this would have happened if I hadn't been sleeping with our bodyguard behind my mum's back. It was my fault Scarlett was on the operating table. I had her blood on my hands. Now I could only hope and pray she lived to see another day.

I had to stop myself from letting out a sigh of relief when Rio turned on his heel and disappeared through the automatic door of the entrance. I couldn't help noticing before he walked away that his dark eyes were glistening with tears. I hadn't taken Rio as the sentimental type, but I knew my sisters and I were more than his former employer's daughters; we were like family to him, the children he'd never had.

As soon as I walked into the room, the feeling of utter desperation smothered me like a fire blanket extinguishing flames. The air was suffocating; every corner of the small space was filled with my family's despair. They looked broken, and for one awful moment, I thought there had been an update on my sister's condition, but I was too scared to ask.

Mia was on her feet in an instant. She rushed past Rio and Todd and threw her arms around me. Relief flooded my body when I realised she wasn't angry with me for not returning her calls sooner. She knew how close I was to

Scarlett; if I'd known for one second that my younger sister had been attacked, I would have dropped everything to be by her side.

'Thank God you made it,' Mia said, burying her face into my hair.

I pulled myself out of my older sister's embrace and looked into her eyes. 'Is there any news?'

Mia shook her head.

'Have you seen Scarlett yet?'

'No, she's still in surgery. It's been hours now. What if she doesn't pull through?'

Mia was looking to me for reassurance, so I said what was expected even though I wasn't sure I believed the words as they came tumbling out of my mouth. 'She will; Scarlett Saunders is a fighter.' I'd done my best to sound optimistic, but I didn't think I'd been very convincing.

Mia gave me a weak smile before she crossed the room and sat down next to Mum. I followed in her footsteps a few moments later, pulling a plastic chair over so that I could sit on the other side of our mum. I leant towards her, threw my arm around her shoulder and kissed her soft cheek. Mum didn't even acknowledge me but continued staring into space, gripping onto a disintegrating tissue as though her life depended on it. She was clinging on so tightly, no doubt willing my sister to hold on. Life was fragile, and a person's grasp on it could change in an instant. I couldn't imagine what was going through her head right now. It was bad enough for Mia and I, but it must be ten times worse for Mum. It went against nature; a parent shouldn't outlive their child.

As the hours dragged by, a whole range of emotions

began swimming around inside me. I struggled to keep my head above the rising tide of sadness, anger, numbness and guilt that kept threatening to pull me under. I knew it was essential to stay positive, but it was virtually impossible to do so when surrounded by so much negative energy. It was a challenging time for all of us, and we all had our own way of dealing with the stress. Mia's was palpable. She was shaking like a leaf. I could feel the tremor of her chair vibrating against the solid floor. Rio, in contrast, was pacing the floor with his fists and jaw clenched like a prized exhibit at London Zoo, barely able to keep a lid on his pent-up anger.

I glanced over to where Todd was positioned with his back against the wall. His arms were hanging down by his sides like a sentry standing to attention. His posture was stiff, and I could see by the look on his face that he was troubled. I had a sudden urge to get to my feet, cross the room and throw my arms around him. I hated seeing him like this; Todd was a tough guy, a former marine who wasn't fazed by anything. But it was clear what had happened had rattled him.

I didn't want to consider the fact that Scarlett might die. If she did, my family would be baying for blood, and Mum would undoubtedly turn to Rio for direction. It was my fault Scarlett wasn't in Todd's care. If the truth came out that I'd fabricated a job so that we could spend the night together, there'd be hell to pay. An enormous wave of guilt crashed down on me; I wouldn't be able to live with myself if Scarlett didn't survive her injuries. I didn't want to face the future without the little sister I adored so much.

As I wrestled with the thoughts that threatened to

overwhelm me, the door suddenly swung open. My eyes scanned over a man dressed in blue scrubs standing at the entrance. This was the moment we'd been waiting for, but instead of relief flooding my body, anxiety started to claw its way up from the depths of my stomach. If the lines of worry etched on his face were anything to go by, he was the bearer of bad news. He paused to compose himself. The sight of him preparing to face my family made a huge lump form in my throat. I wasn't sure I wanted to hear what he had to say.

54

Mia

In the early hours of the morning, the surgeon came to the small room where my red-eyed family members were gathered, waiting for news. I should have been elated, but his appearance made fresh anxiety rise up within me. I braced myself for what he was about to tell us. His body language wasn't giving anything away.

'Scarlett has undergone seven hours of surgery to repair her injuries. The large blade penetrated very deeply, causing extensive damage to her internal organs.' The surgeon paused so that we could take in what he'd just told us.

'Oh dear God. Is she going to be all right?' Mum asked.

'Stab wounds to the abdomen usually have a much better prognosis than gunshot wounds,' the surgeon replied.

I had a sudden flashback to my dad lying in a pool of dark red blood after a single bullet penetrated his head. He hadn't survived the attempt on his life. All we could do was wait and hope that the medical professional's forecast was correct.

The surgeon waited several seconds, and when there were no more questions forthcoming, he continued to drip-feed us the update on my sister's condition.

'Scarlett lost a lot of blood, so the fact that she survived this vicious attack is truly a miracle, but I'm afraid the same cannot be said for her unborn child. The uterine perforation she sustained in the attack caused her to miscarry. I'm sorry to have to tell you that Scarlett has lost the baby,' the surgeon said. He didn't fumble his delivery, but his unexpected words bounced off every wall in the small room.

You could have knocked me down with a feather, and judging from the wide-eyed expressions my bewildered family's faces were wearing, this was news to all of us, Kelsey included. It wasn't the surgeon's fault; he clearly hadn't realised Scarlett had kept her pregnancy a secret. His eyes slowly scanned each of us in turn while he waited for his message to sink in. But none of us knew how to react. The fact that Scarlett had survived the surgery should have elicited a collective sigh of relief and much whooping and hollering from all of us, but we were so shocked to hear that she'd been pregnant it somehow overshadowed the joy we should have been feeling.

I was glad the surgeon hadn't continued speaking and had allowed us some time to try and absorb the facts. As the silence dragged on, my thoughts became scrambled. I wanted to ask questions, but I couldn't seem to form any sentences that would allow me to do so. We were normally a talkative bunch; I'd never known us to be so lost for words, but all of us were completely dumbstruck.

'Is there anything you would like to ask me?'

The surgeon's eyes swept over us again. I wanted to know

about the baby, but I wasn't sure that would go down well with the others, so I tried to push the thought from my head. My sister's miscarriage should have been unimportant in the grand scheme of things. Despite her injuries, Scarlett was still alive. When nobody took the surgeon up on his offer, he began speaking again.

'We will be admitting Scarlett to the intensive care unit because she will need constant, close monitoring.'

'My daughter must be in a bad way if you're admitting her to intensive care,' Mum said.

That was the first time anybody had spoken since the surgeon entered the room. Her hand flew up to cover her mouth as she tried to stop the sob escaping from her lips, but she was too late. Poor Mum. I wasn't sure how much more she could take.

'Scarlett is still in a serious condition, which is why we have put her into an induced coma. She needs time to heal and has a long recovery ahead of her. Go home and get some rest; it's been a traumatic day for all of you.'

'Can't we see Scarlett first?' Mum asked.

'It's going to take some time to get Scarlett settled on the ward, so you'll need to come back later. There are no set visiting times, but in the early days, visits are restricted to close family and friends. Only two people are allowed at a patient's bedside at any one time.'

The surgeon had given us more information to absorb, but my brain was reaching saturation point at this stage.

'I don't feel comfortable going home and leaving my daughter here. I'd really prefer to stay,' Mum insisted.

'I understand that, but I can't let you see Scarlett for the moment. She's in good hands and will be monitored around the clock. It's been a long night for all of you. The best way to help Scarlett is by going home and getting some sleep. The nursing staff will phone you if there's any change in her condition,' the surgeon reassured us before he gestured to the door.

We obediently filed out one after the other. Jack and I travelled with Mum in Rio's car while Kelsey went with Todd. Mum and I got in the back and sat side by side. Nobody spoke on the first part of the journey; we just stared out of the windows. But then curiosity got the better of me.

'Did you know Scarlett was pregnant?' I asked, turning to look at my mum.

I hadn't been able to shake the thought from my mind since the surgeon had told us, and although my sister was gravely ill, it seemed unnatural for us not to talk about it. Avoiding the subject wouldn't make it go away.

'I had no idea,' Mum replied. 'I didn't even know she had a boyfriend.'

Neither did I.

'I hate to think of her keeping something as important as that to herself,' Mum said with tears glistening in her eyes.

I could see Mum was hurt that my younger sister hadn't confided in her. 'Perhaps she didn't know,' I said, hoping that might make her feel better.

'Really? How could she not know?' Mum stared at me with a puzzled expression on her face.

'The surgeon didn't say how far along she was; if she was in the early stages, I guess it's a possibility.'

Mum didn't look convinced by my suggestion. 'I sensed I was expecting all three of you before I even did the test. I felt different somehow, off-colour.'

Not having ever been in that position myself, I'd have to take her word for it.

'I can't believe this has happened. First your dad and now Scarlett...' Mum said.

I squeezed her hand as I saw tears begin to roll down her cheeks. When I looked away, I caught Rio's eye. He was looking at Mum in the rear-view mirror with concern written all over his face.

55

Kelsey

I felt like I was being buried alive. Todd and I were up to our necks in shit, and if we weren't careful, we were going to go under.

'First and foremost, we need to get our story straight. Rio's got a nose like a bloodhound, and if anything seems off, he'll sniff it out straight away,' I said as Todd drove us away from the hospital.

We didn't have long to come up with a convincing cover story, so we'd have to use the time we had alone wisely. We might not get another opportunity before Rio's interrogation began.

'Did you hear what I just said?'

Todd briefly turned his attention away from the road and glanced at me with a blank expression on his face before his eyes snapped back to the windscreen. He didn't need to reply; his vacant expression told me everything I needed to know.

'It's only a matter of time until Rio corners us and

demands an explanation, so we better make sure we're singing from the same hymn sheet.'

'I know that, Kelsey.' Todd threw me a look over his shoulder.

Rio wouldn't stop till he got to the bottom of this. He hadn't bought the excuse I gave him earlier. Todd was meant to be working, so turning his phone off wasn't acceptable under any circumstances. Rio would never have done something like that. He took his role seriously; his job was everything to him. It was more than just a paycheque at the end of the month. He'd grown up with my dad, so we were like family to him.

I was racking my brains, but it was hard to concentrate on anything other than Scarlett. Every time I tried to divert my thoughts away from her, they kept going back again. How would she cope when she regained consciousness? Her life had been upended in the blink of an eye.

'I seriously don't think we'll be able to talk our way out of this; Rio's not stupid, and it doesn't take a genius to work out that something's been going on between us,' Todd said.

'What are you suggesting? We come clean?'

I was horrified by the prospect of having to tell the truth, but we'd been backed into a corner. Todd might be right; owning up might be the only solution. But we'd be taking a huge risk. My mum might have accepted our relationship if I'd told her sooner, but Scarlett was fighting for her life because I'd lied and said I was working so that Todd and I could sneak off together, which meant he wasn't available to accompany her. That was unforgivable. Todd's head would be on the block; he'd lose his job for sure. And I'd lose my family's respect. The more I thought about it, the more I knew I couldn't go through with it. Lying was the only option.

I began pressing down on my throbbing scalp with the pads of my fingers to try and relieve the tension headache that was building inside my skull, no doubt caused by a combination of no sleep, too much champagne and trying to deal with the stress of the situation. I felt overwhelmed by it all.

Todd and I had managed to keep our affair a secret for eighteen months now. But I couldn't help feeling this might be the beginning of the end. Rio would be watching the two of us like a hawk from now on, so slipping off to hotels when I was meant to be working would be a thing of the past. We both thrived on the thrill, and without the excitement I wasn't convinced we had a future together.

We weren't the only ones keeping secrets. I was shocked that Scarlett hadn't told me she was pregnant. We used to be so close. I have to say, it hurt that she didn't feel she could confide in me. At one time, I would have been her go-to person. We might not have been seeing eye to eye recently, but I still had her back. I couldn't allow my wounded pride to get in the way of our relationship. Scarlett hadn't shared her news with me, big deal. I had to get over it; it wasn't the end of the world.

Rio was waiting for us in the driveway when Todd and I arrived. My heart sank at the sight of him. I glanced over at Todd. His hands gripped the wheel, and the skin on his forehead was creased with concern. He was a handsome young man, but he suddenly appeared older.

I let out a long sigh; it was time to face the music. 'Let me do the talking,' I said before I got out of the car.

One thing my sisters and I all had in common was that we'd inherited the gift of the gab from my dad, so I'd psyched myself up to spin Rio a line. Despite what Todd thought, I could nearly always blag my way to a favourable outcome; I had a great track record. If you were given a superpower, it would be rude not to use it, wouldn't it?

'There's no need to speak on my behalf. I'm happy to fight my own battles,' Todd replied.

'I know, but I'm the boss, so Rio will take it better from me.'

Todd was unaccustomed to letting a woman take the lead.

'Can you give us a couple of minutes? I need to talk to Todd in private,' Rio said as I drew closer.

My heart pounded in my chest when I came to a stop in front of the man, who was a solid wall of muscle.

'There's something I need to tell you,' I said.

Rio gave me a weak smile. 'I just need to speak to Todd first. Can it wait?'

I shook my head slowly from side to side as I tried to collect my thoughts. There was no point stalling any longer; it just delayed the inevitable.

'Kelsey, please, this is important.'

Rio didn't bother to hide the irritation in his tone as he tried to dismiss me. I couldn't ever remember a time when he'd spoken to me like that. It was clear he felt very strongly about the situation.

I saw a flash of anger spread across Rio's face before his dark eyes searched mine. 'Your sister is in intensive care, and when I tried to alert Todd to that fact, his phone went to voicemail. That might not be a big deal to you, but it is from where I'm standing. Todd failed to do his job properly. He needs to be contactable at all times when he's on duty. I don't care if he's hobnobbing with the rich and famous, his phone needs to be switched on. What have you got to say for yourself?' Rio put his hands on his hips while he waited for Todd to reply.

'I'm sorry I didn't answer my phone. I should have known better,' Todd said.

I tossed my hair over my shoulders and glared at him. He'd better not mess this up.

'Kelsey and I weren't at an event last night. Our phones were switched off because we'd checked into a hotel...' Todd let his sentence trail off.

I glared at Todd with fury burning in my eyes. What the hell did he think he was doing? He knew damn well I wanted to keep our affair a secret. He'd done this to spite me because I'd pulled rank on him. I was sure of that. I moved my attention away from Todd when Rio turned his accusatory gaze on me. I felt myself buckle under the strain, so I cast my eyes towards the ground, fixing them on the gravel.

'What did you just say?' Rio questioned.

I tore my eyes away from the ground when I felt his glare bore into the top of my skull. Then Rio's eyes flicked between Todd and I. There was no point trying to deny it now that Todd had blurted out the truth. This was going to be a damage-limitation exercise, and thanks to my job, I knew a fair bit about how to handle pear-shaped situations. It was a shame I was the only member on the crisis management team. I wouldn't be able to rely on Todd for help; he'd done quite enough damage for one day.

'Todd wasn't free to keep tabs on Scarlett because he'd checked into a hotel with me.'

This time I held Rio's gaze; my heart was in my mouth when I saw Rio suddenly switch and lunge at Todd, gripping him around the throat with one of his massive hands.

'You stupid fucker.' Rio held on to each word, and his deep voice came out in a growl. 'I've got a good mind to tear you limb from limb. If Davie was still alive, he'd want your head on a plate.'

'Get off him,' I shouted as Todd gasped for air.

Even though I was furious with him, I didn't want to see him come to any harm.

'Your days with this firm are numbered.' Rio got up in Todd's face before he shoved him backwards with the palm of his hand, which rocked the bodyguard on his feet.

Todd dusted himself off, then laughed in Rio's face. 'What's up, big man? You jealous or something?'

Rio didn't reply; he stomped out of the room, clenching and unclenching his fists as he walked.

'Why did you tell Rio the truth? I told you I'd handle things.' I put my hands on my hips and glared at Todd.

'And I told you I fight my own battles,' Todd replied before he turned on his heel and headed out of the door.

I was seriously losing my touch. First with Mia and now with Todd. What the hell was happening to me?

If I didn't sort myself out, things were only going to go one way. I knew I had what it took to run a criminal outfit full of violence and threat, but my confidence had taken a knock, and it was affecting all aspects of my life. Mia had surprised us all when she stepped up to the challenge. She was smashing things, and if I didn't start to push against her, I'd find myself left out of the frame.

Now that the truth had come out, I'd have to steel myself to face the backlash my actions had caused. Todd could walk away from his job, if he wasn't pushed first. But there was no way I was going to step away from my family and responsibilities no matter how difficult things became. My dad hadn't raised a quitter, so it was time to prove that.

56

Mia

The hours that followed our return from the hospital were dark. I would wager a bet that none of us got a wink of sleep even though that's what the surgeon had suggested we do. I was physically and mentally drained, but thoughts were whirring through my head at a million miles an hour, so getting some shut-eye wasn't going to be an option for me. I was staring at the bedroom wall when Jack stirred in the bed next to me. I turned to look at my handsome husband over my shoulder, and as I did, the Egyptian cotton pillowcase rustled beneath my head. He was lying on his back, blue eyes wide open, gazing at the ceiling, so I rolled onto my other side and propped myself up on one elbow.

'Did you manage to get some sleep?' I asked.

'No. How about you?'

I shook my head.

'I didn't think so. You look pale.' Jack ran his fingertips down the side of my cheek. 'Why don't you go and have a shower? I'll make us all something to eat. Then we could go back to the hospital if you like.'

The corners of my mouth lifted slightly as I gave Jack the biggest smile I could muster. He was so thoughtful and always put my wants and needs before his own.

'That's a good idea,' I said as I threw back the covers and clambered out of bed.

I padded across the bedroom floor and into the en-suite bathroom, then turned the tap on the shower before stepping out of my pyjamas, waiting a couple of seconds for the temperature to adjust. As the hot water ran over my weary body, I felt it re-energising me, which was a relief as I was running on empty. I wasn't surprised Jack thought I looked pale. I had the type of skin tone that became almost translucent when I was ill or tired. I wrestled with anxiety on a daily basis, so it didn't take much to send it into overdrive, which took its toll on my health.

I hadn't felt as bad as this since my dad was murdered. As the water cascaded over my body, my mind jumped back to a time I'd battled hard to forget when getting out of bed in the morning was such a struggle, I wasn't always willing to put myself through the ordeal. If it hadn't been for Jack, I would have been tempted to give up. But he'd helped me through the bleakest time in my life. I was lucky to have him.

My wedding day had started off as such a perfect day. I can still picture the look of pride on my dad's face when he gave me away. His beam stretched from ear to ear as he faced Jack at the altar. 'Take good care of her,' Dad had said, and Jack had kept his promise. I hadn't known at the time they would be the last words I would hear my dad speak.

I was too busy gazing into the eyes of my future husband to concern myself with anything else. From the way Jack was looking at me, I could see he loved me as much as I loved him, and as I allowed myself to get lost in the moment, I forgot that anyone else was in the room.

I would give anything to spend just one more day with Dad. I wished I could tell him how much I loved him and that he was the best dad in the world.

Mum and Kelsey went into intensive care first while Jack and I waited outside in the corridor for what seemed like an endless amount of time before they reappeared.

'How is she?' I asked. But the looks on their faces told me everything I needed to know without them replying.

'Not good,' Kelsey said. 'I'm going to take Mum outside for some fresh air.'

My mum looked ready to keel over. The colour had drained from her face as the pressure of the situation mounted. I felt beads of sweat break out on my upper lip as I watched Kelsey and Mum walk away, knowing that any minute now, it would be my turn to face what had distressed them.

Jack held on to my hand as we made our way towards Scarlett's bed. Seeing my little sister hooked up to all those machines and wires made my breath catch in my throat, and tears started to flow fast and furious in tracks down my cheeks. I wasn't sure what I'd been expecting; I think at the back of my mind, I'd been hoping she would look like she was asleep because they'd sedated her, but when I got my first glimpse of Scarlett, I jolted, like I'd just stepped under a cold shower. Seeing the machines brought it all home; I couldn't help feeling alarmed by the amount of equipment that was necessary to keep her alive. Her existence was hanging by a thread.

It was just as well Scarlett was sedated. She'd never be able to rest with all the activity and noise going on around her. But it was to be expected; critically ill patients needed high levels of medication and support, especially in the early stages.

A lovely nurse had been put in charge of Scarlett's treatment, and even though my sister was unaware of what was happening around her, I immediately felt more confident that she would pull through. I could see she was in good hands, and that brought me a lot of comfort. I swallowed the lump in my throat before I leant forward and gently kissed Scarlett's head, willing her to fight with everything she had.

Mum and Kelsey were sitting on a bench opposite the main entrance to St Thomas's when Jack and I emerged from the clinical space. I had a bad feeling that something else had happened. Mum had been like a zombie when she'd left intensive care, and now she was sobbing her heart out in full view of the curious pairs of eyes trained on her. But it was very out of character for her; she was normally so poised, even in a crisis. My heart began pounding in my chest as we drew closer. My gut was telling me this was more than just a reaction to seeing her youngest child hooked up to life-saving equipment. Kelsey had her arm draped around Mum's shoulder and was doing her best to comfort her, but my mum was inconsolable.

'Jack, can you stay with Mum, please?' Kelsey stood up

and took me by the hand so that we were out of earshot. 'Mum's just had a call from Detective Inspector Stewart. She told her that the police investigation is going nowhere, and despite not having found the person responsible for murdering Dad, they're scaling it back.'

Now I understood the reason behind my mum's public meltdown. 'Oh, for God's sake! Talk about bad timing. How much more can she take?'

'I know. Let's get her home. She wants to talk to Rio,' Kelsey replied.

Rio was waiting at the bottom of the front steps when we returned from the hospital.

'Are you OK, Amanda?' he asked when Mum got out of the car.

Mum shook her head. 'I don't know why I bothered to tip them off. I should have known the police weren't going to solve the case, but the idea of them scaling back the investigation without arresting the culprit has hit me hard,' she said as she dabbed at her bloodshot eyes with a damp tissue.

'That's understandable, especially with Scarlett being so ill,' Rio said as we climbed the steps into the house.

We filed through into the dining room, and all took seats around the table.

'I just can't believe the investigation has ground to a halt. The detective said they'd investigated five hundred lines of inquiry. She told me the police had renewed their appeal several times, but they were still no closer to solving the case. And when I pressed her on the information I gave her, she kept insisting that there was a lack of forensic evidence at the scene.'

'That's utter bullshit,' Rio replied. 'They don't need forensics to trace the identity of Davie's killer. What was the point of putting Victor Coleman's name in the frame if the coppers weren't going to use the information you gave them?'

'I think they tried to. The detective admitted the key to solving the case lay within the underworld. She acknowledged that Davie had been a victim of a gangland execution and remarked that his murder bore the hallmark of a contract-style killing,' Mum replied.

'And yet they still didn't manage to tie the Colemans to Davie's murder. Like every clued-up wealthy villain, Victor must be using his money to evade arrest.' Rio's words were laced with bitterness.

'The DI had hoped some allegiances might have changed since Davie's death, and she said the police had urged members of the underworld to come forward. But they hadn't established any new lines of inquiry.'

Mum looked broken. It was beyond frustrating because there was no doubt about it; my dad had been murdered in cold blood.

The sound of the doorbell ringing put an end to the heated discussion.

'I'll get it,' Jack offered.

My husband returned a couple of moments later, accompanied by a police officer. I knew the police had a duty to keep the family informed while they investigated the attack on Scarlett, but they couldn't have picked a worse time to deliver an update. I saw Mum swallow hard at the sight of the officer, bracing herself for more bad news. The rising tide didn't seem to be stopping any time soon; it just kept coming.

'There has been a development in your daughter's case,' the officer said. 'Two independent witnesses have come forward and given us their accounts. We already knew that Scarlett was walking along Hay's Lane, heading towards the Thames with a young man, when two motorbikes mounted the pavement. One of the men tried to snatch Scarlett's bag. When she resisted, the rider on the second bike stabbed her in the stomach with a large knife. Moments before the attack, Scarlett was seen strolling hand in hand, chatting away, unaware of the impending danger. The couple were sharing a kiss when the attackers struck.' The officer paused to allow the information to sink in.

I glanced at Mum; she was wringing her hands in her laps, no doubt wishing he would get this over with sooner rather than later.

'After Scarlett was knifed in the stomach, the young man she was with left her bleeding on the pavement and ran after the attackers.'

Rio was shaking his head. 'How could he leave her on her own?'

'Both witnesses agreed that a rider and passenger were on the first bike with just a rider on the second. Once the motorbikes turned the corner and were out of sight, the driver of the second bike stopped in the middle of the road. Scarlett's companion jumped on the back, and the bike sped off, away from the scene of the crime.'

We all fell silent. The tension in the room heightened as the police officer's words hung in the air.

'He did what?' Rio asked before clenching his jaw. His body was wired with rage. My dad's best friend looked like he was going to explode.

'The man Scarlett was with got onto the back of the motorbike and took off with her attackers. We'd originally thought that he'd been running after them to try and apprehend them or gather information to help us with the investigation. But it looks as though he was somehow involved.'

'There's no "looks as though" about it. I'm convinced the robbery was a smokescreen, and those fuckers would have stabbed Scarlett whether she'd let go of her bag or not. The scumbag she was with was definitely involved,' Rio fumed, nostrils flaring wildly. 'Have you found out who he was yet?'

'Not yet, but we're working on it. We have a good description of the man from witness statements,' the officer replied. 'I'll be in touch when we know more.'

Rio's chest expanded, and his posture straightened as he watched the officer leave.

'I think I know who Scarlett was with,' Kelsey said.

Every pair of eyes in the room turned to look at her.'

'Who?' Rio demanded as he clenched his fists by his sides.

'A guy called CJ,' Kelsey replied, and I saw her and Todd exchange a look.

'What makes you say that?' Rio asked.

'She met him at Bluewater, and I think she's been going out with him in secret,' Kelsey said.

'And you didn't think to mention this before?' Rio wasn't impressed that Kelsey hadn't shared the information with him.

'I'm sorry.'

'That's it? You're sorry?' Rio was fuming. A muscle twitched in the side of his jaw while he waited for Kelsey to reply.

I wasn't sure how my sister would react to his tone. She wasn't in the habit of taking shit from anyone. But Kelsey didn't seem herself; she was usually brimming over with confidence. Her self-assurance seemed to have deserted her as she stood in the firing line. I was normally so envious of her backbone of steel; right now, I wouldn't have wanted to be in her shoes.

'I told her not to go out with him, but she wouldn't listen. Maybe if I'd spoken up sooner, this wouldn't have happened,' Kelsey looked out from under her eyelashes, but Rio hadn't calmed down.

'Too right you should have spoken up sooner.' Rio slammed his fist down in the middle of the table, and I jumped out of my skin.

Kelsey bowed her head in shame. I couldn't blame her for wanting to break eye contact. The weight of Rio's glare was crushing.

'First Davie and now Scarlett. This is too much of a coincidence. The Colemans must have had something to do with this. That family won't stop until they've taken out each and every one of us,' Rio warned.

A shiver ran down my spine. The underworld was a maze of lies and deceit, and Rio was right; we were all in danger. We couldn't wait for the police to handle the situation, not after they failed to charge anyone with my dad's murder and allowed the case to go cold. They'd let my family down, and we couldn't let that happen again.

'This needs sorting one way or another. We can't sit around and let the boys in blue fuck up a second time. We need to bypass the system and take matters into our own hands,' Rio said.

Mum opened her mouth to speak but then paused, pondering over what she was about to say. 'Do what you have to do,' Mum replied, giving him the green light. 'But make sure you don't get caught.'

57

Mia

I was mildly terrified on the drive to Essex; nerves were bubbling up inside me the closer we got, but when Rio stopped his Range Rover outside Victor's neo-Georgian monster house, I realised I wasn't afraid any more. My fear had been replaced with hatred and a need for revenge. My dad was dead, and my sister was barely clinging to life because of this family. They deserved everything they had coming to them. Payback was long overdue. If Rio was right, my sister had become a victim of an argument she wasn't even involved in, so now the Colemans were going to have to pay the price.

My pulse was pounding in my neck as we walked up the block-paved driveway in silence, accompanied by the long shadows of approaching dusk.

'Open the front door, you fucker.' Rio pounded on the composite with his clenched fist.

When Victor obliged and swung open the glossy black door, the huge man grabbed his much smaller and older opponent by the throat and pushed him back through the house. Lorraine let out an ear-splitting scream while Kelsey and I stood on either side of Todd, watching the scene unfolding with eyes like saucers. We'd rushed into the house just in time to see Rio's fist connect with Victor's lower jaw. Blood and saliva flew out of his mouth and splattered onto the designer wallpaper.

'You wanker, you're the scum of the earth. People like you always take it out on an innocent member of the family if things don't go their way,' Rio shouted, unable to contain his pent-up rage for a moment longer. 'Where's Craig?' Rio grabbed the front of Victor's shirt and pulled him onto his tiptoes.

'I don't know,' Victor replied.

'I thought the two of you were meant to be fronting this firm, and yet we've never set eyes on the man. Get him here now. I want to have words with him.' Rio rammed his face into Victor's.

I knew the signs only too well, so I realised Lorraine was beginning to panic before she backed herself into the corner of the room furthest away from her husband. Moments later, her face was sweating profusely, and a menopausal hot flush wasn't the reason: she was scared out of her wits. But I couldn't feel sorry for her. Mum had experienced far worse when she'd had a gun held under her chin. Lorraine was getting off lightly if you asked me; we hadn't come here to harm her; our business was with Victor and Craig, and as long as she stayed out of the way, she'd live to see another day.

A chair leg scraping on a hard floor caught everyone's attention. When Lorraine's eyes darted sideways, Todd shot out of the room, and the sound of a struggle followed. He reappeared shortly afterwards with a dark-haired man in an armlock.

'Get the fuck off me,' the man shouted, his face contorted with pain as he struggled to break free.

'So this is the elusive Craig, is it?' Rio threw the man a glare. If looks could kill...

Kelsey and Todd made eye contact before she rushed forward, drew her arm back and slapped the man around the face with all her might, leaving red marks behind on his skin. What the hell was going on?

'You were right, Rio. The Colemans definitely had something to do with Scarlett's stabbing. This is the guy she met outside Bluewater,' Kelsey said.

My thoughts bounced backwards and forwards in my mind like a ball in a game of tennis. 'Are you sure? I thought his name was CJ.'

'Craig Jordan or CJ for short,' the dark-haired man proudly confirmed, his words full of bravado.

He seemed delighted that he duped my family, but his smugness wasn't going to last long. Rio would make sure of that.

'How could you do that to her?' Kelsey shouted in Craig's face.

When he smirked, Todd responded by tightening his grip, hyperextending the man's shoulder joint, which left him screaming like a schoolgirl.

'He was hiding in the kitchen like a spineless coward, hoping Mummy and Daddy were going to take the flak for his actions. He tried to make a run for it rather than face what's coming to him like a man,' Todd said.

I shuddered. My thoughts flashed back to Scarlett lying in a hospital bed hooked up to life-saving equipment. If I focused on that, so I could condone what was about to happen. Rio wasn't exactly dressed for the occasion, wearing a three-piece suit – he looked as though he'd arrived for a business meeting, not a slaying.

'Why did you hurt Scarlett? What did she ever do to you?' Kelsey questioned.

'I didn't do anything,' Craig replied.

Kelsey shook her head. 'You deliberately targeted her at the shopping centre.'

'It was a chance meeting.'

Who was he trying to kid? While holding on to Victor with one hand, Rio produced a gun from the back of his waistband. He then took a couple of steps forward and got up in Craig's face, ready to use his powers of persuasion.

'Really? Do you expect us to believe that? Scarlett just happens to be the daughter of your family's biggest rival, so I have to agree with Kelsey; I don't think the two of you meeting outside Bluewater was a coincidence. It's time to start talking, CJ,' Rio said, digging the barrel of the gun into Craig's stomach.

'I'm not telling you anything,' Craig replied.

He was trying his best to act the hard man but failing miserably. You could almost smell the fear seeping out of his pores. He knew he was about to pay for what he'd done.

'You might want to reconsider.'

'I swear to God, I don't know what you're talking about.' Craig's Adam's apple bobbed up and down.

He was doing his best to deny any involvement, but it didn't wash.

'Scarlett was a sitting duck. You actively pursued her, grooming her until she trusted you. Then you got someone to stab her to get back at us. She had no idea you were a Coleman. If she had, she wouldn't have gone within a million miles of you,' Kelsey said.

'And after you'd had her assaulted, you tried to make it look like you were being a hero running after the attackers, but witnesses saw you getting onto the back of the motorbike and riding off with the man who stabbed Scarlett. What have you got to say about that?' Rio said, jabbing the gun into his stomach with such force, Craig let out an involuntary groan.

My mind started wandering in a haze. The situation was toxic. Early on, I realised I didn't want to listen to a word this man was saying. Nothing could change the fact that Scarlett was fighting for her life because of him.

'You left her bleeding out on the pavement, surrounded by gawping strangers,' Todd added, repositioning his lock, which made Craig squeal.

'My sister could have died because of you,' Kelsey added.

'But she didn't, did she?' Craig replied in a cocky tone, suddenly recovering from his bout of amnesia.

'No, but she lost her baby. It's good to see your memory's returned. I'm sure you know what I'm thinking. An eye for an eye,' Rio said.

'Hold on; rewind a minute. What baby?' Victor said. He appeared to be more interested in hearing what his son had been getting up to than taking heed of Rio's threat.

'Scarlett was pregnant. Didn't Craig tell you?' Rio replied, calling Craig's bluff.

We didn't know for certain that he was the father of my

sister's unborn child, but everything was pointing in that direction.

'Is that true, Craig?' Victor questioned.

'Yeah. But the kid wasn't planned.'

As if that justified what had happened. His throwaway comment made my blood boil. I'd heard enough. Whatever was about to come his way, he deserved, but I knew I would struggle with being a spectator to the violence Rio was about to unleash. I started to concentrate on tiny details, such as Victor's ever-so-slightly too long fingernails and the sheen of his shirt's fabric, which matched the shine of his shoes, so that I didn't have to see what was happening to Craig.

'It's time to teach this little fucker some manners. Let's swap,' Rio said to Todd before he placed a silencer on the end of the gun.

I heard Lorraine whimper, but I didn't look in her direction. I tried to keep my eyes on Victor, but they were automatically drawn to Craig.

'Wait,' I said, and I felt the weight of all the eyes in the room fix on me.

'For God's sake, Mia, get a grip! We all agreed this needs to be done,' Kelsey shouted, misunderstanding my intentions.

'I know that, but Mum's worried we're going to get caught, and I don't know about you, but I'm not prepared to do time for the Colemans. I think Rio should make Craig's execution look like a suicide, which under the circumstances would be very befitting. Now that we know it was Scarlett's so-called boyfriend who organised the hit on her, he'd have good reason to want to take his own life, wouldn't he?'

Kelsey wound her neck in long enough to consider my proposal. 'That's a good idea,' she said, giving me credit for once.

'Get down on the floor with your back against the wall,' Rio demanded.

Craig did as he was told, bending his knees up and covering his face with his arms as he attempted to make himself a smaller target by curling into a ball.

'Mia's right; we don't want the cops sniffing around, so we'll make this look like you couldn't live with yourself after what you'd done. Nobody could blame you for wanting to take your own life. I mean, what kind of lowlife would kill their unborn child and leave their girlfriend for dead?' Rio swung his leg back as though he was going to kick Craig into the ribs but thought better of it. 'Tempting as it would be to give you a hiding, it will raise questions at your autopsy, so I'll have to restrain myself.'

'Oh, God, please don't kill my son,' Lorraine wailed.

'Shut the fuck up, or you'll be next,' Rio warned, waving the gun in her direction. 'Now where was I?' Rio grinned.

The clock ticked by painfully slowly, which I was sure added to Craig's suffering. Rio repositioned Craig's legs, then placed the gun in his trembling hands. He prised open Craig's mouth with the barrel, closing his hand around Craig's fingers. I wanted to look away, but my eyes were glued to the scene as it unfolded. My hands began sweating, and I could feel my pulse throbbing in my neck.

'This one's for Scarlett,' Rio said before he squeezed the trigger.

I gasped as the bullet blew a huge hole in the side of his face leaving teeth, bone and tissue splattered all over the wall and one of his eyes hanging down onto his cheek. It was a gruesome sight, and I felt the contents of my stomach rise.

Kelsey immediately reached towards me and took hold of my hand to offer me some support, easing the tension between us. Now that we were faced with settling the score with the Colemans, instead of pulling against each other, we were standing together, united by our collective desire for vengeance against the family that had caused us so much pain.

Lorraine started screaming. She was hysterical.

'Shut up,' Rio said over his shoulder before getting up from the floor. He slowly reloaded, then crossed the room to where Lorraine was standing with her hands over her mouth. 'Don't make me do this,' Rio said, pointing the smoking barrel of the gun at her. 'I'm going to let you go on one condition. You leave the house right now, and you never come back. Go into hiding for your own protection. If the police start asking questions, you didn't see or hear anything. Got it? If you don't stick to your side of the deal. I'll come after you. Do I make myself clear?'

Lorraine nodded as two black mascara rivers ran down her cheeks. She didn't put up any resistance and edged along the wall until she was out in the hallway. I heard her pick up her car keys from the hall table before the front door opened and closed. Moments later, a car engine started, and the sound of screeching tyres faded into the distance.

'Listen, mate, if you let me go, I'll cover for you. I'll call the cops and say I came home and found Craig like this. As you said, he had good reason to feel suicidal after what happened to Scarlett and the nipper, so nobody will think anything of it,' Victor said, selling his soul to the devil.

I'd never had a high opinion of Victor, but I hadn't realised how low he would sink. He was despicable. His son's face was splattered across his living room wall, and he was trying to cut a deal with the person who had done that to him.

'You'd do that for me?' Rio cocked his head and put his hand over his heart.

'Of course I would.' Victor nodded his balding head and smiled.

'That's so sweet of you, but I'm afraid no can do. I need to get justice for Davie, so you have to pay the price,' Rio said.

'I swear to you I had nothing to do with Davie's murder,' Victor replied with desperation coating his words.

'You would say that, wouldn't you? My boss wasn't the first person to be killed in cold blood, and he won't be the last. It goes with the territory.'

'Victor still owes us one hundred and fifty thousand pounds. I think we should make him pay it back before we kill him,' I said. The suppressed accountant within me couldn't resist the opportunity to recoup the debt.

'Great idea! You're on a roll,' Kelsey replied.

'Where's the safe?' Rio jabbed the barrel of the gun into Victor's right kidney.

He walked across the room, took the gaudy mirror off the wall, then began twisting the dial to the left and the right. Lorraine had left in such a hurry she'd forgotten to take her Gucci shopping bags with her. They lay discarded by the side of the velvet sofa, so I tipped the clothing onto the floor and began unloading the contents of the safe into the empty bags.

'Hey, that's way more than I owe you,' Victor protested.

'You won't be needing it where you're going,' Rio replied as he frogmarched Victor towards the front door. 'Who fancies a trip to Coalhouse Fort?'

As we walked past the table in the hall, I spotted the two sets of keys belonging to the Audis in the glass dish, so I picked them up for good measure. My family deserved to be compensated after what the Colemans had put us through.

It was a glorious June evening when we stepped out of Victor's house, leaving the grisly scene behind us. I sat in the front passenger seat as Kelsey drove the Range Rover. Rio and Todd took up position in the back on either side of Victor.

Rio directed Kelsey to a disused landfill site close to East Tilbury. On the way, I looked to the left, the scenery was pleasant even though the tide was out. The last rays of the sun were glinting on the water channels left behind in the mudflats. But when I looked to the right, all I could see was the rusting metal of an industrial landscape, and smoke fumes coughed out by the factories that lined this stretch of water. They were no doubt essential to the local economy and workforce, but they weren't very pleasing to the eye. Once we'd arrived, Kelsey parked in a bay outside a decaying lock-up.

'I thought it was only fitting that we brought you to where your brother took his last breath,' Rio said, forcing Victor out of the car.

'Please don't do this,' Victor begged. 'I'll give you everything I own if you let me go.'

'Ahh isn't that nice? But you've got nothing I want,' Rio replied.

Rio turned Victor around and pushed him inside the shipping container. 'This one's for Davie,' he said before he pulled the trigger.

Rio shot Victor in the back of the head at point-blank range with a pump-action shotgun, which left a gaping wound large enough to put a fist inside. Victor fell to the floor, landing on his left side, then Rio turned the barrel of the smoking gun back on him. The next bullet entered behind his right ear, and the slug exited between his eyes. Victor was clearly already dead, but Rio didn't stop shooting until he'd fired the last round. Then he began to stamp and boot Dad's rival even though he was lying motionless on the ground.

'Wesley, there's a job at the landfill site that needs cleaning up. Make it your top priority,' Rio said before he led the way out of the rusting shipping container.

'You're back sooner than I expected,' Mum said when Rio, Todd, Kelsey and I filed into the kitchen. 'How did it go?'

'You won't have any more trouble from the Colemans.' Rio smiled grimly.

'Take a seat. I've made beef Stroganoff; I thought you might be hungry,' Mum said as she started taking plates out of the kitchen cupboard.

I couldn't speak for the others, but food was the last thing on my mind. There was nothing like having a front-row seat at a bloodbath to make you lose your appetite. Mum had gone to so much trouble, I didn't have the heart to tell her that as she served up white rice piled high with Stroganoff before she took a seat at the head of the table opposite Dad's empty seat.

I'd been scared to get involved in the murky side of the business; watching Rio calmly blow our enemies brains out had shocked me to the core. I'd had to dig deep and remind myself why we were in this position to stop myself from going into a meltdown. The Colemans had done the same thing to Dad in front of us, and Scarlett's baby had lost its life too before it had even really begun. My sister wasn't out of the woods yet either, so that made the brutality sit easier with me.

The atmosphere in the kitchen felt awkward. Nobody was speaking; the only sound was our cutlery clinking on the porcelain plates. When Mum's mobile began ringing, I jumped out of my skin. My nerves were in tatters after witnessing Rio in action. He'd been desperate to complete the job, so he wasn't going to settle with firing just one bullet. He'd left nothing to chance and had really gone overboard. But I wasn't going to dwell on it; that kind of behaviour went with the territory. Danger and glory walked hand in hand.

'Hello,' Mum said, then she mouthed, *It's the hospital.* 'That's wonderful news. Thanks for letting me know.' Mum ended the call, and a huge beam spread across her face. 'Scarlett's come out of the coma.'

58

Scarlett

The doctor was checking me over when Mum and Kelsey walked onto the ward. Mum's face lit up at the sight of me.

'You gave us quite a scare,' Mum said, stooping to kiss me on the side of the head.

I managed a weak smile in response.

'Scarlett has no recollection of the attack. Perhaps one of you can fill her in on the details later,' the doctor said, talking about me as though I wasn't in the room.

Mum nodded before she took a seat next to the bed.

'Are you OK?' Kelsey asked before she sat down next to Mum.

I tried to shrug my shoulders, but even the slightest movement caused me pain.

'You underwent extensive surgery to repair your internal injuries, but the uterine perforation you sustained in the attack caused you to miscarry. I'm sorry to have to tell you that you lost the baby you were carrying.'

My hands instinctively went to my stomach. Then my face crumpled, and my hands began shaking uncontrollably; I was too overwhelmed to speak. The news had come completely out of the blue. As the doctor's words registered in my brain, I felt the bottom drop out of my world. This wasn't the way I'd wanted my family to find out I was pregnant... had been pregnant. Tears rolled down my cheeks. I'd initially been devastated when I'd found out I was expecting, but that didn't come close to the feeling of utter despair that was gripping me now. I hadn't realised how much I'd wanted the baby until the choice had been taken out of my hands.

'Everything will be OK, sweetheart.' The sound of my mum's soothing voice did little to ease my suffering.

Overwhelming feelings welled up inside me as tears continued to flow down my cheeks. Mum reached towards me and gently stroked the skin below my little finger to the side of the cannula embedded in the back of my hand.

'Scarlett has a lot to cope with. Now isn't the right time to talk about the attack. Perhaps it would be better if you let her rest and came back later,' the doctor said.

He was talking about me again as though I didn't exist. But I didn't have the energy to protest. It suited me fine if my family left; I wanted them to go. The only person I wanted to see was CJ, but I knew I couldn't ask for him without having to explain everything to my mum, and I wasn't in the right frame of mind to do that. I was trying to come to terms with the loss of my baby. I covered my eyes with my hands when the doctor led Mum and Kelsey away. I couldn't bear to see the look of pity on their faces.

As I lay in my hospital bed attached to tubes and wires,

I had a sudden flashback to that fateful day. I'd felt so overwhelmed, but planned or unplanned, being pregnant for the first time must be scary for everyone; you had no idea what to expect and were entering uncharted territory. It wasn't just the physical changes; it was also the emotional ones. My hormones had been all over the place, and I'd only been in the early stages. Becoming a mother was going to be a massive, life-changing experience. Or so I'd thought.

I'd found myself stuck on an emotional rollercoaster and had struggled to get my head in order and put things into perspective. Panicked thoughts kept invading my brain as I plucked up the courage to have the talk with the man I'd only been seeing for a month. I was worried that the stress and the shock might kill our relationship before it had had a chance to get off the ground.

My life had changed beyond recognition. Once the initial shock had worn off, I'd started to become excited by the new chapter I was embarking on rather than being terrified by the prospect of being a young mum. It was going to be challenging getting to know a new partner and our baby at the same time. But I'd been up for it.

Despite my initial hesitation, I was sure things would have turned out OK in the end. I'd felt like I'd met the one. My twenty-year-old brain was confident that we would have made it work. I never imagined I would end up in this position. I ran my hand over the empty space where my baby had been, and a huge sob escaped from my lips. I felt empty and hollow inside and wished I hadn't survived the attack either.

59

Mia

'Can we go and see her now?' I asked when I saw Mum and Kelsey coming towards Jack and I.

'I'm afraid not. Scarlett was devastated when the doctor told her she'd lost the baby. He told us to go home and let her rest,' Mum replied.

'So she must have known she was pregnant then,' I said.

Mum nodded. 'I'm going to ask her about it when the time's right.'

'Now that she's conscious and her miscarriage is out in the open, Scarlett's bound to want to see CJ. What are we going to tell her?' Kelsey asked as Jack drove us home from the hospital.

'We'll have to tell her what's happened,' Mum replied.

'The truth's so awful; I don't think she'll be able to cope with it. Her state of mind is too fragile.' Kelsey shook her head.

'I don't like the idea of lying to her, but I think Kelsey's right. She has enough to deal with without finding out that her beloved CJ was one of the Colemans, that he arranged the hit on her and that he's dead. It could push her over the edge,' I added.

'What are you suggesting?' Mum asked, shifting in the front seat so that she could see Kelsey and I as we sat in the back.

'We could tell her part of the story. We won't hide the fact that CJ was involved in her attack. We couldn't even if we wanted to; it's been reported on the news and in the paper, so it's out in the public domain. And the police are going to interview Scarlett about the incident once she's well enough,' Kelsey said.

'Hopefully, when she finds out that CJ set her up, she won't want anything to do with him,' I said.

'Exactly, but if we tell her CJ was the nephew of Dad's biggest enemy, and Rio killed him for what he'd done to her, we'll run the risk of making a martyr out of him,' Kelsey replied.

'I'm still not sure. I feel more than a bit uncomfortable about keeping Scarlett in the dark about this, but I suppose you girls are right. It's probably better that she doesn't know the truth. At least not at the moment,' Mum agreed.

'It's the only way, Amanda. You'll never be able to tell Scarlett that CJ was Craig. Let her carry on believing they were two different people. Rio managed to make it look like the guy committed suicide, so we don't want it to come out that that wasn't the case. Do we?' Jack said, turning to look at Mum before training his eyes back on the road. 'Nobody knows how Scarlett would react if she knew the full story. She might tell the police, and then all of our necks will be on the line. Rio isn't the only one with blood on his hands. We'd all be considered accessories to the murder.'

'I hadn't thought of that,' Mum replied.

'None of us want to do time for the Colemans. That family were the scum of the earth. Because of them, you've lost your husband and unborn grandchild, and your daughter almost didn't survive the brutal attack on her,' Jack pointed out.

'I can't help feeling like I'm betraying Scarlett.' Mum turned to look at Jack.

'You're not betraying her; you're protecting her by holding back the most painful details. It's for her own good. Scarlett's got a long recovery ahead of her; she's not in the right frame of mind to deal with all of this,' Jack said.

Mum was listening intently. I could see my husband's words were starting to sink in; he was more than qualified to pre-empt the situation. Jack was an expert at dealing with mental health issues; he'd got me to thank for that.

'Thank you, Jack. It does make me feel better to think that I'm sparing Scarlett more heartache by shielding her from the truth.' Mum seemed content to go along with the plan.

Every family had something to hide, didn't they?

60

Scarlett

Now that there had been a significant improvement in my condition, I'd been moved out of intensive care.

When the doctor had finished examining me, he gestured over his shoulder to a man waiting by the double doors at the front of the ward. 'The police officer would like to speak to you if you're feeling up to it,' he said.

'I can't see the point. I don't remember much about the attack,' I replied, looking across to where Mum, Mia and Kelsey were sitting by my bedside.

The doctor didn't answer. He hung my notes back on the end of the bed and carried on with his rounds.

'I'm Detective Constable Price,' the young man said a few moments later when he approached me. 'I'm glad to see you're on the mend. I was just wondering if you've managed to remember anything about the attack?'

I'd been racking my brain trying to think of something that might be helpful, but I'd drawn a blank. 'All I know is that the motorcyclists were wearing black helmets and were dressed head to toe in black leather...' I trailed off.

In hindsight, I realised I shouldn't have tried to hold on to my bag. Life was more important than money, but it had all happened so quickly, I wasn't thinking straight. It was a gut reaction.

'Your recollection fits with what's been reported. Some of the witnesses noted that neither of the bikes had number plates. Our investigation is continuing, but it's not clear at this stage whether this was a random attack by biker bandits or a targeted attack, as your family believe. Say, for instance, their theory is correct, and the assault on you was linked to your father's murder. How would your father's enemies have known that you would be in that very place, on that day, at that time?'

'I have no idea.' I turned to look at my mum with pleading eyes. I had to make this stop. The young detective was clearly keen to crack the case, but his overzealous behaviour was making me feel unduly pressured. 'I don't feel up to being questioned at the moment. Can we do this another time?' Tears began to roll down my cheeks as I tried my best to put on an Oscar-winning performance, and it struck a chord with my protective Mum.

'Absolutely,' Mum replied, getting out of her seat and handing me a tissue. 'As you can see, talking about the attack is distressing my daughter. I'm afraid you'll need to resume this at a later stage.'

The DC didn't look happy, but there was little he could do about it. I wouldn't consent to being questioned, so he had no choice but to abide by that decision.

'That's not a problem,' Detective Constable Price said, but the expression on his face didn't match his words.

'Can I talk to Kelsey in private for a minute?' I asked once the detective had left.

Mum looked hurt by my request, but she didn't protest. Mia threw Kelsey a sideways glance before she got up from her chair, and they both walked out of the ward without making a fuss.

'I need to ask you a favour. I want to see CJ, but I haven't got his number. My mobile was in my bag when it was stolen. Can you get hold of him, please?' I asked.

Kelsey's posture stiffened.

'I know he's not your favourite person, but you don't know him like I do.' I smiled, hoping to appeal to her better nature.

'There's something I have to tell you. CJ set you up,' Kelsey began. She swallowed hard before she continued to speak. 'After you were stabbed, witnesses saw him get onto the back of the motorbike and take off with the men who attacked you.'

The contents of my stomach started to rise. 'That can't be true. The witnesses must have got that wrong.'

But then I thought back to our date at the Shard, and I felt an overwhelming feeling of dread rise up inside me. CJ had left the table moments after we'd decided where we would be spending the rest of the evening to make a phone call in private. Could he have been arranging the attack?

'I'm sure you don't want to believe it, but that's what happened,' Kelsey replied.

I'd previously brushed aside Kelsey's concerns, but

now that hard facts were staring me in the face, they were difficult to ignore.

'CJ wouldn't do that to me; I was pregnant with his child. When I'd told him about the baby, I'd thought he might run for the door or put his head in his hands and say, "Oh shit, why me?" But he hadn't. Admittedly, he'd been very shocked, but he'd been incredibly supportive, saying he'd stick by me whatever happened.' When I began to cry, Kelsey tried to comfort me, but I shrugged her away.

'My heart bleeds for you,' Kelsey said, but her sincerity seemed false somehow.

Kelsey was the most self-centred person I knew. She wasn't a bit considerate and was usually so absorbed in her own little universe she didn't stop to think about how others were feeling, let alone what they were thinking about. I suddenly swiped my tears away with the pads of my fingers.

'The baby wasn't planned, but CJ hadn't tried to pressure me into having an abortion; he'd held my hand and told me everything would be OK. Why would CJ tell me that I was the best thing that had ever happened to him if he was going to arrange for somebody to stab me?'

'That's the part I don't understand. He could have targeted you without having a relationship with you.'

'We were happy together.'

I knew the odds had been stacked against us, but I was sure we were going to be OK. Tears welled up in my eyes as I pictured the scene. I broke down at the thought of what might have been. Life had so many twists and turns. Who knew for certain what would happen in their future?

'Don't cry, Scarlett. He's not worth it,' Kelsey said.

'You'd look for any reason to throw CJ under the bus, wouldn't you?'

'I'm not making this up, Scarlett.'

'Can you go and get Mum and Mia?

Kelsey walked away from the bed. While I waited for her to return with the others, I kept hoping when they came back they'd put a different spin on what she'd been saying.

'I know you feel devastated, darling, but you're going to get through this,' Mum said, sitting down on the edge of the bed.

'So it's true then? I glanced sideways at Kelsey, and when I saw her slowly shake her head and tut, it brought fresh tears to my bloodshot eyes.

'I'm not that much of a bitch. I wouldn't have told you CJ was involved with your attackers if it wasn't true.' Kelsey had her hands on her hips and a look of anger on her face.

'That's enough, Kelsey.' Mum threw my sister a look, warning her to back off.

'Maybe you can get her to see reason; I've tried, but she's in denial,' Kelsey replied, crossing her arms over her chest. 'I warned you about CJ right from the start. I could sense there was something dodgy about him from the first moment I clapped eyes on him.'

Fresh resentment began bubbling up inside of me. My world had come crashing down around me, and I really needed to be surrounded by positive thoughts at the moment. I didn't want to listen to I told you so; I wanted somebody to say everything would be all right.

'I know you did, but he swept me off my feet. I'd thought he was the perfect guy for me,' I sobbed.

'Shhh, it's OK, Scarlett. We all make mistakes,' Mia said, running her hand over my hair to comfort me.

The truth, whether I wanted to accept it or not, was I hadn't seen any of this coming. I wasn't sure why I was so shocked that I'd been blindsided; I couldn't put my hand on my heart and say I knew CJ inside out. We'd only been together for a month; that was no time at all. The man whose child I'd been carrying was little more than a stranger, and the thought of that terrified me and sent a fresh wave of panic flooding through my body.

CJ's words came back to haunt me. *Don't look so worried; I'm not a serial killer scouting out my next victim,* he'd said. At the time, I laughed his comment off, but it had made me feel uneasy. My gut told me to proceed with caution, but I'd chosen to ignore it. If only I'd listened; it would have saved me a lot of heartache.

Seeing the look of pity and concern on my anxious family's faces was making things ten times worse. They'd already been through so much. I didn't want to add to the burden. But before I could stop them, tears sprang from my eyes, and I began to sob uncontrollably. I couldn't prevent the meltdown; my body was still flooded with the now redundant pregnancy hormones, so my emotions were all over the place.

'Let it all out, my darling. You'll feel better when you've had a good cry,' Mum said. 'I know it seems like this is the end of the world, but trust me; it's just a bump in the road; you have your whole life ahead of you.'

If that was the case, why did I feel so wretched, as though my future was bleak? I couldn't believe I'd been so blind to the deception. CJ must have had all sorts of skeletons hiding in his closet if I'd bothered to take a closer look. But I'd been so delighted that he was showing me some attention and taking my mind off what was happening at home that I'd gone into the relationship wearing blinkers. My mum and sisters had intentionally kept me out of the loop, denying me access to the family business, and that hurt more than I could say. I'd felt shunned by their behaviour, which had driven me into CJ's arms. My mind was whirring. There was so much to take in, and I couldn't think straight with everyone gathered around me.

'Can all of you go now? I want to be on my own.'

My words were cold and self-indulgent, but I didn't care what they thought. After what I'd been through, I felt my behaviour was justified. My mum looked a bit shocked, but I didn't want her sympathy or, worse still, her pity.

'If you're sure that's what you want,' Mum said, with a look of concern on her beautiful face.

I nodded. I didn't trust myself to speak. I could feel fresh tears welling up in my eyes, and I wanted my family to go before they started leaving tracks down my cheeks. I wasn't comfortable playing the role of the victim. I felt like a complete idiot. Kelsey had tried to warn me about going out with a stranger, but I was too pig-headed to listen and now I had to pay the price.

Flashbacks to our time together started bombarding my brain. All the signs had been there; I'd just chosen to ignore them. On our very first date, CJ had taken me to The Three Sisters. He'd said, *When I realised what this place was called, I couldn't resist bringing you here*. I'd wondered how he knew I had two sisters; he'd met Kelsey, but I was almost certain I'd never mentioned Mia. The question had sprung into my mind at the time. Why didn't I speak up? I knew the answer; I hadn't wanted anything to spoil the moment. Then I thought of something else; CJ had used my surname that night too. That should have definitely rung alarm bells, but instead of taking heed of the red flags, I'd decided to bury my head in the sand and ignore them. I'd been an idiot; no wonder I'd been burned.

I felt hollow inside and had cried more tears than I'd ever thought possible. I needed a break from the truth. It was too awful to take in, so I tried to focus on something else, but the memories kept coming, bombarding my brain like missiles. I couldn't seem to stop them. Each of them was more damning than the last. The night before I was stabbed, CJ had been very off with me when I'd paid him a surprise visit. A frosty atmosphere had stretched out between us. He'd said he'd had a stressful day at work. At the time, I'd wondered if he was having doubts about us and if his feelings were genuine; now, I knew that was the case.

A wave of nausea washed over me, and humiliation hung around my shoulders like a lead cloak; the weight of it was crushing. Love had made a fool of me. I wanted to climb into a deep hole and hide away from the world.

61

Kelsey

'What made you tell Scarlett about Craig?' Mum asked as Todd drove us home from the hospital. He'd been waiting in the car while we'd gone in to visit my sister.

'You can't call him that, Mum. As far as Scarlett's concerned his name is CJ,' I replied.

'Sorry, I wasn't thinking. Why did you tell her about the attack? I was expecting to break the bad news to her,' Mum said.

'I didn't have a choice. She was asking to see CJ.'

'Poor Scarlett, she's been through so much.' Mum looked pale and drawn. Scarlett's ordeal was taking its toll on her too.

'I know. I felt like such a bitch having to tell her what he'd done. She didn't take it well; she was adamant that CJ wouldn't have done that to her. I had to drill it into her brain that he was involved in the attack.'

'We probably should have realised she might not believe it,' Mia said. 'It must have come as a terrible shock to her.'

'Scarlett views CJ through rose-tinted glasses, so she can't visualise the scumbag the rest of us see. She told me he was happy about the baby and was convinced they were going to stay together and be one of those lucky couples who beat the odds stacked against them,' I said.

'Love's young dream,' Mum said with a downcast look on her face.

Mia let out a long sigh. 'I'd hate to be in her position; it's just so sad. I hope she's strong enough to cope with all of this.'

Out of all of us, Mia could probably relate the best to Scarlett's fragile state of mind. She always seemed to be battling demons of some sort or another.

'Scarlett is made of strong stuff; she'll get through this. She just needs time to come to terms with what's happened so that she can get everything into perspective,' Mum pointed out.

I wasn't sure it was going to be as simple as that. Scarlett's world had been tipped on its head, and everyone had a breaking point, didn't they?

'Even though they hadn't been together that long, Scarlett had strong feelings for CJ, so she doesn't want to accept what I told her,' I said.

'She will in time.' Mum gave me a half-smile. 'She's got a lot on her plate. She's still recovering from her injuries. The doctor said she's not out of the woods yet.'

'Physical wounds heal much quicker than emotional ones,' Mia said.

'Scarlett needs to know we won't give up on her, even if

she keeps pushing us away,' Mum said. 'We'll give her an hour or two to get herself together, and then let's go back to the hospital.'

'I can't even begin to imagine what she's going through,' Mia said. 'Being betrayed by your partner like that must be completely devastating. Jack's helped me through the worst moments of my life. I can't imagine not having him to lean on.'

'He's a good man. You're lucky to have him. In some ways, I'm glad your dad wasn't alive to see what's happened to Scarlett. You know how protective he was of all of us. It would have torn him apart.' Mum shook her head.

62

Scarlett

When I looked back at it, I think I knew I was pregnant before I'd taken the test. I'd completely gone off alcohol, and certain food that I'd previously loved turned my stomach. Not to mention the fact that I was overly emotional and suddenly offended by the slightest remark that would normally slide off me like a fried egg in a non-stick pan.

Even after it had been confirmed, my mind had been whirring with thoughts. I'd been scared to tell my family I was pregnant in case they pressured me into having an abortion. And if I was totally honest, I was embarrassed because CJ and I hadn't been an item for very long, so it seemed a bit scandalous. I dreaded to think what my dad would have said about the matter. But in the grand scheme of things, all of that seemed ridiculous now.

CJ and I had been blissfully happy; well, at least that's what I'd thought. Now a question mark hung over our entire relationship. After what I'd been through, my faith in the opposite sex had been obliterated. I didn't know how I was going to deal with this. There were so many unanswered questions spinning around in my head, but I couldn't seem to filter what was important or not. How could CJ do this to me? I'd never be able to move on with my life if I didn't confront him. I deserved an explanation. He owed me that much.

'I need to speak to CJ,' I said when Mum, Mia and Kelsey came back to the hospital.

They exchanged awkward glances before Kelsey spoke up. 'There's no way we can get hold of him.'

'I know his address. I'll give it to you. I'm not going to accept what you told me until I hear it from his mouth.'

'If CJ shows up here, the police will arrest him,' Kelsey replied.

I paused for a minute. 'Get him to phone me then.' Mum had bought me a new mobile to replace the stolen one.

'And what if the police trace the call?'

Kelsey seemed to have an answer for everything. But I wasn't going to be fobbed off that easily.

'Just do it, Kelsey. It's important.'

'How are you feeling?' Mum asked, rubbing the back of my hand with her soft fingertips.

It was the question that everyone I came into contact with asked, so I'd become an expert at answering it now. With the help of an expressionless face and a shoulder shrug, I didn't need to utter a word. Why did people even bother to ask? How did they expect me to be feeling? I wasn't going to lie and tell them I was OK when that wasn't the case. Life as I knew it was well and truly over; it wasn't panning out as I'd once hoped, and I found myself lashing out at the people who loved me most. I couldn't seem to stop myself.

'Do you really want to know how I'm feeling?'

'Of course,' Mum's lips stretched into a smile, but it soon slid from her face when I broke into a rant.

'Physically, it hurts to move even an inch; I feel like I've been run over by a bus. But that's the easy part. Mentally, I'll be scarred for life. The man I was in love with left me for dead on the pavement, and I don't think I will ever get over miscarrying in such tragic circumstances.'

'Yes, you will, darling. Just give it some time,' Mum soothed. She was smothering me, but deep down, I knew her concern came from a place of love.

'I feel guilty for being alive when my baby isn't. You can't even begin to imagine what that's like. I hate myself. Survivor's guilt or whatever it is they call it is a destructive force, and it's currently hollowing out my insides like a maggot in a piece of decaying flesh.'

Mum looked aghast as my words hit her full force. 'My heart bleeds for you, darling. Once you're well enough to come home, we'll get you some therapy.'

As if that was going to make everything OK. Nobody understood what I was going through. The last thing I wanted was men in white coats poking their noses into my innermost thoughts.

'You look exhausted. We'll let you get some rest,' Mum said before she kissed me on the cheek.

Just as my family were about to leave, the doctor appeared at the end of my bed.

'Mrs Saunders, have you got a moment?' he said.

'Of course,' Mum replied.

'Scarlett has made fantastic progress, so we're going to be discharging her in the next couple of days,' the doctor said.

'That's great news! We can't wait to have her home.'

When Mum beamed at me, I smiled. The thought of getting out of hospital suddenly made everything seem a bit brighter.

63

Mia

I didn't think I'd ever seen Scarlett lash out at Kelsey before. But at least Kelsey hadn't attempted to retaliate; she'd accepted the verbal onslaught with good grace, which wasn't easy to do. I was proud of her for turning the other cheek.

The hospital visit had been draining. Scarlett's distress was palpable; my family's collective sympathy had done little to ease her suffering. She was heartbroken to the point of wanting to self-destruct, and that was difficult to witness. I'd felt redundant and had been looking forward to some time on my own away from all the anguish. Sadness was contagious. Scarlett's misery would infect my mental state if I wasn't careful.

A feeling of contentment filled me when Todd drove the car along the gravel driveway. I was only moments away from reaching the sanctity of my bedroom, where peace and quiet were waiting to greet me.

As we approached the front door, I could hear a woman's

raised voice coming from the other side. I felt myself groan; we'd had enough drama to last us a lifetime.

'Get out of my way,' the woman said.

'You're not going anywhere,' I heard Rio reply as Mum opened the front door.

An attractive, dark-haired woman was standing in our hallway engaged in a standoff with Rio. Her eyes immediately flicked towards Todd before she focused her glare on Kelsey.

'What's going on?' Mum asked.

'I found this woman hanging around in the lane. She was acting suspiciously and became aggressive when I started questioning her, so I thought it was best to detain her under the circumstances.' Rio turned his attention away from Mum and fixed Todd with his dark eyes. 'She reckons she's your wife.'

I had a sudden churning feeling in the pit of my stomach; I'd always been a martyr to my nerves.

'Your wife?' Kelsey questioned, looking daggers at Todd. 'So nice of you to share that with me.'

'As if you didn't know. Women like you always know.' When the woman delivered the scathing attack, Kelsey switched.

'You're really beginning to piss me off,' Kelsey said, turning on the woman.

'Likewise,' the woman replied.

'I had no idea Todd was married. Not that I have to explain myself to you. He should be the one sitting in the hot seat.' Kelsey jabbed her finger towards Todd. She was a professional when it came to shooting filthy looks, and he was practically squirming in response. 'Start talking.'

'I would, but you two won't let me get a word in,' Todd replied.

'I can't wait to hear this. It will save me the trouble of having to confront you over her.' Todd's wife scanned Kelsey from top to bottom with a bitter expression pasted on her face.

Ever since we'd been little, Kelsey had always pushed boundaries; it looked like she'd gone too far this time.

'I'm not sure what's going on here, but why don't we go through to the living room?' Mum suggested.

Over the years, Mum had had plenty of practice dealing with the situations Kelsey got herself into, so she was an expert at handling them by now. Kelsey never got a rise out of Mum, regardless of what she threw in her direction. Even when my sister was a door-slamming, hormonal teen, Mum stayed calm and didn't let Kelsey's antics ruffle her feathers. She chose her battles wisely, knowing that some things were worth letting go of for the sake of having harmony at home. Mum was a great believer in allowing a person to be independent enough to make their own way and mistakes in life. And Kelsey had made more than most. But I wasn't sure how she was going to react when she found out that Kelsey had been having a relationship with Todd, especially as he was a married man.

'Take a seat,' Mum said to Todd's wife. 'I'm Amanda. What's your name?'

'Michelle,' the dark-haired woman replied.

'You seem to have a problem with my daughter. Would you like to tell me what's going on?' Mum asked.

Todd stood staring into space. His dark eyes were like hollowed-out black sockets.

'My husband's been having an affair with Kelsey,' Michelle replied.

Mum's posture stiffened. 'Please tell me I heard that wrong? Are you serious?'

When Michelle nodded her head, Mum turned her attention to my sister. But Kelsey didn't say a word. She cast her eyes to the floor instead.

'Don't you dare give me the silent treatment! What have you got to say for yourself?' Mum shouted as her composure disappeared into thin air.

She was fuming. I couldn't ever remember a time when I'd seen her so irate. Her cheeks were flushed with colour as rage flowed through her like molten lava.

'Why on earth did you get involved with Todd? He's your bodyguard. How could you be so stupid?' Mum threw her hands out. Her eyes were blazing. 'They'd be hell to pay if your dad was here. He would never have stood for this!'

Kelsey tossed her hair. 'Dad knew Todd and I were seeing each other,' she replied. Her retort was full of bitterness.

Mum jolted backwards as though Kelsey's words had slapped her around the face.

'What do you mean he knew?' Mum looked shell-shocked that her husband had kept their fling a secret.

It wasn't fair of Kelsey to imply that Dad had known about the situation and done nothing about it. If the timing and circumstances had been different, there would have been another outcome. He'd been furious when he'd caught Kelsey and Todd out the night before my wedding and was going to fire Todd once we were back in London. But he'd obviously decided to wait until after the wedding to tell Mum and then never got the chance. So Kelsey and Todd had taken advantage of that and carried on seeing each other, hiding in plain sight, right under everyone's noses.

'I don't understand why you're so angry with me. I'm one of the wounded parties. I had no idea Todd was married, so I'm also a victim,' Kelsey replied, trying to join forces with Michelle against the man who'd wronged them both. 'Todd's been lying to all of us.'

'I suspected he was cheating on me again a while ago,' Michelle said.

'Wait. Rewind that. This has happened before?' I could see anger flash across Kelsey's face.

'Aww, poor you, were you thinking you were special? Todd's one and only?' Michelle's words had a sarcastic edge to them.

Kelsey clamped her mouth shut, but I had a sinking feeling that it was a temporary measure, and pretty soon, the mud-slinging would begin.

'I didn't want to believe he was back to his old tricks.' Michelle's jaw clenched as she spoke.

'How long have you suspected?' Mum asked.

'Within days of Todd starting to work for your family,' Michelle replied.

Mum straightened her posture and stared at Michelle with wide eyes. 'That long?'

Michelle nodded. 'It's been going on for some time. I'd hoped it would have fizzled out by now.' Michelle was simmering with resentment. 'People are sometimes guilty of only seeing and hearing what they want to. I tried to turn a blind eye to it, but deep down, I knew I was deluding myself.'

Scarlett suddenly popped into my thoughts. She was

suffering from the same issue, pinning her hopes and dreams on a lost cause.

'The first time Todd cheated on me, I'd thought he'd picked up a random stranger in a bar after having one too many. But my husband wasn't that mysterious. All the times he's had an affair, it's been with someone he knew.'

'All the times? How many affairs have there been?' Kelsey put her hands on her hips and glared at Michelle, suddenly turning on her.

When Todd's wife began to laugh, I thought my sister was going to wipe the smirk off her face. But she had no right to get physical. Michelle was the victim here, not Kelsey.

'Todd's always been a lady's man. He's a serial cheat,' Michelle announced as if it was something to be proud of. 'He's been unfaithful to me more times than I care to mention; it's proving to be a hard habit to break, isn't it, darling?' Michelle said.

Todd bristled in response.

Kelsey didn't always take other people's feelings into account; it looked like she'd met her match with Todd judging by what his long-suffering wife had put up with over the years. He was just as self-centred as she was, cheating on Michelle with countless women.

'I think you should know, when I apprehended Michelle, she was in possession of a gun,' Rio said, changing the direction of the conversation.

Mum's hand flew up to her chest; her eyes were like saucers.

'Don't look so worried, Amanda; I've confiscated the weapon,' Rio continued.

'Why were you armed?' Mum asked.

Michelle let out a maniacal cackle. 'I came here to finish the job.'

'What's that supposed to mean?' Mum tilted her head and fixed Michelle with a quizzical gaze.

'The last bullet that had Kelsey's name on ended up in somebody else.'

Mum gasped. 'Davie,' she said before her eyes welled up with tears.

Michelle nodded her head.

My heartbeat went into overdrive. Dad's murderer was standing mere feet away from me. The police believed he'd been killed by a sniper, but I hadn't expected it to be a female assassin who was responsible for firing the fatal bullet.

'Oh my God, I can't take this in. You destroyed my family.' Mum's words came out as a heartbroken sob. She had to grip onto the edge of the table for support. Mum swiped her tears away with the back of her hand as fury replaced her anguish. 'You took my husband's life to get back at the vile man you married.'

Mum shot Todd a venomous look.

'I'd been trying to catch Todd and Kelsey together for ages, and I'd flown into a jealous rage when I saw them sneaking off together the night before the wedding. I couldn't face the thought of losing him to another woman. My days of being in a love triangle were over. I wanted revenge. Todd has messed with my head and my heart one too many times. Kelsey had to go.' Michelle's words sent a shiver down my spine.

'So why did you shoot, Davie?' Mum's voice caught in her throat.

'I hit him by accident,' Michelle admitted.

'I'm not buying it,' Todd piped up. 'I met Michelle when we were both in the Army. Thanks to her training, she's a crack shot. Her aim was always perfect. There's no way she would have missed a static target.'

Michelle's eyes were blazing. 'I didn't expect to miss either, but your bit on the side decided to move right at the last moment, so my positioning was slightly off, and I accidentally hit Davie.'

Kelsey's hands flew up to cover her mouth, then she dropped her hands and clasped them in front of her chest. 'I remember leaning towards Dad just before he was shot. I was about to tell him something when I heard the sound of gunfire.'

Kelsey looked grief-stricken as she thought back to the moment.

'Who would have thought that tiny movement would make a difference?' Michelle threw Kelsey an evil look.

Mum suddenly stood up and steadied herself on the edge of the table. She looked deathly pale.

'Are you OK?' I asked.

'I think I'm going to be sick,' Mum said before she rushed out of the room, covering her mouth with her hands.

'I'm not listening to another word. Don't let her out of your sight,' Kelsey said to Rio as she stood up. She stood glaring at Todd for several moments, no doubt trying to take it all in before she continued to speak. 'I want to talk to you in private.' She spat out the words as though they were coated in acid before she stomped out of the room.

64

Kelsey

My feet pounded across the room. I felt like I was going to explode as a mixture of rage and humiliation battled for supremacy inside me. I was brazen by nature and usually brimming over with self-assurance, but I couldn't bear to be in the room with Todd's wife a moment longer. The way her beady eyes kept sweeping over every inch of me made me want to lash out at somebody.

I suddenly pictured Todd's tattoo with the initial M over his heart. When I'd asked him about it, he'd told me it stood for all the things he loved: his mum, the marines and the military. *What a nice tribute*, I'd thought. He hadn't bothered mentioning the most significant detail; it was also the initial of his wife's name. What an idiot I'd been. As the realisation hit me like a slap around the face, my blood began to boil.

Rio had everything under control and was more than capable of guarding Michelle, so Todd's presence wasn't necessary. He was surplus to requirement, which was just as well. By the time I'd finished tearing a strip off of him, he'd be good for nothing.

'I'm just going to check on Mum,' I heard Mia say as I disappeared out of the front door.

Todd caught up with me as I was heading down the lane that led to the river. It was my go-to place when I was stressed out. I loved being close to water; there was something very therapeutic about it.

'So when were you going to tell me you had a wife?' I asked, sitting down on the first wooden bench I came to.

Todd dropped down next to me, put his head in his hands and began rubbing his hair with his palms. He was usually so cocky. I couldn't remember him being lost for words before. If Michelle was to be believed, he'd done this countless times, so you would have thought the excuses would have rolled off his tongue. But he didn't utter a sound.

So Todd didn't think I deserved an explanation. Did that really surprise me? I couldn't say it did. It would appear I was just another notch on his bedpost. I wasn't sure how I felt about that. I like to be the one in control. As we sat side by side in silence, I looked back on my time with him. It had never been the hearts and flowers, candlelit dinner type of romance; it had all been based on stolen moments. The first time our eyes had met, I'd felt a sudden jolt, then a rush of energy. There was a strong physical attraction between us, so it was instinctual to want to rip his clothes off and see what he was made of. I was powerless to resist the pull; it was inevitable that we were going to end up in bed together.

After Dad had died, I'd tried my best to connect with Todd on a deeper level, but something was stopping me from opening up. I'd put that down to the fact that I was a commitment-phobe who loved my freedom and hated it when someone invaded my personal space too closely. Todd had never told me much about himself. I'd thought that was because he didn't want me to know things that made him vulnerable. What I hadn't realised was that he was keeping me at arm's length because he was cheating on his wife. I had no idea he was living a double life. He was just as selfish and self-centred as I was.

I was shell-shocked when I'd found out I'd been Todd's bit on the side. If I'd known he was married, I might not have become involved. Although given my attraction, it was more than likely our affair would still have happened. I knew some people would be appalled by my attitude and call me a homewrecker, but if Todd and Michelle had been happy together, he wouldn't have been tempted to stray. He'd betrayed me just as much as his long-suffering wife by not allowing me to make an informed decision.

It wasn't my fault Todd chose to seek his needs in the arms of another woman. It was true I was a life-long flirt and was not opposed to a dalliance with a good-looking guy. But I hadn't forced him into anything. As far as I knew, it was the first time I'd been involved with a married man. That got me thinking, for all the affairs that partners discovered, there must be plenty of others that remained a secret.

Men like Todd kept their home lives private. I'd never seen him wear a wedding ring. Even if he had, it would have had its limitations. It was just a piece of jewellery; a metal band didn't have the power to repel somebody away from the person wearing it. The attraction wasn't all one-sided.

I could feel Todd's eyes on me. Always. And when we were together, he only ever had one thing on his mind.

I'd been mulling something over while I'd been waiting for Todd to try and redeem himself, but I couldn't fathom it, so I decided to put the question to the man who could potentially shed some light on the matter.

'How did Michelle know where Mia's wedding was being held?'

Todd turned to look at me.

Mia had insisted that she wanted a quiet ceremony, so only a handful of guests were invited, and for security reasons, they'd been given the details of the location at short notice. I had a sinking feeling that Todd knew more than he was letting on.

'Thistledown Castle was as far removed from civilisation as you could get. A gun-toting lunatic shouldn't have been able to stumble upon it accidentally,' I said.

'I agree with you. It was a carefully planned operation. That's why I'm convinced Michelle wasn't the shooter,' Todd replied.

'Why would she admit to killing my dad if she hadn't done it? That makes no sense.'

'Because she's trying to frighten you off by telling you she hit your dad while she was aiming for you. The woman's got a screw loose. The things she saw when she was on active duty messed with her head,' Todd replied.

I didn't doubt that, but there was nothing for her to gain from her admission.

'Your dad wasn't shot by accident. Whoever pulled the trigger did so with the accuracy of a marksman. A single bullet killed him; all the subsequent rounds were deliberately fired away from the main party. The aim was to cause panic and confusion amongst the guests, which was precisely what happened,' Todd said.

I couldn't dispute what he'd just said, but then Craig and Scarlett's situation suddenly popped into my mind. A shiver ran down my spine. Maybe Todd was involved in all of this. And now that Michelle had confessed, he was trying to make me think she was crazy to cover his tracks. I didn't know who to believe. We'd all been convinced the Colemans were behind Dad's murder. But something seemed off. Victor had vehemently protested his innocence and involvement before Rio had snuffed out his life. What if he'd been telling the truth? It was too awful to contemplate.

Todd slung his arm around my shoulder, so I shrugged him away. I didn't want him near me, so I stood up and fixed him with a glare. 'Don't touch me. As far as I'm concerned, it's over between us.'

I'd drawn a line in the sand after his behaviour with Paige. I'd promised myself if Todd crossed it one more time, he'd be history. I wasn't about to go back on that.

'Listen, Kelsey, I know what Michelle's like. You're reacting in the exact way she wants you to. She's trying to split us up; that's why she's messing with your head.'

I didn't know what to think. But one thing that was crystal clear in my mind was my affair with Todd had caused my family nothing but trouble. Because of him, an unstable woman had come into our lives, and we'd lost my dad as a result of it. It could so easily have been me. The thought of that sent a shiver down my spine.

'Take it from me, Michelle's not the shooter who killed

your dad. She's cooked all of this up to scare you off. Don't play into her hand,' Todd said as he tried to convince me he was telling the truth.

His eyes were pleading, but he was so arrogant, he didn't feel the need to apologise for lying to me and bringing shit to my door. He seemed to be under the illusion that finding out he was married wouldn't make any difference to me. He was mistaken. I was worth more than that; I didn't want a man who'd show me so little respect in my life, or in my bed for that matter. There were plenty more fish in the sea.

'As of now, you can consider yourself fired. Your services are no longer required.'

The look of utter shock on Todd's face was so satisfying, I had to stop my lips from stretching into a broad grin. I could be a total bitch when the mood took me. I knew in the past, my words and actions had hurt people, and I didn't care about that as much as I should have. But in this case, I felt my behaviour was justified.

There wasn't much connecting us, so cutting Todd out of my life would be no loss. We had very little in common, apart from the mutual desire to tear each other's clothes off. The sex I'd had with Todd was off-the-charts amazing, which was why he'd lasted so long. But I shook that thought from my mind. I wasn't going to be Todd's bit on the side. I liked a man to treat me well, return my phone calls, remember my birthday, and not just tend to my orgasms. Todd had failed miserably in all departments apart from one.

I felt more stupid than heartbroken. I hadn't just lost my soulmate, so I'd be over him before I knew it. I wouldn't waste my tears on a man like Todd; he didn't deserve them. And they say that the best way to get over somebody is to get under somebody else, don't they? Wise words indeed.

65

Mia

'I don't know what to make of any of this,' Mum said when she walked into the kitchen.

I'd been getting worried about her. She'd locked herself in the bathroom for what seemed like an age, but she had more colour in her cheeks than she'd had earlier, so that was a good sign.

'Do you think Michelle's telling the truth?' Mum pulled out a chair and sat down opposite me.

'I have no idea, but why would she lie?'

'Todd's just been trying to convince me that she cooked all of this up to scare me off,' Kelsey said when she entered the room.

'Do you think that's possible?' Mum quizzed.

'Who knows? You can't believe a word that comes out of his mouth. He's caused us an untold amount of grief, so I decided to fire him,' Kelsey said.

Mum and I exchanged a glance. That wasn't Kelsey's decision to make; she should have discussed it with us first.

But I knew Dad had planned to terminate Todd's employment when he'd caught Kelsey with him, so I was happy to let it go, and I was pretty sure Mum had no objections. I couldn't say I was surprised; Kelsey was impulsive, and Todd had humiliated her, so she was bound to want to get back at him after the way he'd treated her.

There was no point dwelling on the matter; we had more important things to worry about. Learning that Michelle was ex-military had been a shock to all of us. She claimed she'd taken Dad's life by accident because Kelsey had moved. But if she was as good a markswoman as Todd said, she would never have missed her target, would she?

'I'm struggling to make sense of it all.' Mum's brows knitted together.

'You're not the only one,' I agreed.

'Rio was convinced the Colemans were behind your dad's murder,' Mum said.

'And they had a motive, so that backs up Todd's theory,' I added. 'Maybe Michelle was in league with the Colemans, and they paid her to take Dad out.'

We were going around in circles.

'Or maybe Todd was working for the Colemans all along too…' Kelsey's words trailed off.

Mum's hands flew up to cover her mouth. She held them there for a few moments before she crossed her arms over her chest and began to speak.

'I hadn't thought of that. I'm sorry to have to say this, Kelsey, but I'm not at all sure I trust Todd. Your dad had his reservations about him as well.'

'There's no need to apologise; he means nothing to me,' Kelsey said with bitterness coating her words.

'There's only one way we're going to get to the bottom of whether Davie or Kelsey was the real target; we need to question Michelle,' Mum said.

Michelle was still sitting at the dining room table when we walked back into the room. Rio's huge frame was looming over her like an avenging angel.

'How did you know where Mia's wedding was being held?' Kelsey began.

'My husband is very methodical and likes to keeps notes on everything,' Michelle replied.

I remembered my dad had been unhappy about our new bodyguard's incessant scribbling. Dad hated the idea of leaving a paper trail. Now it was clear he'd been right to be concerned about it.

'You and Todd thought you were being so secretive, but I gathered a lot of information from his notebooks so that I could piece together your movements and keep tabs on you,' Michelle said to Kelsey. 'I'd been tormenting myself with the details of your affair and was being eaten alive with jealousy. But when I saw Todd's hands roaming all over your body before you disappeared inside your room the night before the wedding, something flipped inside me.'

The result of one bad decision lasted a lifetime. Michelle had known about the affair for ages, but when she was confronted by the sight of her husband and his mistress, it was more than she could bear. The incident kick-started a chain of events that had changed the course of our lives and devastated all of us. What should have been a celebration turned into a tragedy.

'Can I speak to the two of you in private?' Kelsey said to Mum and I.

'Of course,' Mum replied as we followed her back into the kitchen.

Kelsey looked terrible; the colour had drained from her face.

'You look awful. Are you OK?' I asked.

Kelsey shook her head. 'My gut was telling me not to believe a word Todd said, and it was right.'

'Right about what?' Mum questioned with a look of concern on her face.

'The only way Michelle would have known Todd and I went to my room the night before Mia's wedding was if she saw it with her own eyes. She was the assassin, and I was the target. My affair was meant to be a bit of fun; it wasn't meant to cause all this devastation. So many lives have been affected. It's all my fault; Dad's dead because of me.' Kelsey buried her face in her hands and broke down in tears.

Mum rushed to comfort Kelsey as she crumbled in front of us. She threw her arms around Kelsey's shoulders and held her close, but she was inconsolable. I couldn't bring myself to go to her. My dad had lost his life because of her affair. I stood rooted to the spot, lost in my own grief.

Mum looked up, and her eyes searched mine. 'If Michelle was your dad's murderer, Victor was innocent…'

My breath caught in my throat as her words registered. We'd all been convinced the Colemans had killed my dad. Despite what we'd thought, we were wrong, which made this all the more horrific. Victor Coleman might not have committed the murder, but I wasn't sure anyone could accuse him of being innocent.

'What the hell are we going to do now?' I asked.

Kelsey broke free from Mum's embrace and straightened

her posture. 'I'm going to finish the bitch off,' she said with a look of fury on her face.

'Don't do anything hasty,' Mum replied, catching hold of Kelsey's arm to stop her in her tracks as she began to pace across the floor.

'Mum's right. We need to think about this carefully. We don't want a repeat of what happened with the Colemans, do we?' I added, hoping to talk some sense into her.

'I can't stand by and let Michelle get away with what's she's done. She tore our family apart,' Kelsey continued. Anyone could see her desire for revenge was eating away at her.

'I'm not suggesting we let her walk away, but we need time to think. I'll ask Rio to detain her until we decide on the best course of action,' Mum said, walking out of the kitchen and leaving Kelsey and I to our thoughts.

66

Scarlett

I'd been desperate to get out of the hospital, but I already felt claustrophobic, and I'd only been home a couple of hours. My family were trying to flood my mind with positive thoughts, but it was a bit overwhelming. I understood their reasoning. They didn't want me to withdraw into the depths of despair. It was hard to break free from depression and a downward spiral. Nobody knew that better than Mia, and she considered herself an expert in these matters, so she was determined to reach out to me.

Mia rapped on the door with her knuckles, then opened it before I had a chance to tell her to go away. I was lying on my side with my knees bent towards my chest, hugging my pillow.

'It's heart-breaking to see such a bubbly person reduced to this. Can I offer you some sisterly advice?'

I looked up at the sound of Mia's voice, then wiped my eyes on the back of my hand.

'People say, time heals, but pain doesn't go away, you just

learn how to accept it,' Mia said. 'But you're a performer, so you're made of strong stuff. Try and dig deep and rally your sheer determination. Don't allow yourself to sink into the depths of despair like I did.'

When I started to cry again, Mia walked towards me, sat on the edge of the bed and took hold of my hand.

'There's nothing I can do to ease your suffering; words are inadequate in a situation like this. But I know from experience, the power of touch brings much more comfort than anything I could ever say,' Mia said in a soothing voice.

'Look at the state of me. I look like a drug addict. I'm full of puncture wounds and bruises left behind by the needles. It's a constant reminder of the time I spent in hospital,' I said, glancing down at my arms.

'I know you're conscious of them, but the marks are only superficial. You're doing brilliantly. Don't lose sight of that,' Mia encouraged.

'Am I?' My eyes filled with tears again.

'You're putting too much pressure on yourself. You will get over this, but it won't happen overnight.'

'The hardest thing for me to accept is that our relationship was totally one-sided. All of it was fake. CJ was so convincing; I believed every word he said.'

When silent tears began rolling down my cheeks, Mia wiped them away with the pad of her thumbs.

'And after everything he put me through, he's walked away without a backward glance.' Anger started to boil in the pit of my stomach.

'It's better that way,' Mia said.

'It's as though I never existed.' I felt my lip start to quiver.

'It might not feel like it now, but you're better off without him,' Mia tried to reassure me.

'It makes me feel sick every time I think about what he did. Part of me never wants to see him again, and the other part wants to confront him.'

'CJ was a coward and took off at the first sign of trouble. He's long gone, and if you ask me, he'll never come back. There's too much at stake,' Mia said. 'The best thing you can do is forget you ever met him and move on with your life.'

67

Mia

'Thanks for coming,' Mum said to Rio when he walked into the office in the garden. 'It's been a terrible few days. I'm glad we found out the truth about Davie's death, but it hasn't brought me the closure I was expecting.'

Rio bowed his head for a moment, then he tilted his chin up and looked Mum in the eye. 'That's because the person responsible is still breathing. I'm sorry I got it wrong, Amanda.'

'It's not your fault. I thought the Colemans were responsible too. They had a strong motive to want Davie out of the picture, and we didn't know about Michelle at that stage, so we had no reason to doubt their involvement. I do feel bad about what we did to Victor, but Craig is another matter entirely. He deserved everything he got.' Mum's words were bitter.

'Poor Scarlett's still heartbroken. She told me part of her never wanted to see CJ again, and the other part wanted to confront him,' I said.

'Oh dear God. How are we going to get around that?' Mum looked like she had the weight of the world on her shoulders.

'I think I've sorted it. I told Scarlett that CJ was a coward who took off at the first sign of trouble, and I doubted he'd never come back.'

'Let's hope she believed you,' Mum said.

I'd felt bad lying to Scarlett, but we'd all agreed not to tell her that CJ and Craig were one and the same and let her carry on believing they were two different people. We couldn't go back on that now without making matters ten times worse. The most important thing was that Craig was out of her life and would never be able to hurt her again.

'The less Scarlett knows about the business with the Colemans the better. Let her concentrate on getting well instead,' Rio said.

Mum nodded. 'Now that we've had time to mull things over, we need to decide what we're going to do with Michelle.'

'There's only one option. She has to die for what's she's done,' Kelsey said. Her words were so cold they chilled me to the bone.

'I agree with Kelsey,' Rio said. 'We have to get justice for Davie.'

Mum swept her blonde pixie-cut across her forehead and straightened her posture as she prepared to speak. 'Nobody wants that more than I do. What about you, Mia?'

I paused for a moment. This part of the job would never sit easy with me, but sometimes it was necessary when you were running a criminal outfit. Kill or be killed was the rule of the game.

I nodded to show my agreement. 'If we let Michelle go, she might come back at a later stage...' I said.

I left my sentence unfinished. I didn't think it was necessary to add, *to finish the job*. Michelle had used those very words. Kelsey would always be in danger if we let Todd's wife walk away. She was completely unstable. And the others were right; we needed to get justice for my dad.

'So that's settled then. Nothing would give me greater pleasure than evening up the score,' Rio said.

'Thanks, Rio, but I want to be the one to pull the trigger,' Kelsey said.

'So do I,' Mum replied.

'Michelle tried to kill me, so I think it's only right that I do it,' Kelsey countered.

'And she killed my husband, so I want to see her suffer,' Mum replied.

Mum and Kelsey were facing each other in a gangster edition of *Top Trumps* to see which of them would win the right to end Michelle's life. They both had valid reasons for wanting to be the person.

'I thought I was sparing you ladies the unpleasant task, but if you're both hell-bent on taking part in the execution, why don't you both do it?' Rio suggested. 'I can teach you how to fire a gun if that's what you want.'

Kelsey was behind the wheel of the Range Rover as we made our way to Coalhouse Fort. I was sitting beside her, wringing my hands in my lap. Mum and Rio were positioned on either side of Michelle. A tense atmosphere stretched out between us. Rio had arranged for Wesley to watch over

Scarlett just to be on the safe side. Since Kelsey had fired Todd, he'd disappeared off the face of the earth, and as none of us trusted him, we didn't want to risk him taking revenge while she was home alone.

As we neared the disused landfill site close to the area in East Tilbury that was one of my dad's favourite childhood haunts, I couldn't help noticing that it looked very different than the last time we visited. The tide was in, and if it hadn't been for the smoke fumes and the industrial landscape, the way the sun was glinting on the water would have been picturesque.

Once Kelsey had parked in a bay outside the decaying lock-up, she turned off the ignition and stared out of the front windscreen, still gripping onto the steering wheel, no doubt collecting her thoughts.

When I heard the back door open, I looked over my shoulder and saw Rio getting out of the car, pulling Michelle with him. She wasn't trying to resist. Kelsey and I followed suit.

After Rio switched on the rechargeable work lights, I closed the door on the shipping container.

Michelle had her back against the furthest wall; her hands were bound in front of her. Mum and Kelsey stood in front of her, both armed with .22 calibre revolvers. Rio had selected them because of their light trigger pull; they were easy to shoot and would stay on target. The revolvers also had a low recoil and wouldn't jump around as they were shooting.

I'd expected Michelle to fall to pieces and plead for her life, but she remained stoic even though she was facing the firing squad. I was in a worse state than she was, but I tried not to show it. My hands were sweating, and my temples pulsated in time with the second hand on my watch, which I checked constantly. We needed to get this over and done with; there was no point in delaying the inevitable. The longer we were here, the greater the chance somebody would notice the Range Rover parked outside.

I could see Kelsey wanted to make her sweat and prolong the agony. But eventually, she tore her glare off her rival and glanced over at Mum. They locked eyes for several moments. Then they turned their attention back to Michelle. My heart started pounding when they stepped forward and took aim. As they pulled the triggers, I jumped in response. I'd never get used to the sound of gunfire.

Both of their bullets had hit the target. One had penetrated Michelle's skull, and the other had hit her in the chest. She slammed against the corrugated steel, then slid down the wall.

'Once we get back to the house, I'll send Wesley over here to clean up,' Rio said as we climbed into the Range Rover.

We sat in silence on the drive home, lost in our own thoughts. The tension that had stretched out between us earlier had dissipated. And now that Dad's murderer had been brought to justice, he would be able to rest in peace.

Kelsey and I had jumped into the deep end when we'd decided to head the firm. Thankfully, Rio had been on hand to guide us through the turbulent water. We wouldn't have got through the tough times without him. We'd been underestimated at every step of the way, but the war with the Colemans was over. We'd proved our rivals wrong. The Saunders sisters were so very different, but a common theme flowed through our veins. None of us were short of determination. Dad might not be around any more, but his girls would make sure his memory lived on through his business.

Acknowledgements

Thank you to my fabulous editor, Martina Arzu. It has been an absolute pleasure working with you.

Thanks to all the team at Aries Fiction and everyone involved in the production of this book, especially Thorne Ryan, Lizz Burrell, Lydia Mason, Helena Newton, Cherie Chapman and Emily Reader.

A special mention should go to Deryl Easton. Thank you for everything you've done to help promote my books. All the shares and posts are greatly appreciated.

Last but not least, the Gangland Governor (NotRights) Bookclub members deserve a shout out too. All your fabulous reviews and lovely comments make the hard work worthwhile.

About the Author

STEPHANIE HARTE writes thrilling gangland fiction. She lives in London with her family.